STEELTON

A NOVEL

by

Keith Warner Hall

Steelton

Copyright © 2017 Keith Warner Hall

Cover design by Tugboat Design
Formatting by Tugboat Design

For Janet

1

"I can't believe I am going to go right past my house and yet still not be home for two more days," Harry sighed. "Right by it".

The Pennsylvania Railroad car waddled its noisy way up from Philadelphia. Once out of the Philly suburbs, it was an express to Harrisburg. Harry knew all of the little towns as they rolled by...Mt. Joy, Elizabethtown, Middletown, Highspire and then his home town, Steelton. He pressed his nose against the grimy window as he saw the lower end of the steel mill come into view. He recognized the backyards of his neighbors, and as the slowing train lumbered past, he mentally ticked off the family names of the people who lived in those homes hard by the tracks – Kaufman, O'Reilly, Bruckner, Milosevic - until the gas works came into view and the train sighed into its final crawl into Harrisburg.

The three years spent in the Army seemed wasted. Two stripes on his arm to show for it and a string of boring duty stations in the Army towns of Oklahoma, Texas and a final year in Augusta, Georgia. No real skills learned, no love life started, no friendships made that would endure.

He had joined in the middle of the Korean War. Several of his friends and co-workers who were older than he had gotten called back up for active duty even though they did their time in World War II. Steelton had sent a very high percentage of its eligible men to fight in the second Great War, and had its share of guys who didn't come home, including one of the Medlin kids just up the street from his home. Harry felt signing up was the right thing to do. He never was posted outside of the States, though, a fact that provided his mom with no end of relief.

Harry thought about his so-called military career as he and about twenty other soldiers grabbed their duffels and followed the sergeant's orders to muster near a platform where they were called to attention. No smoking, no talking, no piss break, no looking around at women. A half hour later they boarded a waiting bus headed out to Indiantown Gap to be processed out of the Army.

The final interviews, last mess hall meals, physical exam, and inventory of his Army property passed without incident, and upon receipt of his DD-214 he was honorably discharged....with some pocket money and a ticket for the bus back to Harrisburg where he arrived a couple of hours later.

Harry stretched his neck to get a view of the bus platform and when he saw his Mom and Aunt Louise, he knew he was a civilian once more.

"Where's Dad and Tim?" Harry asked after getting teary-eyed hugs and kisses from the two sisters.

"Your brother is working three to eleven. Your dad didn't want to ride the bus up here; said he'd see you when you got home."

The three of them decided to do it up right and celebrate with a nice dinner at the Alva, a family owned Harrisburg institution beneficially situated right next to the train station and bus depot. Harry had the potpie and two beers and treated Doris and Louise to the meat loaf. The conversation was lively and dominated by the women. Harry's Mom seemed mostly concerned about his loss of weight and his Aunt Louise asked him four times about his love life. They asked polite questions about Georgia although neither of them had been any farther south than Baltimore.

After the big meal, Harry could not face one more minute carrying his large duffel bag so he hailed a taxi to Steelton and the family home on Myers Street. The cab cost him a dollar with the tip but was well worth it.

Doris and Louise joined Harry in the family kitchen, where his dad Hap was waiting for him at the old Formica table. Even the ladies had a glass of beer poured from Hap's quart of Ballantine. They talked a little about the family, the latest news in town, and the Phillies. Harry didn't say anything about his last few months in the Army and Hap didn't ask. Doris and Louise left the men alone after a bit, but the conversation didn't improve.

"Will you be heading back to the mill then, or taking some time off?" Hap inquired.

"Figure I'll take the summer to think it over, Dad."

"Mill's busy. You get back to the bar mill, they're workin' lots of overtime. Good money."

"Yeah, well, we'll see. Got some things to think about." Think Tim'll be home soon?"

"He goes out for a few beers after his shift. I got no idea when he comes in."

It was close to eleven, Hap was yawning. It had been a long day for Harry, and soon he made his way up the brown carpeted stairs to the small bedroom at the back of the house. Doris had the bed made with the same blankets he had slept under as a kid. Harry thought the room smelled the same, too, as he slipped into bed and off to sleep.

Myers Street was one of four north–south streets on Steelton's West Side. The Burger family had been in the same house for over forty years. Harry's grandfather Harold Burger moved in to the brick row house at number 216 prior to World War I several years after his Dad, Harold Junior –who everyone knew as Hap - had been born. Many of the Burger's neighbors had a similar history, moving into newly built brick or frame homes during the period of affluence that steelworkers enjoyed with all of the overtime and production demands for Bethlehem Company steel prior to and during the Great War.

The Burgers were very much like many other families in the neighborhood with a working man of the house and a house-keeping mom. Hap worked as a millwright. They had been married 26 years. Doris' family was also from the West Side. She had ten years of school and when she was sixteen got a job at the cigar factory down on Front Street. Doris had two boys and then a daughter who died soon after difficult birth. The infant was buried in Steelton's Baldwin cemetery but Hap and Doris had not been to the gravesite in nearly twenty years. They belonged to the Steelton Moose and were both active in the Lion's Club. Hap helped coach the Lion's little league baseball team and Doris was in the Ladies Auxiliary. Hap was one of the volunteer fire truck drivers. He lived a half block away from West Side Number Three and could be behind the wheel of the red pumper within five minutes of the siren.

The homes were almost all very neatly kept, windows clean and sills painted. Most of the residents had replaced the red brick sidewalk that had been between their front stoop and the street when the street itself had been paved a couple of years ago. Myers Street had a domed effect to assist water run-off into the gutters that lined each side of the street and emptied into the sewers at the end of each half block. Traffic was next to non-existent as only about one home in four had a car. The biggest excitement in the middle of the street was the local kids playing ball or riding their bikes, an assortment of barking local dogs chasing them.

This block of Myers Street was all residential. It was anchored on the north end at the Conestoga Street intersection by the West Side Hose House and the skating rink, a concrete playground with a foot high curb all around that the firemen filled with water in the winter.

Just on the other side of Conestoga was the Mennonite Mission, and across from that Yetter's Beer Garden. There was no other business, store, bar, or church. The block was entirely white. The white kids walked two blocks to West Side Elementary, the black kids on the West Side hiked eight blocks up the hill to Hygienic Elementary. All of the older kids – black and white - had a mile walk to Steelton High School, which had long been integrated. Most of the men worked in the mill, but alongside the Burger household mortgages were paid by a barber, a beer truck driver, a guy who worked at Dundoff's market, a plumber, and a shoe salesman. The only woman on the block who worked a regular job was a WAC veteran who had a good job at the State and drove to work every day in a green '54 Chevy.

This was the street that Harry woke up to every morning. It was summer, and he took his coffee out on the stoop, where he could easily hear the radios, the vacuum cleaners, the moms yelling at their kids to get out of the house and get some fresh air. After just a few days, he could almost predict the summer routine of his neighbors: who went to work when; where the kids played and who had bikes to ride and who didn't; the neighbors who were friends with one another and the neighbors who had a petty feud of some sort. He got reacquainted with all of the neighborhood dogs, many of which had two names...the dog's name and the family name, like Pooch Adler or Trixie Yovanovich. Nobody seemed to mind that the dogs ran loose; they all went to their respective homes at dinner time and didn't seem to cause much trouble.

Harry had planned to take the summer off before going back to work, but after just a couple of weeks of this routine he was bored and felt lazy. There wasn't much to do for a young single guy. He had no real interest in any of the girls on the West Side. About the only thing he did enjoy was the freedom he had to sleep late and to eat what and when he wanted...a big change from his Army life. His mom's cooking was better, too.

Harry expected that he would have a lot of catching up to do with his mom and dad in his first weeks at home. They were not exactly the talkative type and Harry soon realized the main reason was that there was damn little to talk about. Life was the same day after day. Hap went to work Monday through Friday, all day shift. Doris was up early, packed his thermos and lunch bucket and then worked around the house. She had dinner ready soon after Hap got home. They ate, watched a little TV and by nine thirty they were in bed.

Smoking a cigarette and finishing the last of the suppertime coffee on a warm Wednesday evening, his belly full of Doris' tuna casserole, Harry decided it was time to go back to work. Work in Steelton meant Bethlehem Steel, his prior employer. He confirmed his decision with a last cigarette, and trundled up the old stairs to bed.

The next morning, Harry placed a call to the main employment office and asked for an appointment, explaining that he was a prior Bethlehem employee who had just been honorably discharged from the Army. An agreeable secretary promised him a return call, which came the next day. Business at the mill was very good, and as a veteran and former employee, Harry was welcome to come down for an interview. After another phone call to make the arrangements, Harry found himself two days later with an appointment down at the Main Office on Swatara Street waiting for a Mr. Willis, who was overseeing non-union hiring.

While waiting in the large lobby, Harry wondered what the neighbors would think of him sitting here with his new necktie and hopeful expression. Normally the first place a former employee (Harry worked a couple years in the bar mill before joining the Army) would go was to the Union Hall to go through the re-employment process. Harry had already bumped into Rocky Garber, Local 1688 President and a fellow West-Sider, but Harry did not want to go back to an hourly union swing shift job. He had his eyes on something better. The nights back sleeping in his childhood bed had awakened a bit of ambition in him that had first stirred during the last months of his Army service. He had visions of a white collar job – maybe wearing this new necktie to work – and he hoped to parlay his Army experience (with a little exaggeration) into a position with a future.

He had some things going for him. His grandfather, dad and two uncles were lifetime Bethlehem Steel Company employees…in union jobs admittedly but they held skilled jobs in the maintenance department as millwrights. His brother was a rail department foreman and one of the youngest supervisors in the mill. Harry knew he was fortunate to have German heritage despite the uncomfortable years for the "Krauts" during the war years. Northern Europeans had the best opportunities for skilled work in the mill, and thanks to departmental seniority in the labor agreements blacks, southern and eastern Europeans, and other ethnic groups had no way to break out of the labor and semi-skilled occupations which were contained in specific departments. Harry was proud of his brother Tim, who had a steady work record, made foreman after just a couple of years in a union job and was a popular guy in Steelton; that kind of family reference should help him. Harry's completed application that he handed to the secretary as requested was full of names of relatives employed by Bethlehem in the space conveniently provided on the official employment form.

So it was that a few minutes later Harry found himself talking to Mr. Willis in a big office that smelled of wood polish and pipe smoke. Harry thought about how cool it was in there on a hot and humid day and how easily he could adapt to an office like this himself. Willis gave him the once over twice, quizzed him about his Army time, asked him if he could type (he couldn't). Willis asked about any union activity and if he had plans to marry (none and none). Harry started to squirm. The new necktie he was wearing suddenly felt a little tighter. The more Willis puffed on his pipe, the tighter the tie became. Harry felt some sweat on his forehead.

"You know gate eight down the street?" he asked. "I do" Harry responded.

"All right. Take this card down to the open hearth department tomorrow, eight o'clock. Ask for Mr. Robert Hernley. Leave the tie at home."

Harry headed out onto Front Street and stopped into Bernardo Brothers for a pack of cigarettes and a Nehi. The Nehi was gone in three gulps and Harry made a bee line for Katy's Tavern just down the street and directly across from gate eight. His plan was to see who came into the bar who would know something about this Mr. Hernley and anything else he could learn about the work situation there. Harry ordered a Schmidt's and before long men came in by twos and threes and the bar was filled in a matter of minutes. Harry didn't talk to the bartender but it was soon obvious that this was a regular crowd as no orders were taken but a variety of beers and shots were promptly placed in front of appreciative customers. Harry recognized a guy he knew as "Scrappy" who he had gone to school with and soon struck up a conversation. Scrappy remembered Harry, and that he had gone into the service, and after some small talk Harry began his line of questioning. Scrappy helpfully introduced Harry to several of the men at the bar, and when Harry told them of his upcoming meeting with Hernley, he asked what the gate eight employees knew about him. The word on Hernley among the union guys was that he was demanding, always pushing for more production and trying to impress the big shots. One guy at the end of the bar named Charlie said that Hernley was not very popular with the workers and liked it that way. "I think the foremen like him less than the union does," Charlie added, and nods and murmurs of agreement echoed up and down the bar.

Scrappy had a different view: "I find though" he said quietly, "if you do your job and stay out of his way, he's okay". Turns out Scrappy was not union, but had a couple of years of college and worked in management. Harry thought it a little odd that a management type would be in the bar having shots and beers with the plant guys. He thanked Scrappy and bought him a beer. Harry walked out of Katy's into the bright sunshine and headed home. He'd change, have dinner, ask his dad if he knew of Hernley and then head up to Yetter's that night to see what else he could learn about the open hearth operation. He decided he wouldn't tell anyone – not even his dad – why he wanted to know.

Hap had heard of Hernley but knew nothing about him. "I stay away from the open hearth as much as possible. Too hot and too dangerous, and too many crazy guys workin' in there," he offered. It was clear Hap was more interested in his spaghetti than in talking, so Harry let it go. Maybe Yetter's would be more productive, and after helping his mom with the dishes, Harry walked up a quiet Myers street to the bar.

Yetter's Beer Garden was a West Side Institution. "Buddy" Yetter and his wife ran it; he tended bar and she cooked. Like many Steelton taverns, the bar itself was in what would have been the front room of their house; the dining room was next to it, and then the kitchen. The Yetters lived upstairs. Harry took the three familiar steps up to the tavern's entrance, an imposing heavy wooden green door with three frosted rectangular windows set at a jaunty angle. The marble top bar, on your left as you entered, had about fifteen stools. There was a cashew machine on the near corner and two big glass jars sat prominently in the middle– one with pickled eggs and one with hot sausage – and three taps adjacent. Harry smelled the cigarette smoke and looked down the bar for an empty red leather stool.

Yetter's had a devoted local following. The food was good, prices fair. He carried Schmidt's, Schlitz and Ballantine on tap. The language on the West Side could be pretty rough, but all of the bar regulars felt like they were in Buddy's house, not a barroom, so more or less gentlemanly behavior was the norm. If you had too much to drink, you got flagged and sent home. Harry sat down across from Buddy who was already pouring Harry's glass of Schmidt's. Harry told Buddy to set up the bar and Buddy pulled out six shot glasses and placed them upside down in front of each of the seated bar patrons. "On Harry" he grunted.

Most of the guys in Yetter's that night didn't know of Hernley. Harry did find out that the majority of the open hearth jobs were filled by blacks or Hunkies and that it wasn't a place most guys wanted to work. Jim Marshall, seated near the far end of the bar, told Harry that Hernley went to the Lutheran Church on Pine Street where his family went and he saw him in there from time to time (knowing Marshall, Harry thought, only Christmas and Easter). He said Hernley always sat way up front –never a good sign.

"Oh yeah, one more thing," Marshall said, "He's got a really good looking wife".

"Well, that's not much help," Harry thought as he bid everyone a good night and headed home early, wishing his walk was more than half a block so that he'd have some good thinking time to himself. Myers Street was quiet, the macadam of the street still warm on a very humid evening. Hap and Doris were in bed when he got home. Tim was on his regular three to eleven shift and rarely came home until the wee hours.

Harry climbed into bed but stared at the ceiling for most of the night. It was hot and no breeze came through the one window in his bedroom. The Phils had a day game earlier at St. Louis but there was a Yankee night game on WKBO that he listened to. The Yanks beat the pitiful A's on a Whitey Ford shut-out. Even Mel Allen had a tough time exuding enthusiasm calling an eight to nothing rout for the Yankee faithful. Looking around his room he thought he could have still been seven years old with the flowered wallpaper, the old chest of drawers, one of those metal wardrobe things where his hanging clothes were…now containing one good suit, one summer suit, five or six old and one brand new necktie draped over their shoulders. The only nod to his adulthood was the burgundy Bakelite GE radio he bought with his first Bethlehem paycheck nearly five years back. He tried to think of something about himself that he could make reference to in his interview tomorrow, but he came up empty. Everything about him was mediocre. Average student in school. An average worker who punched a clock for almost two years in the bar mill, a nameless shift worker like a hundred other guys. Then his undistinguished time in the service…three years in the Army with no recognition of any kind. Everything about him was average. "Average people do not get ahead in this world, they get left behind" he concluded before finally drifting off to sleep.

Harry got up early so that he could get some bathroom time to himself, have a close shave and leave the house before seven thirty to make sure he was plenty early for his introduction to the new and now feared Mr. Hernley.

Out of the house by seven fifteen, Harry got to gate eight fifteen minutes later and was pleased to see George Clark at the gate. He had known George for many years. George was well thought of among the volunteer firefighters in Steelton…he was a long-time driver for Citizen's hook and ladder. George was badly injured in World War Two, and Bethlehem did a good thing by handing out these security guard jobs to guys who were solid employees and then went off to war and came back not quite the way they went in. George had some scars on his face, and walked with a heavy limp. His left arm sort of hung by his side most of the time. He recognized Harry right away.

"I heard you were back…going to work in the open hearth this time?"

"I'm not sure," Harry replied, "have an appointment to see Mr. Hernley…do you know him?"

"Sure, sure…I work all daylight and he does too. Pretty much all business; lives up on the hill. He's always one of the first guys here and I'm gone by the time he leaves. Drives a big Olds. Know where you're going?"

Harry shook his head and George pointed out a low brick office under a large yellow "THINK SAFETY" sign and said "You'll need a hard hat and glasses to get through the gate…do you have a pass to see Hernley?" Harry had forgotten about the card Willis had give him even though he had tapped his pocket a dozen times on the way down to make sure he had it. "Yeah, here you go!"

George signed Harry in and Harry found himself holding his pass card in an air conditioned but empty office. There were four metal desks and a row of army green filing cabinets along the wall. There were broken venetian blinds half covering the dirty windows. The place smelled like motor oil and coal dust. Harry thought he'd better wait outside. He really needed a cigarette but he was pretty sure this was a no smoking area. The noise coming from deep underneath the huge structure was crushing. Sirens blared from the overhead bridge cranes and railcars could be heard squealing along the rails. From ground level, the tops of the furnaces towered maybe two hundred feet…and an acrid orange smoke could always be seen from almost any part of Steelton. Harry remembered how his high school science teacher, Mr. Depper, taught his class about weather observation and he used the billowing smoke and flags flying from the mill down the hill below the school to help determine wind speed and direction.

Harry was lost for a minute thinking about his high school days when he was snapped back to reality. "You Burger? I'm Hernley. Come on in."

Hernley took off his white hard hat and safety goggles. His was face was full of sweat and he pulled out a red handkerchief and wiped his eyes. Hernley was maybe in his late thirties, about five foot ten or so, wiry build. He wore a long sleeved khaki shirt and green khaki gabardines. His steel toed boots were shin high and he had his pants cuffs tucked into the boots. He wordlessly opened a manila inter office mail envelope and Harry recognized his employment application and some other papers in the packet. Hernley did not offer coffee. He did not invite Harry to smoke despite the big steel ashtrays he could see on the desks. Hernley began the interview abruptly.

"Most guys don't want to work in the open hearth and most guys don't want to work for me. What makes you different?"

Harry figured best to be honest because he was pretty sure Hernley would see through any line of bullshit. "Well, I went to see Mr. Willis because I am interested in entering into management. I really didn't know your name and I didn't ask about the open hearth. I thought my best chance would be back in the bar mill where I worked before I joined the service. I just got out a few weeks ago."

Hernley asked a hundred questions. He asked if Harry was good at math, if he had science in high school, if he had neat handwriting, again the typing question, was he married, what did he learn from three years in the army, did he respect his officers, ever in trouble with the law, why didn't he just stay here at the mill instead of screwing up his union seniority by going in the army.

"I see you live on Myers Street. That's on the West Side, right?"

"Yessir."

"A lot of troublemakers and boozers over there. We got a couple of union men here who are West- Siders and every one of them would rather drink than work."

"My family has all clean work records Mr. Hernley. Long service, too. You can that on my application there."

Harry tried to point out his brief record in the bar mill... showed up, took overtime, no injuries or lost time. He told

Hernley he was well liked in the Army by his sergeants and officers and got along with everyone. He said he was not afraid of hard work and was eager to learn. He didn't have the smarts for college but wanted a management career at Bethlehem. He again mentioned all of his relatives including his brother who was one of the youngest foremen in the plant.

This back and forth went on for forty-five minutes when Hernley abruptly stood up.

"I've got a safety meeting to run. I'll talk to Willis. That's all for now; give me your pass." No thanks-for-coming-in, no handshake, no mention of what job was open or what he might be considered for, no idea how he did. Hernley signed Harry's pass card along with the time and pointed Harry toward the gate.

Harry saw George on the way out. "Well?" George asked. "I have no idea" Harry said and he meant it.

Later that day Hernley walked up to the big office for his meeting with Willis. A phone call would have done just as well, but Hernley never missed a chance to go to the main office in hopes of bumping into and saying hello to one of the big shots. Willis' secretary showed Hernley in.

"He's no ball of fire, but pit recorder is not the most exciting job in the world either. It used to be a union job you know. He comes from a good family I understand, and he's at least smart enough not to want a life in the union. His brother made foreman. He seems a little more of a go-getter than most of those West Siders. We have that big IBM machine project coming up and it might be good to have some fresh blood working on it with Stone. I honestly don't see anybody else we have down there… all of the regular guys are always opposed to any new ideas right off the bat. I say we give him a try and have him work alongside Melton for a month so he can learn the job the right way".

15

"All right", Willis said while tapping his pipe in the ashtray. "I'll get his physical lined up with personnel, have him sign the paperwork, and he can start a week from Monday. We'll have to inform the union that he's not going back to a rank and file job. Let me know how he does."

Harry had a job but he didn't know it. He figured he screwed the interview and might as well head up to the union hall tomorrow. He might see Rocky Garber at Yetter's tonight and Rocky would set him up with the USWA and a return to the bar mill.

2

Harry was surprised when the call from Mr. Willis' secretary came the next day. He went down to the main office, signed the paperwork, and had his physical. His first day on the job came quickly. He said hello to George Clark who shook his hand at the gate on the way in and Harry picked up his safety gear. He reported to Hernley's office and was introduced by Hernley to a fellow named Melton and before he knew it, Harry was into training and a new work routine.

The first four weeks on the job went pretty well. Harry thought he had the basics of the pit recorder position down in two weeks. Melton did a good job of telling him what to worry about and what to ignore. The work itself was more like record keeping, essentially keeping track of all of the raw materials coming into the open hearth and the finished products going out. Harry's office space was adjacent to the washroom and lockers and near two time clocks, one for union and one for people like Harry who were neither union nor management. He didn't have to go out into the real heat of the furnaces that often, nor did he have to interact with many of the supervisors. Melton reminded him of the sergeant he had during his last post in Georgia, where the overriding rule was to keep the paper work moving and not make any clerical errors. There apparently was no room or interest in suggestions, new ideas, or any criticism of the way things were done. Harry thought "This is the job, there's one way to do it, that's it."

Harry's office was a dirty, noisy and crowded room with old heavy steel desks jammed against one another. The shift foremen all worked out of this office (they shared one desk) as did Melton, a couple inventory control guys, two junior Industrial Engineers, and a space for the summer college kids who were doing time studies. Since the office was occupied 21 shifts a week, there was always uneaten food, trash from the prior shift and piles of papers that seemed to have been there for years. Next to his office and down the side of the plant were all of the other offices: maintenance supervisors, then shipping and rail, and at the very end, the QC labs and in the smallest and shittiest space was the union office for the shop stewards. Harry's work rarely took him out of his own office. He would stretch his legs a couple of times a day, and ate lunch at one of two old picnic tables out toward the entrance past the time clocks. Harry hated that he had to punch in and out.

There were a few other disappointments early on. Harry was upset to learn that Melton had been a pit recorder for eight years before getting a promotion, and then he had to go onto third shift to get that promotion to production scheduler. Melton did that job for six years before getting his current job as production planner. Even now, Melton was still one rung below being eligible for the Bethlehem Steel Management Club, a goal Harry thought would have been within his own reach after a couple of years.

The General Foreman, a guy named Karl Long, had his office in with Hernley. Harry had not been in that office since his first day on the job, but that was going to change in a couple hours. Mr. Long stopped by to tell Harry that Hernley wanted to see him in their office at four o'clock.

This was the kind of thing Hernley was famous for that pissed guys off. It was a Friday afternoon. Hernley knew that all of the day-turn office guys worked seven to three-thirty so Harry would have to hang around for the meeting, the subject of which occupied Harry's mind for the afternoon. Harry was pretty sure he wasn't in any kind of trouble. Melton had told him he was doing fine; he came into work at least fifteen minutes early every morning and stayed ten or fifteen minutes past quitting time every day. He thought he had gotten along pretty well with everyone he met. He made up his mind to be professional and calm no matter what Hernley had to say.

One game Hernley did not play was keeping men waiting. Punctuality was a point of pride for him. Four o'clock meant four o'clock and that's when he met Harry who was standing outside his office door. "C'mon in Burger" Hernley said without making eye contact.

Harry waited for Hernley to sit down before he did. Karl Long was in the office along with another guy Harry recognized as the general maintenance foreman. Hernley, of course, got right down to business.

"Listen up, Burger, Melton tells me you have picked things up okay. I'm going to take you off your probation. Everything else should be about the same, only Melton will not be spending so much time with you. You still go to him with your pit recorder questions. Did you have any Army experience with what is called data processing equipment…things similar to the new batch cards we are using for the pit?"

Harry's mind was racing. The Army had used a similar

method of keeping track of equipment inventory and maintenance schedules, but Harry did not know much about it and neither did anybody else in his unit.

"Yes, quite a bit" Harry found himself saying, "We used systems like this at Fort Gordon, and I helped get it started and then we used it to handle maintenance schedules and inventory."

Hernley weighed Harry's response and Harry could see him studying his face.

"Next week, there will be a guy named Stone working in the same office you and Melton are in. Stone has been at school up in the main office learning this new system. You work with Stone; this should help us replace a lot of the paper and pencil stuff we do now. There is likely to be some overtime involved. Any questions?"

Well, Harry had about a hundred of them, but he asked just two as he could see that Hernley had already mentally dismissed him.

"Do I still punch in and out or do I record the overtime differently"?

"No. Punch in and out. You're not management."

"This guy Stone, does he go by Scrappy?"

"You know him?" Hernley asked, looking up from his paperwork.

"Not really…I went to high school with him and he's also from the West Side."

"Yeah, I know, but Stone went to college and is making something of himself, not like the rest of the drunks and loafers up there!"

Harry had a lot to chew on. He was really surprised to find on his first day of work that he had to punch in and out just like the union guys he was trying to get away from. His new job was not the first step to management and a position with a necktie as he imagined. Most of his co-workers, even though they weren't in union jobs acted as if they were, and they showed little pride in their work. His working environment was hot and noisy, and there were five different kinds of smells a day, all of them stunk. His job wasn't that challenging and he figured that if he knew ninety percent of the total job after just a couple of weeks, how much was left to learn?

"Now that I'm out of the Army and I have a new job, I should be looking forward to every day and enjoying myself" Harry thought. "I'm still living at home and eating Mom's cooking. I sleep in the same bed. Compared to Tim, I'm at a standstill here."

His brother Tim was doing better than Harry. Tim had bought a car, a late model Mercury and Harry helped Tim clear out the backyard so that Tim didn't have to park his car on the street. Tim had a couple of girlfriends from outside of Steelton. He was popular with the guys as well and the couple of times they went out together on a Saturday night, Tim bought rounds and all of the bartenders and tavern owners knew him.

Harry hadn't really cared much about dating. There were a couple of girls from the West Side he used to screw before he went into the service, and he saw them around the neighborhood. One of them, Mary Ann Kukowski, had gotten married but she seemed to make it pretty clear to Harry she was still available, and mentioned her husband worked three to eleven on a steady basis. But Harry had no interest. Part of his plan was to make a move up in class with everyone he dealt with, especially women. He also needed a car and he hoped the overtime at work would get him the extra cash he needed. He was helping out with the bills at home, but thought a lot about getting his own apartment….one up on the hill; not on the West Side.

The next day Harry took Tim's small boat out onto the river. He packed a big lunch, a cooler with ice and a couple of poles, but his plan was to motor over to one of the islands and fish from the shore there spending the whole day thinking about what he wanted to do. A six pack of Schmidt's was along to help the process, and a very productive day it was. As Harry loaded up and locked the boat onto the small trailer they kept at Chambers' launch area, his path forward became clear. After his first week with Scrappy, he would ask if he could borrow all of the textbooks or papers Scrappy had received in his training for the new system. He might go to the library and study more. Then, he was going to work all the overtime he could and save enough for six month's rent for his own apartment...the car would have to wait.

And...he decided he was going to go to church on Sunday. The Lutheran church on Pine Street.

3

Harry was up, took a bath, had a shave and put on a pair of dress pants, shirt and tie. It was too hot for the suit jacket and the church was a good fifteen minute walk and half-way up Pine Street. Sunday school was at nine-thirty, church services an hour later. Harry got into the sanctuary about twenty after ten and sat down in the middle rows, but close enough so he could see up front. There was a Sunday school class underway toward the back of the big room, but soon the organ started and people started filing in. The services began with a prayer, some singing, and then the minister took the pulpit. Harry strained to see if he could pick out Hernley and he finally did, sitting in the third row over to the right. He wore a brown suit. There were some older people to Hernley's left but on his right…that had to be his wife. Harry could only see her long dark hair. He fidgeted around throughout the sermon, and when the congregation stood for the final prayer and benediction, Harry got a good look at Mrs. Hernley. She WAS pretty, and younger than Hernley. It was at that point that Harry decided to make sure that he saw Hernley after the services. He hustled out quickly and stood outside on the sidewalk. It was really a hot day. Most of the congregation lit up cigarettes but Harry didn't. No one paid much attention to him, and he saw nobody he recognized or knew. Then Hernley and his wife stepped out into the sunlight. He moved toward them and said softly "Mr. Hernley"?

Hernley was taken aback. "Yes? Burger? Is that you"?

"Yessir. Good morning. Hot today!"

"What are you doing here?" Hernley almost demanded. "You are not a member here!"

"No Sir" Harry responded. "I have been looking for a new church since I got out of the service, and a friend of mine suggested Pine Street." Harry was lying.

"What friend…do they belong here?"

"The Marshall family, from Myers Street on the West Side."

"Don't know 'em. Well, let's go honey. We'll be late for lunch at the Management Club"

His wife interrupted…"Bob, aren't you going to introduce us?"

"Oh, yes, of course. Burger, this is my wife Cynthia…sorry, I don't remember your first name."

"Harry, Sir. Pleased to meet you Mrs. Hernley. Your husband gave me a job in his department after I got out of the service. I'm really lucky to have it."

"Well, good luck to you Mr. Burger". With that, Hernley did a quick pivot, took Cynthia by the arm and walked her down Pine toward Second Street. As soon as they turned the corner, Harry started down Pine himself. Despite the fact that not one person had welcomed him or said hello to him, Harry had found a new church. He thought about Hernley and Cynthia all the way home. She looked quite a bit younger than him. She had on a bright yellow dress, and her shoes and pocketbook were yellow, too. "Now that's real class" Harry thought to himself. He made it a point to try to find out more about Hernley the following week…

if he had any hobbies, if he had kids, where he grew up; Melton would know. Harry knew that Hernley had a college degree; his diploma was on his office wall. He also knew he had been in the Navy and had been an officer.

As he walked up his front steps, the door was open and through the screen door he could smell Sunday dinner, roast beef most likely. He yelled to his Mom and Dad that he was going upstairs to change when his Dad came out to the front room. "C'mon in the kitchen; we have some bad news."

At the old table, Harry's mom Doris was crying. A cup of coffee was beside her, all of the food for dinner was on the top of the stove but no burners were on. There was a half drunk bottle of Schmidt's in front of Hap's chair.

"What in the world…did somebody die?" Harry hadn't seen his Mom cry since he shoved off for basic training.

"No, it's Tim. He's in jail. He never came home last night and we got a call from him about an hour ago. He's up in Dauphin County detention."

"Is he hurt? Bar fight? Did he wreck his car?"

"No, his car is out back; he didn't drive last night" Hap said. "We don't know what happened. Timmy said everything was just fine, that there was some kind of mistaken identity or something. He said he should be home in a couple of hours."

"Does he need me to go get him or pick him up someplace?"

"Nope, he said he is okay and that he should be home before too long. That's it." Hap said, moving toward his beer.

"Well, he'll have some explaining to do" Doris said, her voice firming. "Once I make sure he's all-right that is."

With that Doris moved toward the oven and announced dinner should be ready in about half an hour. Harry went up to change and Hap returned to his beer, and Harry joined him when he came back downstairs to the warm kitchen. This time they pulled out a cold quart bottle to share.

"Dad, do you have any idea what's up with Tim, 'cause I don't. I know he makes decent pay in supervision, but he seems to have a lot of money. I think he paid cash for the Merc out there, and the times we go out he must spend fifteen or twenty bucks buying drinks and tipping everybody in sight. He goes out two or three nights a week but we hardly ever see him at Yetter's, or Pete and Betty's, or Martzie's or any of the West Side places. When I go out with him, it's always the private clubs like the St. Lawrence or some expensive place in Harrisburg. And I've heard he hangs out up at Arthur's."

This one got Doris to turn around so fast her apron strings spun like an airplane propeller. "ARTHUR'S?"

Arthur's was a colored bar up above Franklin Street. It had a reputation for gambling, after hours drinking, Sunday drinking, and probably prostitution. It was much more respectable during prohibition when its clientele was mostly white. It had somehow survived for more than thirty years, largely due to the owner Arthur Howard. Arthur owned colored grocery stores on the West Side and on Lincoln Street and on the top of Mohn Street. He owned the colored funeral home that bore his name and a large trucking and hauling business and a junk yard up between the gas company and the railroad tracks. His scrap operation was substantial, taking in junked cars and appliances all easily handled by Arthur's two large mobile cranes and fleet of forklifts. Arthur tooled around town in a big white Caddy that matched the funeral home's Fleetwood limousine and pearl white Cadillac hearse. He and his wife lived above his funeral home at the corner of Front and Franklin.

Arthur was revered by the Negroes on the West Side. He could fix any problem it seemed. If good people had trouble paying the heat or water bill, he would help. Hams, turkeys, and kegs of beer would show up for the colored poor on holidays, weddings, and funerals. He'd see that the dear departed got a first class send-off even if the family couldn't pay right away. If you needed your sidewalk fixed, sewers cleaned out, or maybe found yourself in the Steelton jail after a Saturday night indiscretion, Arthur could fix it. His beneficiaries often couldn't pay, so Arthur collected favors. Lots and lots of favors.

"Well," Hap said, "we'll just have to wait and see what Timmy has to say when he gets home."

Harry thought it best to hang around the house even though it was a ninety degree day and air-conditioning in the house was limited to two big floor fans downstairs and a couple of window fans in the bedrooms. He and Hap watched the Phillie game and shared another beer or two. Doris cleaned up after dinner and sat out on the back porch where she said an up-river wind was blowing, meaning a storm was coming for sure. About four o'clock rumbles of thunder were heard and Harry took his glass of beer out to the front stoop to wait for Tim and the rain. Dad fell asleep on the divan in the seventh inning, as he usually did, thereby saving his blood pressure when the Phils blew a two run lead to the Pirates in the ninth inning.

Just before five, a Steelton police cruiser came down Myers Street from Conestoga. It pulled to a stop in front of the house, and from the passenger seat, out popped Tim. "Thanks Phil" Harry heard Tim say to the officer driving. A nod to Tim and the cruiser pulled away. "Don't look so worried, big brother" Tim said with a grin…"everything's all right. Just a misunderstanding."

"Well," you better have your misunderstanding explainable in plain English, 'cause Mom's waiting to hear it."

4

The work week started at six-thirty the next day for Harry. The previous night's thunderstorm had finally cooled things off and Harry enjoyed a brisk walk to the office. He wanted an early start so that he would make a good impression on Scrappy Stone. He could tell that there was something about him that Hernley clearly liked, so if Harry could emulate that, it might help him in Hernley's eyes. Harry met Melton at the coffee pot. The guys all chipped in two bucks a month and Melton bought the coffee, sugar and canned milk and brought it in. The mill was too cheap to provide coffee for the guys, but it did have a coffee vending machine that made the world's worst coffee and also provided a commission for somebody somewhere in upper management. There were also a couple of machines for chips, candy bars, and so on that did a brisk business with the captive employees. Thankfully, there was Gus's hot dog wagon, a truck that offered hot and cold sandwiches that usually rolled up around when the hourly guys had their lunch break. Harry figured he'd ease into his line of inquiry about Hernley with Melton, so he began by asking if Melton knew Scrappy Stone and anything about this new project. He also thanked Melton for all of his help, and told him that it was due to his training

28

and experience that he was now off probation (which he never knew he was on, by the way).

Melton knew Stone for several years. "Scrappy played football in high school and went to Penn State for a couple of years. He's a helluva fisherman and always on the river. His first job in the mill was in the QC lab and everybody liked working with him. He was a science major in college and a smart guy who picked things up in a hurry."

"It's funny" Harry said. "His family lives real close to mine on the West Side. We are about the same age yet I don't know him that well. I remember him from high school, but that's about it." Harry didn't have to wait too long, as he turned around to see Hernley and Stone coming in through the office door. There were four or five other guys in the office, all bullshitting about their weekends. Hernley surveyed the room with a look of disapproval and everybody got their heads down, clammed up and started looking busy. Hernley made certain that Harry knew Stone was in charge, would report directly to him on this automation project. He looked at Harry and Melton both and announced that all of the top guys in the big office were interested in this project, and that the open hearth had been picked for an expansion of the new batch ticket program that was using machines to replace paper and pencil records.

"I want this thing to go off perfectly. You can work all the overtime you need to as long as Stone here OKs it. This implementation phase should take six weeks, and I don't want any vacation requests until this is completed."

Harry looked at the calendar. Six weeks would take them right up to Labor Day.

"Any questions?" Hernley asked while clearly expecting silence in response. He got it and walked swiftly out of the office.

"Looks like you didn't take the advice everyone gave you at Katy's awhile back" Scrappy said to Harry with a smile. Scrappy started by giving both men assurance and helped them get comfortable with him and the project. He said that the recently adopted batch ticket system was working well and that all of the inventory, production planning, QC and ultimately purchasing and accounting would all tie in to this automated data processing approach. "Let's get acquainted, review everything we are doing now and Mike you can bring me up to date on anything unusual that's happened since I've been at school."

That was the first time Harry heard anybody call Melton anything but Melton. The name on his hard hat spelled out MELTON. Harry thought he'd start calling him "Mike" as well.

"And then," Scrappy said, "we'll go across the street to lunch and then up to the main office for the afternoon. I want to show you the machinery behind this project and give you an overview of why it's important and how this is going to improve our efficiency, our quality…and our value to management."

When Harry heard that last phrase, he knew he was tied at the hip to Stone. He not only liked him, but there was an instant respect. Harry was going to work harder on this project than he had worked on anything prior. He foresaw lots of overtime, extra money, and a chance to get on his own two feet.

They had lunch at the counter at Rea&Derrick and Scrappy bought. They spent almost three hours in the big office in the basement where a bunch of large and noisy machines whirred around, shuffling large amounts of what looked like post cards at a rapid rate. Harry saw the multi-colored batch tickets on one machine that crossed his desk in his pit recorder job. At one point, Scrappy said casually to Harry, "You've probably seen processing machines like this in the Army." "Not exactly like this" Harry stammered.

Over the next couple of weeks, the three men worked shoulder to shoulder despite the fact that Hernley said Melton would not be closely involved. Harry figured Stone told Hernley he needed Melton. Their days tended to go to five or six o'clock. Mike Melton didn't like this very much, but Harry ate it up. The project went well and Harry particularly liked the chance it gave him to get into other departments in the mill. Scrappy took him to the bar mill, where of course Harry knew lots of guys but hardly anyone in the office. They went to the pipe mill, bar fab, the railroad offices, and even the local limestone quarry that was near the south end of the mill. From the very top of the quarry in the offices there, the Bethlehem Steel Management Club could be clearly seen perched high above on a beautiful green knoll. It was a modern building constructed soon after the war.

"Ever been inside the Club?" Harry asked Scrappy. "Quite a few times. A lot of meetings and events for the top guys are held there. I don't go much on my own, though. I was up there last year for a wedding reception-it was Bob Willis' son's wedding. Hernley likes to have lunch up there once a week, and sometimes I tag along with him."

Harry took this all in. Bob Willis was the former Superintendent of the open hearth and he was the guy Harry met at the Main Office. The mention of the Hernley lunch at the Club really got Harry's attention and he figured this was the opening he needed.

"How well do you know Hernley, Scrappy? What's the story on him? He's a tough guy to figure out."

Scrappy was too smart to talk about what he knew Harry wanted to know. "Well, I got my original job in QC because I was good friends with Bob Willis' son Bill. We went to Penn State together. He was in their mining school –probably the best in the country -and graduated. He's working now for Bethlehem's quarry group in Scranton. I knew Hernley before he got his current job. He was in engineering and got assigned to some kind of efficiency project when I first started. They needed a QC guy for the project team, and since I had some college, I got picked. The project was a big success and Hernley got promoted to head up all production support and a couple of years ago he got promoted again. He went to Drexel in Philly, signed up for the Navy, got into officer's school there, and finished college on the GI bill. I think his family is from down around Coatesville. He lives up on the hill. He goes to the same church my Mom and Dad go to."

They piled into the company panel truck Scrappy somehow had use of during the day. Harry thought it best not to ask any more questions. Stone was a good teacher and Harry thought that he approached this project correctly figuring that Harry didn't know a damned thing about this data processing or automated systems of any kind. They both relied on Mike Melton's terrific knowledge of the department and its history. He knew why things were done the way they were ten years ago, what worked and what didn't. More important – and this was his real contribution – Melton, from his time in the union and then after his promotion, knew all the short cuts and tricks. Scrappy was able to eliminate all of the cumbersome, approved it's-in-the-manual methods and substitute the off-the-books fixes and incorporate those into the new system. This kept the project from merely making the old bad practices and errors multiply with the new devices.

At the end of the fourth week of the project, Scrappy had a Friday status meeting up at the Main Office. Harry and Melton figured they'd find out what happened the following Monday morning, but they were surprised to see Scrappy come into the office just after three that same afternoon. "Well, everyone is happy with what you guys have done. We're not working late tonight. I'm taking you guys over to Katy's for a beer at three thirty. Let's go wash up so you can punch out on the dot."

It was at this point that Harry noticed that Stone did not have to punch in and out (Melton still did). They walked the couple of minutes to the gate where Harry saw George Clark and wished him a nice weekend. Instead of sitting at the bar, Scrappy motioned them over to a table. Harry and Mike had a Schmidt's; Scrappy a Ballantine. Round two was also on Scrappy and then Mike said he had to get home to his wife and kids. Scrappy and Harry had one more beer – Harry's treat this time.

"You ever go fishing, Harry?" Scrappy asked.

"Not much. I understand you spend a lot of time on the river, though."Harry said.

"Well, if you don't mind getting up early, I'm going out right around five tomorrow morning and you're welcome to join me. My boat is right behind my house in Highspire."

"I'd really like that, but as it happens, I've got a fishing date of my own…with my brother. He has a john boat with a small Evinrude and we've got a date for tomorrow. You won't see us on the water, though. My brother's idea of an early morning on a Saturday is eight o'clock."

"Well, all of the fish will be gone by then" Scrappy said.

"We do more talkin' and drinkin' than we do fishin'" Harry said. "And I expect tomorrow will be more of the same."

And how, Harry thought. Tomorrow was the day he was going to get the whole story from Tim, not that line of bullshit he gave Mom and Dad a month ago about his night in jail. Harry had let things settle down all this time, giving his brother a chance to tell him the full story. He didn't, and now Harry was not accepting any fish stories from his little brother.

5

It was closer to nine when the two brothers eased their small boat into the Susquehanna. The river was at its usual low level at end of summer, and it seemed to have more rocks than water. Tim guided the boat downstream toward the turnpike bridge that crossed the river on the Steelton-Highspire line. Fish sometimes could be found along the abutments, but if the fish weren't there, shade from an already hot sun was in abundance in the bridge's wide shadow. Harry dropped the anchor and with fishing lines in, the first beers were popped around nine-thirty.

Harry thought he'd wait to the third beer before proceeding with his line of inquiry. Tim was talking about his plans for that evening, and tried to get Harry to join him. He planned to head up to Bar-B-Cue Cottage on Front Street in Harrisburg, then to Quigley's on Cameron Street on the way down to Steelton. Tim said he planned to meet a couple of girls at Quigley's, but he allowed as the chance of meeting willing dates at the Cottage was a good possibility. "It's about time you get out with some women, big brother" he said over his shoulder while re-baiting his hook. "You've had what, one or two dates since you've been home? Unless you're having some secret fun on the side you need to get out and enjoy some female company."

"I've had my opportunities but I have been concentrating on work and saving some money to move out of the house and maybe get a car. All of this overtime has helped, and I have some savings from the Army."

"Well, if you need some cash, just ask...I'm happy to help out, Harry."

This was the opening Harry needed. "Where DO you get all of that spending money Tim? You seem to spend four or five times what you make and yet you paid cash for the Merc didn't you? There's something not right about all of the late nights on the weekends, and I'm still waiting to hear the full story about that arrest a month ago. Mom and Dad may have bought your version, but I didn't. Guys don't get arrested and locked up for being in an after-hours place, they get fined. How about giving me the truth on that one as a starter?"

Tim stared at the end of his fishing rod for a bit. "All right. First, I wasn't arrested. I was picked up and held. I'll tell you about that night and that's it. I don't want you asking about anything else, it's my private life and I intend to keep it that way." Harry said nothing. "I was with five or six other guys up at a liquor house on Christian Street. You know Bob's grocery up there?" Harry nodded. "Well, Bob's serves beer during the day and evening. He doesn't have a license. People bring in jars or milk bottles and Bob has a keg set up. He lives right next door to his store beside that big empty lot alongside the main railroad tracks, and the downstairs of his house is an after-hours liquor house on weekends. He has sandwiches, there's beer and booze. People usually walk up there so there's not a lot of late traffic to attract attention. Bob and his son run a tight ship, there's no loud partying to bother the neighbors. Any neighbor who complains, there's usually a free bucket of beer or a bottle of liquor in it for them. If they complain a second time, they get a visit to their house, and that stops the complaining."

Tim continued without looking at Harry. "The night we had the problem, some LCB agents busted into Bob's house about four in the morning. They took all the liquor and beer, and loaded us and the alcohol up in trucks. We were put into a holding cell but not booked. Since this raid was done in Steelton, the Steelton cops should have been notified but they weren't. I was able to make one call just before we were booked, so I called Ernie Linta."

Harry almost dropped his beer. "You called the Chief of Police when you were about to get arrested?"

"Yep. I knew Ernie would be pissed to hear that LCB guys were raiding his town without him knowing about it. About an hour later, all of us guys except Bob were let go with a lecture and a warning. Ernie sent Phil Weaver up in a squad car to bring me back to Steelton. That's when I was able to call the house. Bob got bailed out later that night. That's about it."

Harry listened to this but figured it was the tip of the iceberg. "How do you know that Ernie Linta didn't know about the raid and how do you know him so well?"

"Remember his son Anthony…the big kid whose Mom made him play the violin? Anthony and I are good friends. That's the connection and that's all there is to it."

"Was Anthony Linta the other guy with you who got in trouble at Bob's?" Harry wanted to know.

"He's not that stupid, Harry. Now let's either fish, or drink beer, or head back to the house. I came out here to relax."

"How did you know that Ernie Linta was not aware of the LCB raid?"

Tim said nothing. They sat in silence for maybe 20 minutes.

Harry drained a beer and said to his brother, "They're not biting; might as well head in." He brought up the anchor.

"Before you start the motor, given any more thought to going out tonight? I think you need to relax a little Harry." Tim's avoidance of his questions rankled Harry. "Nope, no thanks. Besides, I have to get up early for church tomorrow."

The locals always said that the Susquehanna was a mile wide and a foot deep. It took Tim close to an hour to navigate upstream, trying to find and then losing the channel. A couple of times the small Evinrude motor clanged against the bottom. They could see the ramp where they stored the little boat, and the Chambers kids(who owned and ran the little launch and storage site) were unmistakable as they were hustling boats in and out of the water. Twice Harry and Tim had to get out and push the boat in water that didn't reach their knees. When they finally got to the ramp and had it pulled onto the trailer with the help of Denny Chambers, Tim turned to Harry and said "I think that's the last fishing trip of the summer." Harry figured that decision had more to do with being alone in a boat with his brother than any hassle with low water. "Yeah", Harry said. "a lotta rocks in the water."

The rest of the Saturday passed quietly enough. Hap and Doris went up to Yetter's for crab cakes. Tim took a nap, had a bath, got dressed and jumped into his car just before seven. Harry had a beer at the house and figured he'd go over to Martzie's on Front Street for something to eat. He also wanted to see what he could find out about Bob's and the liquor house, but he was afraid to ask too many questions because he had a feeling his brother was mixed up in something that Harry didn't want to call any attention to. Harry thought back to his Army days, when his sergeant told him "When in doubt about what to do or say, don't do or say anything."

Harry sat at the bar at Martzie's, ordered some steamed clams and then a hamburger. He saw a couple of guys he knew but most everyone was with their wives or girlfriends on a Saturday night. The bar was busy, but about ten the dinner crowd thinned out and the single people went to the clubs to continue their nights. Harry ordered one for the road from Martzie, and as his bottle of Schmidt's was served with a fresh glass, Martzie gave him his tab. As he paid it, Harry asked Martzie, in a lowered voice, what he knew about an after-hours bar next to Bob's grocery up at the end of Christian Street. Henry Martz, who had been in the bar business with his wife since Prohibition just shook his head. "That kind of fooling around doesn't hurt my business, 'cause I close at midnight every night and I don't open Sundays. But all of that moon-shining and serving beer that fell off the back of trucks, well, that's just not right. This ain't the 1920's."

Harry walked across the Steelton & Highspire railroad tracks and the three blocks to his home. Mom and dad were in bed, and that's where he headed now, up to listen to the radio before getting up the next morning at seven. He was going to Sunday school.

6

Harry plotted his strategy for the morning. He would sit on the right side of the church, about ten rows behind the Hernleys. He wouldn't seek them out. He'd look for a friendly face prior to the start of services to ask where the men's Sunday school class met. He also wanted to see if someone could point out Scrappy Stone's father so that he could introduce himself.

As he crossed Second Street on his way up the hill, Harry had a stroke of good luck. He recognized his dentist, James Becker, who was parking a really nice DeSoto along the curb. James' dad, Reginald Becker had been the Burger's family dentist for years and Harry was James' patient prior to turning his dental care over to the U.S. Army. James himself was a Navy vet who had benefitted from an ample opportunity to practice his new dental degree on reluctant but captive seamen. He had his wife and two little girls with him.

"Hello Doctor Becker!" Harry extended his hand, "Good morning".

"Well, good morning Harry, how are you? Going to church?"

"Yes," Harry replied, "I was here last week. I have been look-ing for a new church since I got back from the service."

Becker introduced his wife and his two daughters. He had

on a beautiful summer suit and his family was very well dressed and polite. "Why don't you walk in and sit with us?" an offer Harry readily accepted. With Doctor Becker, Harry now had his Sunday school host and source of information, and it certainly wouldn't hurt if Hernley saw Harry in the company of a very well known professional family.

"I came to the church service last week but wanted to visit the men's Sunday school class this week. Will you be able to show me the way?"

"Of course, Harry. My wife takes the girls to their class and she helps out sometimes with teaching. My Dad used to teach the adult men's class, but most weekends in the summer now he goes down to the shore. He's not quite retired, but he's working on it!"

After the minister's opening greeting, a prayer and a couple of hymns by the choir, Harry walked to a large room to the rear of the church. No sign of Hernley. The Sunday school lesson taxed Harry's attention span and ended just prior to 10:30. As it ended, Harry asked James about Mr. Stone, explaining how he worked with Scrappy and heard that his family was a member. "Yes, I know him but he wasn't here today. He comes a couple times a month with his wife Marilyn. One of his other sons, Kenneth, is really active in the youth group."

As they moved into the main auditorium of the church itself, young Dr. Becker looked for his family, and it was just then that Harry saw Hernley and his wife talking to some people as they entered the church.

"Thanks, James for escorting me around. I know you want to find your family, but first do you know Bob Hernley and his wife? I work with him, too. I just noticed him over there just inside the door."

"Of course. They are both patients. Bob sees my Dad and

Cynthia is a patient of mine. We have a couple of minutes before the service begins, let's go say hello."

With that, Becker and Harry moved toward the Hernleys and in an instant Bob Hernley saw them advancing. The look on his face was not exactly welcoming. He made eye contact with Harry and then quickly went back to his conversation. It was James who spoke first, saving Harry some potential embarrassment and certainly rescuing him from an awkward moment.

"Hello Cynthia!" The dentist had a big smile on his face as he greeted her and no wonder. She was wearing a beautiful light blue dress and pearls. As she extended her hand to Dr. Becker, Harry noticed her perfectly matching robin's egg blue gloves. She really was very pretty.

"Well, good morning Dr. Byrant" she smiled and then recognized Harry. "And…it's Mister…."

"Burger, Mrs. Hernley, Harry Burger" he stammered. He didn't know if he should be happy because she remembered him or unhappy because she couldn't recall his name.

"Yes, of course, sorry. I am just so awful with names."

At this point, a clearly annoyed Hernley turned to Anthony and Harry. "Good morning, James; back with us again, Burger?"

"Yes Sir", Harry almost shouted as if he were back in his Army days reacting to a Sergeant's bark. "Dr. Becker here showed me to the men's Sunday school class."

"Yes, well, we better sit down Cindy. Good to see you again, James. Send my best to your Dad." And with that Hernley grabbed his wife's elbow and almost pushed her to their pew. Harry turned to Dr. Becker, who was craning his neck toward the rear of the church. "Well, Harry, nice to see you…there's my wife and girls." Becker really was a nice man. Polished, educated, friendly.

"Thank you. By the way, I need to make an appointment

with you now that Uncle Sam is no longer providing free dental care for me. I think I'll stop by this week and set up a date for a check-up."

"Good, Harry…see you soon" and with that he turned toward his family while Harry remained at the back of the church, and as everyone took their seats, he slid quietly out the door. He took off his jacket and flung it across his shoulder as he thought about the morning.

"Hernley's a real prick" he thought to himself.

That summer Sunday on Myers Street passed like most. Everybody took turns reading the paper. Mom had a big dinner in the oven. Tim was still asleep when Harry walked upstairs to change clothes. Harry's dad was helping somebody fix something up at the Fire House but you could set your watch that he wouldn't be one minute late for Sunday dinner. The house was a little warm already as the temperature on the big Coca-Cola thermometer in the backyard slowly climbed above eighty. Harry took several files and a big three ring binder out on the back porch to study. The big project was winding itself down and they were still ahead of schedule. Harry didn't want anything to go wrong at this late date…and he certainly didn't want Hernley to find fault with anything he did on the project.

Doris had baked a ham, made potato salad; there were green beans and a pineapple upside down cake for dessert. She reminded everyone that it was supposed to be the hottest week of the summer coming up, and the family should expect cold cuts and leftovers for dinner. "Too damn hot for the stove" Doris announced.

"I'm still on three to eleven anyway" Tim said with a forkful of potato salad. "Don't worry about lunch Mom…I'll eat from the lunch wagon."

"How about if I take you and Dad up to Yetter's or over to Martzie's one night Mom? We can let them do the cooking for you and sit in an air-conditioned room." Harry was pleased with this offer to his parents.

"That might be the best idea you've had since you've been home." Hap grunted. "Let's go Friday night so I can have a few beers. By the way, what were you reading out there on the porch?"

Harry told them about the project and how well it was going. He told them that if everything went well his overtime would probably be cut back after Labor Day. He kept his other thoughts and plans to himself.

After dinner and the dishes, Harry went out to the back porch in search of shade and maybe a little breeze. He sat there for a while and thought about his view of the world from the back yard where the Burger family had lived all of these years. All of the back yards on either side of 216 were essentially the same...the only distinguishing feature was the amount of junk that varied from yard to yard. In addition to Tim's Mercury, there were two other cars parked in the alley or in makeshift back yard parking places. Everyone's garbage cans were lined up in the alley, and every yard had a flimsy clothes line of some kind for the women to hang their laundry on. Mrs. Rohacek, three doors up, was famous for letting her family sheets, towels and underwear hanging outside for days. Her gigantic bras and her old man's shorts were well known and recognizable to everybody on that side of Myers Street. Across the alley were the similarly crummy backyards and the rear of the triple decker row houses on Christian street. More than a few still had the sheds that had been outside toilets before indoor plumbing made its way into the rest of the West Side after the depression. He could hear the noise from the rail yard just down and across Trewick Street. He was struck by how little green there was to be seen. No grass, no flowers…their own backyard taken up by Tim's car and junk that Hap was going to get around to using some day. Every backyard had a fence and every fence was in some sad state of disrepair… broken boards, cut wire. This was a view of the world – his world – that Harry intended to change.

Harry dozed off, his binder full of progress reports at his feet. He was awakened when he heard the familiar "FWANG" of the screen door slamming shut beside him.

"Sorry Harry, I didn't know you were out here". It was Tim. He had on a pair of khakis and a plaid short sleeved shirt. "Sorry to wake you up…why don't you head into the house and stretch out in front of one of the big fans? Dad's in there snoring away."

Harry straightened himself up and tried to get his eyes accustomed to the sunlight. "Naw, think I'll get out and stretch my legs…maybe take a walk down to the river to see if I can catch a breeze down there, then maybe head over to the pool hall and have a soda."

Just then a car pulled up the alley from Trewick Street. Tim headed down the narrow cement path toward the back gate. He didn't say good-bye. The car pulled up…a late model Buick-black-and Tim jumped in the back seat. Two big guys sat up front and the big Buick pulled away. Harry recognized the guys up front… Ernie and Anthony Linta.

7

Harry had been getting to work around six as often as he could and when he rolled in early on Monday Scrappy Stone was sitting at the engineering desk with a paper coffee cup and two large folders in front of him. He acknowledged Harry but went back to his papers. Harry went back out to the vending machine for his own coffee and checked a couple of inbound rail cars to see if they had the new inventory tags affixed to the load sheets... they did.

Melton walked up and Harry told him Stone was already in the office. "Probably here to give us our bonuses" Melton offered without a smile. They both knew Stone was happy with the way things were going, but he still paid attention to every detail and wouldn't take anything for granted. Melton and Harry went back into the office; it was cooler and quieter than the walkway.

"Missed a hell of a day to fish yesterday" Stone said to no one in particular. "Muskies like the hot weather. Instead of a day on the river, I'm locked inside this crummy office. This place is even more desolate on a Sunday, you know that? The only good thing about it was that I was able to change into a pair of shorts and brought in a radio. Remember when you were allowed to have a radio in here, Mike?"

Melton turned to Harry. "We used to have a radio in here for music and the ball games. When the Phils were in the World Series in fifty, we had the game on and Hernley came into the office here while a bunch of us - including Carper the union steward – were listening to the game. He raised hell, turned the radio off and that was the last of it. The next day, all the guys went down to the bar fab foremen's office after lunch and listened to the game there. Well, Hernley found out about that, too so he got Willis to confiscate their radio. The guys started calling this "Radio Free Steelton."

Scrappy piped up: "Well, boys, working yesterday was worth it. I sorted out a couple of problems and I also finally found out why we were getting those QC errors on the shipping tickets. The QC guys were entering the old codes with capital letters for some reason, and the machines did not recognize them when the data was entered on the cards. We should have that fixed now."

Mike Melton recognized the history behind this: "We used to have to write all of the QC codes in large block letters on the graph sheets that the production reports were attached to. I'll bet that's the reason."

Scrappy nodded: "This is the week that we have every department upstream and everyone post production through final shipping tied in. If we get through Friday's overnight batch, let's see, that's order number sixty-two, without any problems, it looks like we have the full system ready to recommend for approval. That gives the big shots in the Main Office and the guys up in Bethlehem a week to check it out. If that all goes OK, we beat our Labor Day deadline. You know what that means?"

"We get a new Caddy as a reward? Melton wondered sarcastically.

"Hernley shakes our hands?" That was Harry's contribution.

47

"Nope" Scrappy beamed, "it means I get to take a week off and nail those muskies I missed yesterday."

They all worked until six every night that week. Scrappy spent the mornings in other departments, then would check into the big office, then join Harry and Melton around four. Friday afternoon, Scrappy called Harry and Mike on the plant phone at 3:30 and told them not to leave, he was on his way. About an hour later, Scrappy walked into the office with Hernley and with them, Karl Long the general foreman, and Willis, who probably had not been in this office for three or four years.

"What a pig sty this is" were the first words out of Willis' mouth. "I don't think this place has been cleaned since I was last here." The six of them were the only men in the office. Willis continued, "Stone here has made his final report on the open hearth project. He measured the efficiency improvements and analyzed the data. He's recommended that we expand the new methods and procedures from the data processing system you've been working on to another department. We will be taking a good look at it first thing Monday morning, and we are driving up to Bethlehem HQ next Wednesday to make a presentation. Stone will be going with us. We're happy with the job everybody did."

Hernley was next to speak. "Melton, you'll be back on your regular assignment Monday. Burger, you can finally concentrate on your pit recorder duties full time."

That was it. The three big shots turned and left. Stone stayed behind. "Thanks for all the help men. I thought we did a good job for the Company. Let's head up to Katy's for a beer." Melton begged off; Harry accepted.

At the bar, Scrappy had some nice things to say to Harry. Harry was sincere in returning the compliments. "I hope everything goes well for you next week so that you get your week on the river, Scrappy" he said. Harry continued, "You know, you are the only guy who can get the shop workers to help you. Every other guy in management gets resistance or bad information when they approach the hourly men…but they not only answer your questions, they seem to offer suggestions. How do you do that?"

"I don't act like a know-it-all to begin with. I recognize they know more about their jobs than I do. I let them complain and then ask them how they'd fix it. I have good relationships with many of the union guys. Rocky Garber, the local president, I have known all my life. We have fished together since I think we were ten years old. That helps. I played football since the pony league and our high school team, you'll remember, lost two games in three years. With my music and from growing up on the West Side, I have colored friends, Catholic friends, Serbs and Croatians; it just doesn't matter to me. I try to treat everyone the same. I think people see that. You're from the West Side, Harry, you know how it is."

Harry felt like a little kid compared to Scrappy's maturity and common sense. He spoke softly with sincerity: "I appreciate the chance to work with and learn from you, Scrappy. I hope the big project all turns out all right for you."

"I think it will" Scrappy said, looking down at his beer, "You know, that pit recorder job isn't the most exciting thing in the world. I have no idea what is next for me, but it wouldn't surprise me if I get another project assignment similar to this one. If that happens, would you be interested in working with me on it if I could swing something?"

"You know, I would" a very surprised and interested Harry responded. "To be honest, I'd be happy to get away from Hernley…

you saw how appreciative of us he was back there in the office."

"Hernley's OK. He's very good at what he does. He has been successful at just about everything he's touched. He's going places and he knows it. He's a little frustrated to be in the same job now for several years…thinks he is overdue for promotion. He has the skill, and the experience, and he knows his politics. His personality does not allow him to be grateful to others, or to show appreciation. I think he believes hard work is his own reward. He's always been square with me, and I've learned from him. His engineering skills are really something. He'd just rather work with numbers and solve problems and not have to deal with people at all. The most I ever get from him is a nod of agreement, although he is always willing to listen to an opinion from someone he respects. It might take a long time, but you've got to get him to respect you and your ability, and your dedication. Once he does, he won't be such a headache."

Harry thought about that and told Scrappy he'd work hard on building that respect from Hernley. Scrappy picked up the tab for the beers and they walked together back to gate eight. "I'll give you a ride to Myers Street. I'm going to stop in to see my mom and dad. Scrappy had a late forties Ford two door parked outside the gate. Harry was surprised to see a green card tucked behind the windshield…it had a big "U" on it that stood for Unrestricted. This parking card was used only by the top guys…it allowed Scrappy to park just about anywhere in the entire plant, including the best spots behind the big office. Hernley didn't have one. Harry didn't say anything about it. On the short drive to the West Side, Harry asked Scrappy where in Highspire he lived.

"Just below the turnpike bridge. I rent a small house right beside the rail road tracks. I keep my boat on a concrete ramp there with a couple of other guys. I can go from my kitchen to

being on the river in fifteen minutes. I'm five minutes from the
Highspire Diner and five minutes from the Route 230 Diner...I
don't do much cooking. Elsie's tavern is two blocks away, so I
have it pretty good there. The house is a single so I can play my
records and my trumpet without driving anyone crazy. We're
trying to get the band back together too although that's been a
struggle. I hope I get enough time away from work to get back
into it." The Ford pulled up to the Burger's house. "Well, here
we are...have a good weekend and see you after Labor Day. You
have plans for the holiday, Harry?"

"No not really, you?" It was questions like this that made
Harry instantly realize how dull his life was. A big holiday, everybody had something to do, to look forward to; he didn't.

"There's the big picnic at the Management Club Labor Day
itself and a dinner dance the Saturday night previous. I have a
date for Saturday, and if I don't feel like fishing, I'll go to the Club
on Monday. My friend Bill Willis is down from Scranton and
he and his wife will be both at the dance and picnic, so it will be
good to catch up with him."

"Bill Willis, that's Bob Willis' son?" Harry asked.

"Yeah, we have been good friends since we were thirteen. I
spent a lot of time at his parent's house when we were growing
up. They even took me on vacation with them down the shore. I
was best man at his wedding. "

A light bulb went off it Harry's head; Scrappy's projects, his
parking permit, Hernley's admiration for him...it all started to
fall into place. Scrappy had a sponsor at the big office.

As Scrappy pulled away Harry walked into the house to see
Hap and Doris standing in the front room. Hap was not too
pleased. "Did you remember what tonight was? Tonight's the
night you were taking us out to dinner. It's almost seven o'clock."

"Oh, shit...I'm sorry. We worked overtime again and then I had a beer with Scrappy Stone. Sorry, Mom. We can go right now."

"This is going to cost you" Hap said, warming up. "Forget the beer; I'm on the Canadian Club tonight. Your mom too. Let's go to Yetter's, it's closer and I'm starving."

Dinner time at the Burger's, like most of Steelton, was normally five o'clock. Hap and Doris had been waiting two hours.

"If they are out of crab cakes, you're not going to hear the end of it."

Harry, Doris and Hap walked up the street and into Yetter's. The place was jammed, every bar stool taken, most of the tables filled with families and couples finishing their dinners. The smell of fried fish, cigarette smoke and spilled beer was in the air. Two small wheezing window air conditioners tried in vain to cool the place down. Everybody who wasn't chewing or swallowing was smoking. The men at the bar were generally cleaned up and shaved. Buddy himself had his red short sleeved shirt and his apron tied up under his arms. The TV was on but no one was watching.

The Burgers knew just about everybody in the place. Conversations were loud and familiar. The customers bitched about the weather, talked about the high school football team's prospects for the coming season, and bemoaned another end to the baseball season with no World Series for the Phils, all the while wishing the Yankees good luck. Doris saw the Karstetters leaving so she said thanks and how are you as they grabbed the table. Ted Milokovic, his mom and wife were at the table beside them and everyone exchanged hellos. It was close to ten when dinner and the drinks were finished. Buddy's son Donald cleared off the table while Harry got up to pay Buddy. Bellies full, they all set off down Myers Street. On their left as they crossed Conestoga, half a dozen guys were sitting on folding chairs in front of the hose house. There were fireflies and a thousand moths buzzing around the street lights. Many of the houses had people sitting out on the front stoop, the guys drinking beer from quart bottles. A few residents had the blue glow of their Zeniths and Sylvanias illuminating their front rooms as Hap, Doris (who was just a little tipsy) and Harry walked by.

They went in through the unlocked door of # 216. Hap and Doris went to bed. Harry thought he'd have one more beer on the front stoop. He drank that, and was himself in bed by eleven.

8

The big Buick pulled into an abandoned shipping dock behind the defunct Robbins Door and Sash Company on South Cameron Street. Already parked there was a white Caddy, Ben Cohen's old Chevy and a bright red Olds 88. Tim and the Lintas got out of the Buick and headed toward the former shipping office, tucked into the left side of the loading dock area. Waiting for them were Arthur Howard, Cohen and Sonny Donato who was sporting the new fire-engine red Olds. Somehow the old office stayed reasonably cool, despite the fact that it had no electricity and non-opening windows that had been painted shut years ago. The old chairs in the office, including the leather swivel job behind the metal desk smelled bad and looked worse. The accommodations were conducive to short meetings, and brevity was as required as secrecy.

Ben Cohen was the most incongruous member of the group. Barely over five feet tall, and weighing maybe 125 pounds, he was a career civil servant, hired by the Pennsylvania Liquor Control Board not too long after prohibition ended and the LCB was established. He had risen to the head of the department of bonded warehousing and had responsibility for overseeing the in-bound shipping, storage, inventory, and transport of liquor and wine from suppliers as well as all shipping from the Commonwealth owned warehouses to their retail outlets, which everybody in Pennsylvania called a state store. The LCB was a liquor monopoly and was the largest single customer in the U.S. for many wine importers and liquor producers. The LCB was formed essentially to discourage alcohol consumption by making the products expensive and inaccessible. State stores were loathed by just about everybody for their inconvenience, limited hours and crappy service.

All spirits suppliers to the LCB had to survive a rigorous vetting process. They had to ship their products to LCB owned bonded warehouses and survive a bureaucracy that insured slow payment and a host of rules, policies and complex restrictions. The PLCB also oversaw an arcane labyrinth of laws including licensing of breweries, beer wholesalers, distributors, public taverns and private clubs. Cohen had mastered every element of these systems during his twenty four years of service, and had devised and implemented many of the procedures currently in use by the LCB.

Cohen's most ingenious program, and the reason he had been coming to these meetings for several years, was an inventory management procedure of his design that codified the loss of alcohol due to breakage and damage through the shipping and storing process. Through years of analysis and thorough reporting, he had established a universally accepted principle that .0096 per cent of all shipments would be lost due to breakage during handling and shipping in transit, bottles bursting in hot warehouses, or destroyed in the movement of spirits from warehouse to state store. (Once products were inside the stores themselves, the retail department took control of inventory security and reporting).

Losing only one out of a hundred bottles of booze or wine seemed like pretty good performance. In fact, no one complained or bothered to check Cohen's figures. Bottles or full cases destroyed were nothing but broken glass, the contents lost. No supplier wanted to pay for or try to retrieve or keep track of broken bottles; the LCB certainly wasn't going to pay for any retrieval or storage of busted glass of stinking wine or liquor. The figures were all accepted as just a cost of doing business. Cohen kept a running report back to the suppliers who accepted his findings, not wanting to question their best customer. The senior management of the LCB couldn't care less; they just passed along any costs to the consumer. Oversight was lacking at every step of the process.

The beauty of the program-as Cohen had designed it-was that actual breakage was usually less than half of what Cohen's system reported. The cases and bottles counted toward the breakage standard that actually survived were somehow not accounted for in Cohen's programs that he dutifully reported to management every month. Each month he would privately calculate actual breakage versus his magical .0096. The difference was alcohol that everyone else had written off, but Cohen knew about and controlled. Usually this meant the equivalent of thirty to forty cases of liquor or wine each month in the two Harrisburg area warehouses alone.

He kept his plan to keep control of that "surplus" liquor limited to the two warehouses closest to Harrisburg. Cohen also had the authority to approve the shipping companies and trucking firms that moved products from warehouse to warehouse to balance inventories, protect against distribution issues such as strikes or weather problems (flooding and the like). The approved trucking company for Harrisburg was owned by Arthur Howard.

Each month, the designated inventory that disappeared ended up in a Howard truck, and ultimately into the bars, clubs, and liquor houses controlled by the men sitting that warm August day in the Robbins shipping office.

Beer supply was a separate channel and in Sonny Donato's hands. Most of the beer in cases or kegs was stolen by Sonny's organization, and supplied to the Steelton enterprise with a mark-up. Some of the beer was received as payment for other services or loans that Sonny's group provided to legally licensed distributors. Sonny also helped expand the customer side of the enterprise with the private club contacts he had. Three of the Knights of Columbus clubs in the area, and some of the private (usually church affiliated social halls) clubs in Steelton were all cash paying customers. Linta of course provided the security and made certain that none of the protected premises had any difficulties with the law. Howard handled delivery to the clubs through his trucking business. Howard kept the delivery slips, Tim and Sonny collected.

Tim Burger was responsible for the third income stream in Steelton. Burger oversaw the theft of scrap steel, over-aged or forgotten inventory, misplaced or mislabeled raw materials and sometimes finished steel. The rail mill where he worked as a foreman was the northernmost department of the mill, and Howard's scrap operations sat five blocks north and immediately adjacent to the Steelton & Highspire Railroad (totally owned by Bethlehem Steel). Some of the stolen goods would be moved by rail car to a rail siding track accessible by Howard's cranes. Rail cars sat idle on these side tracks for weeks at a time. The rest of the stolen goods were loaded onto unmarked Howard trucks by unknowing workers, thanks to Tim's removal of inventory tags, shipping documents or any other record of the material itself. Bethlehem's antiquated inventory and production planning system made this all laughably easy.

Tim's other responsibilities were to monitor the activities of some of their Steelton bar customers and to collect the cash payments for the beer and liquor from the owners of the bars and clubs that Donato didn't handle, including a couple that he had developed on his own, mostly through life long West Side connections. Linta, as Chief of Police, and his well known son could not be seen in after hour's places buying drinks in clubs. The Howards were black, so they couldn't do it either. Tim's three to eleven shifts at the mill allowed him to visit his paying customers from midnight into the early hours without interfering with his regular job.

Ernie Linta spoke up. "Anthony will hand out all of the figures and make your payments as usual, but first we need to go over the latest from the raid at Bob's. Ben, were the enforcement guys ever able to track back any of the liquor or beer they took that night that Tim got busted?"

Cohen spoke softly. "Not that I have been able to determine. As I told you gentlemen right after the raid, there's a new gung-ho enforcement head – he's an ex-Army Colonel named Warren Walker – lives in Carlisle and he makes it a point to keep his mouth shut about everything. I can't guarantee that there won't be another raid in Steelton. The people I knew who were always able to tip me off in the past are kept in the dark now. I'm working on finding a way to get their agent schedules for Dauphin County. My contact in enforcement is keeping his eyes open. Confiscated liquor is never returned to the warehouses, it's kept in a separate facility under enforcement's control as potential evidence. But I'm working on a way to get that stuff under me, too. I'm telling my bosses we need the security that my proven system provides." Cohen thought that was funny but nobody else in the room seemed to get it.

Ernie Linta again. "Sonny, while Cohen works his sources why don't you see what your people can find out about Walker. See if he likes the ladies or the horses or anything else we can use. By policy, LCB agents are supposed to contact us four hours in advance of a raid. I have all of my force on notice to call me directly no matter what time of night if any place in Steelton is targeted...all the legitimate places as well so that we don't arouse any suspicion. I made sure Peter the Assistant D.A. will call me if any of our joints are on a schedule of some kind. He always tips us off when he knows something's cooking as you know. By the way, son, we need to send Peter a little extra next month with the election coming up; it's a good time for him to be able to pass some cash around the court house. Everyone OK with that?"

"We don't have to worry about the confiscated beer being tracked back to us. The bottles can't be traced and we file the serial numbers off of the kegs when we get them." Howard said. "There's no way to identify where it came from. As usual, we had all of the labels scraped off all of the liquor and the wine jugs as we received it and before we shipped it out to the bar sites. Bob's a reliable guy. We bailed him out with money my son Claude got to one of Bob's sons. We are also paying for his lawyer. As you know, he was back in business two days later. He's told the law he can't read or write, which is mostly true. He told them he gets his liquor from different guys he don't know who sell it from the trunk of their cars or back of trucks. He can't remember what anyone looks like or what kind of vehicle they drive. He uses that Mississippi sharecropper accent of his that nobody can understand, including me and I've known him over twenty years. We don't have to worry about him. Me and my sons personally handle all of the liquor and beer storage and it is as safe as it ever was in the morgue at the funeral home. I don't see any LCB agents wanting to get in there soon, with or without a warrant."

"There's one more thing we need to know about for threats to the business." Tim offered. "Bethlehem may be adopting some new inventory management system. If it ever gets implemented, it may make it harder for me to keep our scrap and materials moving at the same level. The only positive is that my brother is involved with this project, so I might get an inside track on it. I will keep you all posted. I expect this month's deliveries will be about at the same level. Arthur, I've got an idea or two for a couple of big jobs that maybe we can talk about at Bob's one night. I need to know more about your crane lift limits and ability to do some heavy cutting after dark. Stuff is too boring for the rest of the guys. That's it for me."

Ernie's son Anthony stood up. "Here are the reports with all of the numbers since the last meeting. Take a look and then hand them back to me. Give me your receipts and paperwork. Dad has your shares." This was about the only thing Anthony ever said at any meeting. Nobody complained because he did all the paperwork and no one ever suspected any skimming or cheating by the Lintas.

"That's it." Ernie said as Anthony collected everything he just handed out. He handed out the shares in white envelopes. "Next meeting twenty-fifth of September…and for God's sake Sonny, drive something less noticeable next time. Arthur's Caddy is enough of a problem. A fucking rookie cop on his first day of duty would follow that red Olds if he saw it pulling into a derelict building like this."

"Hey, I got an image to protect!" Sonny laughed, and everybody else did, too.

9

The last week of summer was going to be a good one for Harry. He had it all planned. He was going to spend as much time at work as he could get with the college engineering students. He was taking Scrappy's advice to earn Hernley's respect and he intended to start that process by getting an introduction to engineering from the college kids. His paycheck at the end of the week would have quite a bit of overtime on it and when he stopped at the bank he was going to deposit the entire overtime amount into his savings account for rent for his own apartment. He was getting a haircut prior to Labor Day weekend at Toot's and walking up the hill to Dr. Becker's to make his dental check-up appointment. He was also stopping into Fromm's menswear for a new fall weight sport jacket, and pair of grey woolen slacks. Next door was Morrison's where he'd buy a new pair of dress shoes to complete the outfit. Then to the State Store at Front and Pine for a bottle of Canadian Club for Hap as a birthday present.

The industrial engineering guys pretty much kept to themselves despite sharing the crowded office with Harry and the foreman. It was the last Monday in August and Harry cornered one of the Lehigh students at the vending machine just after seven. "Before you head back to school, could you give me a little introduction to industrial engineering? I'm hoping I can learn to use some basic knowledge to help me support the full time I.E.s here."

The kid's name was Shelton and he and his fellow Lehigh student Markowski could not have been more helpful. They took Harry out into the plant a couple of hours that day and gave him the basics in job observation and motion and time management. They showed how they analyzed the worker and machine for inefficiencies. Back in the office on Tuesday they showed him the charts and reports they produced. Harry understood maybe twenty percent of this, but it was a start. Markowski showed Harry several books that were in the office that probably hadn't been touched in years. One was on the Bessemer process for steelmaking, its history and how it worked. There was a smaller manual on quality control that had been written by Bethlehem engineers. Harry found several binders of reports that had been produced at Steelton, including one that listed Hernley and Willis as contributors. Harry pulled those and put them on his desk.

His pit recorder job took him four hours a day at most. He was often bored and found himself talking to and learning as much from Melton as he could. Harry determined that he would faithfully spend two hours every day on his on-the-job education.

Wednesday was the day the big shots were driving up to Bethlehem to make their reports and recommendations. Harry and Melton had not heard anything more from Scrappy or Hernley since last Friday. Harry figured he could get away with leaving the office for a couple of hours since all of the management was either away or on vacation. About eleven, he walked up through the plant as he didn't want George Clark to see him leaving the plant at gate eight (he did not punch out). Harry went out the main gate to Front Street and made a left and headed up to Toots

Yanchileff's barber shop. He was thinking he shouldn't have a wait on a weekday morning and he didn't. Toots had one guy on the chair and within a half hour Harry, with his snappy new trim and a spring in his step, was stopping into Rea & Derrick's for a hamburger and a milkshake at the counter. Then it was a one block walk up Locust Street to Dr. Becker's.

The entrance to the dentist's office was on Second Street and as Harry turned to walk up the three steps to the door, he saw the sign: "Apartment for Rent". He opened the door and entered a cool and smallish vestibule with black and red linoleum tiles, clean as could be. He smelled the unmistakable scent of a dentist office. To the right was the entrance door to the Becker dental offices, with Reginald and James' names etched in black on the frosted glass. Straight ahead was a flight of stairs. Harry could see a sturdy door at the top. He paused and opened the door to the waiting room. Just as he did, he was stopped in his tracks. It was Cynthia Hernley.

He could see that she was pre-occupied and looking down into the small green pocketbook she was carrying. Harry heard his own voice "Hello, Mrs. Hernley."

She was obviously taken aback and took a second or two to respond.

"Oh! Oh. It's…Harry right? Harry Burger?"

"Yes, how are you?" Harry found himself talking without thinking.

"Fine, just fine…I was just looking for my car keys…sorry I did not see you."

"I hope you are not having any dental problems" Harry offered. And immediately thought it was a rude question to ask.

"No, thank you, I just had a filling replaced."

Harry looked at her for a moment. Every time he had seen

her she was perfectly dressed with a beautiful outfit and not a hair out of place. "I'm here to make an appointment myself with James... we all met at church if you'll remember."

"Yes, of course. I'm sorry I am a little confused here, I just do not do well with Novocain and I'm afraid I'm not speaking clearly."

"No, it's fine" Harry responded. "Did you find your keys?" and then he bravely added, "Would you like me to walk you to your car?"

"Oh, it's just down the block...it's OK...I am fine, really."

"It's no trouble at all; let me get the door for you."

Harry held open the office door and then the outer entrance door. Cynthia walked ahead down the three steps. "I'm really fine from here, but thank you Harry. Very kind of you. By the way, will you be going to the dance or picnic at the Club this weekend?"

Harry felt as if a knife had been thrust through his ribs. "No. No... unfortunately my position at work does not qualify me for membership. I would very much like to be invited to join some day, but that is a ways off I suppose."

"That is too bad, I didn't know. I'm sorry. It would be nice if you could come."

"Well, maybe see you at church Sunday. 'Bye Mrs. Hernley!"

"Please, call me Cindy. All my friends do", and with that she turned and headed south on second toward Walnut Street. He watched her walk away. She had a pale green blouse with light tan slacks. She wore a matching pair of tan Ked's sneakers. She had her hair tied into a pony tail. The slacks really showed off her figure and Harry thought he'd better turn away before she looked over her shoulder and caught him staring at her rear end.

Harry would replay this meeting and conversation a

hundred times over the next several days. He would find fault with just about everything he said and did, but he couldn't shake the memory of her face when she said: *"Call me, Cindy. All my friends do"*.

At that, he went back into Dr. Becker's office and spoke to Peggy, his assistant. He set up the appointment and then asked about the apartment for rent sign. Peggy said it was the apartment above the office and that it was going to be available later in September. "Do you think I could talk to Dr. James about it?" he asked.

"He's with a patient and as you see we have two people waiting." Harry, in his flushed state of having suddenly seen Cindy failed to even notice the two people in the waiting room. "Of course, but, you see, I may be looking for a place for myself."

Peggy handed him his appointment card and said, "OK, have a seat, maybe I can get a couple of minutes for you after the doctor is through with his patient. His father is on vacation this week so he is the only one here."

Harry sat in the waiting room. His mind was too occupied to read a magazine. How much would a nice apartment like this cost? Would they rent to a single man? Did Cindy really mean that she was sorry Harry couldn't attend the Labor Day events at the Club?

"Harry?" it was Peggy. "Dr. James can see you for a minute." She turned and told the young kid sitting across from Harry that he was next and Dr. Becker would be with him shortly.

"Harry, hello!" Dr. Becker extended his hand. "Nice to have you back in the practice. Peggy said you had a question about the apartment upstairs."

Harry expressed his interest and James was both encouraging but cautious. "Well, my Dad handles the apartment; he owns the building and won't be back until next week. The family that's in there now is moving down to Middletown, and I know it will be available by the first of October.

"Do you know what the rent is?" Harry asked, expecting the worst.

"No, I don't, sorry Harry. Why don't you ask Peggy to set up a couple of minutes with my Dad late next week and you two can talk about it?"

"I'll do that" Harry said, shaking James' hand. "Thanks for the time today."

Harry set up an appointment for four-thirty the following Thursday to see the senior Dr. Becker, said good-bye and thanks to Peggy, and headed down Locust Street, past Bernardo Brothers, showed his badge at gate seven guard house and went across the S&H railroad tracks past the shipping clerk offices and into the bowels of the plant. The noise, heat and smells of the mill quickly brought him down to earth. Harry's head was swimming with thoughts of him watching TV in his apartment on the hill, with a sophisticated cocktail in his hand…and Cindy Hernley snuggled up on the couch by his side.

10

Harry spent his Thursday with Melton until lunch and then tried to engage the college kids to help him with his engineering orientation. The kids were more interested in thinking about their return to school, as the next day would be their last at the plant 'til next summer, so he went back to Melton to see what he could do for Mike, who had scheduled a week of vacation for Labor Day week. Some of Mike's regular work would be picked up by the second shift guy while Mike was out, but Harry offered to help pick up the slack. Just when Harry was thinking about how slow next week was going to be, the phone in the office rang and one of the shift foremen yelled to him. It was Stone on the line. Stone told him to get Melton and to be in Hernley's office first thing in the morning. Willis would be there too. They had their results from the meeting up in Bethlehem.

"Anything I need to prepare for or to bring, Scrappy?"

"Nope. You and Melton bring yourselves." Harry couldn't tell if Scrappy was happy or mad and before he could ask, Stone hung up. This set Harry's mind spinning. What happened up in Bethlehem? Would there be a new project, or perhaps an expansion of this one that would get him working with Scrappy on something exciting? Did something go wrong? Was Scrappy in some kind of trouble? Was Hernley getting a promotion as a result of the project? All of these things kept Harry thinking until three that afternoon, when he got himself cleaned up in the locker room and punched out precisely at three-thirty. This was his big shopping day on Front Street.

As he walked out of the plant and up Front, Harry took a look down toward Katy's. One storefront after another had people window shopping. All of the little businesses, side by side, seemed to be doing well. Ort's bakery. Brownie's beer distributor. O'Malley's hardware. The Bon Marche beauty shop filled the sidewalk with the smell of permanents. The bottom of Locust Street on Front was anchored by the two large banks-concrete edifices with columns and marble steps. The Steelton Trust had a large, three-sided clock with ornate iron hands and large steel finials on each corner. The only slightly less imposing Steelton Savings and Loan had bars on the windows and a steady stream of customers trying to beat the four o'clock closing time. Rea & Derrick's was next, and then came a solid block of Steelton's finest retail shops. Harry stopped into Fromm's and thirty minutes later had been fitted with a snappy grey herringbone sports coat and a pair of grey flannel slacks. He gave Mr. Fromm ten bucks down.

Right next door was Morrison's shoes. In fifteen minutes, Harry walked out with a shoebox under his arm, secured with the twine from the big spool next to the cash register…in it a pair of size 10 cordovan oxfords – his first pair of Florsheims ever. Mr. Morrison threw in two cans of Kiwi shoe polish and three pair of socks to seal the deal. Harry was feeling very pleased with himself. His original plan was to get Hap's birthday gift at the state store but Harry had spent most of his cash on the Florsheims…he'd stop in tomorrow after he made his bank deposit.

As he cut across the parking lot behind Rudy's gas station the noise from the rail mill banged and clanged through the large open bay doors. It was as if there were a thousand blacksmiths in that building, each hammering out a bar of steel on a heavy anvil. An S&H railroad engine pulled three empty flat bed rail cars north toward Trewick Street. The parking lot was full of Fords, Chevys, Dodges, and Plymouths driven by the union guys working second shift in the heat. All of the West-Siders could walk to work, including Harry's brother Tim who was now somewhere within the bowels of the rail mill, wearing his white supervisor's hat and probably sitting in one of the few air conditioned offices drinking his coffee.

How was it that he and Tim had turned out so different? They were pretty much raised the same. Give Hap and Doris credit-they never played favorites. He and Tim had about the same grades in school, but Tim was out-going and very popular. He always had girlfriends and cute ones too. "We both went to work in the mill right after high school, but I went nowhere while Tim made foreman in just a few years" Harry thought. Tim had no interest in military service and thought guys who signed up ought to have their head examined. "Maybe he was right" Harry thought to himself. "I spent three years in the Army, I saved a little money. Tim's rolling in the cash. Maybe it's just luck; maybe the luck will even out...I'm trying to do the right things and I'm due for a break."

Harry needed a pack of cigarettes so he cut up Main Street to the pool hall. Jack Stoyanoff was behind the counter. Jack lived above the pool hall that was owned by his brother "Mooch". Jack had the worst complexion Harry had ever seen, and he wore his coal black hair combed straight back. Jack called everybody "Slick". The pool hall was a thriving enterprise, the place to pick up the milk or bread, sodas, candy and cigarettes. They had a freezer with Hershey's ice cream and popsicles. There were pinball machines and in a dark and smoky room in the rear two pool tables, a separate card room with no windows, a back door to the alley, and beer and liquor(supplied by Howard) if you were a regular. Harry knew he could bet on a horse race, a football game, and in a pinch get a cash advance here if he needed it. He never shot pool though, and never went into the back room. Tim did, though, and Harry thought it was just another little difference in how the two of them spent their time and money.

Harry got his L&Ms and on the way out almost bumped into Darlene Decker. Darlene was one of the girls Harry spent a little time with before he went into the service. He hadn't seen her since he got back.

"Darlene...how you doin'? It's been awhile".

"Harry Burger. My brother told me you were back...he saw you at Yetters. You know, you could have called or stopped by. I'm still living at home. You lost a little weight in the Army?"

"Doris is trying to put the weight back on me, that's for sure. Yeah, I saw Charlie at Yetter's. We talked a little. What's new with you?"

"I got a job up at Kormushoff's...running the cash register and helping out. You know the West Side, nothing much changes. I just needed to pick up some hamburg buns for tonight from Mooch." She noticed the shoebox under Harry's arm. "Been shopping?"

"Yes, needed a new pair of shoes. OK, Darlene, I gotta get home...maybe we can go over to Martzie's some night if you like."

"I can do better than that" Darlene said, smiling. "Charlie is taking my mom and dad down to Reading for the weekend to visit my uncle. I have to work. Why don't you come over Saturday night and we can watch some TV. Maybe we can catch up a little."

"I, uh, well, uh, yeah, um…sure. OK. I'll bring something over."

"I won't be cooking, but I will be thirsty!" Darlene was clearly flirting now. I have to work 'til six on Saturday, come over about 7:30."

"OK Darlene. See you then."

"Oh shit". Harry was already beating himself up over being so stupid and now he was talking to himself, too. "I told myself I was not going to fool around with girls from the West Side and now here I am right back in it. It's the same damn story. Every time I try to get myself out of here, I screw up. I just hope everything goes OK with this meeting tomorrow morning, because I can't see myself being a pit recorder for the rest of my life."

Harry and Hap ate dinner together with Doris and while Doris cleaned up Hap had a seat on the big overstuffed chair in the front room. He had taken his after work bath –sometimes in the summer he would shower at the plant-and it seemed like all he could do to stay awake. "Well, Dad, big birthday coming up Saturday. Mom baking a cake?"

"I guess so, she usually does. Anything's better than those god damn hot dogs and pork and beans we got tonight. Too hot to cook proper I guess. Saturday night there's a floor show at the Moose so I promised I'd take her. We'll probably celebrate the birthday on Sunday. Monday's the Lion's Club picnic and you can join us if you want. The kids need new uniforms for next year and we're trying to raise some money for them. Your Mom and the ladies auxiliary have tried to sew those old uniforms up every year but they are just about shot….they're close to ten years old I think. It's embarrassing as a coach to send those kids out in those shitty things every game. As it is we make every kid buy his own hat every season."

"How's work going Dad? I never hear you talk about it."

"What's to talk about? I punch in, I fix shit that breaks down, something else breaks down, I go fix that. Then I punch out."

Harry envisioned this same life for himself over the next twenty years. "And how about Tim? Does he ever talk to you about his job? He made foreman so young, he must have ambition to rise up in management."

"Tim don't say shit."

And that was pretty much the end of the conversation.

11

Harry awakened at five-thirty. He had had a restless night, even though his bedroom was quite a bit cooler than it had been the previous weeks. He was able to get into the bathroom before Hap did, always a good thing. Today was payday, but more important than that was the seven o'clock meeting in Hernley's office. Harry put on a long sleeved dress shirt, and a pair of his best pants; he went through gate eight, paid his respects to George Clark, and punched in at six thirty-five. He got a cup of coffee and Melton was right behind him. Harry was a little on edge but Melton was his usual not-get-excited -about -anything self.

"Any idea about what will hear this morning, Mike?" Harry was hoping for something positive.

"Nope, no idea, I just don't want anything screwing up my vacation next week."

"Thank you, Melton" Harry thought to himself.

They walked into Hernley's office at 6:55 and Stone, Long, Hernley and Willis were there along with a couple of other guys Harry had seen at the main office when they were up there during the project. There wasn't room for everyone to sit down, so everybody stayed standing. Willis had a big blue binder beside him and then he spoke.

"On Wednesday we went up to Bethlehem to Headquarters to go over our work and our recommendations on the production planning project. Two of the Company Vice Presidents and the General Superintendent – Ledbetter – were there. We had sent our recommendations to them by courier a couple of days in advance so that they could have time to go over all the data. There were also several management personnel from the open hearth operations at the main Bethlehem facility. It turns out they had made separate reports to Ledbetter and the V.P.s themselves on their own project that paralleled ours. What we didn't know while we were working on our project here in Steelton over the past couple months was that HQ had the same project – a duplicate – running up at the Bethlehem Plant. It was kind of a quality control check, but also a way to see if overall efficiencies were measurable and realized, and if recommendations from the two plants matched up. We didn't know they were working on this and the management up in Bethlehem-other than the VPs - didn't know we were working on it at the same time. Bob?"

Hernley took the binder from Willis and cleared his throat. "Results of the two studies were similar. Just about every aspect of work flow– QC, inventory, shipping, production scheduling - showed the benefits of the new data processing methods we tried. The only real difference between the two plants came in the management recommendations. We here at Steelton thought the results were significant and that the new DP approach should be implemented plant wide, with budgets approved for training and equipment so that we could begin in January. We proposed Steelton as the pilot site for the entire Corporation; if things went as expected, then the new methods and procedures could be adopted within all of our facilities across the country."

Harry thought to himself: "This is great. Maybe I will be

selected to work on this and maybe Stone will be in charge."

Hernley continued. "The other project team from the other plant was more cautious than we were. They thought that implementation should go on a department by department basis, instead of plant-wide, and of course it should be done up at Bethlehem. They told the VPs and Ledbetter that local supervision up there could take advantage of the executives' personal oversight and expertise much easier if everything was done at the HQ facility. This was mostly ass-kissing of course, but the cautious approach seemed to resonate with the top people. The final decision is that the project, that we will now officially call PEP –for Production Efficiency Project – will be implemented by departments. We are fortunate that we have the opportunity to participate here in Steelton, but only in extending our open hearth work to one other department, instead of plant wide. Mr. Willis and I, along with Stone and the office staff, will decide which department we will bring on next. Melton, you are OK for your vacation next week. Burger, you are still on pit recorder. Stone will be in touch with you if he needs you for anything. We expect Stone will be in charge of PEP for the next department we select. That's all for now."

Everyone filed out. Melton was happy because his vacation was preserved. Harry could not read Scrappy's face. He could tell, though, that Hernley seemed to have been knocked down a peg and Willis didn't seem too happy either. Harry decided just to keep his head down, say nothing. He thought he remembered Scrappy telling him that he wanted to extend the project only into another department, not the plant wide approach that he heard Hernley talking about.

Harry figured it was best just to think about the next three days off. He'd get his paycheck at lunch time, punch out at exactly three-thirty and get to the bank before closing.

Back in his office, Harry saw that the student engineers had planned a little party for their last day of work. One of the kid's Moms baked a cake and everybody had a piece with their mid morning coffee. Harry had some extra work for the three day weekend schedules but he was pretty much done by lunch time, when he went to the cage to pick up his pay check. Melton was beside him but had mentally checked out already and Harry made it a point not to ask Melton anything about the meeting.

Harry walked out to the picnic tables just behind the gate eight guard house with his lunch. Doris packed him a proper lunch just about every day so that Harry wouldn't have to pay for lunch from the hot dog wagon. There were a couple of men already seated at the table when Harry saw George Clark by the gate.

"Hello George. Have plans for the holiday?"

"No, Harry, I'm working Monday. Most of the guards do not have holidays off; the plant still runs, trucks in and out, that sort of thing. "George gave Harry a good, long look. "Big meeting this morning, huh?"

"Why, yes, yes there was George. " Harry was kind of surprised George knew about these things, or cared. "How'd you know?"

"Harry, here's a little advice. If you ever need to know what's going on around here, ask the guards. We see everything and everybody come and go. People talk to us because they think we're harmless. They see me as sort of a beat-up old guy and are careless sometimes with what they say to me. I'm trained to always have my eyes and ears open. I saw Willis come in this morning with Stone and that big binder under his arm. As he got out of his Olds and rushed by, I could tell Hernley was in a sour mood. The word is those two were up to the main HQ in

Bethlehem on an important project and had their asses handed to them by Ledbetter and his men. The guard working the main office second shift heard them discussing it in Willis' office late Wednesday evening. Yesterday, one of the inter-plant truck drivers brought that replacement oxygen sensor platform down from the open hearth at the Bethlehem plant, and he told me everybody was up there talking about some kind of production efficiency contest they had with Steelton and that the Steelton guys lost a big investment decision to the HQ group."

"I see. Well, that seems to make some sense George. Thanks. By the way, Doris put a TastyKake in my lunch box and I already had some cake with the engineering kids…help yourself."

"Thanks, Harry. I know you've been working with Scrappy Stone. He's a good guy and he walked in and out the gate and up Front Street with Willis. I heard him tell Stone to make sure they get together at the picnic Monday. I'd stick close to Stone if I were you."

"I do like him, George, and I respect him. Us West-Siders have to stick together, right?"

"Yeah, I guess…you DO have the second best fire house in Steelton!" George said with a big grin."

Harry ate his sandwich and then took a long walk around the open hearth. He did a lot of clock watching that afternoon. He had his hands and face washed, changed out of his steel toes and into a pair of loafers and stood by the time clock, punching out at quitting time on the button.

He did his banking and stopped into the State Store to buy Hap's Canadian Club. The day was warm but not humid. Steelton was bustling. The sidewalks were full and the State Store was doing a booming business. There was a line at the cash register as everyone was trying to beat the store's five o'clock close.

Every customer had the same cold, impersonal interaction with the clerk, who couldn't care less. Harry ordered the half-gallon bottle and had his cash ready on the counter, and the clerk rang it up without a word. His purchase complete, Harry jay-walked across Front, past the gas station, and down Trewick to Myers. The rail mill was still humming, the parking lot still full. A couple of people were in the Balkan Bakery to pick up their half priced bread that Mr. Stefanovich put on sale at four o'clock every day. A north bound Pennsylvania passenger train with two electric engines zoomed up the tracks, its horn blowing for the Franklin Street crossing just a few blocks away.

It was Labor Day weekend, the end of summer nineteen fifty-five. A summer that had seen Harry discharged from the service, returned safely to his parents' home and his own little bedroom. A summer that produced a steady if unrewarding job and visits to a church used solely to help advance his stature in the community. The bright spots were his new found friendship with Scrappy Stone, and the introduction to Cindy Hernley. His relationship with his brother, never that strong, seemed to be strained. His romantic life was essentially empty, not that he cared that much. The weekend ahead presented him with no interest, no enthusiasm, no optimism… his only event a date with a West Side girl he had sex with a couple of times before he went into the service and would probably have sex with again tomorrow night. Harry thought about all of these things as he entered the house, where he heard Doris humming a tune in the kitchen and Hap listening to the end of a Phillies game; they were in Chicago and getting killed by the lowly Cubs.

12

Ben Cohen was the only person remaining in the warehouse office on the Friday afternoon before a holiday weekend. He was waiting for Arthur while reviewing the month end reports for August, and he paid particular interest as always to inter-warehouse shipments for the two Harrisburg facilities. Volumes were up, but not so much as to attract any unwanted attention. He next looked at the invoices from Howard Trucking, Arthur's firm that had recently been awarded a second three year contract under the Commonwealth's competitive bidding process that Cohen oversaw. Howard, always the shrewd businessman, had presented invoices exactly in keeping with the recorded products shipped. It was the unrecorded wine and liquor that provided a very nice income to Cohen, Howard, and their Steelton friends.

Cohen thought back to the first time years ago that he had been introduced to Howard; it was through Cohen's father Jake. The Cohen family ran two very successful scrap yards in Harrisburg: A-1 and Central. Ben's grandfather started the business and his father and two brothers now ran the operation. Before Ben was appointed into his current position, he oversaw trucking and transport for the LCB and was looking for reliable local trucking firms to bid on the LCB business. Jake told him about this Negro in Steelton who was the cheapest around, and who was a reliable supplier of scrap materials, junked cars, and other refuse to their Central scrap yard. Ben liked the idea of helping a colored guy out, and soon Ben met Arthur at the family's Central yard to talk about the bidding process. Arthur, subtle but smart, made sure that Ben knew that if he was able to know a number that Ben thought would win the bid, he would be sure to submit it. A month later, Howard had passed a State review of his fleet and business licenses and a three year contract to move LCB inventory between the two Harrisburg area warehouses was his.

In those days, Ben often went down to the warehouse shipping areas to keep an eye on shipments and to make certain that his inventories were accurate. He already knew that his direct boss was oblivious to partial cases of broken liquor that had been totally written off the inventory and charged back to the supplier. There was a growing area in each warehouse of this off-the-books product…some wine but mostly liquor. It was during one late afternoon when Arthur himself was loading one of his trucks with about 30 cases of liquor and wine for transfer that he struck up a conversation with Ben, who he frequently saw on his trips to the warehouses.

"Mr. Cohen, is that inventory stacked against the far wall something I should be moving? I have been coming to both of the warehouses for about four months now, and each one has a growing store of stuff that doesn't seem to move. I want to make sure I'm doing everything you expect under my contract."

"That is obsolete inventory Mr. Howard. I am working on a plan to dispose of it."

"Is it spoiled or ruined?" Arthur's eyebrows were raised and his mind was already working.

"Well, some of the wines may be affected…I'm not certain of that. But there's nothing wrong with the spirits, no."

Howard already had an idea but he thought he would save it for another time. "Well, OK, Mr. Cohen, sure is a shame to see all that good liquor go to waste…I'm sure someone would pay good money for it even if the cartons were damaged. I got to get going, Sir. Will I see you next time I pick up here? It's been about every other week."

"I try to keep an eye on things, so maybe we will see each other next trip. Drive carefully, Mr. Howard." Howard had planted two ideas in Ben's head. The first was that he might have to watch Howard in case he would try to steal some of the damaged goods…he would be certain to be at the dock for Howard's next pick-up. The second thought Ben had was that Howard was right…someone WOULD pay good money for that liquor…liquor that everyone had just forgotten about…everyone except him.

Ben thought back to that original idea of Arthur's, and how well it had paid off for him and his family. He had three kids and a modest home in the sixteen hundred block of Second Street in Harrisburg. His father and brothers lived above Division Street, where the homes were bigger and nicer, and closer to their temple. Ben's family had to walk about a dozen blocks to temple, his father and brothers just a couple. The brothers were all very successful, as was Ben's sister Ruth who married a lawyer and lived in Reservoir Park. By taking a civil service job, Ben condemned himself and his wife to a middle class life at best, and his father never forgave him for not coming into the business as his brothers did. Everyone else in the family belonged to Blue Ridge Country Club, the Jewish club in Harrisburg; Ben couldn't afford it as his wife Arlene constantly reminded him.

Ben's career had gone well, but his recent promotion would be his last. There were no Jews above his current grade at the LCB, and this was as high as he could go. The very steady, tax-free income he was making though Steelton assured his kids of college, and he and Arlene a comfortable retirement if things kept going. He liked the idea that he did not get too greedy, and that he kept his side business with Steelton small enough so that it would not bring unwanted attention. He trusted Howard and Burger, and the Lintas gave them protection. He thought Donato was the one member who might get them into trouble, but Donato had his own bosses among the Italians and Ben figured that they would keep Donato in line.

Just then Ben turned his attention to an unmarked Chevy panel truck that pulled up to the loading dock outside. Ben watched as Arthur and his son Claude backed it up to the side of the loading ramp. Ben had a hand dolly waiting for them. Arthur took a walk around the front of the truck while Claude sprinted up the steps and grabbed a dolly, nodding to Ben as Ben pointed out that day's shipments. Within ten minutes, Claude had the truck loaded and Arthur was back behind the wheel. No paperwork changed hands and not a word was exchanged between the three men. Ben kept his handwritten records of what was shipped and Arthur did the same for his receipts. There had never been one discrepancy between the two of them when they handed their monthly totals to Anthony Linta at the regular meetings at Robbins.

"There will be some happy people in Steelton this weekend." Ben thought to himself as he double locked the shipping dock gate and doors and headed back to office he kept at the warehouse to lock it before departing for the three day weekend.

Arthur and Claude pulled into the porte cochere alongside

their funeral home. There were two entrance doors into the funeral home itself: one into the public rooms for viewings and services, one in the rear for coffins and bodies picked up on "death calls" as they were known in the trade. There was a tall row of hedges on the other side along Franklin Street to provide privacy for grieving families as they left the funeral home…and the same privacy was afforded Arthur and Claude as they unloaded the liquor from the Chevy and carried it downstairs to the morgue. The morgue had a second exit on the rear of the building, and it was blocked from view by tall wooden fencing on three sides. The open side of the fencing was next to the rear of Farina Motors, one of two Steelton new car dealerships. Farina parked a lot of old trade-ins back there; some that couldn't sell were sold to Arthur for scrap. There was an alley behind Howard's and Farina's and along the alley Arthur's scrap operation stretched for two full blocks north from Franklin, sandwiched between the S&H railroad tracks, the gas works and some warehouses that Arthur also owned just on the other side of Farina's. This set up was perfect for liquor pick-ups at his location by the handful of white customers Arthur trusted. The deliveries to the bars and clubs Sonny and Tim managed were carefully scheduled and made in Arthur's trash service trucks to avoid suspicion. Arthur's sons collected the bottles they sold as part of their trash collection service and would often pick up some regular garbage and trash from the customers to help the cover-up on their deliveries, which had to be done carefully. There were also some places (like Mooch's pool hall) where any black guy –let alone Arthur or his sons who were well known on the West Side- would stick out like a sore thumb and attract unwanted attention, and these customers came to Arthur's funeral home on designated dates and times that Arthur controlled. He always varied them. Arthur and his sons made personal deliveries to the colored grocery stores and after-hours bars that he owned outright or in partnership with old friends like Bob. Arthur liked that there was always a low level of traffic between his home and the scrap yards.... enough so that liquor customers wouldn't be noticed and not too much so that people would get curious or snoop around, not that people liked to hang around a colored morgue and funeral home to see what was going on. There was always a fair amount of distracting movement from Arthur's own scrap and junk yard. He had two mobile cranes, several large forklifts, a Caterpillar bulldozer converted to a claw-loader and a number of dump trucks. He picked up trash and scrap, bought it from others, and sold it to the Cohen's operations plus just enough to two other large scrap dealers in order to keep the Cohen's payments at a fair level. Customers felt safe and protected doing business there.

Arthur had two liquor pick-ups scheduled that evening and then he had three deliveries to make later that night to his own places. His last stop would be to Bob's where he had an appointment to meet Tim Burger around two that morning.

13

Sonny Donato was at the bar for last call at the Steelton Knights of Columbus next to St. Ann's on the lower end. Many of the private clubs stayed open to four in the morning but this K of C closed at two. There were a handful of members at the bar enjoying the last round of the night. The kitchen had been closed since eleven, and Pete the bartender and Sonny waited for the last of the lingerers to leave. This K of C was more of a family centered operation, with good food that resulted in a thriving dinner business. It sold a higher percentage of wine than most Steelton establishments, with the Gallo in the gallon jug the most popular selection. The patrons remaining at the small bar this early Saturday morning were in their forties and fifties, and they knew Sonny only by his first name, a guest of Pete's who showed up from time to time.

Sonny was there to pick up his payments for his deliveries for the month. Like most of the clubs Sonny served, Pete supplemented his legitimate purchases with stolen liquor from Arthur Howard and the beer Sonny supplied off the books and at a cut rate price. The clubs had to show above-the-table purchases from the beer distributors and the state store for the books. Pete handled all of the ordering from Sonny and made a tidy profit in the process that the club didn't know about. As the last of the men shuffled out, Pete locked the main entrance door and returned to the bar and poured himself a V.O. and water.

"Let me get all the lights, Sonny, and we can wrap things up and get out of here." Pete said over his shoulder. Pete took about fifteen minutes to turn off all the beer signs, lights, pinball machines, and juke box.

"Take your time, Pete. I have everything ready for you." Sonny sipped the last of his beer.

"Let me get the deposit and what we owe you Sonny. And I need your guy to get here Tuesday or Wednesday to collect the bottles. Have him here when I open at four sharp."

"OK, let's make it Tuesday" Sonny made a coded note in the little book he kept in his shirt pocket. Howard's sons collected the liquor bottles, but Sonny had to arrange for beer pick-up. Beer was always in returnable bottles, so there was a deposit and some cash in it. Sonny had a couple of sources, including a distributorship that he and his friends controlled, who could accept the bottles. The beer bought by the K of C and other clubs through Sonny could not be returned as empties for deposit to the legitimate distributors who also sold to the K of C and other clubs. They would wise up in a hurry if brands of beer started showing up that they did not handle.

"That last shipment from you had six cases of Stegmaier and I can't return that through our regular channels. Shorty's would know they never sold us that beer and would wonder where we got it."

"I get it!" Sonny was a little annoyed. He had been in this business long enough to know not to make rookie mistakes. "Four o'clock Tuesday; the usual guy will call at the back door. Count on it."

Pete continued back behind the bar and took the cash from the register, filled out the deposit slip and put in into the night deposit bag that he would drop off at the Savings and Loan on his way home. He looked at Sonny's handwritten invoice, detailed by brand and type as well as quantity, and he paid Sonny the hundred and twenty-five bucks totaled up for the month's beer and liquor and cigarettes. He handed the written invoice back to Sonny along with the cash.

Sonny took the cash and folded it into his jacket pocket. "Here's a little something for the month, Pete. Let's try to make September a little better." Sonny kicked back a ten spot to Pete as a thank you. They shook hands and headed out toward the back door. It was double bolted on the inside and Sonny watched as Pete pulled out a key chain and fumbled through a dozen or more until he found the one for the door knob lock. Pete pushed open the door and immediately noticed that the light over the door was burned out. His old Dodge was parked right beside the door…Sonny's red Olds was at the edge of the parking light under a street lamp at the corner of the alley. As Sonny was just about to walk around Pete a firm voice barked out from behind them.

"Don't turn around." Sonny felt something poke him – hard – in the small of the back. "You, hand over that bank bag!" All of a sudden, there were two guys coming out of the shadows, one guy has his hand menacingly in his right jacket pocket. "Let's have the wallets, too, and your watches!"

Sonny had lived his life not to take any shit from anyone and never backed away from a fight. As soon as one of the guys got close enough to reach for Sonny's wallet, he took a wild swing and hit the guy on the side of his head. He tried to jump on the guy when Pete watched in horror as another guy –still behind them-cracked Sonny over the back of his head with a baseball bat. Sonny crumpled to the ground.

"Hand me the fucking bag and get down on the ground"

Pete did not want any part of that baseball bat.

"OK OK OK!" he yelled as he threw the deposit bag a few feet in front of himself. He felt a hard push in the small of his back and was pushed face first into the stony ground.

"Get their wallets!" he heard one of them say....Pete was face down and expecting to get the same baseball bat treatment any second.

"Fuck the wallets, man, let's go!"

Pete stayed down, for a couple of seconds, and looked up to see three guys running across the parking lot and up the alley. It was dark, he was stunned. Sonny looked bad, his head was cut open and he was not moving. There was some blood on his face. Pete grabbed his handkerchief and held it on Sonny's bleeding head. Sonny did not move.

Pete yelled out for help, hoping one of the neighbors would hear. Across the way, he heard a voice from a second story window.

"What's going on? You OK down there?"

"Call the cops. I need an ambulance" Pete was yelling while he was trying to find his keys. Maybe he could get back inside and get some ice for Sonny.

A porch light came on at the house next door. Pete saw that it was Tony Coletto, one of the guys who was just in the bar for last call.

"For God's sake Tony, get on the phone! Call the cops! This guy needs a doctor!" Tony ran back toward his house. Sonny was still not moving.

Pete's head was clear enough to remember the cash in Sonny's wallet. He held Sonny's head but reached inside Sonny's jacket. There must have been three or four hundred in it. Pete took the cash, and threw the empty wallet about ten feet away, toward the side of the building.

A couple of the neighbors started to come out to see what was going on....one of them had his own baseball bat in his hands. Tony rushed back. "I got the cops...they're on the way...I told them back of the K of C... they said they'd radio for an ambulance...is that guy dead?"

Pete saw that Sonny was breathing but he still had not come back around. "Let's just try to keep him from bleeding and wait for the ambulance."

Pete heard sirens. Sonny was starting to stir a little bit. A Steelton police car pulled into the lot, its headlights shining on the small cluster of people gathered around Pete and Sonny. Pete was sitting on the ground. Two of the neighbors had returned with flashlights and they helped the cops see what was going on with Sonny. One of the cops had a first aid kit and bent down over Sonny. The other cop took in the situation and turned toward the crowd.

"What happened here? Who saw what?"

Tony Coletto spoke up. "This here's Pete, the bartender from the K of C. The other guy was a customer. I heard somebody yelling for help and ran out here. That guy was knocked out and Pete here was giving him first aid. His head is all bloody."

"All right...anybody who saw or heard anything here, you stick around. The rest of you people can go back home." The ambulance could be heard wailing and getting closer. The cop continued his orders: "Everybody back off and make room for the ambulance. Anybody who didn't see anything go back home."

"I'll stick around" Tony said to Pete.

Two guys in the ambulance got Sonny on a stretcher and with the other cop's help got him into the wagon. Sonny was stirring and mumbling, but never quite came around. The cop who seemed to be in charge talked to the ambulance driver just before they sped off and then returned to Pete, who was still sitting on the ground.

"Can you talk? What happened here? Robbery?" Pete saw that the cop's nametag was Karmilov. He was a corporal. Pete took a minute to try to think how to play this.

"My name's Corporal Karmilov…my partner here is Dolan. Why don't you start with your name and how you got here."

Tony spoke up. "I told you, this is Pete Posetti. He tends bar here. We…"

"OK Thank you. But I'm asking this guy." Karmilov was not going to let a bystander tell him what happened. He wanted to hear it from the man involved.

"Uh, well, I uh…I was locking up. I had the night deposit bag and a couple of guys jumped us from behind. They whacked this guy over the head with a baseball bat I think it was…he took a swing at one of 'em. They pushed me down on the ground and took the deposit bag and our wallets. They took off across the lot and up the alley, toward Mohn Street."

"How many were there? Did you get a good look at them? How old? Colored or white?

"Three I think. I was a little woozy. They jumped us as soon as I came out the door. They must have broken the light above the doorway…it was dark. They must have been young guys, they ran fast. I couldn't tell if they were colored or not."

"Who's the other guy?"

"Uh…he goes by Sonny…he's a customer; I don't know his real name." Pete was starting to worry about getting a story that the cops would buy. Karmilov did not seem like a dummy.

"Why was Sonny back here with you?"

Pete knew it was time to clam up. "Mr. Karmilov, I'm a little dizzy, I feel like I'm gonna pass out. Can I get something to drink and maybe can we talk about this tomorrow? I'd kind of like to rest up a bit."

Karmilov looked at Pete for a good long while. "All right. Where do you live? We can give you a lift home. I don't want you driving or trying to walk home if you're in bad shape."

"If it's OK with you, maybe I'll just stay overnight at the club. There's a big sofa in the office and it's air conditioned. I can just let myself back in and lock up. I should try to call Mr. Cantore, he is the club manager. I'll have to report the money that's missing...I'm responsible for that."

Karmilov did not like this idea. He thought Pete was covering something up. Just then his partner Dolan came hurrying back to him.

"Mike, We got another call just came in on the radio...car crash over on Lincoln Street and some kind of fight breaking out over it."

"OK. Look, Pete. We got a lot more we need to know about this to try to track down who did this. It's OK for you to stay here...maybe your friend here can give you a hand. Karmilov turned to Tony Coletto. "What's your address?"

"I live right here, next to the club, number 535, lived here twenty years. We ain't never had no trouble here before. I'll help Pete."

"All right, Pete. Make your report to your manager. Expect a visit from us sometime tomorrow. By the way, is that big red Olds yours?" Karmilov didn't miss much.

"No, that Dodge there is mine. I'm on duty tomorrow. Mr.

Cantore will probably be here first thing in the morning. We'll help you out any way we can."

With that Karmilov and Dolan jumped back in the patrol car and sped off. Tony helped Pete find the keys and they went into the club. Pete turned on a couple of lights.

"Thanks for all of your help Tony. I think we could both use a drink…on the house!"

"You read my mind Pete. Shot and a beer for me."

Pete had a V.O. for himself. He thanked Tony and showed him out the back door. Pete sat in the darkened bar for a bit and then quietly opened the back door where the robbery occurred. He made certain that no one was around…it was almost three thirty in the morning. Pete emptied the cash out of his own wallet and threw the empty billfold as far as he could down along the wall of the building, in the same direction he threw Sonny's. He called Nick Cantore from the office phone and made his report. Cantore listened to Pete's story, made sure Pete was OK, and told him he'd be down about eight that morning.

"Okay Nick. I'll probably be sleeping on the couch in the office." Pete hung up, washed his face in the men's room sink and stretched out on the couch for a couple hours' sleep.

14

Arthur kept the inventory as two of his sons loaded up the panel truck. There were three stops plus Arthur's own bar. The bottles of liquor for his own place had their labels still affixed; the others were stripped but marked with a heavy yellow wax crayon "1" or "2". The number one bottles were the premium brands so that Arthur's outlets would know to charge a little more. Regular customers knew to ask for number one or number two. The number ones sold well on paydays. For Arthur's own place, the labels were kept on until poured into empty or nearly-empty bottles he had purchased legally from the state store. Arthur still bought a little more than half of his liquor the legal way for his own place, which was properly licensed. As soon as one of Cohen's bottles was poured into one of the "legal" bottles it was smashed and put in a large trash bin that Arthur's garbage operation hauled away.

Arthur's bar was protected by the Steelton police and Arthur's own community influence and powers of persuasion. For the most part, it seemed like an above-board operation. It drew a mostly colored crowd from Steelton and Harrisburg, but more than a few white guys –mostly locals – were regulars. Ernie Linta liked the fact that Arthur kept a tight grip on the operations. The rumors about prostitution had no basis in fact. Arthur kept his circle of insiders tight. He donated to the right politicians but in a low profile way that preserved his influence.

"Make the hill deliveries first and then drop off ours last" Arthur barked instructions to Claude, his oldest. "Let's go over these numbers once more". The shipment having been double-checked, Claude and his younger brother Lawrence took off down the alley. Arthur went in for a pork chop dinner with his wife and his two youngest children and just before ten walked the two blocks west on Franklin Street to his bar.

Arthur's was on the north-west corner of Myers and Franklin. There was a neon Ballantine Beer sign above the door…each one of the circles in the three ring sign lit up one at a time, and then the three interlocking circles of the logo would all flick on together. Arthur always walked in through the front door. As he did so this late Friday evening, the place was humming with happy customers. The juke box was playing and smoke was heavy in the air. Arthur was happy to feel the nice cool air being noisily pumped out of three new window air conditioners that he bargained for from Schindler's Electric. He greeted everyone he saw and moved behind the bar to have a private word with Anthony Wright, his long time bar manager.

"Claude and Lawrence should be here in a little bit. I'll take care of the truck in the back when they arrive. Are you running out of anything?

"We ran out of Cutty earlier, but everything else is OK. The kitchen has been busy but Etta should be closing it any time." Etta had been his cook for many years, and now two of her daughters were old enough to help out with the cooking and waiting on tables. The place offered mostly sandwiches and fried chicken and fish and the clientele seemed happy with that. Etta brought in some pies now and again and Arthur let her keep all of the money she made from those.

Arthur reached under the bar and grabbed two empty bottles of Cutty Sark and walked into the kitchen which had to be 20 degrees hotter than the main rooms up front. "Etta baby, you got everything under control tonight? Anthony said you was busy."

"Yessir, Mr. Arthur. We out of fish and the barbeque. We sold two pies but I saved the last one for you and Mrs. Arthur and the children. They peach and turned out real good."

"Thank you, Etta. My boy Claude will be pulling up back here in a bit with some supplies. I'll get him and Lawrence to help you with the dishes and pots and pans so you can get home. Tomorrow night should be a busy one too. Make sure you tell Anthony what you need for the kitchen order so we can get it in for you." Arthur went out behind the kitchen to the alley and waited for his sons. He smoked a Camel and then helped Etta move a couple of garbage cans out from the kitchen to the alley. Claude pulled up, backing the truck in as Laurence opened the metal gate they had installed last year. The boys and Arthur carried the liquor, which was in plain brown cardboard boxes, and put it in a broom closet just off the kitchen. Arthur reached into one of the boxes, and with the door closed, opened two bottles of Cutty Sark and poured the contents into the two empties he brought back from the bar. He tore the labels off of Cohen's stuff, took them out to the garbage cans and smashed them into the cans. He put the two bottles of re-filled Cutty into a brown bag, walked into the bar and bent down to put them near Anthony's feet, giving Anthony a nudge in the process.

Arthur walked back into the kitchen to see son Lawrence washing some pans but Claude in the corner flirting with Etta's young daughter. "Those pots don't wash themselves" he barked and Claude snapped to. Etta's daughter got out of there as fast as she could. Arthur turned to Etta, "We gotta watch them two…I can some the sparks flyin.'"

Arthur walked back over to the broom closet and pulled out a bottle of Four Roses. He tore the label off and put the bottle in a paper bag by Etta's pocketbook. "There's a little something for you Etta, I appreciate the pie."

Arthur spent the next several hours with his customers and helping Anthony at the bar. He didn't drink anything himself other than a couple of nickel cokes from the machine. He didn't buy any rounds and he didn't talk to any individual more than just a couple of minutes. Some of the old time regulars would be making their way over to Bob's after last call, as Arthur would be himself. That's the place where Arthur bought drinks for his friends and best customers.

Tim walked up to and across Conestoga and then the two blocks up Christian Street to Bob's. It was a couple minutes after two. Two cars were parked in the dirt lot next to the main rail road tracks, the one dim street light on the far corner casting shadows across Mr. Washington's old blue Packard and another car Tim did not recognize. He was thinking about how to approach his new idea with Arthur. Tim had worked an hour or so past his regular eleven o'clock quitting time. He took a long walk around the perimeter fences of the rail mill and then he walked along the S&H railroad sidings and took a mental note of the rolling stock inventory. One goat engine sat idle, its engineer and helper reading girlie magazines in the cab. He stopped into Pete and Betty's tavern for two beers and a bag of pretzels. He had all business on his mind when he entered Bob's, nodded hello to the three men at the small bar, and ordered a draft beer. He was the only white guy in the place and sat down at a wobbly table toward the rear of the room. Arthur came in a few minutes later, talked to Bob for a second, and pulled up a chair beside Tim.

"Arthur, I've been thinking about some ways that we can bring bigger money into the business. We have been doing OK with the shipments between us, but I have something I want to talk to you about without bothering the other guys at our regular meeting."

Arthur eased a little closer but at the same time his guard was raised. "I'm interested in bigger money, what've you got?"

Tim made certain that no one was within earshot. "You know how I ship up the steel and wire rope, and the rusted parts in those old gondola cars that the mill railroad runs? Well, there's three of those cars always parked on a siding by my department…it's just outside my office. There's the one engineer-you know him-who just follows my orders when we make a delivery to you. He thinks it's all legitimate, that Bethlehem is selling that shit to you, not that he cares. A couple months ago I saw a physical inventory report and those three gondola cars were not on it. Somehow, although they were supposed to be on the S&H Railroad's asset books, for a couple of years they were recorded as part of the rail mill's rolling inventory, like the yard cranes and so on. The point is, as far as Bethlehem is concerned and as far as I can tell, nobody has any record of those three gondola cars. They must weigh, what six or seven tons, all steel?

"Guess so, don't have any idea really," Arthur was waiting for the money making part of Tim's story.

"Two weeks ago, I took a bucket of acid and a metal brush and in an hour or so a night over three nights I pretty much erased all of the old painted-on car numbers on one of 'em… they were half rusted away to begin with. So I have a gondola car that nobody knows about or cares about, there's no record of it and now there's no identifiable registration numbers on it." Tim waited for Arthur to say something but essentially got a blank stare in return.

"What I'm thinking of is we move that car up to your business and cut it apart, the whole car. That's got to be worth a bunch of money, right?"

Arthur started thinking about six tons of steel and what the Cohens would pay for it.

"What I need to know is can your guys handle that? I can get the car moved up there and parked. These cars stand idle and empty a long time sometimes, and the engineer who I deal with – and you remember he's the only guy I use – would forget about the car and never notice it was missing. I'm guessing you'd have to cut it apart at night, right? I mean there's enough S&H rail traffic and car traffic on the alley that someone would be bound to notice that you were cutting apart a Bethlehem rail car if you tried it in broad daylight.

"Guess so" Arthur wasn't sure at this point if Tim had a great idea or if he was going crazy.

"Do you think you could figure out a way to make this work Arthur? I can be sure to get the car to you and that nobody will notice that it's gone. Don't forget the rail car wheels are a very high quality alloy steel, and you would be able to get a sweet price for those, right? Right??"

"Let me get you another glass of beer" Arthur got up and moved toward the bar, which now had close to a dozen men smoking cigars and drinking small water glasses of brown whiskey. Bob the bartender was hustling to keep up with the demand. Tim thought to himself that Arthur had cold feet. Arthur was a cautious guy. He came back with Tim's beer and a wrinkled brow.

"I gotta think about this. When can I expect your next

shipment of the usual stuff? It's been close to two weeks since we got all of that big rebar. We had to spend a lot of time cutting that shit into smaller lengths that would fit on the dump truck."

"Maybe next week…" Tim was thinking about where he had squirreled away Arthur's stuff throughout the plant since the last shipment. "We got maybe two tons now, we could get lucky with some rail ends. But say two tons for now."

"When you ship this stuff up, why don't you put it in the no-number gondola you've been workin' on. Arrange with the rail road guy to leave the car on the siding closest to my funeral home if you can. Don't schedule a pick up and return of that car for at least a week. I'll have my crane guy give it a look. I also need the cutters to see how they'd take it apart. That mobile crane of mine has a three ton limit with the magnet, so we can't pick the whole car up and move it into a closed in part of the operation."

"Could you just hook it up to the Cat and drag it off the tracks and into your building?"

Arthur thought about this for a minute. "Maybe. Get a message to me like usual through Bob on the shipment date and we'll take a good look at this thing. All right?"

Tim nodded. He slipped Bob a buck on the way out and headed home. There were still a bunch of ways this car deal could go wrong but it seemed solid enough to give it a try if Arthur thought he could get the thing apart. Tim glanced at his watch: quarter to three. He retraced his steps back home and entered through the unlatched back screen door. He turned on the kitchen lights and opened a can of beer from the Kelvinator. He'd have a last cigarette or two and call it a night. He had Monday off, and then four shifts of 3-11. After that, the heavy vacation schedules would be over, the sub foremen would return to their union jobs, and Tim would be back on rotating shifts. That meant a third of his shifts would be on day turn, with the big bosses around and that's a pain in the ass for his business with Arthur.

15

Ernie Linta's phone rang just before five Saturday morning. "Chief? Sorry to wake you up, it's Karmilov."

"It's Ok what is it Mike? You and Dolan OK?"

"Yessir. We had a busy night…everybody's getting a head start on the holiday. You wanted to know about bar or tavern raids or break-ins. It's not the same but we had a robbery at the K of C down on the lower end around two thirty this morning. One guy got whacked pretty good and they took him to Harrisburg Hospital. The bartender, a guy named Pete Posetti, got pushed around but he's OK. I thought you should know. We're going to need some follow up on the scene because me and Dolan got called to a big mess up on Lincoln Street and couldn't finish our investigations and questions. We had to haul in three colored guys over the Lincoln Street fight. The other car had a busy night too; we got seven guys locked up."

"All right, thanks Karmilov. You guys don't worry about the K of C robbery. I'm around all weekend, I'll take care of that one myself. I know Nick Cantore who manages the lodge and I'll call him."

"Right Chief. Cantore…that's the name the bartender gave us. You'll see our report when you get into the office. It's really brief, nobody saw much of anything and as I said, Dolan and I got yanked to another call. We could use a third patrol on these holiday weekends, Chief."

"Yeah. Got it, Corporal. If you're not out on a call, I'll see you at the station before seven."

Linta apologized to his now awakened wife and got dressed. He put on civilian clothes. He knew that the K of C was one of Sonny Donato's places but a robbery there was better than an LCB raid. At worst, they may have lost a monthly payment. He told his wife he would get coffee and breakfast at Knaub's diner. He was out of his house by five thirty and had a plate of ham and eggs in front of him fifteen minutes later.

Ernie looked through the Harrisburg Patriot at the diner, had a second cup of coffee and soon pulled his dark blue unmarked Plymouth into the Steelton Municipal Building parking lot. Neither of the squad cars from his force was in the lot.

"Morning, Mickey. Busy night last night." Mickey Hauser was overnight Officer in Charge. He was the only member of the Steelton P.D. with the rank of lieutenant.

"Yes it was Chief. I've got hearings for all of the guys we've got locked up. Looks like most of 'em will post bail and be out of here by ten. Remember the desk is uncovered now until Tuesday, so the uniforms will have to do their own paperwork for lock-ups."

"I haven't forgotten. Can you stay on until all the cells are empty? I've got to make a couple of calls and head down to the lower end. Had a robbery at the K of C...did Karmilov tell you anything about it?" Hauser nodded. "Just that some guy got his head bashed in and had to go to the hospital. No suspects."

Linta settled into his desk and took a look at the overnight arrest reports and log. He paid particular attention to the K of C report that was of little value. He looked at the wall clock and decided to call the manager Cantore despite the fact it wasn't quite seven. He pulled up the number and Cantore answered on the first ring.

"Nick? Ernie Linta. I have a report here of a disturbance at your lodge last night. Says here the bartender was to call you. Do you know what happened?"

Cantore said that he was about to head down there. "My bartender Pete called me. I made sure he was OK. He got roughed up and one of the customers was sent to the hospital. Sounds like three guys jumped them just as they were heading out with the overnight bank deposit. All the money's gone and I think Pete's wallet too. Pete slept there overnight."

"All right. I'll be there myself in fifteen minutes. Don't screw around with anything 'til I get there. It's a crime scene that we haven't been able to secure or investigate. Don't you or Pete talk to anybody either. Got it?" Ernie hung up before Cantore could answer. Linta was most concerned about the situation regarding the beer and liquor Sonny supplied to the K of C. He cursed himself for not knowing who Sonny's contact was at the K of C. Cantore? The bartender? Someone else? Linta pulled out of the parking lot and stopped at a pay phone just outside Bernardo Brothers. He tried Sonny's number but no answer. He got back into his Plymouth and drove the five minutes to Mohn Street and then doubled back the alley way toward the K of C. He could have shit his pants when he saw a new, bright red Olds parked at the corner of the K of C lot. His training told him to check out the car first. Was anything in it that could cause him a problem? The car was locked with nothing visible on the inside. He tried the trunk and that was locked too. He thought he'd wait until Cantore arrived. There was nobody else around and in a minute Cantore pulled up to the front door.

"Thanks for coming personally Chief. This is the first time we've ever had anything like this. Let's go in."

Cantore unlocked the door and they entered a cool, dark dining area. The place still smelled of garlic.

"You and Mrs. Linta haven't been in for dinner in a while, Chief. Would like to see more of you." Nick called for Pete and Pete stumbled sleepily from the office back in the corner behind the far end of the bar. "You OK, Pete?" Cantore was genuinely worried. "Do you know Chief Linta of the Steelton Police? His officer made a report but they didn't have time to complete their interviews. How much money did we lose?"

"I'll take it from here Nick. Why don't you make us all some coffee?" Linta wanted the two of them separated until he figured out which one-or both – had the Sonny connection.

"All right Pete, why don't you give me the whole story?"

Pete recounted the events but carefully avoided Sonny's name. He called him "a customer" which immediately had Linta's attention.

"Why was a normal customer hanging around and leaving with you and the money after you closed? What's the guy's name and how do you know him?"

Linta wasn't stupid. His imposing size alone often intimidated people into telling him the truth, but they overlooked his ability to read people and situations. From years of dealing with liars, thieves, scam artists, wife-beaters and drunks he could sniff out a lie in ten seconds.

"Uh, guy's name is Sonny something...don't know his last name. Comes in couple of times a month, usually for last call. He was talkin' about his new car, a big Olds and offered to show it to me after closing, so I invited him to hang around. Never hurts to have another guy along when I'm carrying the bank deposit.

Do you guys have any report on how he's doing? He was still out when the ambulance arrived."

"Was he able to say anything to anyone after he was hit?"

"Nope. We got jumped, he took a swing at one of 'em like I told you and then he got smashed. They pushed me to the ground, got the bag and our wallets. I had almost twenty bucks in tip money in mine."

Just then there was a loud pounding on the door. "We're closed" Pete yelled. From the other side of the door he heard a guy yell. "It's me Tony Coletto! I found your wallets!"

Pete let Tony in and introduced him to the Chief. Cantore came out of the kitchen with the coffee pot. Pete spoke up: "This here's Tony Coletto. He's a Knight and a regular. Lives next door. He's the guy I mentioned who helped us out last night when he heard me calling for help. What have you got, Tony?"

"To be honest, I thought there might be some loose money somewhere on the ground after last night. Thought I'd check everything out first thing this morning. I was walking along the far side of the building, way to the left of the back door, when I saw a wallet…then about five feet away another wallet. There's no cash in them. Honest. I found them just this way." He started to hand the wallets to Pete but Linta intercepted. "Hold on…that's evidence. Let me take a look." Linta did want anybody learning anything about Sonny. He looked through the wallet and then tucked it into his shirt pocket and buttoned it up. He looked at Pete's wallet. Driver's license, some cards, a picture, coins but no folding money. He handed it to Pete. "Anything missing other than your money?"

Pete looked through the wallet and shook his head. "Glad to have it back, though."

Linta turned to Coletto: "Did you look inside their wallets?

Did you take anything out?"

Tony started to shake. "No, Chief, honest. I saw one on the ground, then the other. I did open them to see if there was any folding money in them…they were empty. I didn't look at anything else, I just figured they belonged to Pete and Sonny. I saw Nick's car out front and that's when I knocked on the door."

"All right, let's have a look outside. Pete, show me where you were jumped and Mr. Coletto, show us where the wallets were found. What you can tell me about the guys who jumped you?" Linta went through the motions but he had two things in mind. First, see if either Cantore or Pete would tip their hand over the Sonny relationship. Linta was betting on Pete. Second priority, get this over as fast as possible and get to the hospital to see Sonny. Normally Linta would avoid being seen with Sonny, but under pretense of investigation of a serious crime, no eyebrows should be raised at the Chief interviewing a victim who could easily have been killed.

"OK boys, thanks for all the help. I'm going to have one of the officers who responded to the call come by over the next couple of days to complete their reports. Anybody hear of any talk in the neighborhood…bragging…someone suddenly spending a lot of cash…let us know. Any tips on the suspects of any kind, call the station. I'm going to have that Olds towed. It's evidence as well. I don't want any of you talkin' to anyone about any of this… understand?"

With that, Linta made two calls from his Plymouth. He radioed Lowry's towing, the contractor who did all of the borough's towing, thanks to Ernie's influence. He got Sam Lowry on his tow truck radio.

"Sam. There's a new red Olds parked behind the Steelton K of C on the lower end. It's evidence in a robbery case. Tow it up to the public works garage where it's out of the way. I don't want it to attract any attention…see if you can find an empty garage for it up there. I put an evidence card underneath the windshield wiper so I don't want any snooping around with it. Radio me back after you drop it off."

"Should be within two hours, Ernie." Linta and Lowry were old school friends. "I heard somebody got away with a bunch of money last night. I'll keep my ears open for you." Lowry was a terrific source of information. He always had his radio on to the police and fire frequencies and sometimes beat the cops to car wrecks and fires. He had more than a little experience with stolen cars and the organizations who stole them, his history with them known to Linta.

Linta's second call was to the Harrisburg Hospital. He identified himself and asked about the robbery victim with a head injury brought into the hospital by Steelton ambulance about three in the morning. The switchboard connected him to the Emergency Room, and after a wait, he spoke with a nurse who told him the patient was moved to a room on the fifth floor.

Ernie zoomed up Front Street and hit his siren when he needed to run a light. He whipped into the front entrance of the hospital and quickly found his way up to the fifth floor nurse's station. He showed his badge and I.D. The nurse asked him to wait a minute while she paged the attending physician, Dr. Atwood. Ernie paced around the hallways for a good twenty minutes until he saw a kid approaching him in a Doctor's white coat with "Dr. Atwood" written in red script. He couldn't have been older that Ernie's son Anthony. "Chief, I'm Alan Atwood. I understand you want to talk to the patient in 507. I'm afraid he's in no shape to talk to anyone today; maybe tomorrow."

"What can you tell me about his condition? Was he able to

say anything about his attackers? Is he awake and alert?"

"I can't say much…he came in here without any identifica-tion. Do you know who he is? We haven't been able to contact any family."

Ernie thought it best to play it cautiously. He wanted to be the first to talk to Sonny when Sonny came around. He didn't need any pain in the ass family or worse-newspaper people- trying to get to him. "We are trying to I.D. him through his car which was at the scene of the robbery. It's a Saturday of a holiday weekend so the State is a little slow responding. Nobody knows who he is. His wallet was stolen in the robbery." Of course, Sonny's wallet was in Ernie's shirt pocket all the while. "It's really important that we speak to him as soon as he's able. This is an active crime inves-tigation. A lot of money was stolen and this gentleman could've been killed. He is going to be OK, Doc?"

"He has a small fracture of the skull that will not require surgery. He broke his nose when he hit the ground, and he has facial abrasions. Can you please notify us here at the hospital immediately upon learning his identity? His family should know. He will be OK but he's going to be in here a couple of days at least. Please leave all of your contact information at the nurse's station and we'll let you know when you can see him."

Ernie stopped at a pay phone in the hospital lobby and called the Knights of Columbus. Cantore answered. "Nick, this is Chief Linta. Listen, the guy who got knocked out last night is in bad shape. I don't want you or Pete or anybody else there talking to anybody about this. Especially any newspaper people. We have a lead on the suspects and I don't want our investigation screwed up. Don't mention this guy Sonny's name to anybody until I tell you it's OK. Make sure Pete gets the same message and that guy Coletto. I don't like criminals thinking they can get away with this kind of shit in Steelton, so I am taking on this case person-ally. If you guys learn anything, you contact me and only me. Understand that?"

"Yessir. Yes Chief." Ernie knew now he needed Tim Burger to see if they could get more info on Sonny. That meant using son Anthony as the connection. Ernie drove home and told Anthony the story. Anthony got on the phone to the Burger's. Doris answered the phone.

"Mrs. Burger? This is Anthony Linta. Is Tim around please?" He heard Doris yelling for Tim and after a bit Tim was on the line. "Tim, we need to meet for a bit. How about Ray's for lunch at twelve?" Tim knew better than to ask over the phone why Anthony wanted to meet. "OK, see you there at noon." Tim hung up and knew that something had gone wrong somewhere. Another LCB raid? Whatever it was, he'd find out in an hour.

Tim went into the kitchen for a cup of coffee. His Mom was already making a tuna salad for lunch. "Where's dad? I wanted to wish him a happy birthday."

"He's up at the fire house. They are planning a trip down to Lancaster next Saturday for the football game. Hard to believe another season is rolling around already. I want him to take a nap so that he's not falling asleep on me at the Moose tonight."

Tim took a look at his Mom. She had been to the beauty parlor yesterday and had her hair done up in a new way. Doris and Hap only went out a few times a year, so this was a big night for her. "Mom, I was thinking, how about if I join you at the Moose tonight for a bit? I might get a date...is the show sold out?"

"I don't know Tim...your dad got the tickets. I think there's two shows and we are going to the early one at nine. We're eating there before the show. I hope the food is better than the last time. And what kind of girl would go out with you on a Saturday night if she wasn't asked until Saturday afternoon? I know I wouldn't."

"Mom, you are past your time for dating. Don't worry, I won't have any trouble. I'm heading out so don't worry about making lunch for me. Where's Harry?"

"Well, speaking of dates, I think Harry may be seeing a girl tonight. He asked me to press a shirt and slacks for him and he left a little bit ago to go to Dundoff's for some ice cream and to Yetter's to pick up a six pack of beer. He hasn't said anything about it though."

"Ice cream and beer? I can tell you one thing for sure, he's seeing a girl from the West Side."

Just then Harry came in through the front door and as he entered the kitchen he put a brown paper bag into the freezer, and pulled out a six pack of Schmidt's out of a second brown bag and put it in the Kelvinator.

"Seeing a West Side girl tonight, Harry?" Tim was always ready with the needle.

"Nah, I figured you guys were all going out, so I'd just have a party here myself. By the way, Mom, I have a birthday present for Hap...do you want to give him his gifts today or wait 'til tomorrow?"

"I thought we'd do it tomorrow right after dinner. It's a little more relaxed. I just told Tim I don't want the old man getting worn out this afternoon and then crappin' out on me tonight at the Moose."

Tim piped up: "Maybe you're more worried about him crappin' out on you after you get home from the Moose, Mom!" Even Doris laughed at that one.

Harry went over and smelled the tuna fish, got the Patriot and sat down at the kitchen table, waiting for Hap to get home for lunch. Tim was out of the door soon after, walking down to

Ray's Luncheonette on a beautiful September day. Tim mentally went over his talk with Arthur from late last night, and shifted his concentration to the meeting with Anthony.

Ray's, at the corner of Front and Pine was the most popular night spot with the high school kids in Steelton. It was a sandwich and soda shop with a beautiful Wurlitzer jukebox that had all of the big hits of the new Rock n Roll sound. During the day, Ray kept the jukebox switched off, and the popular place did a good breakfast business, and was always crowded at lunch for the employees and owners in Steelton's main business district. The owners, Ray and Elinore were in the place morning, noon and night six days a week. There was a long counter with fifteen stools and booths all along the wall. Steelton's football and basketball pennants, banners, and pictures of heroes past and present adorned the walls. Even on a holiday Saturday, the counter was mostly filled. Tim spied Anthony sitting in the back booth, with a large chocolate milkshake already in front of him.

Anthony Linta was a puzzling combination of features and personality. He was one of the biggest kids in the class all through school, both height and weight. Now he stood six foot three or so, and probably weighed 275. He had thick dark hair. He never played sports. He had some kind of a heart condition as a kid and his mother was very protective of him. Tim and Anthony were always close friends, living just a few doors apart on Myers Street, although Anthony went to Catholic High when he reached ninth grade and Tim went to Steelton. Anthony's mother made him take lessons on the violin all through his childhood, which caused no end of humiliation to his man's man dad Ernie. Ernie, who was progressing through the ranks of the Harrisburg City police while Anthony was growing up, was always forced to explain to people that his giant of a son was medically unable to play football. Most people thought he was a big sissy whose Mom was afraid he'd get hurt.

Anthony was an outstanding student through school, and he earned a scholarship to Villanova, graduating in three years with a degree in accounting. He returned home to Steelton and secured a position with Mr. Cackovic, a Croatian with a thriving tax and accounting practice down on Second Street, a few blocks from the Linta home. Cackovic went to St. James, where the Lintas attended. Anthony still lived at home. He never dated and didn't have a driver's license. He didn't drink, smoke or use bad language…the antithesis of a West Side kid in every respect.

When Ernie secured the Chief's position for Steelton Borough five years ago, the family moved from the West Side to the hill, as all successful people did. Tim did not know when Ernie brought Anthony into his confidence with Ernie's side interests…but Tim was pretty sure Anthony figured everything out before his dad confirmed what he already suspected.

The waitress took their order –cherry coke and a grilled cheese for Tim, hamburger for Anthony. Anthony filled Tim in on the Sonny situation. His voice and demeanor was calm in describing his dad's concerns, and Sonny's condition.

"Have any idea who's Sonny's contact at the Knights?"

"No, I don't Anthony. Your family is a member there, your Dad doesn't have a clue?"

"He thinks it's the bartender not only because the manager,- Cantore, who he knows, is a straight arrow but also because my dad thought Pete was lying to him about what happened last night, and the old man's instincts are pretty good."

"Well, I can't go in there and snoop around because I'm not a member. Your dad told everybody there to clam up anyway, right? So I think we just sit tight and see what we can learn from

Sonny once we get to him. We need to get his keys to find out what might be in the trunk, you know. I think I also need to fill Arthur in on this."

"My dad thought of the trunk so he has the Olds marked as evidence and has it hidden away at the borough garage. Sonny had some slips of paper in his wallet that my dad has and will go through later. I think Arthur should be told as well, if you can take care of that."

"I'll get up there right after I leave. I got one more thing though. We all trust you in managing the books and the shares, and that's why we don't ask a lot of questions. But are Sonny's contributions worth the risk? I wonder if we could do as well without him, and eliminate some of these unknowns. All of us pretty much know all of our original revenue sources, but we don't know all of Sonny's. Plus he's got those Italian family connections. I'm a little worried about that and I wouldn't be surprised if Cohen and Arthur didn't feel the same way."

"You're in a gray area here Tim. All I'm willing to say is that we get a big mark-up on the beer he supplies. He also has opened a half dozen liquor accounts that also pay more than Arthur's stores and bars....a dollar a bottle more in several of his accounts. We see his sales numbers but not his contacts. We are all in this together, unless someone wants to get out. That's the agreement we made."

"Yeah, I remember. Look, I'll head up to see Arthur. Can you give me a call tomorrow and let me know if your dad gets to talk to Sonny? I'm off until Tuesday at three so if you guys need anything just let me know. I'm probably going to hit a few of the clubs this weekend, and I'm going to the Moose tonight to check up on their operation."

"Make sure you get to the St. Lawrence. They are a month

behind."

"I know, Anthony. They're on my list."

Tim thought about his conversation with Anthony as he walked up Front Street. Arthur's son Claude would be able to describe who he delivered to at the Knight's. That would help. Tim knew from Anthony's monthly accounting that the Knight's was a liquor only delivery for Arthur, and that Sonny handled the beer. Tim got within sight of Arthur's and the first thing he noticed was all of Arthur's white fleet, including the hearse, parked alongside the funeral home. As he got closer, he realized a service was underway so his talk with Arthur would have to wait.

16

The Burger house was buzzing as everybody jockeyed for the bathroom late that afternoon. Doris had informed everybody to clear out by five, so Hap, Tim and Harry rushed through their baths and shaves. The men sat around the kitchen table and shared a quart bottle of Ballantine and toasted Hap's birthday. "Everything at the Moose is on me tonight Dad. I didn't get a date so I will sit with you and Mom. I'd invite you along Harry, but I think that would disappoint one of our local West Side beauties."

Harry kept to himself. "I'm sure you will all have a good time. Don't worry about me."

Doris came down the steps just after six. She had on her favorite dress, a black and white checked sleeveless number with a short black jacket. Hap wore his brown sports coat, brown pants, brown shoes and a lively burgundy colored, patterned tie.

"Well, do we want to ride or walk to the Moose?" Tim asked.

"I'm not walking down there in these shoes!" Doris declared, and that was that. Harry went out back to hold the Merc's door open for Doris. "We'll celebrate your birthday tomorrow, Dad. Have a great time tonight." Harry called out and waved to Tim. Harry closed the gate after Tim backed out.

He went in and clicked on the radio in the kitchen to listen to some music. He thought about his upcoming date with Darlene, and he still wasn't able to muster much enthusiasm for it, but a promise is a promise. At 7:30, he pulled the beer and ice cream out of the icebox and put them in a paper bag. He went out the back door and walked up the alley to Darlene's place. He knocked on the front screen door…the main door was wide open. "C'mon in Harry!" he heard Darlene calling from inside. "I'm still upstairs changing. I didn't get out of Kormy's until almost seven. There's beer in the icebox!"

Harry walked through the house and put the beer in the refrigerator and the ice cream in the small freezer compartment. Not much appeared to have changed since the last time Harry was in the Decker house, probably four years ago. He decided to wait on the beer until Darlene came down the stairs. He sat on the old faded red sofa with the cheap doilies. A DuMont television console occupied the corner of the front room. He heard Darlene come down the steps. He stood up and she walked directly to him and gave him a big hug. "I'm happy you came, Harry. Where's your beer?"

"In the kitchen… I brought some too." Harry looked at Darlene. She had on black slacks and shoes and a white sleeveless top with a frilly front. Her dark hair was pulled back under some kind of black band. She seemed to have put on a little weight now that he got a look at her ass, as she walked into the kitchen with Harry close behind.

"Well, I am going to have a Seven and Seven. What do you want, Harry?"

"I brought a six pack of Schmidt's. Did you get to eat something since you had to work late?" As soon as the words were out of his mouth Harry regretted it.

"No I didn't" Darlene replied. "We were really busy since we are closed tomorrow. Did you have supper? Do you want to go out for a bite?"

"Well, I uh, we could I guess." Harry was now thinking which was worse…a whole night here alone with Darlene or being seen out with her on a Saturday night.

"I know!" Darlene gushed, "Why don't we walk over to Sal's and get a pizza, and bring it back here?" This seemed like a good idea to Harry. Darlene picked up an old pocketbook and they walked the four blocks over to North Front Street to the pizza joint. Harry paid, and they took it back to Darlene's place. He drank a few beers and she had a couple of seven and sevens at the kitchen table. Harry excused himself to go up and use the bathroom, and when he came back down the stairs Darlene was on the couch with the TV on, fresh drinks sitting on the coffee table and the front door and window blinds now closed.

It wasn't fifteen minutes until Darlene had her hand on Harry's thigh. He kissed her and started feeling up her breasts. Her nipples were hard and Darlene was pushing Harry down on his back on the couch. She was kissing him harder and her hips were starting to grind against Harry's.

"Let's go up to my bedroom", Darlene said as she stuck her tongue in his ear. Harry followed her up the stairs and down the hall to the back bedroom. Darlene turned to kiss him and he reached under her blouse and unhooked her bra. His hands went up under her blouse and she pulled the blouse over her head without unbuttoning it. Harry had seen her tits before and he remembered that Darlene liked to have her nipples pinched. He couldn't help being aroused himself and he was on top of her fumbling to get her pants off. She had black panties and they were thrown to the floor. Harry screwed her the best he could and pulled out of her before he came. He thought Darlene had a climax but wasn't certain. "Why did you pull out of me?" Darlene was panting..." We got into it so fast I forgot to put on a rubber." Harry had put a couple of rubbers in his pocket that he had from his Army days. The last thing he wanted to do was to get Darlene pregnant. West Side girls were famous for getting knocked up in order to snag a husband if they hadn't married by their early twenties. Harry was not falling for that old trick. They lay there side by side for a bit. Darlene went into the bathroom and then came back to the bed. Harry was thinking about getting dressed when Darlene grabbed his dick and started pumping away. "You're going to need the rubber after all! Where are they?"

She got into Harry's pants on the floor, pulled out the condoms and put one on him. She got on top of him and Harry thrust his hips up into Darlene as hard as he could. Her make-up was a smeared mess as she sweated over him. She was no Cindy Hernley. Her fat tits bounced up and down, faster and faster. She had her hands on Harry's shoulders, pinning him down. Darlene came and Harry did too. She rolled over onto her side and had her arm across Harry's chest. She didn't say anything and Harry didn't either. Harry wondered how long he would have to lay there until he could leave. He certainly wasn't going to stay the night. Darlene's neighbors would be all eyes and ears, and then he'd have to face Tim and Doris; Hap wouldn't give a damn.

Harry got up and told Darlene he would let himself out. Darlene did not protest. He quietly opened and closed the front door, and walked down toward home. He had no thoughts or feelings for Darlene one way or the other.

They never did eat the ice cream.

* * *

Tim's morning at the other end of town was still going strong. He was at the St. Lawrence Club…a private club that was affiliated with the Croatian Church but open to any white person over twenty-one who paid a five dollar annual membership fee. The place was jammed tonight with the Polka Quads playing well past their normal two a.m. quitting time. Tim sat at the corner of the bar, the club's cash payment in his pocket after the manager, Mike Jamnov, had paid him in full for the liquor and beer deliveries that Arthur's sons had made over the previous month. Tim also had Jamnov's order for the upcoming month in his wallet. Tim was nursing a beer and keeping a couple of tipsy but not attractive young ladies at bay when he noticed a familiar face at a table across from his bar stool. It was Scrappy Stone, fellow West-Sider and topic of daily reports from brother Harry. Scrappy was with a very pretty blonde and another attractive couple; the guys had coats and ties and the ladies fancy dresses, not the usual attire for the St. Lawrence. Tim made his way over to their table.

"Scrappy…it's Tim Burger…haven't see you in quite a while but your name is frequently mentioned in the Burger house." Scrappy looked up and did recognize Tim. Conversation in the bar at this early hour of the morning required a small shout.

"Tim, good to see you. Yeah, Harry and I have spent a little time together. He's done a good job; very conscientious."

"I understand he worked with you on some kind of production and inventory project that might be extended to the whole plant. You remember I work up in the rail mill."

"Yeah, well, the project itself is still being evaluated." Scrappy was too smart to talk about his work with other employees. He was careful talking about his work, despite having had a bunch of beer at the Management Club dance earlier that evening and now at the club. "Let me introduce you..." At that he introduced his date Susie and Bill Willis and his wife. "This is Tim Burger... works in supervision at the mill and a fellow native of the West Side."

Tim's hopes of getting something he could use out of Scrappy rapidly faded. " It's nice to meet all of you and thanks for taking good care of my big brother, Scrappy. He really thinks a lot of you." On his way back to the bar, Tim flagged the waitress and bought a round for Scrappy's table. He finished his beer and thought about picking up one of the friendly girls still making eye contact with him, but decided against it and paid his tab. On his way toward the exit, Tim saw Jamnov waving to him to come over. Jamnov took Tim into the small office back by the kitchen.

Mike Jamnov knew Tim since they were little kids. Mike was working hard to save up some money to start his own bar. The side cash he was able to skim off the Tim business helped him out, and Tim knew Mike would be a good, loyal, and trustworthy customer once he did start his own place.

"What is it Mike?"

"A couple of my friends are talking about a robbery last night at the Knights. It's got some of us late night club guys a little concerned. Anything you can tell me about it?"

"Not really Mike. I did hear about it earlier today, but I don't know anything other than the bartender got jumped and some guys got away with the day's receipts. Anybody you know have any clue who was behind it?"

"No. Word is Pete Posetti the bartender had some other guy with him when they were jumped. Two members were in here earlier who were at last call at the Knights, and they said the guy with Pete was named Sonny and he showed up there every once in awhile and always right before last call. Pete kicked everybody out at closing but this Sonny. I've known Pete Posetti for awhile and he is connected with some rough characters. Don't misunderstand me Tim, but this Sonny guy acted with Posetti a little like you do with me...showing up to collect and always at last call. I just don't want you –or me- to be in any kind of danger if there's any connection between Sonny and you."

"Look, Mike. I have no idea. The cops must be on the case. It was probably some colored guys from down on Mohn Street who were casing the joint and knew Pete's routine. I'm not a K of C member and I don't think I've ever been in there. And, if it makes you feel better, I'll start spending a little more time in here...maybe bring a date. And if I were you I'd have somebody you trust with you if you are making night deposits."

"Shit, NIGHT deposits? We usually throw the last people out of here around 4:30. It takes the staff here until six every morning to get things cleaned up. On weekends, I almost never get out of here before seven...so I'm locking the place up in daylight. Anyway, if you hear of anything unusual, would you let me know?"

"With your sources, Mike, you know more about what's going on in Steelton than I do. See you soon." Tim left Mike's office with an uneasy feeling. If Jamnov thought to make a connection between Tim's work and Sonny's, who else might do the same? This reinforced Tim's suspicion that Sonny presented too much risk for the group. Tim fired up the Merc and carefully drove the couple of miles to Myers Street. He parked in the alley but didn't bother to put the Merc in the yard. Tomorrow the family would celebrate Hap's birthday after Doris' big mid-day meal. Tim had no plans for the day other than to try to see Arthur, who was never much interested in doing any kind of work on a Sunday. The more he thought about it, seeing Arthur was probably rushing it and seemed a little panicky. He'd wait to hear from the Lintas and decide what to do once he had more information.

As Tim walked to his bedroom he heard Hap snoring away, and noticed Harry was tucked into his room as well. He wondered what kind of evening his big brother had. He hoped that Harry had spent the evening with a woman…it would help to take some of the edge off of him. Tim kept thinking about Harry. What would Harry make of Tim's side enterprise? Could he use Harry to get more information about the Stone project in case it presented a threat to his scrap business with Arthur? Would there ever come a time when Tim might approach Harry about being a partner with him? Tim laughed quietly to himself at that last thought as he turned out the lights.

17

"Sonny, you are in one tough spot" Anthony Donato thought to himself from his semi-private hospital room in Harrisburg Hospital. He had started to come out of his dream world a few hours ago. He heard the nurses talking. He heard people on the other side of the curtain. He wasn't really in pain but he had some tubes coming out of him, including one coming out of his dick that he didn't like at all. He had a big band aid of some kind across his nose. He had a memory of the fight in Steelton and that was about it for his recollection of the night. He wondered what he may have said. He did not see anyone he knew. He thought it best to play like Sleepy and Dopey and see what he could learn from the others around him. He was thirsty, though, and planned to ask the next nurse he saw for some water…maybe he could find out more.

It was just after twelve on Sunday. The Lintas were about to sit down to dinner. Ernie Linta had Sonny on his mind. If he didn't hear from the hospital by two, he was going up there. He had talked it over with Anthony, and they both thought that getting to Sonny first was important enough to risk some nosey SOB wondering why the Chief of Police was personally handling a bar robbery.

"Well, look who's awake? How are you feeling? Are you in any pain?" A nurse with gray hair tucked under a big white pointy hat was talking to Sonny. Her name badge said Esther Yoder. "Do you know where you are? Do you remember your name?" She was smiling at Sonny.

"Uh, no Ma'am. I'm thirsty. May I have some water please?"

"Yes, water is permitted. I'm going to call Dr. Atwood. He will want to talk to you. We do not know your name. You had no identification on you when you came in with the ambulance. The Steelton Police are trying to identify you. Do you remember your name?"

"I'm…I..uh…I'm not really sure of anything. I really am thirsty." The nurse returned in a minute with the water. "Dr. Atwood will be down to see you. He is in charge of your care. I have other patients to see…it's a holiday weekend and we are short of staff."

Sonny took the water. He thought about the right time to call his people and who in particular he would call….probably Frankie or Nick Messina …they knew about the K of C beer deal but not about the cigarettes. He'd have to get to Posetti as fast as he could. The Steelton guys would want to know what was going on as well. Then he needed to get some help from the big people to find out who stole his money and smashed his head in. He wanted his guys to find out who the robbers were before the cops tracked 'em down. His thoughts were interrupted by a knock on his hospital room door.

"Good afternoon, Sir. I'm Dr. Atwood. I am in charge of your case. Can you tell me your name?"

"Uh, I don't remember much of anything. Can you take these tubes out of me?"

"Let's go over first things first…can you hear me and understand me?"

"Yes, Doc, I can."

"You were attacked in a robbery. You were hit on the back of the head and have a small fracture of the skull back here" Atwood pointed to a spot behind his right ear. "You will not need surgery for that, it will come around on its own. You also had your nose broken. We fixed that, it was not severe and you should be able to get rid of the packing and bandages in a day or two. I'll see about removing the catheter but you need to stay on IVs for a bit. Are you hungry?"

"More thirsty than hungry, but yes, I could eat something."

"I'm going to send another physician in here later. He is going to ask you a lot of questions. We need to evaluate your cognitive abilities – your memory – and we also will have some more tests for you. Do you feel any numbness in your hands or feet?"

"No"

"Do you think you could sit up in bed?"

"Yes"

"All right, let's see how this afternoon goes and I'll be back to see you tomorrow. If everything goes OK, you can be released in a couple of days…but…"

"But what, Doc?"

"Well, if you can't remember your name, and no one shows up who knows you, we'll have to release you to an intermediate care institution…probably Dauphin County Home."

Sonny's first inclination was to tell the Doc "No Fucking Way! I'm not goin' to the nuthouse!" but that outburst would result in the doc quickly determining Sonny's memory was quite a bit sharper than he let on. He just let the young Doctor's comment slide, and tried to maintain a blank expression as best he could.

Dr. Atwood walked back to the nurses' station with Mrs. Yoder. "That guy's in better shape than he's letting on. I've had a good look at his eyes and his reflexes. Call that Police Chief from Steelton; he has my OK to talk to our patient. I'm writing an order for the intern to run him through the standard neurological and memory protocols. My guess is his memory will come back in a hurry once we set up his discharge to the County Home."

Ernie got the call just before dessert. He went upstairs to change into his full uniform. He got into the Plymouth and headed up Cameron Street and presented himself to Nurse Yoder at 2:30. "Dr. Atwood asked to talk to you after you've had your time with the patient, Chief. Please let me know when you're done. We have a shift change at three so it's going to be a little hectic around here."

"Yes, Nurse. I will. Is there any way I can talk to the patient in private? This is a police matter and with the investigation being active, I have to protect confidentiality."

"The other patient in the room does not have visitors now. I think he's asleep…I'll go in with you." Nurse Yoder walked into Sonny's room, quietly pulled back the curtain and gave the Chief a nod. As she closed the door behind her, she whispered "Press that button if you need me."

"How you feelin', Sonny? You hear me OK?"

"I can hear you Ernie. I'm just thinkin' a little slow. Doc says I got a fractured skull…be in here a few more days I guess. I ain't said nothin' to nobody…played stupid like I lost my memory. They have no idea who I am."

"Why don't you fill me in. I take it you were at the K of C to collect? Is the bartender your contact there?"

"Yeah, yeah. The bartender handles the beer and liquor."

"Name's Pete Posetti?"

"Yep. That's him. You been down there?"

"I decided to take care of this one myself once I heard about it yesterday morning. I've told everybody down there to clam up…I know the manager there. What can you tell me about Posetti?"

"I've known him a while. He's been bartending or around bars most of his life. He used to work for some friends of mine uptown Harrisburg. He's a bit of a gambler, likes the ponies and the fights. He's been involved in some low level hustles…but I can trust him to keep his mouth shut."

"What kind of hustles?"

"Things the average Joe don't think about…records and juke-boxes, bar supplies, he had a brother worked in a food service operation who stole kitchen supplies…ketchup, mustard, coffee, that sort of thing, and he'd peddle it to small bar owners."

"He have a record?"

"I think he did some time in County. Most of the guys have a prison connection one way or the other."

Ernie made a mental note to check on Posetti's record when he got back to the station. "Look, anything we need to worry about here? Were you followed to the Knight's? Could you have been jumped by someone you know, or worse, someone who sent somebody after you? Have you gotten cross-ways with any of your other connections?"

"No, Ernie, no. We were jumped by a couple of niggers who must have been watchin' Posetti leave every night. They wanted the bank bag and our wallets. When the guy reached toward me for my wallet, I took a swing at him, just grazed his head, then I got whacked. Sons o' bitches…if they got my wallet I had four hundred or so in it, including your money."

"Was there anything in your wallet Sonny that could give us trouble….names, delivery or inventory slips, my name or number, Tim or Arthur's?"

"No Chief. I'm careful. What about my car?"

"What about it? Anything in it that could cause us trouble… anything inside the car or in the trunk?"

Sonny thought about this before he responded. He didn't know what Ernie knew or what he had found out, and had a feeling Ernie knew more than he was letting on. He was a cop, after all. He didn't want Ernie looking in the trunk of the Olds…there was probably 50 cartons of cigarettes in there, and two potato chip cans full of 45 records for juke boxes.

"Ernie, I have no names or numbers or anything written down. I keep almost everything in my head, and deliveries I keep a secret code in a little book. Nobody could figure it out."

"Where's the little book, Sonny, and where are the keys to the car?" Ernie decided he was going to keep Sonny in the dark for a bit…not letting him know the Olds was safely in his possession.

"I guess in my pants or jacket pocket…I don't even know where my clothes are."

"I'll ask the nurse or the doc. They are going to ask your permission to let me look through your clothes. When they ask, just nod and say OK. We also have to decide when your memory is coming back. From what I know, nobody knows you're in here or who you are."

"OK, how about my memory comes back when they tell me I can get out of here? That should work out, and you can get me my car. I hope you have somebody good tracking down the shit-heads who jumped me…better you find them before I do."

"Sonny, is there anybody else who's gonna be trackin' you down when they find out what happened here?"

"No, Ernie…I'm pretty much on my own. I have some connections that help me with different parts of my business, but nobody knows my whole story. The problem for the Steelton group is I don't know how long I'll be laid up, so my part of the business is going to suffer."

"Don't worry, Sonny, you're still in for your full shares…we'll take care of you. Keep your mouth shut and that amnesia going until it's time to be released. Tell them you want to be released to my custody, that you have no one else, no family. Deal?"

"That makes sense Ernie, thanks."

Ernie nodded to Sonny and walked out of the room. He told nurse Yoder that the victim seemed to be coming around. The nurse said to wait until Dr. Atwood arrived, she would have him paged. "Do you have the clothing that the victim wore when he was brought here, Mrs. Yoder?"

The ER would have sent all of his stuff to hospital security since he came in as a result of a crime. There's nothing in his room."

"Oh, shit." Ernie thought. Someone else I have to see and deal with. "Do you have a name or number for hospital security Mrs. Yoder? Is Mr. Christiansen still in charge of overall security here?" Ernie knew Ted Christiansen from his days on the Harrisburg police force…Ted was a bad cop with a drinking problem, squeezed out of the force, who landed a rocking-chair job with the hospital.

"I have no idea, really," Mrs. Yoder was distracted…"Chief, I really have a lot to do here, and Dr. Atwood is the man in charge… ah! Here he comes now."

"Dr. Atwood? I'm Chief Linta of the Steelton Police. Thanks for calling us. I just spoke with the victim. He was responsive but still not remembering his name. We are running a full investigation on this…I've got two men working on finding out who this guy is and who attacked him. We aren't making much progress between the holiday and people with cloudy memories.

Anything you can help us with? Do you have an idea if this guy's memory's coming back anytime soon?" Ernie sized up the young doc. Looked like he hadn't slept in two days, blonde hair, blue eyes, tall and good looking. Bet he had no trouble with the ladies.

"Chief, the gentleman should not be experiencing memory loss given his injury. It's possible for him to have a temporary amnesia, but I'm more inclined to think he's faking it for some reason. We're going to have an intern run him through a battery of tests today and tomorrow. Should know more Tuesday."

"Dr. Atwood, can you connect me with hospital security so that I can get a look at his clothing and any other personal effects that might help our investigation? I know the gentleman who heads up that department, but I'm certain he's off 'til Tuesday. I don't like the idea of a couple of violent robbers wandering around Steelton while we wait for this guy to wake up."

"Chief, did you learn anything that can help us? You said he was responsive…did he remember anything prior to his skull fracture?"

"What I meant was that he said he could hear me and understand my questions. He couldn't come up with anything to help us. I asked him his name a couple of times, where his wallet was, and so on. He did ask about his clothes…he used the words pants and jacket. That's about it…I was in there only about 10 minutes… it's not the most private place to try to conduct a police interview. Would there be anyone in hospital security on duty now?"

"I'll get you the phone and extension. You can ask. If you or your officers find anything out about our patient here that could help us, would you let us know, please, Chief?"

"I will if you'll do the same, doc. Where's the phone?"

Ernie dialed the extension. The guy answering- named Harris -was substituting for the regular staff for the holiday weekend.

He wouldn't do anything without checking with his supervisors and they would not be in until Tuesday. He would not see Ernie or even confirm that he had anything belonging to Sonny. He was 100% unhelpful and Ernie did not like that one bit.

"Do you know Mr. Christiansen, the top boss? He and I served on the Harrisburg Police force together. He is not going to be happy when I tell him about your lack of cooperation. I'm working an active crime investigation, a violent robbery where a guy could have been killed. You are interfering with that investigation. I'm giving you one more chance here."

"Sorry Chief, I have my orders. This is Harrisburg not Steelton. Mr. Christiansen left strict orders not to be disturbed. Those are my orders."

"You are in deep shit Harris." Ernie knew that Christiansen was probably on a three day bender, and that's why he didn't want any calls from work. Sonny's car would have to sit. Ernie thought about going back to see Posetti but decided it best to let things simmer down a bit. He would go back to the office, check messages, get in touch with the on-duty officers, and then plan to see Arthur Monday after he briefed his son on what happened with Sonny. He was going to ask Anthony to do an individual audit of Sonny's work over the past six months or so, to see if anything unusual popped up. He still had a crime to solve, and he was going to get Arthur's son and his man Karmilov on the case.

This was not the Sunday afternoon Ernie expected. He had hoped to have an afternoon filled with nothing whatever to do and a couple of cold beers and a snooze in his living room. The messages awaiting him as he slid behind his desk were essentially routine, but with one glaring exception: Winston Clark, Jr. from the Steelton News.

The Steelton News was a once a week paper that came out Thursdays. It was mostly full of ads placed by long-time Steelton shopkeepers promoting their weekend specials. It always featured good sports reporting on the Steamroller football and basketball teams. There were a lot of soft features about charity groups, churches, that sort of thing. Hard news was pretty much limited to Borough Council meetings and the events related to the Bethlehem Steel Company and the Steelton mill in particular until "Winny" Clark's kid came to work for the paper a year or so ago fresh out of The University of Pittsburgh. Winny Junior went to college in a big city that had a very competitive newspaper environment that was a giant pain in the ass for the police in Pittsburgh. Winny Junior was always digging for what he thought was unreported crimes, people getting off the hook if they had political connections. He would show up at every Borough Council meeting…he believed that crime was dramatically under-reported in Steelton to make the Borough seem safer than it really was.

The Chief picked up the phone for what would be his last call of the day.

"Steelton News, Deputy Editor Winston Clark, Junior speaking!"

"Oh brother", Ernie sighed. "Winny, this is Chief Linta. You called for me. It's a Sunday afternoon and a holiday weekend, you know. What's up?"

"Thank you for calling Chief. We got several reports of a robbery down at the K of C around three o'clock Saturday morning. I talked to a couple of guys who were there, plus the ambulance driver. A guy got knocked out and taken to Harrisburg Hospital. They confirmed that a guy was admitted after the attack. They won't release any additional information. I tried to get statements from the K of C manager – Cantore – but he won't say a word because of police orders. I tried to get to the bartender and he cursed me out and hung up the phone. What can you tell me? Do you have any suspects and any word on the victim and his condition?"

Ernie thought how Winny Junior just made every rookie newspaperman's mistake by telling him everything he knew instead of playing dumb and asking questions to see if the responses matched the facts he already had collected. "Winny, we are in the early stages of the investigation. We have no confirmed I.D. on the guy who was knocked out. We have a lead on him and we are working on a couple of leads on the suspects. Money was stolen from the K of C and from the bartender and the victim. We are having difficulty getting information from some of the other agencies we cooperate with due to the holiday weekend. I have officers on the case. I think we need a couple of days before I will have anything for you."

"Well, there's talk that some wallets were found, and that a new red Oldsmobile was parked behind the club late that night and now it's been towed away. Know anything about that?"

"The car might be evidence that is important to our investigation. That's all I can say about it right now. We haven't been able to trace anything because the State DMV is closed 'til Tuesday and this is not a high priority nor under the jurisdiction of the State Police. Winny, it's Sunday. I am going home. If something breaks, we'll see that you get a call. Tell your dad I said hello."

"We have a deadline Wednesday noon, Chief. If I don't hear from you by Tuesday night, I'm writing the story as we have it. I'll give you a call to run it past you for confirmation as a courtesy."

"Go Fuck Yourself" Ernie thought silently. "Yeah, sure, OK

Winny. Just don't get carried away with wild guesses and uncon-firmed stories. Anybody who was at last call that night at the K of C probably had been drinking all night and I wouldn't trust their stories or their memories. Good-bye."

18

The Bethlehem Steel Management Club was a beautiful new facility built on top of a hill at the far south end of Steelton (half of the total property was actually situated in Swatara Township.) The building itself was in the shape of an arc, and it promoted and featured every aspect of steel construction, with open steel beams, a side wall that exposed re-bar and wire rope, any opportunity to showcase the products of Steelton. To the far right of the sweeping outside veranda, a skeet shooting range faced the limestone quarry owned by Bethlehem. The Club afforded a beautiful view of the Susquehanna River from the large, lower level patio, and had two bowling alleys, a fifty seat indoor movie theater and a large swimming pool. The Annual Labor Day picnic was one of the biggest events of the year…free food and drink, entertainment, and always well attended by the families of the BS management. Activities were scheduled from morning until six in the evening.

As Chief of Police, Ernie Linta and his family were invited to every major BSMC event, and he and his wife Maria were in attendance this year; Anthony stayed home. Ernie usually showed up around noon, made the rounds with the big shots and had a couple of beers while his wife socialized with her Steelton friends. Ernie always made it a point to spend some time with Herman Klein, who was the head of security for the Steelton Plant. They compared crime notes and usually met for dinner a few times a year. Herman oversaw all of the guards, main office security, and provided protection for the senior management when they needed it. Theft was always a concern at a large operation like the mill, and Herman also had a half dozen undercover guys working on one scam or another. Klein had great contacts with trucking and railroad security people, and law enforcement including the Feds. Herman had been in the job for quite a while, and earned high marks from union and management alike for his fair handling of the long 1952 strike.

Willis and Hernley had made plans to meet to go over their project meeting results in a quiet corner of the bar while their wives socialized at the pool. It was a beautiful day and the bar was empty when Willis walked in. Hernley was drinking a coke; Willis ordered a draft. Willis spoke first: "We need to think about and select the next department for the PEP and about how we can repair things with the guys up at HQ. We got good marks for the project itself but they think we really over-reached with the plant-wide proposal. My son told me his boss heard that Superintendent Ledbetter said we were putting our careers ahead of the company by trying to get Steelton to be the flagship for the entire corporation on the PEP."

"I know" Hernley spoke into his coke glass. "Pisses me off they didn't trust us to know about the parallel work up at Bethlehem. It would have been a real feather in our cap to take the lead for the whole Company…Steelton could really use a prestige assignment like that."

"Look, let's be honest here, Bob. You wanted that prestige

as much for yourself as for the plant. Otherwise, you wouldn't have over-ruled Stone and pushed so hard for the plant wide implementation. Our job now is to make phase two of the PEP 100% successful…that's the best way to earn the credibility we may have lost."

"I agree. I've given the next department for the PEP a lot of thought, and the bar fab shop is the right place to really show what we can do. Eighteen sizes of re-bar, straight, bent, sheared, sawed; hundreds of customers every month with multiple delivery sites. It's a department that has had the highest level of inventory reconciliation problems every month since I've been here. The complexity will show what PEP can do, and the improvements will be dramatic. I've been down there several times over the last month and the overall management there is weak and ineffective. I'd like you to approve the bar fab, and I'd like the assignment to oversee the PEP and to put me in charge of that department. I promise you, you won't regret it."

Bob Willis expected Hernley to bid for the next PEP phase, it did make sense given his experience and track record, but he didn't expect the push for a totally new assignment by Hernley. "That's a lot to ask for. I can see a role for you in the next phase, but I'm not wild about a change in departments for you. And don't forget, my recommendation will carry some weight, but Mr. Stevens has got to approve this. It's got enough visibility that I want our General Superintendent in the boat with us. Bar fab is too complex for many of the points you just made. I'm thinking rail mill. A lot easier for us to keep track of, fewer data inputs, fewer QC problems. The rail mill is the department that could get significant future capital given its importance to the corporation. It's visible to the top guys up in Bethlehem. I've talked to Stone about it and he agrees with me."

"Why did you talk to Stone about this without my involve-ment...and why didn't he say anything to me about this?"

"Don't get upset Bob. Stone was with my son at the dinner dance Saturday night. We all sat at the same table. While the women were away we had a chance to talk. My son and Stone are close...like brothers almost...there was no intention to cut you out of anything, the topic just came up. My son's training is just about complete and he will be assigned to HQ next, so that might turn out to be a good source of information for us. Stone is well thought of and if he had finished college he'd probably be a general foreman by now. He admires and respects you, he's on your side; don't start thinking he's against you somehow."

"All right, I understand"

"And we might as well clear the air on the rest of your request. You are going to stay at open hearth because we need you there. You have no successor groomed. 1956 is a strike year and if the guys walk out in July as everybody expects they will, I'll need an experienced manager to supervise the furnace shut downs and then re-starts when the union comes to their senses and the strike ends. You can come and see me to talk some more about this, but that's where I stand. I'm going to give the rail mill a little more thought, and try to talk to Stevens next week. Now, I think we should get back to our wives."

Cindy Hernley could tell that her husband was in a stormy mood. She had a feeling things had not been going well at the mill, but her husband rarely spoke about his work.

"Is everything OK, Bob? You don't look happy."

"Things are fine...we just have a little problem at work that Willis wanted my advice on. It's an important project that all of the top guys are involved in, including Mr. Stevens. You have met his wife Kathleen, haven't you?"

"A few times…she's very nice but keeps to a small circle of friends who are all a good bit older than me."

"Do you know her well enough to invite her to a lunch either at the house or out somewhere? I think it would be good if we tried to get to know the Stevens socially. I thought if you had a nice lunch with her, then maybe we could use that to get together with them for dinner sometime."

"I guess I could, Bob but it would be a little awkward. I'll try if you want me to."

"Can you do it today if the opportunity presents itself? Maybe you could talk to her a bit and if she's alone at some point you could offer the invitation."

"Mrs. Stevens is hardly ever by herself at these social events, Bob. There is always a group trying to talk to her and Mr. Stevens….but I'll see if I can."

"OK, I don't want to stay here too late today…I have a real early start tomorrow and a big week ahead of me."

Scrappy Stone did not make the picnic. He had been on the river since five thirty. The bass fishing was great for the first couple of hours, and then stopped dead. Just prior to noon he pulled up the small anchor and headed for Highspire. He thought about his friend Bill Willis, who was excited about the completion of his training in the field and his new assignment at headquarters. Bill was a persuasive salesman. He spent more than a little time Saturday night trying to convince Scrappy to apply for a position up at Bethlehem HQ. "Don't tell my dad, because he would shit his pants if he knew I was trying to pry you out of Steelton." Scrappy told Bill not to hold out too much hope, as things were going pretty well for him at the moment.

He had his own little house that he rented that was nearby

his boat and the river. He liked his job; he was constantly learning and had a variety of important assignments. He had time for his fishing and his music and his family was close by. He wished there was a college near Harrisburg where he could take part time courses to finish his degree. He didn't see living in Bethlehem in his future, although the Steel Company's long association with Lehigh would provide him a great opportunity to work while he finished his degree…a point that Bill had brought up at least three times Saturday night. Scrappy also had been giving the PEP a thorough mental review. He liked the idea of taking on the rail mill, the scope of the production, inventory and quality demands was ideal. Rail production at Steelton was a vital component of Bethlehem's overall capability. Business was strong and profitable. He knew a couple of guys at the rail mill, but none of the top two or three guys in that department. There was also Harry's brother Tim, who he had just bumped into at the St. Lawrence Club.

Scrappy pulled his boat onto its trailer with the help of a couple of bank fisherman hanging out by the river. He locked everything down, took a shower, got into the Ford and headed over to his parents house for a neighborhood cookout. All the neighbors took over the shady side of his block of Conestoga Street. There would be eight or ten families, including his dad's parents who lived just a few doors away. Hamburgers, hot dogs, hot sausage, watermelon and a half keg of beer bought through Buddy Yetter. A baseball game would be on the radio…maybe a double header. A couple of the older guys would find a football and toss it around after they had a few beers, the alcohol affecting their memories of how well they played the game back in high school. Kids would be raising hell in the lot across the street – a few skinned knees would result. Their moms didn't mind because the little angels were off to school this week, and a few of the West Side homemakers could be seen discreetly slurping their Seven and Sevens in celebration. Around dusk some fire-crackers would be shot off and sparklers lit. Everybody got along well, their dogs too.

It was a quiet Labor Day at the Burger home. Hap was nursing a pretty good hangover after his birthday celebration, so he passed up the Lion's Club picnic. He had gotten into the Canadian Club that Harry had given him. Doris made his favorite yellow cake with chocolate icing and Tim got him a box of Dutch Masters. He was sporting a new Steelton ball cap for the upcoming foot-ball season, another present from Tim. It was the darkest navy blue – wool – with the white block lettered "S". Tim bought the hat at Sam Singer's along with a fungo bat that he had Sam special order for Hap, who couldn't wait to put it to use next spring when the Little League tryouts began. Hap wandered up to the Fire House to show off the new hat.

Doris warned the men that they were cooking the hot dogs for Monday dinner. She'd open some pork and beans, and she made macaroni salad…but that was it. "It's a holiday for the labor of women too!" she advised.

Harry kind of shuffled around the house most of the day. He offered to help Tim wash the car but Tim had no interest in that. Harry was thinking ahead of his week at work, but more so his upcoming meeting with Dr. Becker to talk about the apartment. He planned to have fifty bucks in cash in his pocket if things went well and Dr. Becker asked for a deposit. Harry knew there was a party on Conestoga Street as there was every Labor Day, and he was sure Scrappy Stone would be there as the two Stone fami-lies always helped with the food and drinks. He was counting on

Scrappy to help him at work and hoping that he would ask him to join the production project's next phase. He did not want to be locked into the pit recorder position under the thumb of Bob Hernley. Harry had been trying to study up on some of the materials the engineering kids had given him, and he was trying to do what Scrappy told him to do by earning Hernley's respect. "I'm doing everything I am supposed to be doing to get ahead, but my future seems to be in other people's hands..." Harry did not like thinking about this bit of reality but he swallowed hard and decided to get to work early in the morning, as he knew Hernley would. "It's a six a.m. start for me tomorrow."

Tim slept late. It was about two when he took a walk down to Bernardo Brothers, about the only place open on a holiday. There was a phone booth there that he could use to call Anthony Linta, and he'd pick up a Philly paper while there. He put on a pair of Bermuda shorts and a knit shirt...he figured he wouldn't be able to wear shorts too much longer now that Labor Day was here. The town was pretty much dead although the rail mill was operating and all of the men who worked eleven to seven would be trying to get some sleep this afternoon for their Tuesday shift that started tonight. Tim thought about how he'd be on rotating shifts the following week...and how much time he'd have to himself on eleven to seven. Day turn, with all of the big bosses around, would be a total loss.

The sun was still high and over the river as Tim nodded to "Bernie" Bernardo who was behind the counter. Bernie made sure that Tim knew he was taking World Series action again this year. Tim picked up the Daily News and headed to the phone booth. Anthony answered.

"Any news Anthony? I decided not to see Arthur yesterday. You know how he is with Sundays."

"Dad went up to see Sonny yesterday. They have an amnesia story set up. He told all of the K of C guys to clam up. That pain in the butt kid Winny Clark talked to some people and called my dad Sunday…he seemed to know a fair bit. We know Posetti the bartender is Sonny's contact. Dad will be checking him out tomorrow, he supposedly has a prison record. Dad's going to put one of his guys on the case but instruct him to stay away from the K of C people…he'll continue to handle that directly."

"That's good."

"He wants you to get up to see Arthur today or tomorrow morning if you can. He wants Arthur's kid Claude to go down to Mohn Street and see what he can pick up from the colored bars and groceries down there…see if anybody's bragging or flashing around a lot of cash all of a sudden. You know my Dad, his theory is the criminal element can't stand to have money in their pocket without spending it foolishly and bragging about it when they do."

"All right, Anthony. I'll get to Arthur. What about Sonny's car?"

"Don't worry about it. Dad has it under his control. When Sonny gets released, the plan is for his memory to come back and he'll call Dad right away."

Tim thought it best to keep his conversation with Mike Jamnov at the St. Lawrence to himself.

"I was at the St. Lawrence Saturday night. They are all caught up, Anthony. I'm back at work at three tomorrow, but starting next week I'm on rotating shifts again."

"My Dad and Mom are at the management Club picnic. He'll have a full day tomorrow. Let's connect by phone sometime Wednesday."

Tim had his instructions. He might see Arthur at Bob's later on tonight, but thought it best to try to make the contact yet this afternoon. He walked the fifteen minutes up to Arthur's and went around the back. He saw Claude and another black guy washing Arthur's Caddy. Tim and Claude made eye contact but didn't say anything.

"I'll be right back, Charles. I need to see this guy a minute" Claude yelled to his friend as he and Tim went into the back entrance to the morgue.

Tim made sure no one could see them talking. "Your father at home, Claude?"

"Nope. He and Mom and everyone else is at the church picnic. Won't be back 'til late."

Tim had to decide what to tell Claude. Arthur did not like anybody giving his sons orders and Arthur and Arthur alone determined when and how much his kids knew about what.

"Did you hear about the robbery at the Knights of Columbus down on the lower end? That's one of your liquor deliveries, right Claude?"

"Yessir."

"You know the guy Pete, the bartender? He's our contact there, right?

"I can't say Mr. Burger. I make deliveries to the bartender, yeah, but he never gave me his name. I never gave him mine neither. He ain't friendly and I don't like him much. I don't think he likes dealin' with colored folk. He tries to screw me on the deliveries sometimes, tellin' me I'm short, that kind of thing. I deliver there and get out and we double count every bottle together."

"All right, Claude. Please tell your dad I'll try to call him around eight tonight. I'd like to see him if I can."

"OK Mr. Burger. See you."

144

Harry walked down Franklin Street toward the river. When he got to Main Street, he was surprised to see Kormushoff's Market open. He decided to stop in to get some ice cream for after the hot dogs tonight.

"Hello Tim! What brings you way up here?" Darlene Decker asked with a smile.

"Hi Darlene. It's a nice day so I just went out for a walk and I was surprised to see you are open. Thought I'd get a quart of Hershey's for dinner tonight." Tim walked back to the freezer case and picked out a container of Teaberry- Doris' favorite – and walked up to the register.

"How's that brother of yours doing, Tim? You know, he could call a girl once in awhile."

"He's OK I guess…keeps to himself mostly. All wound up in his new job at the mill. Have you seen him this summer?"

"I guess you could say that. Well, tell him I asked about him and want him to give me a call."

"OK Darlene, I'll do that. Be good!"

"No fun in that." she replied as she turned to the next customer in line.

"Darlene, always the flirt" Tim thought… "I wonder if she's doing more than flirting with big brother Harry?"

Tim hustled home so the ice cream wouldn't melt. He figured he'd wait until everyone was together and that's when he'd mention Darlene asking all about Harry. If Doris heard that, she'd put her West Side mom's network in action and if Harry even held hands with Darlene, she'd find out about it.

Hap finally made his way down to the house around five. Harry had the flimsy steel barbecue grill set up in the back yard, the charcoal hot and a can of Schimdt's in his hand. Doris had the table set and Hap assumed his customary position at the far end with his back to the wall. He had a quart bottle and a water glass in front of him…two Dutch masters sticking out of his shirt pocket.

Tim sat beside Hap and poured himself a short one out of Hap's bottle. "Dogs in ten minutes!" Harry yelled from the back porch over the hum of the window fan Hap had installed in the back kitchen window. Doris was putting the relish, ketchup and mustard out for the table, along with a big bowl of diced onion. Harry brought in eight hot dogs and miraculously only one was burned. "I'll eat the burned one" Harry offered.

Tim waited for the right moment during dinner. "I got you a quart of Hershey's Teaberry for dessert Mom. I walked up past the school and saw Kormushoff's was open."

Harry stopped chewing. He kind of knew what was coming next.

"Saw Darlene Decker in there at the cash register. She was looking pretty good. Asked all about you, Harry, and wondered why you haven't called."

"Yeah, I bumped into her at Motzie's last week. I took her out a couple of times before I went in the service. I'll call her sometime."

"Well, she seemed as though you had just seen her. Anyway, she asked me to relay the message that she'd like you to call."

Harry just nodded…these God damned West Side girls just can't keep their mouths shut.

Doris piped up: "What kind of girl asks for a man to call her? I just don't understand these girls today…they are so forward. They might as well be asking you to jump right into bed with them."

"Maybe she has already, Mom" Tim offered.

"All right…I don't need that kind of talk at my kitchen table." Doris barked back.

The sons cleaned up after dinner without a word between them. Hap went out on the front stoop to finish his beer and smoke a cigar. Doris took a big bowl of ice cream along and joined him. Harry took a look at the Philly paper Tim had brought home, then switched on the TV.

Tim walked up to the fire house so he could call Arthur in private. He dialed Arthur's business line at eight o'clock sharp. No answer. That meant Arthur either didn't get the message from Claude, or he didn't want to talk. Tim hung up and headed home. As he walked down the sloped driveway of West Side Hose, he could easily see down Conestoga Street, where a party was still in full swing. He heard the firecrackers and saw the sparklers. "That's it…the last sights and sounds of a Steelton summer" he thought to himself as he turned to his left and headed home.

19

Ernie Linta and Bob Hernley could have easily passed one another on the way to work early Tuesday morning. At five-thirty there were few cars on the road. Ernie wanted to be sure to get some time with Mike Karmilov, who would be going off duty at seven, and Hernley was on his usual early schedule to talk to his eleven to seven foreman and to get the day shift started. Hernley rushed passed security at the gate and bolted toward his office.

Linta saw Karmilov's squad car in the municipal building parking lot and found him in the patrolmen's office area as he entered the building. "Mike, when you finish your shift report come into my office for a minute." "Be right there, Chief."

Linta got his call list together for the morning…State Police and Dauphin County Records office to check on Pete Posetti's record; Harrisburg Hospital for status on Sonny; Arthur Howard. Herman Klein. Karmilov knocked on the open door.

"C'mon in Mike…quiet night last night?"

"Not too bad chief…mostly traffic stuff, couple of fights. Some idiot at the Legion blew two of his fingers off lighting M-80s with a cigar; no lock-ups."

"Good. I want you to work with me on the K of C robbery… this is a chance to pair up with me on something important. Here's how it breaks down. I was at the Bethlehem Steel Management picnic yesterday and was pulled aside by the security chief there. They've been having a rash of robberies of some of the truck drivers down at gate ten, and their material thefts are up too. He thinks there's a ring of guys from the lower end doing all of this. He heard about the strong armed robbery at the K of C and thinks the people who did it are part of the same operation. He and I agreed to cooperate, but to keep it quiet. I'm a member of the K of C and know the manager there. I'll personally handle all of the investigation and follow up with the membership and management there. I don't want a uniformed presence around the club. Your job is to see what you can find out about who did this. I want you to work the Mohn Street area in particular. See if anyone has been spending a bunch of money in the neighborhood, new car, clothes, that sort of thing. Let me know if you need some folding money to help people to talk…I'll arrange it through Lt. Hauser. Also, the football season starts on Saturday, and the last week of practice is usually well attended by blacks and whites. Get up there and sit in the stands to see what you can pick up. No uniform. Work any overtime you need. You get any leads, you come right to me. Don't talk about this assignment with anyone but me. Somebody told me the Weems brothers might be involved. Check it out."

The stuff about Herman Klein and the theft ring was a total smoke screen; Ernie had to try to throw Karmilov off of the main investigation on the K of C, though.

"Got it Chief. You get any word on how that guy made out who had his head bashed in?"

"He's got a case of amnesia up at the hospital, that's what I hear. The docs up there will let us know when and if he can give us a statement."

"When I went up to the garage to fill up the cruiser, I saw that new red Olds up there…same car that was in K of C that night. Belong to the guy in the hospital?"

"I had it towed up there. I intend to get the license tracked today…no one from the State was working over the holiday. Forget about the car and work on suspects. That's it."

Harry was up at five and through the gate around six. He wanted to make sure Hernley saw him at work an hour early. He picked up a clip board and a binder with an open hearth PEP report and walked out into the plant on the safety walkway that lead to Hernley's office so that Hernley would notice him. A couple of minutes later, Hernley came up from the area of the maintenance offices.

"Morning Mr. Hernley" Harry said. "Have a nice holiday?"

"You're here early Burger. What are you working on there?"

"Reviewing the last couple of PEP status reports, want to make sure I refreshed my memory. I really enjoyed working on that project. Thanks for giving me the chance to learn so much."

"Well, you still have a lot to learn about the pit recorder job, and I suggest you concentrate on that. I am going to be setting some new production and quality goals for the open hearth for the rest of the year, and I need everybody's best efforts, including you and Melton. And by the way, if you have any conversations or meetings with Mark Stone, I want to know about it right away. Understood?" Bob Hernley pivoted back to his office.

"Yes, of course. Understood."

"Well, that was that" thought Harry. "Nothing like putting your best foot forward, showing some ambition and then getting shot down in the first hour of the first day of your plan." He wondered why the sudden attitude – anger almost – at Scrappy Stone. He thought back to what George Clark had said about things not working out so well for Hernley and Mr. Willis at the big meeting last week up at Bethlehem…maybe Scrappy screwed up and they are blaming him? Well, one thing for sure, if I talk to Scrappy or he comes to me, I'm telling him what Hernley said and Hernley can go screw himself. With that, Harry tried to put himself one hundred per cent into his job and his studies. He at least had his meeting with Dr. Becker to look forward to. He hoped he could afford the rent if the apartment was offered. It sounded like there would be no overtime with Hernley's new goals…knowing him it would mean working harder but no pay for it.

Tim got up early and walked up to the firehouse to use the phone. He called Arthur just before eight. Arthur answered the business line.

"It's Tim. Do you have time to talk?"

"Yeah sure…My son said you were up here yesterday…what's new?"

"Two things. Ernie wants to know if you can have Claude spend some extra time down around Mohn Street to see if anybody's flashing around a lot of money, or bragging about anything that might tie back to the robbery at the Knights of Columbus. He also would like you to see if your people can help if they see anything…maybe somebody all of a sudden sporting new clothes, spending big in one of your places."

"All right, Tim. Makes sense. I'll talk to Claude. I know he's had some problems with the bartender at that club. I think we should cut the K of C off for awhile…maybe I'll talk to the Chief about that."

"Yeah, he should make the call…we don't want to piss the bartender off. Anthony told me that Ernie is handling everything personally."

"You said there were two things? I got a busy morning and a funeral this afternoon."

"Yeah, I am going to have those three gondola rail cars pulled up to the siding closest to your place this week. I'll give you a heads up when I get the specific date. The car I have in mind is the one with all of the serial numbers scraped off...you can't miss it. I'll also take a quiet walk up there after it's parked to make sure it was dropped where it's supposed to be. I'm going to try to have some rail sections in it for you as well. I'll be at Bob's after work Wednesday night. Maybe I'll see you there. I've been dealing with Anthony on the K of C matter but it wouldn't surprise me if Ernie contacts you. I don't think he wants Cohen to know anything that might shake him up...that's Ernie's call too."

"All right, man. Maybe see you late Wednesday."

Ernie Linta got the ball rolling on Pete Posetti as soon as the state offices opened at eight o'clock. He had personal contacts and favors he could draw on just about everywhere, but he went strictly through channels on the Posetti thing. He didn't want to attract any special attention, just a routine matter as a part of a normal crime investigation. He had a busy morning with a number of department matters to attend to, and his office braced itself for the barrage of calls it always got the first week of the school year. He took a call from the Borough Council Chairman about the upcoming Council meeting, assured the high school principal he'd have a cruiser escort the football team and band buses to the opening game. He put a call as he promised yesterday into Herman Klein's office to arrange for their periodic dinner at the BSMC. It wasn't until almost eleven when he noticed an item on the daily log about funeral escort for Howard's that afternoon that he remembered to call Arthur. He did that now on his private line with his door closed.

"Arthur? Ernie. Got a couple of minutes?"

"I got a funeral at two and I got five minutes, tops. I can save you some time, Tim called me first thing this morning and brought me up to date. I'll have Claude poke around but only with people we know and trust. I ain't sending him out on the streets. I'm not in favor of telling Cohen anything about this. And I think we should shut off deliveries to the K of C at the lower end until things calm down a bit. Agreed?"

Ernie hadn't thought about that. "Yeah, good idea. The bartender there deals solely through Sonny except for the actual delivery. Let's just take a step back and see what happens. As soon as Sonny is released from the hospital, I'll arrange to have him picked up. I need to spend some one-on-one time with him. I'll let you go. Tim and Anthony are connected on this, too Arthur. By the way, who died?"

"Lady from our church, Miss Emma everyone called her. Eighty-two. Had seven kids. Widow. Should be a big service… getting buried up at Howard Day. We'll need that police escort."

"It will be there Arthur. Don't worry. Let's see if we can find out who robbed Sonny. We need to get to them too before anybody else does. Bye."

Ernie decided to head home for lunch. He knew that Anthony would be there as well…he worked about five minutes from the Linta home and took advantage of his Mom's cooking every day. He brought his son up to date on his call with Arthur and told him that Tim and Arthur had connected, too.

"I'll need some more time on Sonny's production records, Dad. I spent a few hours on it yesterday while you were at the picnic. Nothing really jumped out. I looked at all of the K of C's first. Arthur does delivery and Sonny handles the beer. They are all labels-on accounts, unlike Arthur's places. Sonny seems to hit them once a month for payments, business is steady. We had a couple of bottles discrepancy between Arthur's delivery slips and Sonny's collections when the account on the lower end –our club -first opened but no trouble the last three or four months. They all pay on time. Our K of C sells more wine that any other account, that's the only thing that pops out."

"The three of us are going to go down there for dinner Friday night. Wouldn't hurt to support them, show a little extra level of police interest. I'm going to talk to Nick Cantore sometime this week. I'm checking on Pullitti, the bartender."

Ernie's first call when he got back to the office was to Sam Lowry's radio, the tow truck driver.

"Sam, you have a good weekend? Lots of drunks wrecking their cars? "

Ernie had to strain to hear Sam over the noise from the tow truck. "Yeah, good weekend. How can I help Ernie?"

"Hear anything more about the K of C robbery? Picking anything up?"

"That asshole kid from the newspaper called me Sunday; found out I towed a car away from the K of C and was asking questions. I told him it was a confidential police matter. I'm keeping my ears open for you."

"Thanks Sam. Call me anytime if you hear something."

Ernie worked through his calls and some overdue paper-work. It was the middle of the afternoon when two calls come in, one right after the other. The first he was eager to answer...the second, not so much.

"Chief? Andy Wambach from Division of Records in Harris-burg. I have something for you on a Peter A. Posetti, age forty. We'll need the formal request if you want file copies of course, but

I can tell you what we found. Mr. Posetti has entries here going back to 1936. Mostly property theft, selling stolen goods, petty larceny, that sort of thing. Had a charge pending for grand theft auto, but worked a deal with Dauphin County in forty-one... charge was dropped and he entered the Army. Several more arrests and finally six months County jail for gambling and wire fraud in forty--seven. Another gambling conviction in March of forty-nine, sentenced to three to five years but got out around Thanksgiving in fifty-one. Nothing since.

"Thanks Mr. Wambach, that is all I need. I appreciate your getting back to me so quickly on this. Let me know if I can ever do anything for you."

The gambling charges got Ernie's attention. All of the petty larceny, stealing, that sort of low level crime can be done by yourself or with a partner or two. But gambling and a wire fraud charge requires a network, and almost always somebody deep enough into gambling bumps into organized crime at some point. Ernie thought Sonny was smart enough to keep his independence from that crowd and in fact that's what Sonny promised Ernie when they began their partnership all those years ago.

Ernie's second call was from Winnie Clark Junior, who wanted an update on the K of C robbery.

"I've got nothing much new for you Winny. Still tracking down leads. Trying to keep things under wraps so that we don't scare off the suspects, who we have a lead on. My guys are still working hard on the case."

"All right Chief. Anything new on the hospitalized victim you can share, or that red Olds, or on the amount of money missing?"

"Nope, not right now."

"Anything about the wallets of the two victims being found and turned into the club?"

"That's news to me…you have a source for that?"

"I spoke to several guys who were at last call…I mentioned that to you Sunday."

"Those guys were all probably in the bag by then…if you don't have a confirmed source I wouldn't print it…but you're the newspaperman."

"Well I've got the story written. I'd like to run it past you for confirmation or comment. Can I read it to you? It's going to be written this way unless you have something else to add."

"Go ahead, Winny. I hope you didn't get carried away."

"It will carry a dateline of today – here's the copy. The headline won't be written until we typeset:

"Two men were injured-one seriously-in a violent robbery early last Saturday morning at the Steelton Knights of Columbus. The robbery occurred just after closing, and the attackers fled with a full day's receipts estimated in the hundreds of dollars.

A bartender, Peter Posetti was attacked in the club parking lot along with a customer as the two men left the club about three in the morning. The Steelton News has been unable to get official identification of the second victim, although Harrisburg Hospital has confirmed that he was taken by ambulance to the emergency room and admitted. He is reported in good condition and remains hospitalized according to hospital nursing staff. The driver of the ambulance would not provide any information other than the victim had a serious head injury.

Patrons of the club identified the unknown victim as a guest of bartender Posetti who was known as "Sonny". He was thought to have been driving a new red Oldsmobile which neighbors said had been towed away from the Knights of Columbus parking lot by Lowry towing. Mr. Samuel Lowry, owner, when contacted, had no comment for the Steelton News.

A report that wallets belonging to the two robbery victims had been recovered in the parking lot could not be confirmed.

Nick Cantore manager of the K of C likewise had no comment. Efforts to speak with Mr. Posetti were unsuccessful. Chief Ernie Linta of the Steelton Police confirmed that the robbery had occurred, but refused to provide additional information, citing the holiday weekend and the on-going investigation. He did tell a reporter for the Steelton news that he was pursuing leads on suspects.

The local Knights of Columbus –Council 3625- was founded just over two years ago and previous reports showed a membership of well over one hundred; it is a private club and re-opened for business last Saturday afternoon.

Anyone with information is encouraged to call the Police, or the Steelton News."

That's it Chief….anything to add?"

"I got nothing else for you Winny….I told you before, don't get carried away….stick to the facts. I'd hate to see you or your Dad get embarrassed by reporting some things that a bunch of drunks tried to remember after a night of drinking that turned out later to not be true."

"All right, Chief. I've got a few more hours until deadline if anything comes up. This is going on the front page."

"Sure Winny, it's always slow the end of summer. You can put this piece next to the jaywalker stories."

Ernie was at the office until almost six and as soon as he got home he brought Anthony up to date on the Posetti file and the Steelton News article that would come out Thursday.

"I have a full day tomorrow. If I don't hear anything about Sonny I'll call or head up there sometime Thursday."

20

"Good afternoon, Sir. It's Doctor Atwood. I see by your chart you are progressing well. Sorry I did not get in to see you Tuesday, I finally had a day off, and we were awaiting some of your test results. You feeling better now that all the tubes are out and you're on solid food?"

"Yes Doc, I am. Much better."

"Well then, let's go over all of these tests we put you through the last couple of days. You'll be pleased to learn we found no permanent neurological damage of any kind…no paralysis or impairment of your extremities. Your eyesight, speech and hearing are fine. Your reflexes are outstanding. All of your vital signs are close to perfect. We will take the stitches out of your head later today, and your nose and eyes are healing as expected. You report no pain other than soreness around your incision, right?"

"That's right Doctor."

"Well, Sir. The big question for me is why you have this memory loss. It's not characteristic for your injury. You also seem to have full command of the language, your circumstances here, pain level, hunger, thirst, but your name is a mystery. You know, Doctors do not like medical mysteries…we are trained to solve them. I need some help from you to solve this one."

"Sorry to be so much trouble…I just don't remember anything about myself really. I mean, I do feel good except for the pain in the back of the head, maybe I'll come around."

Sonny was putting on his best acting job and wondering how long he could get away with it. He was hoping Ernie Linta would stop by so that they could put their plan into action.

"Do you remember a policeman being in here, asking you some questions?"

"Uh, Geez, I, uh, yeah maybe. Sorta. I mean I think so."

"Memory a little foggy on recent events, too?" Dr. Atwood was getting more impatient by the second. "You talked to Chief Linta for about fifteen minutes. He told us you were what he called "responsive." Remember talking to him now?"

"I do recall seeing a big guy in here, yeah. But I couldn't remember what we talked about. Am I in some kind of trouble with the police?"

"Not that I know of. That's for the police to decide. I'm simply in charge of your medical care." Atwood took a good long pause and looked his patient dead in the eye. "Are you Sonny? Is that your name?"

"I am totally fucked", Sonny thought. "I need the best acting performance of my life." Here goes: "Sonny…that…that does sound familiar. That could be me. Do you know my last name?"

"The hospital had a couple of calls from the newspaper in Steelton. My nurse took one of them. She protected your confidentiality but the newspaper knew quite a bit about you. Turns out several people knew you from the Knights of Columbus down there. They talked to the newspaper and the editor down there called us about you. That's the place where you got knocked in the head."

"I see…well, this is starting to come back to me a little. Did the police call too…am I in some kind of trouble, because I don't remember being involved in any kind of problem…I hardly even know Steelton."

"Well, Sonny. I am going to do you a favor. I'm giving you tonight to work on your memory. I don't think you have been honest with me and the people who have taken care of you here. Medically, you are OK to be discharged tomorrow. If your memory hasn't improved by tomorrow morning, I'm writing orders for you to be discharged to the County's care. And all of the hospital's bills are going to go along with you. Now, you won't forget THAT, will you?"

"No Sir, Doctor. I get it. Listen, can you do me a favor? Can you call the policeman who you said was in here? I got to know if I am in some kind of trouble. I think that's only fair." Sonny was very pleased with himself. This doctor was no dummy, but he couldn't outwit the master.

"And did I have some clothes on me when I was brought in, and anything in my pockets?" Sonny needed his car and he hoped his car keys and his small notebook were still with his clothes.

"We'll see about your clothing but I think at least for today you don't need visitors. I will stop in tomorrow Sonny.…you have any sort of breakthrough, you let the nursing staff know."

Doctor Atwood had no intention of calling the police until tomorrow when Sonny was getting out of his hospital, one way or the other. He made his notes on Sonny's charts and he'd write the discharge order in the morning.

Tim remembered that he forgot to call Anthony as he walked up Christian Street…he'd connect with him tomorrow. The middle of the week was always slow at Bob's, and a Wednesday after a holiday weekend it was quiet as a church. Everyone was tired out or tapped out. Tim walked into Bob's around 11:30 and there were two other guys in the place. No sign of Arthur. Tim thought he'd have two beers and a bag of chips and if Arthur didn't show, he'd call it a night.

Bob's liquor house could be two different places. On weekends, the place would be jammed – standing room only until dawn, juke box playing, men and women enjoying themselves with cheap booze and familiar company. It would be hot as hell in the summer but no one seemed to mind. Service was always fast and there was never any trouble of any kind. On quiet nights like tonight, Tim noticed all the things he would never pay attention to on a busy night, the faded and beat up wallpaper, the ceiling stained a yellow brown from years of cigarette and cigar smoke. Every bar stool, table and chair wobbled. The floor was swept regularly but hadn't had a proper cleaning in years. Lighting was always kept to a minimum. The two bathrooms smelled of stale piss. A separate bathroom was at the back of the building for the ladies and the kitchen staff, who could be relied upon to keep their mouths shut no matter who they saw in there.

Tim sat at the bar and made small talk until Arthur came in just before midnight. Arthur gave the two guys at the bar a look, and a nod at the bartender and all of a sudden the bar was closed and Bob, Arthur and Tim were the only souls in the place. Bob made himself busy at the bar.

"Arthur, I can get those three gondola cars up there tomorrow, probably right around dark. I've got about a ton and a half of rail in the old brown car with the numbers erased. There's also maybe a ton of frog and switch parts that were intended for re-melt. There all twisted and rusty but still good...I'll have that shit on top of the rails so it really does look like scrap. It will be the most northbound of the cars…the other two still have serial numbers so you can't miss it. I'll have it on the end of the far east siding…I checked it out a couple of days ago when I talked to Claude…the siding is empty. OK?"

"Yeah, Tim. I'll have my guys look at it. We can take our time fooling around with the scrap…that all looks legit in the daytime…and I'll have my cutters take a good look. We can talk when I know something."

"Arthur, I got a bad feeling about the Sonny business. Sometimes I wish it was just you and me, and we could get out of the liquor business."

Arthur said nothing. "We need to give this some time. I'll have my boy see what he can find out, but only so far as we need to protect our business. That's the limit. He ain't no cop and I don't want him to be. Funny how a couple of white guys up to no good at a private white club get robbed and everybody automatically thinks it's a couple of niggers that did it. I only have my sons in the business as far as I WANT them in the business. That's for me to decide and no one else."

Tim understood the conversation was over. "I got to get home Arthur. Thanks for meeting me."

He nodded to Bob on the way out and tipped him the usual dollar. Tim thought about his conversation with Anthony Linta at lunch a few days ago, trying to see if there was any sentiment for cutting Sonny out, and there wasn't, at least as far as Anthony let on. Arthur had his own interests to protect. Tim walked down a lonely Christian Street. He decided that his gondola car deal would be his last for a while. Might be a good idea to lay low, especially if the rail car thing worked out…it should bring a big payday. The changes in his working schedule were going to cause disruptions anyway…Tim never thought of himself as the cautious type, but all the signs pointed in that direction. As he approached his backyard, he made some decisions: "I think I'm going to scale things back a bit, keep a lower profile. Maybe I'll spend a little more time with the ladies....I could always give Darlene Decker a call." That one made him laugh. He had sworn off West Side girls a long time ago...better to let his brother fish in that pond.

21

The Steelton News was delivered with the Harrisburg Patriot and it was waiting for Ernie on his front porch at six Thursday morning. As Winny had promised, the K of C article was on the front page, written just as he had read it to the Chief Tuesday afternoon. Ernie didn't like the use of Sonny's name, or the reference to the wallets, but it was all in the open now. He planned to get up to Harrisburg Hospital to check on Sonny later that day. His first meeting of the morning was at the seven o'clock shift change at the station, when Karmilov was due for an update on the robbery. Karmilov was waiting for him, two coffees in his hands.

"Chief, I'll give you the highlights. Nobody knows nothing, although plenty of people are talking about it. The Weems kids' names never came up from anyone. The owner of Washington's store at the top of Swatara Street said that he heard it was an inside job...that the bartender faked the robbery and split the money with some other guys. None of the people I spoke to whose homes back up to the alley behind the Knights heard or saw anything. No one is flashing around new money that I could find. I took your advice and sat through the football practice yesterday...there's a good mix of white and colored in the stands. I must have talked to fifteen guys...not one reliable lead. If you want me to make some progress, I got to interview all the guys who were in the bar that night, the bartender, and the manager."

"All right, Mike. I don't want anything else done at the moment. The guys who got the money will slip up sooner or later. Let's sit tight for a bit. I'm going to take my family into the Knights for dinner tomorrow night and see who comes up to talk." Ernie's phone rang just as Corporal Karmilov walked out.

"Ernie, this is Sam Lowry. I'm callin' from my office. I just had an interesting call I think you should know about."

"Go ahead, Sam."

"Guy calls me up and says he's Sonny's brother, you know, the guy with the red Olds who got whacked at the Knights? Guy says he heard I towed the car and wants to know where it is. Said his brother is still in the hospital but Sonny wants him to pick up the car."

"You get a name or a return phone number?"

"I told the guy it was a confidential police matter and he'd have to call Steelton Police. And here's the good part: the guy starts threatening me, telling me he knows I know where the car is, it's their private property, and says to me it wouldn't be good for my business if I didn't tell him what he wants to know."

"Then what, Sam?"

"I tell him I turned the car over to the police, I don't know where it is, but if he wants to try anything funny, I know how to handle myself. Then he hung up."

"OK Sam, you need any help from me let me know. If you hear anymore from this creep, call me."

"Got it, Ernie."

Ernie thought he'd better speed up his schedule to go see Sonny. He looked up the number and eventually got the fifth floor nursing station on the phone.

"Ma'am...this is Chief Ernie Linta of the Steelton Police Department. Is Dr. Atwood available please? Can you page him?"

"Oh, yes Chief, I remember you. Dr. Atwood is in surgery. May I give him a message?"

"Yes, thanks, please have him call...he has my number. By the way, is there any change in the patient I came to see over the weekend, the unknown gentleman with the head injury?"

"Oh, you mean Sonny? Yes, he started coming around last evening I understand."

The Chief was taken aback with this, wondering why Sonny didn't call him right away. "Oh, he remembered his name...his last name too?"

"I don't think so, Chief. You really should talk to the doctor about this."

"Of course, nurse, thanks...oh! One more thing...were Sonny's clothes and other possessions returned to him? They are evidence from the robbery, and it is important to try to keep custody of that. If his clothes are not in his room, can you see that they are please when I get up there? We are particularly interested in his car keys, as his car is also vital evidence in the case."

"I will check on it, Chief. I will have Dr. Atwood call you. Goodbye."

The more Ernie thought about this the less he liked it. He decided he wouldn't wait for Atwood's call, but he had to take care of a few more pressing police items before he could leave. He was able to pull out of the station lot at ten thirty and was in the hospital elevator at eleven. As he approached the nurse station, he saw a familiar face, nurse Yoder. He raised his hand, and took off his Captain's hat to wave hello.

"Good morning, Chief. I'll bet you're here to see our famous mystery patient. One day, no one knows who he is, and the next

166

day he has one visitor after another."

"He had visitors? What kind of visitors? When were they here?" His voice was loud and firm. Ernie noticed the nurse take a step back from him.

"He has family with him now…they arrived just a bit ago. They had pictures of him with them and said his full name was Salvatore Donato, but that everyone knew him as Sonny. Told me everybody was worried sick about him. Sonny recognized them when I showed them into his room."

Ernie didn't wait for anything else. He put his cap back on spun around and headed for Sonny's room. Nurse Yoder paged Dr. Atwood…she was afraid she was in some kind of trouble.

Ernie burst into the room to see two men, one on either side of Sonny's bed. They looked up to see this big cop in full uniform staring them down. Both guys looked like they had seen a ghost.

"Identify yourselves!" Ernie commanded.

One guy was dressed in a colorful open collar sport shirt, gold chain, gold watch. The other guy had a white long-sleeved shirt, neck tie, no jacket. The sport shirt spoke up.

"Family, officer. I'm Sonny's family…brother-in-law."

"You?" Ernie was in full angry cop mode.

"Family friend….family friend." Shirt and tie guy said haltingly.

You two got names?

Sport shirt spoke up. "I'm Francis, Francis Messina. Sonny here used to be married to my sister…but we still think of him as a brother. This here's Nick…we've all known Sonny a long time… we just found out this morning he's been in the hospital…read it in the newspaper."

Ernie's eyes were on Sonny. He was sure that if Sonny had been on a bed pan, he'd be shitting in it right now.

"Well, Francis, you and Nick here can go out and wait 'til I talk to our patient here. He was involved in a violent crime that's under active investigation. He is a central witness. If he's medically able he will be in police custody until he is fully interviewed. You can give your names, address and phone number to the nurses at the desk…they can contact you when I advise them we are through with this gentleman. Got that?"

The two men said a hasty good bye and left the room. Ernie gave Sonny a good hard look and closed the door. He went over behind the curtain to check out the other bed…it was empty.

"That guy just got discharged this morning" Sonny said sheepishly. "Just us."

"You can start by telling me what the fuck is going on here, and no bullshit Sonny, I ain't in the mood."

"All right, here it is. Those two guys are part of my beer connections. They found out about me getting whacked a couple of days ago when I didn't show up for a meeting, and they started asking questions. They tracked me down to the K of C and yesterday somebody down there told them I was in Harrisburg Hospital. They tried to get in here last night but the doc had no visitors until today on my records."

"What are their interests Sonny?"

"Well, same as you. The meeting I missed was to pay them for beer delivered to my accounts; they don't like it when people owe them money. That's it."

"C'mon Sonny. They come up here personally for that? If they were talking to those paisanos at the K of C they must have heard your wallet was stolen. They knew you didn't skip out on them if they found out you were hurt and taken out of there by ambulance. Give me the real story on those two."

"Ernie, I still have a hell of a headache, I ain't thinkin' too good. I don't know why they came up here like this. The guy Frank is my ex-brother-in-law, that's the truth. Nick is one of my other connections. He is Frank's cousin. Their last name is Messina. They also know Posetti, the bartender down there at the Knights. I got connected to Posetti that way. They don't know about the liquor side of things, that's between me and Posetti. I pay him a little extra to keep his mouth shut. Posetti has some other deals going too, he has had gambling problems in the past, and had to work off some debts by doing leg work for the Messinas and some others."

"Who are they connected to Sonny?"

"You know how it is from your time in Harrisburg, Ernie. As you go up the line you know less and less about who you're working for."

"SONNY…cut the bullshit!"

"They're mostly connected to the Lombardi guys, but some of them have ties into that gang down in Reading…deFilippo or something like that."

"Lombardi. You too, Sonny? You workin' for them too?"

"Ernie, you know when you checked me out, I work mostly independent. You and I go back a ways. I pay my shares to the few guys who get a piece of my business. Mostly beer, nothing big time. I'm just a little guy that tries not to get noticed. It costs me about 15 cents on every dollar I make but I am a steady earner that don't cause no trouble. I stay out of their way on the big money – gambling and numbers, women, lending money – I don't do any of that and they know it."

"So let me ask again, Sonny, why the big interest and the personal visit?"

"I think it's Posetti, Ernie. I think he squawked. I'm guessing they got to him for some reason and he told them about the liquor scam. Frank and Nick didn't get to ask me much before you came in, but I think they will when I get out of here. If I know them, they won't try to horn in, they'll just want me to pay a percentage on what I'm making on the liquor. We all should be OK."

"Yeah, sure Sonny...well any extra commission comes out of your pockets. Now, what's in the trunk of the Olds. Don't forget, I have it. I'll have it busted open if I have to."

"Shit Ernie, C'mon. It's a brand new car. Gimme a break here!"

"Listen Sonny, and listen good. We are partners. I don't need to know everything about your business, but when it threatens my affairs, I DO need to know everything. Let's review our situation. You are part of a crime investigation. I can keep you under wraps for a couple of days. You got no money, no way of getting out of here unless Nick and Frank come to your aid...and that will cost you. You get out of here with me, I put you up someplace for a couple of days, get you your car back, you're back in business. And by the way we drop the K of C and this Posetti character from our customer list, right?

"Yeah, he's already been scratched off in my mind, son of a bitch."

Just then a knock on the door...Alan Atwood walks through.

"Well, getting re-acquainted gentlemen? Mr. Donato, your memory has returned I understand?"

"Yes Doc, thanks a lot. You did a great job. Stared clearing up yesterday after we had our talk."

"And you've had some company I understand? Family and the Chief here?"

"Yessir, somehow they all found me...something about a newspaper article I think."

"Chief, do you mind stepping outside? I want to check Mr. Donato out here. Shouldn't be but a couple of minutes."

Ernie stepped out of the room and walked down to the nurses' station where Nurse Yoder was filling out a chart.

"Sorry if I got a little gruff there nurse…it's been a long week already. Mr. Donato's family still around?"

"No Chief, they left right away after you came in."

"They leave their names and numbers with you?"

"Why no."

This was no surprise to Ernie. "Any luck with Mr. Donato's things?

"I just had a call. They are on their way up from security. I'll bring them in."

Alan Atwood approached the Chief. "Well, Chief, we just might keep Mr. Donato here for awhile so that I can study him. His miraculous recovery from amnesia-an amnesia he never really should have had in the first place-would make a terrific case study. I could make a fortune on the lecture circuit with him. I just looked him over…he can be discharged. I told him that. He wants to be released to your…what do I call it, custody? He'll be ready once the paperwork clears about an hour. You can see him if you want. Good day, Chief."

"Thank you, Doctor. If you are ever in Steelton, look me up. I think I'll wait until his personal effects come up. I'll have a uniform come by to get Mr. Donato." Ernie walked back to the room just as a porter was delivering a cardboard box. It had Sonny's bloodstained jacket and shirt, pants and shoes, underwear. His car keys and St. Christopher medal were in the box.

"Check my inside jacket pocket, Ernie!"

Ernie felt inside and pulled out a small, green spiral notebook, a couple inches in length and maybe a half inch thick. He held up the keys and book, and handed Sonny his St. Christopher's on its gold chain.

"I'll have an officer up here to get you when you're discharged. He'll bring you down to the station in Steelton. We've got to make this look official. I keep you in my office for half an hour, you'll make a formal statement. Then the officer will take you to your car. I'll be there waiting. I dismiss the officer and then we have a nice long look in the trunk. Unless you want to tell me now."

Sonny had to come clean, but as was his habit, only to a point. "Ernie, there's a bunch of cigarettes in there, another little side businesses of mine. Some of my record collection. Might be a couple half gallons of booze. That's it."

"Um-Hmm. All right, see you in a couple hours."

On his way back to Steelton Ernie radioed to set up the police transport for Sonny to the station. He then radioed the municipal garage to tell them he would be up later without telling them why. He had Sonny's keys and book in his pocket. He hadn't decided if he was going to hand Sonny's wallet back to him; he wanted to go through everything one more time. It was too late for lunch at home; he would have liked to bring his son up to date, but no time for that. He also wanted Anthony's opinion on how to handle the Posetti matter.

Sonny was released by the hospital and escorted to Steelton by one of Ernie's patrolmen. Their meeting in Ernie's office went just as planned and Ernie was waiting for Sonny, Sonny's wallet and keys in hand, at the municipal garage when the same officer dropped him off. Ernie made sure every worker still hanging around had somewhere else to be when he and Sonny opened the door to Sonny's Olds. It was parked in a darkened and covered space with the Borough's snow plows.

"Let's see what Santa brought us" Ernie said as he twisted the key into the Old's cavernous trunk. The content was as Sonny described. About forty to fifty cartons of branded cigarettes, two half gallons of Seagram's V.O., and two Charles Chips cans – one red and one gold –full of forty-five rpm records.

"Told you, Ernie."

"What's the story with the cigarettes?"

"I have a source from my church…a long distance truck driver. He would offer to pick up cigarettes for people in the church on his runs down to North Carolina…did it more as a favor to everybody than to make any real money. I got to talking to him. He has some relative down there who's a wholesaler of some kind, and in any case we were able to start bringing up forty or fifty cartons at a time. I bankrolled the deal and cut him in for a percentage after I sold them. I'm making about a buck a carton selling them to bars and a couple of jobbers who fill vending machines. We average about 200 cartons a month now. I meet him over in Carlisle."

"Anybody else know about this?"

"Yep. The guys I sell to, unfortunately that includes Posetti. Most of the K of C's around here are customers. My guess is Posetti also yakked to the Messina guys…and as I said I think he told them about the liquor deal too."

"You figure Posetti knows anything about the source of the liquor?"

"He just knows it's delivered by an unmarked panel truck by a colored guy."

Ernie thought about this and weighed Sonny's posture and his eyes. "And what do you think the Messinas will do about this Sonny?

"Well, I won't wait long to find out. I'm gonna have to go see 'em right after I get my car. I've been thinkin' about it, though.

My guess is they will be pissed I kept something from them, but that they will want some kind of commission on the liquor and cigarettes. It's easy money for them. They have no risk, no work, just collect. I can't see 'em trying to take this over themselves… too much small potatoes."

"And those records…you have a big collection, all 45's… mind if I take a look, Sonny?"

"Shit Ernie, they're just records. Let's go. I gotta get out of these fucked-up clothes, I gotta run around getting my driver's license and car registration replaced, see people."

Ernie wasn't in a trusting mood. He reached into the gold can and grabbed a bunch of records. "You like Nat King Cole, Sonny?"

Sonny knew he was screwed.

"Because the first eight or ten records I pulled out here, they're all by Nat Cole…and they are all the same song. Says on the label "promotional copy, not for sale."

"Aww, shit, Ernie. Same sort of deal as with the cigarettes. I got a guy who services jukeboxes, vending machines, that kind of thing. He steals the records, I pay him ten cents apiece, I sell 'em to clubs for a buck for their jukeboxes….they make their money back a nickel at a time."

"Messinas know about this little dance party?"

"No, Ernie, just another little side businesses. A man's gotta make a living, you know."

"All right Sonny. I'm gonna help you out, and you're gonna help me out. First, here's your wallet and your notebook. License and stuff still in it. It got turned into me and I've kept it to myself. You can take the car. You're not going into any of our businesses until I tell you to. Come to the regular monthly meeting at Robbins on the twenty-fifth. And I want you to let me know everything you can about Posetti, and exactly what he knows, and who he told it to. I also want you to let me know if your guys pick up any information on the guys who wacked you…it's still an open police matter. And I'll tell you this: we have some good sources telling us that Posetti staged this whole thing and set you up. Maybe your friends the Messinas know something about that. And I'm giving you fair warning: If I track any information about the liquor business back to you, the Messina and Lombardi boys will be the smallest of your problems. We clear on that Sonny?"

"Jesus, Chief. I think you're over-reactin' on this. I'll keep my mouth shut. I'll find out what I can. I'll see you at Robbins like always. Don't forget, I'm the one who damned near got his head torn off, and I'm the one out four hundred bucks."

Sonny crawled in and cranked up the Olds. He backed out of the garage and slowly pulled away. Ernie checked his watch as Sonny disappeared over the hill. It was getting close to dinner time and Ernie needed to bring his son up to date. He pulled his Plymouth down Swatara Street. He drove past one of Arthur's places, the Hill Top, and noticed one of Arthur's green, unmarked panel trucks pulled around the side. For the first time since he became Chief, he was a little worried about his side businesses. He planned to talk to Anthony about cutting Sonny out. Arthur would have to OK it. Cohen and Tim would have no say in the matter.

22

Claude, Lawrence, and Charles sat down in the cool basement of the Hill Top, drinking cokes out of the bottle. Charles and Lawrence had just completed a day's work in the salvage yard; Claude picked them up after his day in the funeral home. They were alone in the dirt floored cellar, one small light bulb hanging from a rafter the only light. Claude was smoking. His younger brother Lawrence had a bag of salted peanuts, and he'd put a couple of peanuts in the coke bottle and then take a swig. Their long time friend Charles was going up to the Steamrollers' football practice at Cottage Hill after their meeting. Charles had been a three year starter on the football team, basketball and baseball too. He was well known throughout the town and worked as a driver and helper for Arthur's businesses. He sometimes drove the hearse, and Arthur had provided him with both black and white tuxedo outfits, right down to the patent leather shoes. He was a fit and trim six footer, but looked small compared to his friend Claude, who outweighed him by close to a hundred pounds.

Claude spoke first.

"My Dad asked me to see if I could find out anything about the robbery last weekend. He told me the cops are working hard on

it too. Charles, that guy askin' questions you saw at football practice the other day was one of the Police Chief's guys. From what I
know, no one has any good information. The cops have a couple
of ideas that the Weems brothers might have been involved, but
they are the first guys people think of when there's any trouble
around Mohn Street. There's also a story going around that the
guy I had to hit- the one who took a swing at you, Charles - was
set up by the bartender who planned the whole thing. I like that
story myself!"

Everybody laughed. Claude continued:

"We've had good luck so far with this thing, considering we
got surprised that two men came out of that club instead of just
that bartender. Nobody seems to have seen us or the truck when
we got out of there. It's important that we keep everything quiet
for a while longer. Nobody spends more than five dollars a week
from your share, understand? They are looking for somebody
who's gonna be stupid and flash a lot of money around. That ain't
us. We too smart for that. We are not gonna do any other job for a
couple of weeks. We lay low for a bit. Is that OK with everyone?"

Charles spoke up: "Yeah, that's OK. If that cop tries to talk to
me this afternoon, what do you think of me telling him I heard
the word goin' 'round is the bartender set it all up?"

"I think it's better to say you don't know anything if he asks
you. Be helpful and polite. It would be great if that asshole got
tagged with settin' up his friend there. In any case, the guy who
I hit is supposed to have lost his memory, so he may not even
remember what you look like Charles."

"Lawrence, all three of us have to be careful around Dad. He
can read us like a book. We don't ask any questions about this.
I'm going to tell him there is nothing on the Weems boys, nothin'
on the street. Dad already knew that I didn't like that smart ass

cracker at the Knights, always accusing me of cheating him and treating me as if I was his boy. We just keep our heads down and that will give me some time to think about our next job. OK? Let's finish upstairs and get back home for dinner. Charles, see you tomorrow."

A few blocks below the Hill Top on Swatara, and just three blocks north on Second, Harry opened the door to the dentists' office. It was four twenty-five. He presented himself to Peggy, who told him Dr. Becker would be out in a few minutes. Harry took a seat in the cool office, the sound of a belt driven drill whistling in the front of the office. There were two school aged kids and an older lady in the waiting room. He knew young Dr. Becker would be seeing the kids…he hoped he wouldn't have to wait for the lady before he saw Dr. Becker Senior. Just then, Reginald Becker, a true pillar of Steelton, came into the waiting room.

"Hello Harry. Welcome back from the Army. James told me he saw you at church. We're very happy to have you back safe and sound!"

"Thank you, Sir. I'm also happy to be back as a patient. My Mom and Dad said to say hello."

"Good, good. Nice family. Well, I have the key. What say we take a walk upstairs."

"Yes, thank you Dr. Becker. Thank you."

Harry was spreading it on kind of thick but the Beckers were true gentlemen. The old man was head of the Masonic Lodge in Steelton, on the School Board, President of the Rotary. Everybody liked him. His son was the mirror image of his dad.

"Harry, this is a very nice apartment. It's mostly furnished. All the utilities are included. It even has a small window air conditioner in the bedroom. No TV, though. Why don't you take your time, walk around, and then come down and have Peggy show you in. Mrs. Morrow down there is my last patient, shouldn't be more than half an hour."

The first thing Harry thought is that he would never be able to afford this place. The door opened to a small hall way with a coat closet just to the right. Straight ahead about five or six steps was a large kitchen with a square green and white patterned linoleum floor. A light green Formica kitchen table with four matching green and white chairs looked almost new. There was a Kelvinator and a two burner gas stove with an oven. Harry opened one cabinet after another. The shelves had a few dishes and plates each, certainly enough for a single guy. There were cooking utensils and even a toaster…an old one but seemed to be OK. There was a coffee percolator as well. The kitchen sink had a window above it, but it looked directly into the back of the solid brick wall of the Steelton Trust building. There was a pass through beside the sink and the refrigerator to a nice room that was probably the dining room but it had no table or chairs. That in turn flowed into a large front room with big windows opening up onto Locust Street. The front room had a nice printed carpet, a sofa and a chair and two tables. The furniture was at least as nice as Hap and Doris had. Harry walked through the right side of the front room, across the small hall way and into the corner bedroom. It too had big windows on both sides. There was a bed frame but no mattress or box spring. A big bureau dresser was against the near wall, and a nice clothes closet. There were two throw rugs on either side of the bed. The bathroom had its door off the hallway. A nice tub in good shape with claw feet. Toilet and sink with a shaving cabinet. There was a new looking steam radiator in the bath that promised a warm cozy exit from the tub on winter mornings. Everything was as clean as the dental office below.

Harry opened several of the windows. They all worked fine. He tried all of the curtains and drapes, and took a look at the small window air conditioner to see how it worked. He tried out every chair and the sofa, and he allowed himself another quick thought of Cindy Hernley on it with him, just few steps away from the bedroom.

He took another look through all of the kitchen drawers, but he did not bother to make a mental inventory of what he would need to purchase to set up house…there was no way he could afford this. He locked the door behind him and ambled down the stairs. He returned the key to Peggy, who told him Dr. Becker would be free in a few moments. Five minutes later, Harry was escorted into Dr. Becker's office. There were diplomas covering every wall, and photos of his family and of him with government officials. Dr. Becker, Senior sat in one of those big burgundy leather chairs with the high back and rolled top, like a judge would sit in.

"Did you like what you saw, Harry?"

"Yes, I did. It's better than I could have imagined, but I'm afraid it might be a little too much for me…your son didn't know the rent for the apartment when I asked."

"We were getting forty dollars a month from the previous family, but I'd like to get fifty. I never thought about renting to a single guy. If we reached agreement, you'd take care of the place, wouldn't you? No big or loud parties?"

"You can count on that. I pretty much keep to myself. The Army taught me to keep my place neat…my Mom, too. I'd really like to take the apartment if you would consider me."

"Don't forget all the utilities are included. I have some other families interested, but honestly families with kids beat up the place and you should see the water and heat bill. Plus, it's really a one bedroom, the previous people used the dining room as the kids' bedroom. The place is available now, the family moved out early. When would you want to move in?"

"I'd need to buy a mattress and box springs, and maybe a couple of other things once I see how it goes. I don't know if I could afford a TV, but that's not a big deal."

"OK Harry. Your family has been with me, and now my son for a long time. You served your country. How about this: We say forty dollars a month for the first six months, then the rent goes to forty-five. Next October it goes to fifty. Can you arrange that? You can move in any time and we will pro-rate the first month."

Harry had been chipping in twenty a month at home to Hap, plus providing his own beer and toiletries. He could swing the forty. "Yes, Doctor Becker, that's very fair. I brought some cash with me as a deposit."

"OK, fine. Call Peggy when you have set your date to move in. She will have a rental agreement for you to sign. I'm going to trust you with a key so that you can let yourself in to help plan your move. Coordinate everything with Peggy. You will pay Peggy in cash for the balance of September, and the full rent is due the first of each month in advance. I will not require a security deposit. I know things will work out just fine between us."

Dr. Becker stood up and they shook hands. Harry stopped by to thank Peggy and told her he was the new tenant. She congratulated him and then Harry went back up to the apartment to look around once more. He would come back Saturday to make a move-in list, and maybe get Hap to come along. He had one more big job ahead of him…telling Doris he was moving out. "Better get that out of the way first," Harry thought.

Dinner at the Burger's was just about over when Harry came through the front door. He would help himself to the leftovers that Doris always kept warm for him. Harry's plan was to tell Hap first, then talk to Doris. He figured Hap wouldn't care, Doris would. He helped with the dishes and then caught up with Hap in the front room.

"Dad, I found a place of my own, an apartment up on Locust Street. It's the floor above Dr. Becker's office. I'm moving out. Thought I'd tell you before I spoke to Mom."

"Is that right? You planning to take any of the furniture in your room?"

"I'm going to have to buy a new bed. The place is pretty well furnished, the kitchen, too. Don't know if I can afford a TV or phone right away."

"What's the rent? Got to be a fortune up there on the hill."

"Dad, don't worry about it. I've been saving up and I have hopes to keep getting ahead at the mill. I can swing it. Dr. Becker was very fair on the rent."

"All right. Your Mom did some crying when you went away to the service. She might not say much, but she likes having you and Tim here. You're not moving up there with that Decker girl, are you?"

"Jesus, Dad. Where'd that come from? I hardly know her. Is that Tim telling you and Mom stories? I'm not stupid, and if I ever get serious about a girl, it's not going to be one from the West Side, I can tell you that!"

Hap took a big pull on his pipe. "Your Mom's from the West Side. I think I did pretty good with her."

"For Christ's sake, Dad, you know what I mean. It's time I'm on my own and I mean ON MY OWN! And I don't need Tim feeding Mom a bunch of B.S. about my private life." Harry almost startled himself when he heard his own voice raised. "Sorry, Dad."

"All right, Harry. Why are you so gung ho over this job and

these big plans anyway? I never understood why you didn't get back in the union after the Army. I think they would have counted your prior seniority. The pay is OK, you don't have all of those headaches of a big job. All my years in the mill, I never had to bring papers home to study or work on my own time the way you do. You put in your eight hours and that's it."

"I want more out of my life, Dad. It's not enough for me anymore. I see how some other people live, and what they have, and I want that. I'm willing to work for it and learn the way that the other people work and live. I guess I just don't want to stay in the same place, be in the same situation for my whole life."

"When did this all come about, Son? You've changed since you went into the service…even when you were home on leave last Christmas I didn't hear any talk from you like this."

Harry didn't really want to get into this, but he thought his Dad deserved an answer. "The Army has everything set up by rank. Each step you go up the ladder things get a lot better for you. I was around a lot of officers, and it was like a different world for them from the enlisted guys. And we had a colonel in our group, he had a guy driving him around in a nice car, he had a beautiful house, he had a million guys doing all the hard work for him. Even the difference between the lowest officers and the sergeants – guys who had been in the Army twenty years or more – the G.I.'s could never have what the officers had. I thought about this a lot the last couple of months. I mean, look at me. I went from private, to private first class, to corporal. Do you know how I advanced? I put in the time, and I didn't screw up. That's it. I didn't do anything great, I didn't make any improvements to anything. I didn't do anything to get noticed. And that's how the low level guys got ahead…by not screwing up, and not doing anything that got special attention over a long period of time. I thought that's just how life is on the West Side and in the steel plant. That's the life I was heading back into, and it was the life I lived all through school. Just mark your time, don't do anything that attracts attention, and you'll move a little ahead, a step at a time, and it will take years and years. I decided that's not for me. I want an officer's kind of life. I want a better job, a nicer house, a prettier wife, a new car and I guess I want finally to get noticed and for people to know I am a success."

Hap took this all in. "I guess we – me and your Mom - were brought up to appreciate what we have. I never saw any need to want more, especially if it might cost you some of what you already have. I like things stable…I guess what you'd call average, but I see it as a comfort to me and your mom. Well…let me know what you need when it comes time to move…me and Tim should be able to help…and now, I guess you better have your talk with your Mom."

Doris was sitting at the kitchen table with her coffee cup and saucer, and half of a sugar cookie ready to be dunked into her cup, which always contained more milk than coffee.

"Mom, can we talk a minute? I have some news…I just told Hap. I found a place above Dr. Becker's office on Locust Street, it's a very nice apartment-furnished- and I took it. I'm going to be moving out of the house here in the next week or so."

"Are you getting married Harry? Is it that Decker girl?"

This time Harry stayed calm. "No Mom. I've been planning on this for awhile-been saving up, too. It's time I stood on my own two feet. I'm doing good at work, and I am working hard to make something of myself. It's important to me. I owe you and Dad everything, and it's just time for me to get out on my own."

Doris just looked down at her coffee. "Is everything OK…I mean here at home for you? I tried to make everything the same for you when you got back from the Army. I wanted things to feel like home for you."

"I know, Mom. I appreciate everything. You and Dad could not be better parents. Everything here is fine, but I have to start a life of my own. I am trying to build a career, and to get ahead. I want to be a success and be someone people can respect...and that you and Hap can be proud of."

"I could not have been prouder when you volunteered for the Army. You know Steelton sent way more than its share of boys to fight Hitler and the Japs. We lost a lot, too. Francis Medlin ain't never been the same without Joey. And we got three families in the Lion's Club lost sons in the big war, and a guy your Dad works with at the mill, his kid got killed in Korea, where we never shoulda been in the first place. I was scared to death you were going to be sent over there. We had Tim here, but you and Tim are two different sons. He always seemed to have things go his way, even as a little kid he was always popular and I worried that you resented that somehow. You never seemed to want that much attention...maybe me and Hap should have supported you more as the number one son."

"Mom, it's OK really. I made my own bed. I just always seemed to go around unnoticed. I didn't really like a lot of attention. Maybe that's why my grades in school were just OK. The slow kids and the really smart kids got all of the teacher's attention. I don't know, but those couple of years right out of high school working the union job, then the Army, I just believe I have more in me now...and much more in front of me. Times are really good for a lot of people, and I want to join them. People are buying new cars, and TVs, they are moving out of row houses to brick houses with yards and stuff. I think that's the life for me. My future is not here on the West Side."

Doris took this all in. "And here I was thinking you were about to set up house with Darlene Decker, and maybe in a couple of years me and Hap would have some grandkids...maybe a little granddaughter..." Doris' eyes welled up and Harry could see her lower lip quivering. "We never talk about it, you can't bring back the dead, but your Dad and I never quite got over the hurt of losing that baby. Two big boys and then a little girl, that would have made my life complete. But that was not in God's plan I guess. Overall, we have done good for ourselves. We have a good marriage, a good home. We have our friends and our activities here. There's a lot worse places to raise your kids than the West Side. But nothing lasts forever...and if you are happy then I am happy for you. When will you move out?"

"Maybe a week or two, Mom. The place is mostly furnished. I need to buy a new bed and a few other things. I'll take you and Hap up to see the place this weekend if you want."

"Your Dad has his football trip Saturday...maybe Sunday? How about kitchen things? Have a list of what you'll need? It takes a lot to set up a house...towels, bed clothes, filling the kitchen cabinets, cleaning stuff. And why buy a new bed? Why don't you just take your bed upstairs...no need to spend all that money on a new one!"

Harry thought to himself, "That god-damned bed is the last thing I want to take with me. Every night I crawl into it it's a reminder that I'm still a little kid, needing Mommy and Daddy to take care of me." "It's OK Mom, time for a new bed anyway. The place is really nicely furnished. Even has air conditioning in the bedroom!"

"OK Harry. I'll miss your help with the dinner dishes."

Harry put his schedule into place that evening. He'd move in on the fifteenth; that would be half a month's rent. That would give him time to shop for and buy a bed and to get Doris' help in stocking the kitchen. He'd ask Hap to get up there with his measuring tapes and tool box in case anything needed attention. He'd need to borrow Tim's car a couple of times but was sure that wouldn't be a problem. The end of his days on the West Side were in sight.

23

Pete Posetti was getting ready for his Friday night shift. He was pleased with himself. He got all of the returnable beer bottles quietly stashed into his car on Tuesday and took them down to Middletown – where nobody knew him - for his deposits. He talked his boss Cantore into buying a second hand safe from Kappy's Jewelers so that his night deposit days were over…the bank runs would be made during the day. The day before, Thursday, he had the meeting he had arranged with a couple of guys from Harrisburg who he had worked with before. Nick Messina was there, too. Pete filled them in on everything he knew about Sonny. As he expected, they were mostly pissed off about missing their cuts on Sonny's side businesses. They didn't need or want to control these small time deals, so Pete thought his liquor arrangement with Sonny would not be interfered with by the Lombardi people.

They asked Pete about the liquor source. All he knew was that he got a delivery once a month, set up for the date and time through a call from Sonny. He never knew exactly what he would get, usually fifteen or twenty bottles of liquor and a mixed case of wine. The delivery was made by some colored guy in an unmarked truck. No money exchanged hands on the deliveries.

Sonny had the receipts and collected once a month in person, always at last call. He and Sonny would have a talk about what was selling, and what wasn't in order to try to get the best order he could. Pete had no idea where Sonny got the liquor or who he dealt with. It was a quiet and efficient transaction. He told the boys he made a couple of dollars a bottle, and that since he was in charge of all booze inventory and ordering, no one else at the Knights suspected anything.

Pete's main interest in connecting with his old friends was that he wanted to get back in the gambling business, and not as a runner. Pete thought there was a lot of money to be made on the softer areas of sports…college basketball and football in particular. Everyone concentrated on the horses, boxing, and the major sports events like the World Series or a famous team like Notre Dame. He had pretty good information from all of his years tending bar about what guys would bet on. He made a little pitch on this to Nick Messina, but Nick showed no interest at all.

They also talked about the robbery and what had happened to Sonny. Pete told them he had no idea who was behind it and told them that he had no enemies of his own…assuring them that it was colored guys who jumped him and Sonny.

Nick Messina said nothing about seeing Sonny in the hospital. He and Francis were going to connect with Sonny in a couple of days and have a sit down. They told Pete his business with Sonny might be interrupted for a bit, but not to worry. That made Pete worry.

"Hear anything from the cops?" Nick asked Pete.

"Not a word since the first couple of days. The Chief was in here himself and one of his officers was back a couple of times asking questions. As far as I know, they don't have any leads. If you guys have an interest, or hear anything, I'd be glad to help out. Those sons o' bitches got all of my tip money that night."

Thursday was Pete's day off. After he left the meeting in Harrisburg he drove down Cameron Street for his next stop: Farina Motors. He wheeled his old dog of a car into the parking lot, got out, and walked into the showroom.

Farina Motors was the Plymouth dealer in town, one of Steelton's two new car dealerships. It occupied a half block on Front Street between Howard's funeral home and the warehouses Arthur owned. Their repair shops and garages had a rear entrance, and shared an alley alongside Arthur's sprawling salvage yard and trucking garages.

Pete was pissed off when he saw Sonny driving the big new Red Olds 88 and here he was, a smarter and more experienced guy who ran in more important circles driving an old Dodge. Pete also had a little over four hundred of Sonny's dollars in his pocket, more than enough for a nice down payment. Pete had his eye on a new fifty-six black and white Belvedere that Ralph Farina had in the showroom. "Now that's a car that makes a statement" Pete thought. He arranged for a test drive the following Saturday and put a hundred buck deposit on it with Ralph.

The clientele at the Knights was loyal and predictable, especially on a Friday. The retirees and disabled would have their after lunch drinks in the afternoon and be out by four. The working guys who quit at three or so would stop in for a couple of rounds, and then leave to be home for dinner at five. The families coming in for dinner would start to fill the place up by five or five thirty, ordering their fish dishes as all good Catholics did. The dinner crowd would thin out by eight or so, and then the bar would be filled with the same men who had just taken their wives and kids home from dinner at the lodge, and finally the real money makers for the bar, those who would come in at eight or nine and stay until close.

It was just after eight when Ernie Linta took a stool at the end of the bar. His wife and son were enjoying their desserts and coffee. Manager Nick Cantore came over, got behind the bar, and poured Ernie a nice glass of red wine. Ernie thanked Nick, shook hands and paid his respects to the good citizens at the bar, but he was there to watch Posetti who nodded in acknowledgement to the Chief. Pete could feel the Chief's eyes on him and it made him jumpy. Best to say hello, Pete thought.

"Good to have you in for dinner Chief…better circumstances than the last time."

Ernie didn't say anything. Pete edged a little closer and lowered his voice. "Anything new on the robbery Chief? Any progress on suspects?"

"Afraid to say things are going slowly. That fellow Sonny was released from the hospital. I interviewed him but he didn't remember much of anything. You have any more thoughts yourself? Any idea why someone would target you?"

"Target me?" Pete did not like the sound of that. "What do you mean, Chief? These guys were after the money…me and Sonny just got in the way. I was afraid it was an inside job there for awhile, you know, maybe a member here who knew my night deposit routine. Hate to say that, but I thought of it."

"Anyone in particular Pete? You got any enemies I should know about?"

"ME? No Chief. There's nobody got a beef with me that I know of."

"Well, you must have met some pretty rough characters given your history, Pete. Am I right about that?"

"Look Chief," Pete got close and almost whispered. "I made

my mistakes and paid for it. I've been on the straight and narrow. I really need this job…please don't say anything to Nick. I'm makin' an honest livin'. I got a steady girl and I'm thinkin' about gettin' married someday. I lost a bunch of the Knight's money and a whole shift's worth of tips that night. That coulda been me instead of Sonny that had his head bashed in."

"Yeah, OK Pete. I'm really off duty here so I should get back to my family. You come up with anything, you let me know personally."

"I will Chief. Thanks. Wine's on the house."

"Thanks, but I'll make sure Mr. Cantore adds it to my dinner bill."

Back home, Ernie and Anthony had a couple of minutes alone at the kitchen table.

"That guy Posetti is trouble, son. Something stinks about him. No more business with that Knights. Let's get Arthur on the same page with us prior to the meeting at Robbins the end of the month."

"I agree, Dad. If we lose all of Sonny's business, we are not going to be able to move the supply Cohen will have for us, not to mention the revenue lost. Sonny may think he's an independent guy, but my guess is those Lombardi people will have other ideas. Is there anyone you can call on back from your days on the Harrisburg force who can give us the latest on what Lombardi has been doing? We can't single out Sonny because people will wonder why we are asking about him. Probably have to frame it as part of the robbery investigation."

"Maybe we ask about our friend Posetti while we're at it. Arthur said there was some talk on the street that Posetti set this whole thing up and split the money. Maybe we might need a story like that someday."

* * *

Steelton enjoyed a beautiful couple of weeks in mid September. After a hot and humid summer, the weather turned cool. The Steamrollers won their first three games. Harry moved into his apartment. Tim kept his promise to himself to take things slowly, and his couple of weeks of day shift and eleven to seven in the rail mill made it easy for that to happen…he even helped Harry get settled in. Arthur and his sons attended to business as usual and Cohen, other than hearing about the robbery at the Knights and Sonny's hospitalization during one of Arthur's pick-ups, kept to his own little world.

24

Cohen arrived first as usual. Then Sonny and Arthur pulled in. Five minutes later, the Linta family Buick with Tim in the back seat, Ernie and Anthony up front. The first thing Ernie noticed was a different car where Sonny always parked. Anthony carried his briefcase up the six concrete steps into the old Robbins shipping office, Ernie and Tim a few steps behind. They all nodded to one another and Ernie looked first at Sonny. "Where's the red Olds, Sonny? Don't tell me you took my advice about driving something less flashy to our meetings."

Sonny spoke softly. "No Ernie. I've had my wings clipped a bit. Had orders to get rid of the Olds…driving that piece of junk Pontiac you saw. Might as well tell everyone here right off the bat what's happened the last couple of weeks…if that's OK Chief."

"Go ahead, Sonny. We got no secrets in this group."

"After getting out of the hospital, I had a couple of meetings with guys in different circles who I do business with. I make some money for them with some small hustles, and of course the major connection is with the beer sources I have. I'm kind of a customer and a partner in the beer thing. Well, as of this week I'm more of an employee. I can't do any freelancing and I've got a regular job working at the beer distributor my friends own. So

I'm kind of under their supervision you could say. My opportunities to work on my own are cut way back. They made me get rid of the Olds, and plus with this new, uh, situation, I couldn't afford the payments anyway."

"OK Sonny, what does this mean for us for the future as far as you're concerned?"

"First, I had their OK to collect on the money that was owed to me. They took a chunk of that but I have enough here to pay you what I owe, Anthony. It should clear the books. After our talk at the garage, Ernie, I ain't done no business or said one word to anybody about the liquor side of things. So, I took no orders and things are pretty much at a stop."

Arthur spoke up. "What do your friends know about the liquor Sonny?" At this point, Cohen was on the edge of his seat. If he had been a smoker, he'd be lighting one up.

"They asked. I told them I had a guy in Maryland who got the liquor out of the D.C. area. I told them I didn't ask him any questions…that he and I would meet in different places every couple of weeks – Gettysburg, York, Waynesboro – out of the way places to make the pick-up. I paid a neighbor ten bucks a day and a tank of gas for use of his panel truck to make the pick-ups. I paid cash out of my own pocket and collected the cash myself… that's what I was doing at the Steelton Knights when me and Pete got held up. They told me right there and then I was out of the liquor business because the interstate thing was too risky…if I got caught the LCB or cops might make a connection back to them. Since I figured you guys were going to tell me the same thing, and since I had no real choice, I told 'em OK. I got the money I owe you and if you guys got anything for me, I'd appreciate it because I'm in kind of a hole cash-wise."

"Arthur, I think we pay Sonny the share he earned. We just all have to eat the cash we lost that night when Sonny got robbed. That OK with you?"

Arthur said nothing, but nodded agreement. "Everybody else OK with this?" Tim and Cohen didn't say anything. "All right. Anthony, get the receipts and cash from Sonny and pay him what he's owed. Sonny, that's it between us, except for two things. Number one, you won't forget the talk we had at the garage when I gave you your car back?"

"I remember, Chief."

"The second thing is, you hear any word of any kind that might affect the men in this room, you call or get a message to me personally; use "Mr. Robbins" as before and call from a pay phone. Anybody you know tries to make any kind of push into Steelton, same deal. I'm not saying we can never do any business in the future, but for now, it's best for all of us to go our own way. And now, you can go."

Sonny went over to the desk where Anthony was sitting. Anthony reached into his briefcase, some cash and paperwork was exchanged. Sonny walked out of the office; no further words were said.

Anthony spoke up. "We're not going to be able to move all of Cohen's inventory without Sonny. We need to address that."

"I thought about it" Arthur said. "I think it's best we just slow down here until Christmas time, when we can pick things up for the holidays. I will continue to take the same level for my businesses, and we still have the same customers doing pick up at the funeral home. Ben, can you keep the excess inventory in good shape for us without any problems for yourself?"

"Of course; it's actually less risk for me, no problem there. I kind of feel better because we have less exposure, but we're all making less money. I always thought Sonny was a little bit uncontrolled to be honest with everyone. But Mr. Howard and I still have a good business and he is a good partner for all of us. My major concern is if someone puts a lot of pressure on Sonny, he might tell them what he knows."

"I have a plan to take care of that, Ben, if it comes to a head. Now let's move on to the rest of the business; Anthony will have your shares and you can give him your receipts and proceeds at the end of the meeting."

Tim spoke up. "I still have a couple of liquor accounts I trust and will keep those going. Two things on the scrap business. Arthur and I worked a new deal on an obsolete rail car. He will give you the numbers but our tonnage will be up. I'm back on rotating shifts and have had to keep a lower profile as I told you, Anthony. But remember when I told everybody the last time about a new inventory tracking system that Bethlehem is putting in? Well, the rail mill is the next department scheduled to adopt it, but there's a chance I might get picked to be on the committee putting the new system in. If that's the case, I'll get to see first-hand how it works and I hope that will help with our steel movements."

Ernie chimed in. "I have my regular dinner meeting with Klein, the Bethlehem head of security this week. I'll have my ears open for anything that he might be up to. Oh, and a final note on Sonny, we have no clue on who knocked him out and took our money. The only thing we learned is that his contact at the Knights, a guy named Posetti is trouble. He's connected to Lombardi people, apparently better than Sonny is. We've heard he set the whole thing up, but have nothing solid to go on…Arthur?"

"I ain't heard nothin' and neither has my son. I just like the idea of everybody staying low for a month or two…we keep our businesses we trust…no expansion. I think it's good to just lay low. The liquor business will really pick up as always in December. As Tim said, we'll have a good month on steel scrap. I say we meet again maybe just before Thanksgiving...anything unusual happens, we get in touch through the usual channels."

"All right. That's our plan. Ben, you hear anything fishy, or anything from those new enforcement guys, you let Arthur know."

"I will Chief. I've got a good guy over in the enforcement department now. He goes to my temple and hates that new guy Walker with all his military orders. We should get tipped off in advance of anything we need to know."

"Next meeting, same time...the Sunday before Thanksgiving. Anthony, finish things up."

The Chief, Anthony and Tim piled into the Buick. Tim spoke up. "Ernie, when is your meeting with Mr. Klein? Please have Anthony clue me in with anything that might help me and Arthur. If everything stays quiet for another couple of weeks, I'm going to try to move another whole rail car up to Arthur. It would help us if Klein or his people are suspicious of anything... he has all of the railroad security reporting to him too, so if they smell something funny, I'll put any big moves on hold."

"I'm having dinner with Klein week after next, Tim."

"OK. I'm going to try to get into a meeting that looks like it may happen about the same time from what I hear. It's about that new inventory and efficiency project I mentioned, the same one my brother worked on down at the open hearth. I'm also going to see what Harry knows that can help us....can you just drop me off at Conestoga Street? I want to catch the Eagles game at Buddy's...he opens Sunday afternoons when they're on...and get this...he's talking about getting a color TV for the bar! Hard to believe a guy could make that much money out of a little place like that to afford a color TV."

Anthony turned around, and said with a smile, "Well, Tim, it IS the West Side."

Herman Klein and Ernie Linta took their usual table back in the corner of the Bethlehem Steel Management Club. It was at the side of the large beautiful stone fireplace that was kept roaring in the winter, but was unlit this quiet, early October evening. The two men talked about the Dodgers big win in the World Series, and the conversation covered politics, the health of the steel business, and the general prosperity that the country seemed to be enjoying in peacetime. Herman had his two glasses of beer – Lowenbrau on tap at the Club – and ordered his usual well done steak. Ernie's plate of veal was put in front of him as the two men got down to the talk of their professions.

"Chief, you make any progress on the robbery at that Italian Club? The guy who was in the hospital come around OK?"

"It's unusual. I expected we'd have the guys who did it locked up in a week. We figure something like four hundred was stolen. That kind of money usually gets spread around in a hurry by guys not used to having it. We had some talk that the bartender himself set it up, but it's just talk. The guy who got smacked was in the hospital for almost a week. I interviewed him…foggy memory. Other than the usual stuff that's really been the only violent crime we've had. Couple of colored guys got in a knife fight and damned near killed each other last week….other than that a pretty quiet summer. You?"

"We have our ongoing problem…theft of our products from trucks and rail cars, usually at construction sites or at the docks. It's the customers' problem of course, but they often call us in for help. We have the usual half dozen or so cases every month of employees trying to steal tools and the like...had one in July that involved a maintenance foreman down at the pipe mill in conjunction with two union guys stealing maintenance supplies, copper tubing, welding machine and rods…they got away with it for a couple of months but eventually slipped up – they all do. All of them fired plus we always press charges…I think one of your officers helped us out on that. The rolling stock is always subject to theft… stolen wheels and tires. We have more problems with vandalism, outright sabotage of equipment, that's expensive and dangerous. We'll start to see more of that a couple of months prior to the end of the current labor contract. That kind of behavior always spikes once new contract negotiation starts. A stolen five hundred dollar piece of equipment is nothing compared to sabotage that could cost six or eight hours production in a key department."

Herman chewed his steak and ordered another beer. "How's the family Chief? Everything going OK personally?"

"Yes, Herman, thanks for asking. My son's doing well at the CPA firm, everybody's health is good…I have a pretty good force now, although I need about four more patrolmen, another squad car…you know how it goes with the budget."

"Yes, I do. I spend more time on the paperwork it seems… we're just starting our budget for next year. I've also got a big project for our strike contingency planning…in case the union walks out again like everyone expects come July first. These union leaders…we have a strike now every contract. You'd think they'd learn after the President had to step in back in fifty-two. We go through another one of those and it will be my last, that's for sure."

"Well, everybody respected the work you did back then Herman…union and management alike, and I don't have to tell you how grateful I was as a new Chief. I learned a lot and the resources you had really took most of the pressure off of the

Steelton PD. Most of my force had brothers, dads, you name it, on strike, so I don't have to tell you where their sympathies were. Anything new or different in particular that you're concerned about…any areas for cooperation between our departments, or anything I should be on the lookout for to help you out?"

"Thank you Chief, but everything is under control. Why don't we meet again for dinner right after the New Year? I enjoy our talks and it's good to have this level of professional cooperation. Of course, we'll probably see you around the Club here over the holidays."

"Yes, the Club is very kind to invite me and Mrs. Linta to the Holiday events. Always a first class party." Herman signed for the check after the dessert and coffee.

"Must be nice" Ernie thought to himself as he drove home…"-just sign for a check like that and have the company pick up the tab." And then he thought about the labor strike in the upcoming summer, and made a mental note to put a request in for some extra budget money to handle what was to be sure another nasty labor disruption the following summer.

Tim Burger was waiting impatiently in rail mill general superintendent Pat Patterson's office along with half a dozen other supervisors and management personnel. The PEP meeting was scheduled for ten o'clock, and with all the big shots attending from the main office, everybody made sure they showed up fifteen minutes early. The men were all of the same opinion: the best meetings were short meetings, so people shuffled around and no one sat down. Cigarettes were lit and the pervasive smell of burned coffee hung in the low ceilinged room. It was luck of the draw for Tim to be in the meeting…he happened to be one of four foremen on day shift this week, but the maintenance foreman and old Harold Wilson begged off. Everybody snapped to when Patterson and big Bob Willis came in the door, accompanied by a couple of guys Tim didn't know and one he did: Scrappy Stone. Patterson spoke up.

"We have Mr. Willis with us today along with several of his key people from the main office. Some of you may have heard about the Production Efficiency Project, or PEP for short. It had a successful trial run down at the open hearth, and our department has been selected for the second important phase of the project. Mr. Willis will provide the overview."

Bob Willis gave a ten minute summary of the project, ignoring all of the parallel work done up at the Bethlehem HQ and concentrating on the great job done at the open hearth in Steelton. He reviewed the project's objectives, and highlighted the importance of the project to not only Steelton, but to the entire Corporation. He touched on all of the functions affected by the new studies, and emphasized the importance of Bethlehem's rail production to the national economy. "Demand for the high quality rails produced here at Steelton – the premiere rail mill in the country- is projected to grow. The Company is considering additional capital investment in expanding capacity, and we want that capacity here in Steelton. It means more profits, more jobs, and more job security. Mr. Patterson will be an important part of the committee overseeing the PEP efforts, which will be under the direct management of Mark Stone, the gentleman here on my right. Some of you know him better as Scrappy. I'm going to turn the floor over to him for additional detail."

Tim looked around the room…when Pat and Willis spoke, people respectfully listened, but when Stone began talking, they really paid attention. Scrappy went into some detail, and surprised everyone by announcing that he planned to have a union man on the PEP committee. He said that he would be forming the committee over the next few days, and expected to spend time personally with all of the rail mill management affected, including those on second and third shifts. He introduced the two young men from the main office who would be assisting him, a young engineer and a newly hired data processing machine technician, a title that meant nothing to everyone else in attendance.

"I'm going to stay behind for awhile for more discussion and your questions. Meanwhile, we have to thank Mr. Willis and Mr. Patterson for their executive support of this important new initiative." Patterson, Willis and the other two left the office.

Tim thought this was a smart move. Stone knew that no one was going to ask a question with Willis and Patterson in the room, so he got them out of the way. Several of the rail mill personnel asked questions of Scrappy, and the majority of those were of the "how will this affect me?" variety. To say the first level management was jaded was to understate their lack of zeal for anything new or different. Tim thought about his own Dad, who liked nothing better than if everything would stay just the way it is now…and forever, thank you. They did ask Stone about the union participation, though, and Scrappy looked them each in the eye as he responded. "I know all of you men are thinking that you've heard all of this before, new efficiency, new procedures and so on and it's all of bunch of BS that blows over sooner or later. And you're management. The union feels even more strongly about these things as you know. My plan is to include one of their respected members on the committee to help us gain acceptance. We all know that the best plans and procedures put in by management can be undercut by the men on the floor. If the union decides to oppose something, they dig their heels in and every step of the way we are fighting grievances and encountering resistance. If any of you have someone to recommend from the union here in the rail mill, I'd like to have the name. It has to be someone the other employees respect. And before you ask, I have gotten union participation OK'd by Willis and by Mr. Garber, Local 1688 President."

Tim waited until everyone else filed out and went up to see Scrappy. "That was a good meeting, Scrappy. You know, my brother Harry really enjoyed working with you down at the open hearth, and he was hoping to get a chance to work with you again on the next phase."

Scrappy, ever careful, looked at Tim. "Harry did a great job for us...but he is really needed where he is."

"He was excited about the work. Scrappy, I'd be very interested in joining your committee if you think a front level supervisor would help."

"Why the interest Tim...most guys don't like the idea of the extra work. There's always a chance things don't turn out so well, you know."

"Well, I'm one of the youngest foremen in the plant. I'm open to new ideas. I've worked in rail final shipping, rail fab, and pre-heat so I know a little about the full process. I have good relations with the hourly guys and I don't know if you thought about this, but I'm happy to work second shift. I expect most of the guys always want daylight."

"Yes, they do. Why is second shift a good idea?"

"Harry told me a little about the batch ticket process, the production and inventory demands. He told me about seeing the computer machinery down at the big office. I thought it might be helpful to round out the work a little. If you had a guy working second shift, he could produce his daily reports and whatever was needed at the end of second shift, and also help flag any issues or problems for night turn. Harry said there were some bottlenecks because all of the open hearth data for all three shifts would go out to the main office all at the same time. I know smooth work flow is essential, and thought it might be the same for your project."

"That's not a bad idea, Tim. Let me think about that. You said you worked in final shipping?"

"Yep. Got to know rail and truck shipments, cooling yard schedules, all of the loading codes, customer numbers, read all of the QC reports, and of course handled all of the screw ups for fab mistakes, and scrap inventory."

"All right Tim. Let me think about it."

"Thanks, Scrappy. You won't be disappointed. And I'll give some thought to the union member of the committee you asked about. I have a couple of guys in mind…won't say anything to them of course. Confidentiality is important, I know. Harry really clammed up when I asked him about his project work."

Scrappy didn't trust Tim entirely, but he did bring some good rail mill knowledge. He was the youngest production foreman by far and did have some sensitivity to the union's interests. That second shift idea was a good one. A lot of men would take a twenty percent pay cut to work all day shift, and here was a man volunteering to work steady three to eleven.

The conversation with Tim did remind Scrappy that he should at least make a personal connection back to Harry… and maybe he could use that opportunity find out a little more about Harry's little brother. He'd have to contact Harry without Bob Hernley knowing about it, though; Willis made it clear that Scrappy was to avoid Hernley unless absolutely necessary.

Scrappy thought he knew why.

25

"Burger! Telephone!" The shift foreman handed the receiver to Harry.

"Burger here."

"Harry, it's Scrappy Stone. I know you can't talk much down there, but I'm calling to see if you'd like to get together for a beer after work…maybe Friday. We can meet down at the St. Lawrence Club…I can sign you in. Maybe we can catch up a bit."

"Yeah, I'd like that. How about four-thirty or so…I have to stay right to the last minute and that will give me some time to clean up."

"OK Harry, half past four. If you get there before me just tell the bartender you're my guest. See you then."

The call got Harry's mind racing. Maybe Stone would be asking for his help on the next phase of the big project. Despite Hernley's orders there was no way Harry was saying anything to anybody about his meeting with Scrappy.

Harry had been in his apartment for a couple of weeks. He bought his new bed and a second hand chair on time up at Miller's Furniture in Harrisburg. Doris set him up with the kitchen stuff he needed, and Hap put together a tool box as a house-warming gift. He bought a second hand table top TV at Billow's (it had been re-possessed) for twenty bucks down and ten dollars a month for six months. He decided to wait on putting in a telephone until he saw how things worked out. He and Doris filled up the pantry with stuff she had at home, and then they did a big shopping trip to Dundoff's. Tim pitched in with use of the car and bought Harry a case of Schmidt's and a half gallon of Canadian Club "for Hap when he comes down here to get away from Mom!"

The arrangement with the Beckers went well. Harry was out of the door for work before the first patients arrived in the morning and the two dentists were usually out of the office by six at night. Everything in the apartment worked fine and when he paid the October rent he made certain to tell Dr. Becker senior how pleased he was with the apartment. All in all, things were working out as Harry had hoped with the new place. He wasn't the best cook in the world, but he got by. His plan so far was to eat at Martzie's or Buddy's Friday and Saturday, and still have Sunday dinner back at the house. Doris always gave him enough leftovers from Sunday dinner for another meal…Harry suspected she cooked extra to be sure there was plenty for him to take back to Locust Street. The other days of the week he put together soup and sandwiches and had a couple of tries with the new invention, TV dinners. He liked to watch TV while he ate. His old radio from Myers Street kept him company in the bedroom.

Harry had been in the St. Lawrence Club a couple of times before he went into the service. He knew Mike Jamnov, a fellow West-Sider, was the manager there. He thought he'd see how it went and maybe he could get Scrappy and his brother Tim to sponsor him as a member. He pressed the door buzzer at four-thirty sharp and went straight to the bartender, who he didn't recognize, and mentioned Scrappy's name. He was told he couldn't be served until Scrappy came in and signed him in. Harry took a seat near the door, and Scrappy came in five minutes later.

"You want a Schmidt's Harry?" Burger nodded and the two of them took a table off to the side of the bar, away from the juke-box. "Thanks, Scrappy. It was good to get your call; this is a good way to start the weekend."

"Glad to do it Harry, I have a little business to talk over, but first, how about bringing me up to date on what's been going on with you. I hear Hernley is on the war path down there with a big production push for the last quarter of the year…he's told everybody he's going to set production and quality records by the Christmas break."

"You heard right about that. He's been even tougher than usual, and he doesn't spare himself from the work either. I hear he's at work by five or so every morning, and doesn't leave to five at night. He's driving everybody pretty hard…no overtime though for anybody. He's generated a couple of grievances from the union and one of the foremen went out last week on disability-everybody said he just got sick of Hernley. I'm doing what you suggested. I don't complain; I give every day my best effort. I come in maybe half hour early and try to stay a little later even though I clock in and out on time. He's brought two college students in from Drexel who are working on some kind of apprenticeship I guess you'd call it…anyway, they are engineering students who are pretty sharp kids…they are eating all of this up with a spoon. I try to get them to teach me a little basic engineering whenever I can. You probably know we have most of the procedures put in place from our project and that seems to be working just fine. And by the way, Hernley ordered me to let him know if you contacted me; did you know that? I'm ignoring him though…who I talk to is my own business."

"I see. And how are you doing personally, Harry? Getting any fishing in?"

"Naw, the boat's put away. My big news is I took an apartment up on Locust Street and moved out of the house a couple of weeks ago. Got a used TV, new bed, a bunch of kitchen stuff from Doris. The place was mostly furnished, though, so I didn't have a lot of expense getting set up. I do some of my own cooking, usually hit the taverns Fridays and Saturdays. I learned how to keep a place clean and orderly in the service. I've get a short walk to and from work, so that's good too."

"Seeing any ladies?"

"Seems like I don't have time…I've had a couple of dates but believe it or not I've been concentrating on work and getting a career started, and now setting up the apartment."

"Things will pick up now that you've got your own place. Makes it easier, you'll see. By the way, I had a meeting at the rail mill on the next phase of the PEP, and your brother Tim attended…came up and talked to me afterward, too."

Harry said nothing.

"He seemed pretty keen on the PEP and volunteered to help out on the team. Think he'd do a good job?"

Now Harry was getting a little pissed, but he didn't want Scrappy to know. It was important to be professional. The very job he wanted so much now seemed to be one Tim had his eyes on.

"Tim's a real go-getter. He was only in the union a couple of years when he got offered that foreman's position…one of the youngest in the plant. He's a little like you, Scrappy, he gets along with everybody, people seem to like being around him, and I mean all kinds of people…union, management, old or young, white or colored. You remember big Anthony Linta, the fat kid on the West Side whose Mom made him take violin lessons?"

"Yeah, sure, the police chief's son."

"He's stayed good friends with him and now Tim is in good with the Chief and all of the Steelton cops. And he hangs out here at the St. Lawrence, but also is a regular up at Arthur's. Like I said, he has friends everywhere. You know Arthur's right?"

"Sure, go up there myself once in a while."

"He's real popular with the other rail mill foremen because he is willing to take second and third shifts…likes it in fact… and that frees up some day turn for the other guys. I tell you one thing, he knows that rail mill inside out and top to bottom. He worked several union jobs before his foreman's position and that tells me he knows where all the trouble spots and bottlenecks are. He bought himself a really nice Mercury and he dates women from Harrisburg…almost never goes out with a Steelton girl. He's even been out a few times with a college girl from the west shore…Camp Hill I think. Point is he's just about the opposite from me personality-wise…he's done well for himself and I think he's got a good future. I think the only thing you wouldn't like about him is he's a lousy fisherman."

"Nobody catches fish if they're not out on the river until nine o'clock in the morning."

Harry thought: "This guy remembers everything you tell him."

"Harry, I wish things would have worked out a little better for you, but I'm afraid you're stuck in open hearth for awhile; I can't help you there. I owe you thanks for the work you did and my best advice is stick it out there for a year or so, learn as much as you can from Hernley and the other guys, and then maybe you can make a move, or maybe some kind of transfer will open up for you."

"OK Scrappy, I trust you but I've been there getting on toward six months and I feel like I'm stuck in the mud."

"Harry, there are plenty of men in that mill with six YEARS of seniority and they are in the same job they started in. Be patient, but always be on the lookout. Take on any assignment you're offered. Don't be a pain in the ass or a complainer. OK? Ready for another beer?"

They had their second beers and the conversation turned to women and fishing.

"Hey, are you still going to church at Pine Street? I think one time you were asking about my Dad…my whole family will be there this Sunday. My kid brother Kenny is the head of the youth group, and he has a part in the Sunday message, so my whole family will be there. If you can make it, I'll introduce you."

"Yes, of course, I'd like that but you know Hernley and his wife will probably be there, so it may be a problem if he sees us together."

"You let me worry about Hernley. I'll settle the tab and I'll see you Sunday."

"OK. By the way, I'm thinking of joining the Club here, can I use you as a reference? My brother Tim will sign for me and I know Mike Jamnov from a while back."

"Sure, Harry. Let's get an application from the bar." Harry filled it out, put his brother and Stone's name as sponsors, and gave the bartender a five spot. He'd hear in a week on his membership.

* * *

Tim drove the Merc up the alley to Conestoga and then up Myers to Franklin. He headed off the West Side and as he went over the S&H railroad tracks he slowed and took a long look to the left, behind Arthur's funeral home and scrap yard. His gondola car was gone. He looked into his rear view mirror and a smile broke across his face. He was headed up to Quigley's for a couple of cold beers to start his Friday night.

Harry shuffled into a pew three rows behind the Becker family just as the services were beginning. He had on his new sports jacket and his Florsheim shoes had a military quality spit shine. He suffered through a long church service that featured Scrappy's brother Kenny reading some Bible verses and then explaining to the congregation what he thought they meant. Harry could see the Hernleys over in their normal spot. He tried to look around the church to see the Stone family but didn't see Scrappy and had no idea what everyone else looked like. Finally the service ended and Harry quickly moved to the back of the church, trying at once to be conspicuous for Scrappy but invisible to Hernley. Then he caught sight of Scrappy, who was wearing a dark grey suit and was talking to two girls. Harry thought they might be family members, cousins or something.

"Hello, Mark! Good morning."

"Hi Harry...nice jacket! Let me introduce you to Patti Dale and her sister Susie. This is Harry Burger, who I've worked with at the mill. Harry returned to Steelton from the Army not too long ago."

"Good morning Patti, Susie."

"Hello Harry," it was Patti who spoke first. "Were you overseas in the war?"

"No, I signed up after Korea got started, but my three years were all spent in the States...that made my Mom happy I can tell you."

"Well, we are happy to have you back safe and sound" Susie said.

"That's nice of you to say. I just started coming here after the

Army…I had been looking for a new church. And I was lucky enough to land a job that gave me a chance to work with Mark here."

Patti again: "You can call him Scrappy…we all do!" And then Patti and Susie sort of looked at each other and giggled. Scrappy said he had to go catch up with his mom and dad and told Harry to stay put for a couple of minutes so that introductions could be made. He made some more small talk with the Dale sisters and said hello to all of the Beckers when they exited the church.

Patti: "Do you know the Beckers, Harry? They are our dentists and James and his family live not too far from us up on the hill."

"Why yes, they have been our family dentists, too. As a matter of fact, I just recently moved into the apartment above their office."

Patti brightened a bit. "We seem to have a few things in common with you, Harry, except of course I have no experience with the Army."

"Maybe that will change, Sis" Susie said to Patti and they both laughed. Harry wondered if he was crazy or were these girls flirting with him in church? They said good bye and soon Scrappy was back with full family in tow. Introductions were made and Scrappy's parents said they had known Hap and Doris for a long time, and how happy they were that Harry came back from the service in one piece.

Scrappy's Dad spoke up: "I saw you talking to the Dale sisters, Harry. You're not trying to cut into Scrappy's time are you?" Everybody had a little laugh, even Scrappy.

"I see Susie sometimes," Scrappy said. They all left the church together and never did cross paths with Hernley.

26

The chestnut, sycamore and elm trees did their best to brighten up the sidewalks and row houses of the West Side as autumn crept in. Coal deliveries started in earnest and the kids reluctantly wore the jackets their moms insisted on for their walks to school. The Steelton Steamrollers were still undefeated and it was standing room only at the Cottage Hill field on Saturday afternoons. Most of the men on the West Side walked to work themselves and did not own a car, so they organized bus trips to the high school away games. When the big end of year tilt against Williamsport was an away game, two train cars were sponsored by the Lion's club for the sixty mile trip up the river. It was the only time the old Steelton train depot and passenger siding at Trewick Street was used.

Pete Posetti pulled his new Belvedere into Farina Motors. He had driven the car for a couple of weeks and had a few things that needed warranty attention, so he called and made an appointment for his Thursday day off. He wheeled the black and white beauty right to the front of the showroom entrance. As he got out, Ralph Farina himself greeted him.

"We're all ready for you Mr. Posetti...just please pull her around back to Bay One. I've got my best man Brown waiting for you back there."

Pete engaged the push button transmission and as he came around back to the service area he saw the mechanic waving him into the service bay. "This shouldn't take more than half an hour Mr. Posetti…I got your check list from Mr. Farina. You can wait in the show room if you like."

"If it's OK with you, I'd like to watch you work on her." Pete wasn't trusting anybody with his brand new car.

"Suit yourself. But there's no place to sit in the garage here."

"That's all right, I'll have a cigarette and stretch my legs."

Pete lit up his Viceroy and looked around at the large dusty stone and rock covered lot behind the dealership. There was a large crane with a round magnet thing on it, and a hell of a scraping metal shriek coming from a large shed with a roof maybe thirty feet high. An old Mack dump truck rumbled out from near some railroad tracks with a load of junked and smashed car parts. Some guy was using a cutting torch on what liked like rusted steel girders, creating a cascade of yellow sparks in the process. Pete walked a little further back toward the alley and to his left he saw a big white Cadillac Fleetwood pulling up behind the building right next door. Then he remembered Farina's was next to that big colored funeral home, the one with the white hearse. He watched as a tall colored kid in a suit and tie got out of the car and headed toward the rear entrance of a pale yellow sided building.

It took Pete a second…"wait a minute, I've seen that guy before." He took another quick three steps toward the Caddy to get a better look. He just glimpsed the kid in profile before he walked down a couple of steps into the lower level of the building.

"Holy Shit!" Pete said out loud. He was sure of it. That black kid was the guy who robbed him at the Knights. Pete lit up another cigarette…he was going to wait until the kid came back out to be certain. The noise from the junkyard and the dust from the truck traffic seemed to get louder, and now a brown and yellow locomotive with some freight cars blew its horn and thundered slowly across the street crossing. Pete wanted to get a good view if the kid came back out, but didn't want to be seen himself. He waited half crouched behind an old Plymouth that was parked behind Farina's garage.

"Mr. Posetti!" It was Brown, the mechanic. "Your car's done. We'll pull it around front for you."

Pete waved OK. He waited another ten minutes, but no one emerged from the funeral home. He walked around front to collect his car. He was pretty sure of what he saw, but he wasn't going to say or do anything just yet. He needed to be certain, and there was an easy way to do that. Just check the papers and look for the next funeral held at the place next door. He looked over at the sign "Howard Funeral Home".

Pete walked into the showroom to see Farina and to get his service sheet. "You got today's Steelton News, Ralph?" Pete thumbed back to the obituaries. He found what he was looking for. A service at Monumental AME Church for tomorrow at 10:00 for Mr. James Washington…service provided by Howard Funeral Home with burial immediately following at William Howard Day cemetery. Pete would park on the other side of Lincoln Street where the white Baldwin cemetery was, and then watch carefully for the procession, the white Fleetwood, and its driver. He thought it might be a nice touch if he had a bouquet of flowers in his hand.

Ernie's private line rang on his desk. "This is Chief Linta."

"Chief, this is Mr. Robbins. Can you meet me? It's important."

"OK. Five o'clock. Usual place. Better be good."

The sun was going down, and it was a little after five when the Chief pulled his unmarked Plymouth into the back of Robbins. Sonny's Pontiac was there…and Sonny got out when he saw Ernie approach.

"What's the story Sonny?"

"I was at a meeting earlier today with Posetti, the two Messina boys and a couple of other associates. Pete tells everyone he knows who wacked the two of us at the Knights and wants to get even. Ernie, one of 'em might be Arthur's kid."

Ernie was trained well enough that he reacted to even the most shocking news as if he was listening to a weather report.

"How does he figure that?"

"Pete was having his car serviced at Farina's…by the way do you know he bought a brand new Belvedere? Two-toned job. Anyway, he's out back having a smoke when he sees a tall black kid pull up and get out of a white Caddy right behind Arthur's. Watched the kid go into Arthur's funeral home…he never came back out so Posetti decides to go to a funeral Arthur ran the next day and staked out the cemetery. The same kid is driving the hearse. Early twenties, six feet or better, athletic build. Pete got a long look at him and he's sure of it."

"What's he going to do about it, did he say?"

"He wanted the Messinas to give the OK to get a couple of guys to follow the kid and beat the hell out of him and try to get the money back. The Messinas wouldn't have anything to do with it, said Howard was too big a target and anyhow it was Pete's and my problem not theirs. I think that was the end of it. Pete is pissed but I don't think he can do anything about it. He tried to get me to join him in tailin' this kid but I said I was on a tight leash and couldn't go free-lancin' after the Messinas just said no.

I told him I was not happy about it but I had no choice, I got orders to follow and I can't step out of line."

"Anything else?"

"I don't know if it was one of Arthur's kids he saw, an employee, I just don't know. I figured you'd want to know."

"When did Posetti buy this new car? And he got it at Farina's?"

"Maybe three, four weeks ago. Sharp, big tail fins, black and white, bought it right out of the showroom."

"OK Sonny, you did good. Let me see what I can find out. I'm not saying there's a tie-in to Arthur based on what this bartender says. I just don't trust him. All I can tell you if there's a connection and we can get some of your money back, I'll do the right thing. Square?"

"Square, Chief."

Ernie did some paperwork the following morning and about ten told the officer on duty he was heading up to Farina's to have a noise checked out on his car. He found Ralph reading the Patriot as he walked in the showroom. "Mornin' Ralph."

"Good morning Chief. Ready to trade that Buick in? I just ordered a black Imperial for the showroom...four door. Beautiful. I think Mrs. Linta deserves to ride in the best, don't you?"

"Good try Ralph. Say, I've just a little shimmy in the front end of my Plymouth out there...think one of your guys could take it for a quick test drive and see what it could be?"

"Yep. Give me a minute." Ralph bounced right back. "Put Brownie on it for you. He's my best. How about a coffee, Chief?"

Ernie sipped his coffee..."What happened to that black and white two tone you had in the showroom Ralph? That was a sharp car."

"I can get another one just like it for you Chief, make you a deal. That one sold right away, bartender down at the Knights bought it. You're a member there right? How much are you paying your bartenders? Tips must be good, too."

"Why do you say that, Ralph?"

"Guy gave me five hundred down, cash. Had a trade-in and financed the rest but didn't flinch at the payments."

"Well, you know Steelton, bartenders are treated better than priests."

"More valuable, too!" Ralph laughed. "Here comes Brownie with your car."

"Couldn't find a thing, Chief. Sorry. Bring her back if you want and we'll get her up on the rack. Don't think it's anything serious."

"Could be my imagination. Thanks, men. Stay out of trouble."

"Come back with the Missus and take a look at that Imperial, Chief. Should be here in a couple of weeks. Make a hell of a Christmas present!"

Ernie had three calls to make once he got back to the office. Arthur was first of course. The second was to the County D.A.'s office. Then, the Steelton News.

"Mr. Howard, Chief Linta here. I understand you've requested a Chief's escort for a service?"

Ernie said this with his office door open and in his best, loud, official voice. "Chief's escort" was code and a cover when a meeting between the two was required. "Right, O.K. Sir. I'll be up there right after lunch."

Arthur was waiting for Ernie in his office, beautiful suit and tie and white carnation pinned to his lapel. He dressed like a black Jackie Gleason. He told his wife "no interruptions" and closed the door. He didn't have to say anything...he just waited for Ernie to talk. There was never any small talk between them... the two men spent words as if they were twenty dollar bills.

Ernie laid out the story.

"You believe Sonny, Chief?"

"This time I do. Posetti's story about last Thursday check out?"

"My employee Charles was driving the Fleetwood that day. Posetti described him OK. You remember him-it's Charles Parker, the football and basketball star? He drives for me and does odds jobs in the junk yard."

"What do you think happened here, Arthur?"

"Chief. I need some time. You're sure those Italians aren't going to try anything funny with any of my boys? 'Cause that would be a real big problem for everybody...and I mean everybody, includin' our sons."

Ernie's jaw firmed. "One more thing. I'd like your OK to call in Peter Lewis. Farina next door tells me Posetti had five hundred in cash that he put down for a new car...bought it right after that business at the Knights. I think we need a back-up plan to take care of Posetti."

Arthur stood up and nodded; meeting over.

"Peter...how are you? Can you talk for a minute, please?"

"Sure Chief, how can I help?"

"Remember the robbery at the K of C down here a month or so ago... a guy got whacked and somebody got away with four or five hundred dollars? I've got a suspect but this case is going to need some special handling. Can we get together? I recommend I come up to your office as it's official business."

"Of course, Chief. If it's urgent we can do it tomorrow...how about ten?"

"I'll be there Peter. Thanks."

"Steelton News, Deputy Editor Winston Clark speaking."

"Winny this is Chief Ernie Linta. I promised you news when I had it for that assault and robbery down at the Knights of Columbus. Well, I can't say much but we do have a prime suspect identified. Plus, the fellow who was injured has fully recovered. We've been able to track some of the stolen money and expect to make an arrest in the next couple of weeks. That's it."

"From what we know it was three Negro men identified as the robbers Chief. Can you confirm that?"

"Winny, I can't say much more but if you printed that story about three Negroes, you'd be misleading your readers and make a conclusion inconsistent with police work. That's all for now, I gotta go."

"One more thing, Chief, we also heard it could be an inside job. Can you confirm that?"

"Well, Winny, I can't confirm it officially, but I'd say that line is closer to the evidence we have. Goodbye."

27

Scrappy Stone sat quietly while Bob Willis looked over the two page typewritten report that Scrappy had gotten back the previous day from the secretarial pool at the main office. Willis' pipe had a mini eruption of smoke every time he exhaled. As he read, he made notes on white lined paper in a large blue three ring binder. Willis put the papers down, took off his glasses and looked at Stone. "I've got a couple of questions."

Scrappy pulled out his own little note book from his shirt pocket.

"Number one, are you sure about this business of having a union guy on the PEP team? Number two, how certain are you of having a final report done by the end of February? And last, why do you have to spend so much time up in Bethlehem at HQ while the project is underway here at Steelton? Seems to me you'd want to be hands-on every day here."

Scrappy anticipated the first and third questions. The second one, he thought he would get pressure to finish his recommendations faster. "I've wired everything with the union president and told the team members we would have a union rep. I've picked my guy, J.T. Squires…he's got twenty years in the rail mill, he's a war vet, and he has the respect of everybody who knows him.

I've met him and he's solid as a rock. On the second point, we've got year-end holidays coming up, and I needed to plug in some days for weather disruptions, illness and so on. With a little luck, we might beat end of February, but open hearth was a simpler pilot project and it took a concentrated three months or so from initial planning to final presentation on that phase. Plus we've got untrained rookies as technicians. I don't want to put a deadline on this that we have to push back. As far as my going up to Bethlehem, I don't like the idea of driving up there in the winter and spending all those nights in a hotel, but we have to coordinate with the guys up there…we were ordered to do that you'll recall."

"Yes, yes, I recall everything about that god-damned meeting, Mark."

"They also have more and better data processing staff than we have and I need to work with those guys first hand. Maybe I can get one or two transferred down here on a temporary basis to help us out. And there are two other reasons that I think you'll like."

"What's that?"

"First, I can keep an eye on those assholes who cut your and Hernley's legs out from under you on the parallel pilot program, and second, I can give you regular reports on how your son is doing in his new big job up there."

Willis gave Scrappy a look of approval. "All right. Let me brief Mr. Stevens on this. He wants to keep abreast of this rail mill phase. He's got his eye on a major capital expansion the Corporation is planning and he wants that money spent here. Stop in here tomorrow and we should have the green light…and by the way, see me about getting a pool car for your trips to Bethlehem. I don't want you driving that Ford of yours up there. Sons of bitches not only make their own steel, now they're starting to sell it on the open market as a competitor. If I was a young guy with executive aspirations here, I wouldn't be driving a Ford. By the way, have you been in contact with Hernley at all?"

"No, I just hear he's on a production rampage; out to prove a point I guess."

"Best to avoid him for awhile."

"I get the picture….thanks. You and Mrs. Willis going to the Halloween party at the Club?"

"Already got my costume…going as Blackbeard the Pirate and I'm carrying a real sword, so nobody better piss me off that night or I'll cut their balls off."

"I'll stay out of your way, Bob. Thanks for the warning and see you tomorrow morning first thing. I've already got a team kick-off meeting set for tomorrow at 2:00 in Patterson's office. Would be great if you come and could say a few words."

"Count on it, Mr. Stone. Any more orders for the day?"

Assistant District Attorney Peter Lewis was a Steelton success story. Valedictorian of his class and cum laude graduate of Temple Law School, he returned to Steelton to set up a store front law practice when most of his classmates stayed in the city or went to work in a big law firm. Peter liked to help the working class of Steelton and he never let a client's inability to pay interfere with high quality legal advice. The professional people of Steelton sent him their business, too. What Ernie liked about him most was that Peter never forgot where he came from. He was loyal to Steelton and supported just about every major charity in town. He had served the town as counsel as a twenty six year old and negotiated more than a few scrapes between the police and the citizenry. Peter was also a pragmatist. The demands on his charitable giving, political obligations and from his young family far outstripped the pay of an Assistant D.A. There was a line he would not cross, of course, but as an attorney he knew that the real world was painted in shades of gray, no matter how much the law preferred black and white.

The Chief showed up in uniform at ten on the dot.

"Thanks for seeing me so soon, Peter. Everything OK with the family?"

"Couldn't be better Chief. I've got to be in court at eleven… how can I help?"

"Peter, I can save you some time…you know about that assault and robbery at the Knights, right? We couldn't find out who did it, even though crimes involving that much cash we usually solve in a week. Turns out the guy who tends bar there shows up at Farina's a couple weeks later and plunks down five hundred in cash on a new Plymouth. I check the guy out, name's Pete Posetti…seems to have been straight for a while but has a number of priors including jail time. Minor player with the Lombardi people. Posetti is insisting it was some colored guys who jumped the two of them, smacked the other guy and stole all the money. He got knocked down in all of this but not hurt. I interviewed the other guy, named Salvatore Donato, in the hospital. He had a good case of temporary amnesia and says he doesn't remember anything about the night and wouldn't be able to identify anybody. He said it was Posetti's idea that the two of them leave together through the back door. We had some word on the street about this being an inside job, and I think this guy Posetti may have engineered the whole thing."

"OK. You want some resources to help nail Posetti? You want me to have him picked up?"

"Peter, there are some, uh, *sensitivities*, around this case. I don't want an arrest. What I need is for you to turn up the heat on Posetti and we put the fear of God into him so that he gets out of Steelton and everybody forgets about this. I'd like you to call Salvatore –he goes by Sonny - Donato and Posetti in separately, Donato first. Get Donato's story. He won't remember much and certainly won't corroborate Posetti's story. I want Posetti to feel like he's all alone here. Suggest to Posetti that the Steelton Police Chief thinks he arranged the whole thing and that I'm about to arrest him. Posetti is not a big enough player to get the Lombardi people to act on his behalf...he's already had a couple of skirmishes with them. I will take care of the situation as far as the K of C is concerned; I'm heading down there after I see you to fill Nick Cantore in. Think you can help us?

"Consider it done Chief."

"Thanks Peter. Call if you need anything from me. And, by the way, I've got a donation for you. Thanksgiving's not that far away and I'm sure a lot of those charities you support could use some extra dough." An envelope with ten twenties went across the desk.

"Thanks Chief. I'll give you a ring after I interview Posetti."

Ernie patched through a call to Nick Cantore from his car on the way back down to Steelton. "Nick? Chief Linta. Listen, I'm coming in for lunch today and I need some private time with you, all right?"

"Chief, I'm glad you called. That kid from the Steelton paper called me at home last night...I was going to call you myself. I'm really kind of worried about all of these rumors and the membership is starting to talk too."

"Posetti on duty?"

"No, Chief, he comes on at six tonight."

"OK, Nick. Don't worry. I'll be there in twenty minutes."

Scrappy was just outside Pat Patterson's office getting his notes together for the two o'clock meeting. He looked up to see Rocky

Garber walking toward him, accompanied by J.T. Squires.

Scrappy shook their hands. "Scrappy, I thought J.T. here could use a little moral support, so I hope you don't mind me tagging along for this first meeting."

"No, Rocky, I'm glad to have you, J.T. is going to be a big help. Rocky, why don't you say a few words at the meeting? Bob Willis is going to kick things off...always good to have you two guys on the same page. I want everyone to know we have union support...this is a job creation opportunity, it's not about job elimination. If this project works out, we get a huge investment in Steelton...maybe another hundred jobs."

"All right, Scrappy. For you, I'll do it." Just then Willis came lumbering down the walkway.

"Mr. Willis, you know James Garber, local 1688 president? And this is my PEP project team mate, J.T. Squires rail mill loader. J.T. has twenty years service in the mill."

Bob Willis just about shit his pants. Here he was, about to kick off a major project that the fucking Superintendent was personally interested in, he was about to enter the meeting with the union president and a colored guy.

"Good to meet you Mr. Squires. Always a pleasure to see you, James." Willis shook their hands as well. "That Stone, he's just one surprise after another" Willis thought to himself.

"Good afternoon, rail mill PEP Team! Thank you for coming to this important kick-off meeting. Before we introduce all of the team members, we are fortunate to have with us both Mr. Bob Willis – who you all know – and Mr. James Garber, local 1688 president. To start us off, Bob would like to say a few words.... Bob?"

Willis and Garber made their opening remarks. Scrappy excused them, and got down to outlining the early phases of the project, its objectives and its importance to Steelton. He brought materials to hand out and every member of the team had a personalized blue binder. Scrappy also handed out new stickers for their hard hats identifying them as PEP team members. Then he opened a large cardboard box and handed out new windbreaker jackets to every team mate. They were dark blue with "Rail Mill PEP Team Steelton Plant" embroidered on the back and their names on the front. Tim looked at his: "BURGER".

"Nick, I know this has been a tough couple of weeks for you. But I can help you. First let me fill you in on our investigation. This is confidential police business, Nick, but I know I can count on you."

"You can, Chief."

"We had some reliable information that your man Posetti was involved in this robbery. He has a string of prior arrests and has done jail time. I guess you've seen that new car of his? Well, he put down five hundred in cash for it."

Cantore was pale. He wondered if the Chief thought that he was somehow personally mixed up in this.

"We know you're in the clear on this Nick. We all know you run a clean business, and that you're an honest family man and a good Catholic. Now look, I'm going to help you out. You start by finding yourself a new bartender. When you do, if you want me to be with you when you fire Posetti, call the office and I'll come down and be with you. You give him a week's pay in lieu of notice, but he gets out of here right away. I don't want to see him in any business in Steelton ever again."

"Chief, if you've got the goods on him, why not just arrest him?"

"OK Nick, I'm going to trust you with something big here,

but I need your promise you will keep it between us."

"Shit, yeah, sure Chief. It's not gonna get me in any trouble is it?"

"No. OK, let me lay it out for you. Posetti is a small fish in a big pond. I am working with the County D.A. on some much bigger fish up in Harrisburg. Sometimes you gotta use the little fish as bait to catch the bigger fish. You get my meaning?"

"Christ, OK, Chief, OK. I just don't want anybody in that kind of circle causing me any trouble…or the club here…or my family…Jesus, Mary and Joseph!"

"Don't worry. I want you to do one thing…tell Posetti when he comes in tonight that I was here earlier today, and asking a lot of questions. He'll want you to tell him what I was asking about, you tell him it was about the robbery and nothing else, that I made you swear to secrecy. Got that? What time does he show up for his shift and when will he close up tonight?"

"I understand Chief. He'll roll in about quarter to six. We lock the doors on a weeknight at eleven thirty, so he'll probably be out of here an hour after that."

As he pulled out of the parking lot, the Chief got corporal Karmilov on the radio. "Karmilov. I got a quick assignment for you. This afternoon, by five-thirty have a uniform in a squad car in the back parking lot behind the Knights of Columbus. Look for a new black and white Plymouth. The owner is Posetti, the bartender. Just make sure he sees you watching him, nothing else. OK?"

"10-4 Chief"

"And then, I want a car in the same spot around midnight… unless there's something hot going on. Posetti should close up sometime after midnight. I want him followed from the Knights to the Borough line. Just make sure he knows he's being tailed.

And Karmilov, you can forget about the K of C robbery and assault case. Don't do any more work on it. The case is closed. Roger?"

"Roger. 10-4 Chief."

The Chief closed the loop with Sonny the following morning, preparing him for the call from Peter Lewis and meeting with the assistant D.A. He told Sonny to stick with the playbook and his Christmas would be a little nicer. Then he called Arthur and brought him up to date. Arthur just listened. "See you Sunday before Thanksgiving, Chief."

28

Out of consideration for his big brother, Tim had decided that he would never wear that windbreaker outside of the rail mill. He thought about how hard Harry worked and how much he wanted the next assignment with Scrappy; he couldn't keep his own selection to the PEP team a secret, but he was not going to push Harry's face into it either. Tim walked into the house through the back door. Doris had a big pot of something on the stove and Tim lifted the lid and took a big sniff… beef stew. "Smells good, Mom. Harry will want the leftovers for sure."

"Have you seen your brother? I just took a phone message for him. The Stone kid was calling for him…the oldest boy you two work with."

"Mark Stone?"

"Yeah, is your brother coming home for dinner tonight? Stone wants him to call."

"I don't know Mom. Tell you what, if he's not here for dinner, I'll take some of the leftovers up to his place after. I can give him the message. He'll be happy about the stew."

"Well, I made enough to feed Coxey's Army. Now that the weather's a little colder, you men are all eating like it's your last meal. I got some Hunkey bread from the Balkan bakery, too. Your dad's up at the fire house."

"He won't be late for supper, Mom. You can bet money on that. What does Harry say when you two are alone? Is he happy up in that apartment? He say anything to you and Dad? I don't think he's seeing that Decker girl anymore."

Doris wiped her hands on a dish towel as she turned around. "You know your brother, he don't say much about anything. In that way he's a little like your dad, although in most other ways he ain't nothin' like your dad...and of course you two are as different as day and night."

"I know Mom. I wish we got on a little better, but Harry is hell bent on this career of his and movin' up the ladder. I think things would be smoother if he had a steady girl...you know what I mean?"

"You don't have to spell it out for me, Timmy. I was young once. He just never seemed to be much of a ball of fire...he was a good kid, never any trouble...but now he comes back from the Army and gets that job down at the open hearth and he's like a different person. I was talkin' to Aunt Louise about him, she says it's just a phase where he's proving he's a man now. I think he's always been jealous of you, how easy you make friends and how good luck always seems to follow you around...not to mention the girls. And that reminds me, when are you going to get settled down? Your dad and me already had a kid and a house when we was your age. There are still plenty of nice girls around."

"Mom, don't count on any grandkids from me anytime soon...and my guess is Harry's in the same situation. At least I'm testin' the waters!"

"I don't need to hear any details, son. There's Hap now. Set the table and open him up a beer."

232

"Mom and I were talking about Harry a little bit Dad… anything new from him on your end?"

"I just know he's tryin' hard to get ahead. He doesn't want to have much to do with the West Side although I hear he's in Buddy's on the weekends. I tried to get him on the football bus last Saturday down to the York game…said he was fixing his apartment up. Maybe he's got a steady girl down there."

That was Doris' cue to chip in: "If he wanted a steady girl, that Decker girl would have filled the bill. I don't know why you boys need to wander away from the West Side. Right Hap?"

"Mmmm…" Hap mumbled as he wiped his bowl with a chunk of bread.

"Well, I'm going to take some stew down right after we finish…I'll give him the message from Stone… maybe we'll get out and have a beer or two."

The downstairs buzzer rang and Harry went down the steps. He was surprised to see Tim; he was Harry's first visitor since he moved in.

"Mom sent some beef stew for you, Harry, and I have a message for you from Mark Stone. He wants you to call him."

"Stone?" Harry's face brightened. "Did he say what he wanted?"

"Mom took the message earlier today. Just asked that you give him a call. How's the place coming along?"

"Good, good. Just finished up some chili and a grilled cheese. Can you stay for a bit? Want a beer?"

"I thought we might go out for a beer or two, catch up a little. We can walk down to Katy's or drive down to the St. Lawrence if you want."

"St. Lawrence is good. I meant to tell you, I filled out an

application to join. I used you as a reference. Stone said I could use his name too."

"Harry, I hate to bust your bubble, but if you've got five bucks and you're a white guy, you could put Jack the Ripper down as a reference and get in. Grab your jacket."

"All right, I can call Stone from the club. I got his home number in my wallet."

The St. Lawrence had maybe twenty people, two couples and the rest single guys of all ages. The juke box was playing Perry Como and Tim waved over Mike Jamnov as he and Harry took a table.

"Mike, you know my big brother Harry? He's back from the service and working down at open hearth now. Moved up from the West Side to a place on Locust Street. He might be a little high class for us now, but he filled out an application and wants to become a member."

"Hi Harry, I remember you. I saw your application; give me a couple of minutes and I'll have your card for you. That way you don't need to lug your pain in the ass brother along every time you want to come down for a drink! Be right back."

"I see Jamnov knows you well, Tim. How about if I call Scrappy now, and get that out of the way. Order me a Schimdt's."

Harry went into the phone booth out in the lobby and dropped his coin in the slot and dialed up the Highspire number. "Scrappy…it's Harry Burger. My mom said you left a message for me at the house."

"Yeah, I didn't have the number for you at your new place there. Listen, how'd you like to be my guest at the Bethlehem Steel Management Club Halloween party? Before you say anything, let me tell you it would be a double date."

"Geez, Scrappy, I'd like to go but I'm not seeing anyone at

the moment, certainly no one classy enough for the Management Club."

"I've got you covered. Remember the Dale sisters from church? Well, I'm taking Susie and Patti will be your date."

"Christ! Sure, that's nice. I liked her. You sure about this? I mean, can you bring three guests, you know, Susie and the two of us?"

"Harry, do you know who the Dale sisters' dad is? Don't worry about it. Look, you'll need a costume too. Saturday the twenty-ninth. I'm going as a Steelton football player…got my kid brother's uniform and my old cleats. Give me a call over the weekend and we'll fix the time. Call in the afternoon, I'll be on the river 'til noon."

"I will Scrappy, Thanks. One more thing, should I call Patti and invite her?"

"All taken care of Harry…she's looking forward to it. Talk to you over the weekend. 'Bye."

"Well, your call must have gone well by the smile on your face. You get a promotion?"

"No, it was social. Me and Scrappy are double dating for a Halloween party."

"I'm happy to hear that Harry….I'd like to see you get out with the ladies a little bit. You takin' Darlene?"

"No Tim, I'm not. Look, we got together once for old time's sake, that's it. I'm taking a girl from up on the hill."

"She got a name?"

"Tim, it's our first date. I met her at church. Let me see how things go first."

"Look, Harry, you've got your own place now so it's good that you're getting out more, but Steelton can be a pretty small town as you know. You hold hands with one girl on Main Street and the next day people have you gettin' married to her…you saw that with Darlene. That's why I go for girls outside of town, plus if something goes wrong they're not bitchin' to everyone in town about what a prick you are. You ever want to borrow the Merc you just let me know. Out of town girls are the way to go, you'll see. Y'know, I really do want you to be happy and to find the success you seem to be searchin' for. We ain't in competition."

"I know that Tim. It's just that things just seem to come easy for you, and I try my best to do all the right things and I don't seem to make any progress. It's like I'm always in the same place, waiting for somebody else to decide what's going to happen to me. At work, I did my best on that project with Stone…everybody said I did a good job. I put in extra time, I studied, I tried to get to know the people at a higher level, and here I am back at the same job, and now it's even worse because the big boss is on the warpath and even ordered me not to talk to Scrappy Stone. I wanted to continue working with him; that guy is going places."

Tim figured this was as good a time as any to tell Harry. He was guessing that Scrappy hadn't said anything about the rail mill PEP team or Harry would've mentioned it.

"Harry, you should probably hear this direct from me…if you haven't heard already…I got picked for the team to work with Stone in the rail mill. He wanted a second shift foreman and I volunteered."

"I figured you would Tim. Scrappy asked me about you, and I recommended you to him."

"You did?" Tim didn't quite know what to say. "Thanks, Harry. I had no idea."

"He woulda probably picked you anyway. Good things like that just follow you around. I know you'll do a good job. How's mom and dad by the way? Dad pissed about the team losing to John Harris last week?"

"Those old timers think the football team should go undefeated every year. They're doing OK…you know what I think is bugging them deep down? I think they want grand kids, and to be honest about it they want a granddaughter. They haven't said as much, but I can see it in their faces when they talk about you and me and our lack of interest in settling down."

"Well, Tim, at least we have one thing in common." They ordered a second beer.

Neither of the brothers said anything for a while.

"Where are you and Stone taking these lucky ladies?"

"Management Club Halloween party. I'm his guest. You know, Tim, that's another thing. As a first level supervisor you're a member of the Management Club, and eligible for all of those great activities, but you never go. I'd be thrilled if I ever qualified for membership."

"Doesn't mean anything to me. I see enough big shots during an eight hour shift. I'm not going to be down there kissing their asses on my own time. I don't want or need their approval and I can make my way on my own. I don't need anybody's help; I rely on myself. You talked about trying to get what you want, but it has always depended on somebody else. Let me tell you, Harry, you want something, you trust yourself to earn it and you don't have to worry about nobody else."

Harry sat back on his chair. He lit a cigarette. "How did Tim get all of his confidence" he wondered, "and why didn't I get any at all?"

"Harry, I need to talk to Mike Jamnov for a second, and I see a couple of guys at the bar I want to say hello to. Be right back."

Harry looked up to see Tim shaking hands and laughing

with three or four guys at the bar. He told the bartender to set everybody up and to settle his own tab. Tim went back toward the kitchen apparently to see Jamnov. He came out a few minutes later.

"We're paid. Better get a move on, day turn tomorrow. I start three to eleven next week, thank God."

Harry told Tim just to drop him off at Front and Locust, he'd walk the block up the hill to his place. "You remember that West Side Hose House fireman's outfit Dad had…the one he used to wear to all the big celebrations before he got his beer gut? If you think of it, ask him or Mom to pull that out. I think it'll fit me, and I'll need a costume for the Halloween party."

Tim relayed the message and the next day Doris found the uniform upstairs and miraculously it didn't stink like moth balls. Even had the matching hat right where it was supposed to be. She gave it a quick press and Harry tried it on and for the most part, it fit. The shirt that originally came with the uniform, with the epaulets and gold buttons was long gone, but Harry put on a white shirt with the jacket and trousers and that seemed to work out fine. He told Scrappy to pick him up at Myers Street and just before seven a freshly washed Ford pulled up to the stoop driven by a guy in a blue and white football uniform, number fifty-five, shoulder pads and all. Harry got in but had to move the helmet off of the passenger seat. Scrappy's black high top cleats were on the floor.

"Little change in plans Harry. We're meeting the sisters at the Club, we're not picking them up."

Harry immediately read this as a bad sign…"Why's that?"

"Don't worry, Harry. Susie said they were wearing some dresses that they didn't want all wrinkled up climbing into my car that, by the way she added, usually smelled like dead fish.

They talked their dad into dropping them off. I told her as long as her dad wasn't planning to pick 'em up, afterwards, it would be OK."

"Can you gimme a little help here Scrappy? This is my first time up there, first date with Patti, I got to admit I'm kind of nervous about all of this, I mean with all those executives and all. Whose idea was it to match up me and Patti? Was that yours? I hate to feel like she was dragged into this."

"This is all easy. Just follow my cues. Patti asked about you after we all met at church and her sister thought a double date would be a good idea. We'll probably sit with Bob Willis and his wife...her name is Nancy. Very nice person. Ask her about her son William and you won't have to ask another question all night."

"Jesus, Bob Willis? Christ! What if he asks me about work, or the PEP project, or worse suppose he asks me about Hernley? What am I supposed to say?"

"You say how much you enjoy your job, what a great opportunity, it's nice to see how good business is. It's a social occasion and guys have their wives. If they start to talk about business, their wives give them shit. And as far as Hernley goes...same thing...all is well, you couldn't be happier, then ask him if he is enjoying the party. You will see Hernley, he'll stop by to see Willis."

"And what about our dates? Are you and Susie serious? Do you know what Patti likes? You mentioned something about their dad."

"Harry...relax! This is fun. You're wearing me out. No more questions. Just smile a lot, don't drink too much, don't eat like a pig, only dance the slow ones, and keep your eye on me. Mr. Dale is the head of construction purchasing for the Pennsylvania

Turnpike…works at the headquarters in Highspire. Do you know how much rebar is in a mile of highway Harry? Do you know how much structural steel is in the hundreds of turnpike bridges? Mr. Dale himself gets invited to every big Club event. He's not exactly the Halloween costume type, otherwise we'd be enjoying a table with the beautiful and exciting Dale sisters and their Mom and Dad. And their Mom's name is Thelma, by the way, and that should tell you everything you need to know."

Scrappy made a bee-line to the bar with Harry two steps behind. Harry made his first social mistake in the first minute, when he offered to buy the beers, fortunately only Scrappy and the bartender heard it. "No charge for anything here, Harry. Let's keep our eyes on the door."

The bar was full and Harry was taking in all of the great costumes. A lot of them were obviously purchased and he wondered if he looked a little shabby. Scrappy introduced him to everyone who stopped by, although he kept his football helmet on for the most part; he had to drink his beer kind of underneath the single bar nose guard bolted onto his helmet. Harry said a lot of "hellos" and "nice to meet yous" while he nervously watched the main entrance while never moving more than two feet away from Stone. Finally, Scrappy turned and said "Harry, you are one lucky boy."

The Dale sisters came through together…one in red, one in pale blue. They looked as if they had stepped out of Gone with the Wind. They didn't have those giant hoop dresses on, but sort of half way. Both of the gowns they had on were off the shoulder types, and each wore a wide brimmed hat and carried a parasol. There was kind of a buzz when they entered the bar area, not exactly searching for Scrappy and Harry, but certainly drawing a lot of admirers…more ladies than men. "Let's let them enjoy the spotlight a little" Scrappy whispered. "OK, that's enough."

Harry was his now accustomed two steps behind Stone as they approached the southern belles. "I don't think we are up to your standards, ladies, but we are pleased to be seen with you this evening. I think we are a little out of our league, Harry, don't you think?"

"Beautiful" Harry said, and he meant it. Somehow, he had stumbled onto just the right thing to say. One word said it all.

"Why thank you, Mr. Burger." Patti said in her best imitation of Scarlett O'Hara. "I must say, Sister Susan, I am absolutely *PARCHED* after that long buggy ride. I could be persuaded to enjoy a cool drink…do you suppose these gentlemen could arrange that?"

"Why yes, sister. I think two large V.O.'s and water would be just the thing." Scrappy took off to the bar; Harry had to carry the conversation. "It really is a sincere pleasure to be invited here this evening. Thank you Susie and thank you Patti for giving me the opportunity to know you better."

"Mister BURGER! What lovely manners you have." Patti said with a warm smile.

"I hope they don't last all night." Sister Susie said with a wicked grin. Scrappy came back with the cocktails. "Maybe we should find our table. That is, if you two ladies can sit down in those contraptions."

"Scrappy, my dear. Please don't tell me you are going to wear that helmet all night. At least Mr. Burger here has the sense to carry his fireman's hat under his arm. And do not concern yourself with our dresses. We are quite accustomed to them, is that not right, dear Sister?"

Harry somehow managed to work his way through the evening meal even with Mr. Willis and his wife at their table.

Willis wore a ridiculous pirate outfit and his wife dressed like some kind of European princess. Harry liked the other couple who made up their table for eight, a quiet middle aged couple who had very little to say. The gentleman, dressed like a Scottish golfer, was in fact named McCulloch and he was some kind of engineer on Willis' staff. His wife, also in some kind of Scottish get up, hardly said two words.

After the coffee there was dancing to a three piece combo, and Harry took Scrappy's advice to sit out the fast ones. The McCullochs left for the evening right after dessert. Harry was enjoying the conversation when he looked up and saw R. M. Stevens approaching their table. Stevens was the very top guy at Steelton, the works superintendent. Harry had never met him, but certainly knew him from the many pictures he had seen.

"Evening, Bob, Nancy. Hello Susan, Patricia. Enjoying yourselves?" Scrappy stood up, so Harry did too. Scrappy's helmet was on the floor, thank God. "Well, Mr. Stone, taking proper care of the lovely Miss Dale I trust?"

"You can count on it, R.M."

Harry just about shit his pants standing upright. Here's Scrappy calling the very top guy by his common name.

"And this is Harry Burger, who is responsible this evening for the other beautiful Dale sister. Harry has worked with me on the PEP project."

"Evening Sir; Ma'am." was about all Harry could squeak out.

"Top priority project for us Mr. Burger. Mind if we sit for a bit?"

Well, no one was going to say no. Stevens' wife Arlene talked to the ladies and in a few minutes they decided to make a move as a foursome to the ladies room. "To be honest, we really could use a little help with the dresses" Patti admitted.

With the ladies gone, the talk shifted right away to work. "The rail mill PEP on schedule Bob? We off to a good start there?"

"We are. Mr. Stone here has his team in place. We are coordinating with HQ and expect we'll hit all of the project milestones. That right, Mark?"

"Our pilot program at the open hearth-Harry here played a big part in that -was an on time success and I don't see why we shouldn't be able to replicate that in the rail mill."

Just then, who should approach the table but Bob Hernley – without Mrs. Hernley. "Good evening Gentlemen, nice party."

"Hello Bob." Willis said. "We'd ask you to join us but we expect the ladies back any time."

It was at this point that Harry's eyes connected with Hernley's. Maybe it was Harry's outfit that threw him off, but Harry thought he literally saw the blood drain from Hernley's face when he recognized Harry enjoying a table with Stone, Willis and Mr. Stevens. He couldn't resist. "Good evening Mr. Hernley. Nice to see you."

"B-Burger?" Hernley stammered. "That you?"

Scrappy spoke up when he saw Harry at a loss for words. "We were just going over the PEP progress with R.M., Bob. Where is Mrs. Hernley?"

"Uh, ladies room I think. Well, I just wanted to stop by to say hello to everyone. Enjoy the party."

Hernley turned and walked away. Stevens watched Hernley walk away. "Third time tonight he's bumped into me and Arlene just to say hello. Look, here come the women. Stone, we have a lot riding on that rail mill….millions in capital, double our production capacity, and a major expansion to accommodate it all. We have any major setbacks, I want to hear about it."

The party wound down after a bit and Harry, Mark and their

dates moved to the bar for a last drink. Harry was watching Scrappy for a sign of what to do and say next while Susie and Patti talked about the upcoming holidays. Just then Harry spied Cynthia Hernley. She hadn't made eye contact but Harry wanted Cynthia to see Patti and vice-versa. Cindy was wearing a Peter Pan costume that fit her perfectly. She had green eye make-up and sparkles in her hair.

"Cindy…Hello Cindy!" Harry was hoping she would at least recognize him. She did. "Well, hello…looks like you're the man to call in case of fire."

"Cindy, this is Patti Dale. Patti, Cynthia Hernley. I work with her husband."

"Pleased to meet you Miss Dale. Haven't seen you in church Harry."

"I've been attending. I usually sit with the Becker families. I've taken the apartment just above their offices."

"Have you? I'm due in there for an appointment in the next week or so."

"That's a great costume, Cindy. You could go right onto TV the way you look."

"That's very kind Harry. Well, I'm certain Bob is looking for me. Goodnight, Miss Dale. That really is a lovely dress. I'd love to know where you got it."

"It's just a family hand-me-down; my sister's too." Harry was not accustomed to conversation between educated women so he missed the dripping sarcasm.

Scrappy sipped his cocktail and turned to Harry. "Susie's ready to get out of her dress, I imagine you are too Patti. What say we finish these and I'll pull the car out front."

"Jesus" Harry wondered, "what on earth did Scrappy mean?"

Harry and Patti crawled into the back of Scrappy's coupe.

Susie turned around from the front seat. "We'll go back to our place so that we can change. We can have a night cap or a coffee there, although my Dad may still be up."

Harry didn't say anything but that solved a lot of problems. He didn't have to think about how to say good night to Patti or to worry about a situation where they'd be alone. He really did like her, she was funny, intelligent, kind of cute but not beautiful. He hoped that he would have the chance to see her again.

Mr. Dale was up and while the girls changed outfits he invited Harry and Scrappy down to his rec room for a drink. It was a nice house with a walk out basement that opened up out onto the back yard. The rec room had a linoleum floor and wood paneling, and a small bar with two stools. There was a portable TV in the corner, almost like Harry's recent purchase. He had noticed a big Zenith console job in the living room before being shown down the stairs. Harry and Scrappy each had a bottle of Ballantine.

After a while the girls came down. They must have consulted on their outfits. Each one had on slacks and a kind of tight sweater, Susie a mid blue but Patti's fire engine red. Both had a string of pearls over the sweater and their hair pulled back. Both of the sisters had plenty to show off in those sweaters.

"Can you make us a rum and coke, Daddy?"

The remainder of the evening went quietly. A second drink for everyone. A tray of snacks produced from behind the bar. The TV was never turned on and the talk was of that night's party, the weather turning colder, and an upcoming trip for Mr. Dale to some kind of conference about tunnel building and maintenance that was being held in Pittsburgh. Harry said he hoped to see the girls at church the following morning; Scrappy announced he'd be saving his prayers for the elusive muskellunge on the Susquehanna.

Mr. Dale was gentlemanly enough to stay downstairs while his two girls showed their men to the front door. A nice hug and kind of a long warm kiss on the cheek for Harry, something a little more exuberant for Scrappy and Susie.

"Scrappy, I can't thank you enough for tonight. I could not believe what you said to Mr. Stevens about me; I don't think anybody in my life ever has given me a compliment like that. And I like Patti, too…I hope she will see me again."

"When you see her at church tomorrow, tell her and her sister what a great time you had, and then get Patti aside and ask if it's OK for you to call her. Don't try to set up a second date right away."

"Thanks again, Scrappy…and thanks for driving."

Stone dropped Harry off and wheeled down Locust to Front and turned left toward Highspire. A last drink or two at the St. Lawrence occurred to him, but then he thought about his alarm clock set for five thirty. Besides, he had some thinking to do. "A major expansion" Stevens said.

Cindy looked over at her husband. "That was a nice party, Bob. Did you have a good time?"

"It was all right. Did you get any time alone with Arlene Stevens?"

"No, I'm sorry I didn't. You saw how people were around them all night. I did see that guy who works for you at the end of the night… Harry Burger. He's very polite."

"Yeah, I saw him too."

29

"Peter? Peter, it's Ira Weintraub. How are you?"

"I'm doing well Ira, It's been a while since we've spoken. Family OK?"

"Yes, thanks Peter. This call's business though if you have a couple of minutes. Has to do with one of your staff attorneys wanting to bring in a guy named Pete Posetti to see you. Posetti's a client, so I'm calling as his counsel."

"Go ahead."

"He's told me the whole story about that robbery down in Steelton and also tells me he's being followed and harassed by the Steelton cops. He says he's under suspicion for the robbery even though he was just an innocent victim. And, he says he can identify the guy who DID do it."

"Is that right? Well, I just want to have him come in for a little talk. I'm happy to listen to his story. You know he was spending a lot of cash all over town right after the robbery? The Steelton Police thinks he's also involved in some other things that they don't want in Steelton, and the fact that YOU are calling me tells me they're right."

"Look, Peter, this Posetti guy is small potatoes but he's getting the short end of the stick here."

"I can make it easy for you Ira. He quits his job down there at the K of C and he doesn't come back to Steelton or try to do business in Steelton, I cancel the meeting with him."

"I see." There was a pause on the phone. "Peter, you have a kid coming up for trial next month named Ricci, Anthony Ricci. Felony grand theft and a couple of other charges. He's out on bail. Ricci's family would like to see him avoid that trial and jail time. This kid had no major problems before his arrest. Anyway he's willing to plead if I can get him an assurance of suspended sentence. Would mean a lot to the kid's family."

"Ira, Ricci got off the hook a couple of times before he finally got pinched because of who his family is. It was a courtesy. The kid and one of his buddies were caught trying to sell a Harrisburg city dump truck, and when we tracked him down he had a couple of stolen cars in his lot too."

"Yeah, I know. Look his family says they'll straighten him out and put the clamps on him. How about it?"

"I'll take care of it with the D.A. Ricci's going to get a fine, suspended sentence and probation. One screw up while on probation, it's County for him."

"Thanks Peter. Posetti is out of Steelton and out of your hair."

"One more thing, Ira. You know Steelton's my home town. All of my family still lives there, and I expect to live there until I die. Please let your clients know I don't want to see any expansion of their enterprise into Steelton. I find out about it, there's no compromise and no one gets off the hook. It's personal for me and I can tell you Ernie Linta feels the same way."

"I understand Peter. Linta and I go way back. Tough nut to crack. Thanks for working with me on this. Let me know if any of your friends need help on Election Day. You know me, always working hard to save democracy."

248

"You should run for Mayor, Ira. Thanks for the call."

It was late on a blustery afternoon when Posetti and Nick Messina shuffled into Ira Weintraub's law offices, a red brick three story townhouse literally in the shadow of the State Capitol. The wind blew the leaves down State Street, and it was already getting dark now that Daylight Saving Time had ended.

"Pete, I talked to the D.A. They are not backing down. They are being unreasonable about this, and that Police Chief in Steelton has you in his sights. The only way out of this is for you to quit that bartending job and stay out of Steelton. You do that, I can make sure that they leave you alone and the matter is dropped."

"For Christ sake, Mr. Weintraub, I need the money. I don't have another job. And I know the son of a bitch kid who took the dough. I told Nick here and you all about it."

"Let's be practical here, Pete. We don't go running to the law to solve our problems or settle our scores. You did the right thing when you went to Nick. He took it up the line and the decision was we are not going to do anything. You just had some bad luck. You bumped into a couple of guys in Steelton we don't want to tangle with. We have our reasons. You just got to take it as a lesson learned. Nick, can you find something for Pete here to do that will let him keep that fancy new car of his?"

"Sure Mr. Weintraub. Pete goes way back with some of us."

"And Pete, get that car of yours serviced somewhere else. Phone in your resignation and do not go into Steelton. Ever. We clear on that?"

"I get it. I took a fall for some guys before the war and I guess I can do it again. I hope I get some credit for this. I don't want any shit job beatin' people up over a five buck debt."

"Mr. Messina will take good care of you. Hold on a minute."

Weintraub opened a lower drawer in his beautiful walnut desk. "Here's a C-note to help ease the pain, Pete." Thank you gentlemen for your time today."

Fridays were paydays for the Howard employees. The regular full time employees got their paychecks just before lunch, so that they could cash them while the banks were still open. Arthur paid his family in cash, except for his wife who was considered an executive with the Company. He often had an extra five or ten dollar bill for an employee who did a particularly good job for him. The three men who worked on Tim's gondola car, for example, got an extra ten each for figuring out the best way to get the thing off the tracks and into the shed. The wheels from the car got a premium price at Central Scrap. Arthur like to hand out the checks to his people personally, and he now had fifteen employees outside of the family. There were three funerals in the past week, so Charles Parker was looking forward to a nice check as he had worked nearly fifty hours covering the day and night services and a long twelve hour shift the prior Saturday. He always waited patiently until Mr. Howard came back to the office from the scrap yards, even though sometimes he had to wait until one o'clock or so to get his check.

"Charles, call Claude up from downstairs; then you two come into my office for your pay."

This seemed a little out of the ordinary but Charles hustled down the stairs, told Claude his Dad wanted to see both of them in his office. Claude just looked at Charles. "Do you suppose we're in trouble?" Charles asked.

"Just be calm. I don't know of anything. Maybe he just wants to thank you...we had a full week. I worked over seventy hours myself last week the way I figure it." Claude washed his hands and he and Charles walked into Arthur's office. Arthur was behind the desk, with a copy of the Steelton news in front of him."

"You boys put in a lot of hours last week. It shows in your pay for this week. Are you both happy with your jobs here?"

"Yessir." Parker said. "Of course, Dad."

"Well that's good, because I like having you two here with me. I hope that we have a long time together. We are a family. You too, Charles. Families have to trust one another. There can't be any secrets. Families have to work together to stay together. And there is one leader in a family, and that leader has to be respected. That leader has to have loyalty. That leader can't have anybody in the family doing anything that might threaten the family. You look at our business here. It's taken me all my life to build it up. No one is going to take it away from me. Anybody who did ANYTHING that might hurt my business or my family, well, they'd have to deal with me. And I would not be a forgiving leader. You two following me?"

At this point both Claude and Charles had their eyes permanently fixed to their shoe tops. "Yessir." "Yes, Dad."

"I was just reading this news article about that robbery down at the Italian Club…you remember that bartender there don't you son?" Claude nodded. "Now this article here says that the Police Chief thinks that robbery was what he called an "inside job". You know what that means? That means that the guy who ran that bar business trusted this bartender, and this bartender betrayed him. Just like Judas in the Bible. I think about what that would be like if it was me, if someone I had in my business betrayed me like that, and did something that would embarrass me or hurt my reputation. I would not be happy about that; and the person who did betray me would never have my trust again."

Arthur just paused and let his words sink in. To Claude and

Charles, it seemed like an eternity until Arthur spoke again.

"I have your paycheck Charles. You did good work for me last week. There's an extra ten in the envelope for you. OK, you can go."

"Thank you, Mr. Howard."

Claude figured he was about to get it from his dad, and he braced himself for the worst.

"You know, son, I made some mistakes when I was young. I was lucky I had someone lookin' out for me, I guess, because I never got hurt too bad by my mistakes. I learned from them, though. And I try to go through every day of my life without making a mistake. A man has to be careful. A real man has responsibilities to his family. I have trusted you and brought you into the business step by step. I don't want to ever have to think that maybe I am makin' a mistake by doin' that. We clear?"

"We clear, Dad."

"See your Mama to pick up your money this week. She is as much responsible for our family's happiness as I am. Maybe you should thank her this week instead of me."

"Yes, Dad. Don't worry. I know how to learn from my mistakes, too."

Scrappy's drive up to Bethlehem from the main office on Swatara Street took just under three hours. He had asked Willis for a panel truck to carry his boxes, binders, and his own suitcase for his travel, but Willis came up with a Rambler station wagon. It was a newer model, a fifty-four, but one of the ugliest cars ever made. "We bought a bunch of these as fleet and pool cars to help out American Motors. They're having a rough go and are good customers. You're not driving this thing to impress the ladies, Stone, it's all about business. You can have it until the rail mill

PEP is over. Don't even think about driving that Ford up to headquarters."

"Understood, Bob, and with this thing, don't worry about me attracting any women."

"You couldn't do better that Susie Dale anyway. Why don't you do the right thing and ask that girl to marry you. It would be good for your career and good for Bethlehem Steel."

"You know me, Mr. Willis, I always put the Company's needs ahead of my own."

"That Stone, never at a loss for words," Willis thought.

Scrappy had plenty of time to think as he drove up Route 22 toward Allentown and Bethlehem. He was invited to dinner at Bill Willis' house that night. Three days up at HQ and then back down to Steelton. The rail mill team was doing a good job on collecting and categorizing all of the existing reports and schedules, and prioritizing them. They had identified reports and files they had been keeping for years that they thought were worthless, or duplicates. They had discovered, for example, that inventories of assets were reported through several different channels, such as maintenance, lab equipment, and rolling stock. Finished goods inventory with delayed shipments were stacked in a haphazard fashion, and if it weren't for experienced men with good memories like Squires, some of the special order rails might never be found. Scrappy's job this week was to coordinate with all of the data processing guys and to see how his Bethlehem counterparts were doing it. He was also taking one of the "efficiency" engineers back with him to Steelton to help with overall project process design. Scrappy knew the Steelton Plant was in competition with the Bethlehem facility, and he had been hearing that the management up at Lackawanna was trying to get in on the action. If a big investment was at stake, he didn't see the

Pennsylvania politicians losing out to New York, but that was for others to decide.

After a long but productive day that had started in Steelton at five, Scrappy checked into the hotel and his friend Bill picked him up at six. Over a nice roast beef and mashed potatoes dinner Bill and his wife Cheryl talked about their house hunting plans. They had been renting in Scranton and Bethlehem was providing them a company apartment for six months as a part of his promotion and move. Cheryl of course asked about Susie Dale as the two of them had become fast friends. Bill talked about the exciting and fast paced environment at the Headquarters operation...he was learning something new every day.

"You know, Scrappy, you have Lehigh right next door. I know several guys who are finishing their bachelor degrees while working full time. The Company cooperates and even pays for books and lab fees. You could have your degree finished in under two years if you were up here. You know there's a point at which your career will get capped without that sheepskin. Me and Cheryl would love to have you and Susie up here."

"I've thought about that, but I've got a pretty big assignment going and I have my family and fishing and....well, you know the story. As for Susie, she loves teaching school and she and her sister are about to get a place of their own. A guy her dad knows is building some new homes...ranch homes...just a couple blocks from Swatara Junior High where she teaches. That's maybe a ten minute drive to the turnpike office for her sister Patti. Their old man is putting up a nice down payment I understand. So, I think maybe Susie is set in Steelton, too."

"I've got to be in Scranton tomorrow and I guess you're heading right back to Steelton after work the day following, so I guess we won't see you til Thanksgiving. We'll be in Steelton Thursday and Friday and then with Cheryl's mom and dad Saturday and Sunday. Let's try to get together maybe day after Turkey-Day. OK?"

"Count on it. I'll be working but we can maybe get out as a foursome at the Club Friday night."

"Let's go somewhere else for dinner." Cheryl piped up. "If we go to the club, Bill's parents will come along and everybody wants to talk to Bill about work. How about the Old Stone Inn?"

"That's a deal Cheryl. I'll confirm it with Susie this weekend."

Scrappy put in one twelve hour day and followed that with another full day. He had a passenger for his trip back to Steelton. He was taking an engineer named Wallace who was going to be in Steelton for over a week studying existing processes and helping out with future production plans. Wallace, who had a Manager's title, was all about business and Scrappy thought if he heard the word "de-bottlenecking" once more he was going to throw Wallace out of the car on the way home to Steelton. He tried to get Wallace to talk fishing, politics, weather, family, nothing worked. He finally dropped Wallace off at the Management Club after seven. The BSMC had a suite of five one bedroom apartments back by the skeet shooting range for employees on temporary assignment as Steelton did not have a proper hotel. "I'll pick you up at six tomorrow and take you to the main office. You can get your pool car there, Wallace. Probably see you in the rail mill later."

"Thanks, Mr. Stone. My schedule is set for the main office, then Mr. Patterson's office at 1:00 pm tomorrow. See you then."

Ernie had his call from Peter Lewis. He called Cantore.

"Nick…Chief Linta here. Fine, thank you. Nick, you're going to get a call from Pete Posetti telling you he's quitting his bartender job immediately. Don't say anything to him other than confirming where he wants his last paycheck sent. He's not permitted to come back to Steelton. That closes this case. Any of the members there –especially the regulars - want to ask you about Pete, the robbery, anything even closely related you tell them you are under police orders not to discuss it. They want to know where Pete went you don't know. And you DON'T. We have an understanding Nick?"

"Yes Chief. Thanks."

"Couple more things…you have anyone in mind or any applications for Posetti's old job…title was bar manager right?"

"That's the title and no I don't have anyone. I'll probably have to cover a bunch of hours myself and see if I can stretch my other two part-timers until I find someone."

"Okay. I'll be in there with my family tomorrow night for dinner. Save me a good table. I'll see if I can help you out on the bartender situation. See you then." Ernie hung up and dialed his next call.

"Mr. Klein, please. Chief of Police Linta calling."

"Chief Linta, this is a nice surprise. Everything going well I hope?"

"Yes, thank you Herman. This call is part personal and part business. Is that son-in-law of yours still looking for a new position, the one working at the Hotel for the Hershey people?"

"Why yes, he is. He and my daughter and their twins have a hard time making ends meet, Hershey is so expensive. They rent a tiny little house…it is a converted garage really. We'd like to get them down here to Steelton, we have three empty bedrooms in that big house." Klein lived toward the top of Pine Street, where some of the biggest homes were built for Steelton's wealthiest families. "The Hershey people make their employees live in Hershey."

"And he has worked in the kitchens, lounges, and the Hotel itself is that right?"

"Yes, he has had good training. He orders supplies, is good with the customers. A very hard worker."

"He's a good Catholic, like you Herman?"

"He is a good GERMAN Catholic my friend."

"What is his name?"

"Klaus Entmann, but people call him Ken."

"OK. Tomorrow, you have Klaus call Mr. Nicholas Cantore at the Steelton Knights of Columbus. The number is WEbster 9-4006. Have Karl mention he is Chief Linta's friend. Mr. Cantore has an opening that Klaus can interview for. I will do my best for him."

"Thank you very much Chief. This is a nice thing you do. Thank you. You said there was business also?"

"I just want to set up a Christmas-time dinner Herman. How about the evening of December eighteenth?"

"Yes, the eighteenth at the Club. Shall we say six-thirty. We will have a good talk. Good-bye Ernest, and thank you from me and Mrs. Klein for this help."

"Nick…this is Ernie Linta again. Tomorrow you will get a call from a Mr. Ken Entmann. He is an experienced bartender and hotel guy now with the Hershey people. I can vouch for him. He would like to apply for the vacant position you have. Right, Entmann. He's German but Catholic…his family goes to St. Marks. Right. See you tomorrow night."

Ben Cohen sat toward the back of the meeting room as he usually did for these staff meetings. The temperature outside was in the low fifties but of course the steam heat system in the state government buildings assured a minimum temperature of eighty throughout the vintage stone building. The meeting room had twenty foot ceilings and hard surfaces throughout so every gathering had the same sound effect as a large railroad station. This meeting was called by Colonel Walker, who despite the fact that he was now a Pennsylvania civil servant insisted on being addressed by his former military title. Diminutive Ben was well over a foot shorter than Walker, whose bald, craggy head made him look like he could have been a model for Mount Rushmore.

"Look at this putz." Ben thought to himself as Walker strode into the room with several aides. He hated these military double-dippers. When they got passed over for a general's position, the colonels retired with their big federal pension and used their veteran's preference to secure high level jobs with the Commonwealth, hoping to get ten years in to qualify for another pension. Walker insisted on having a "Chief of Staff" who introduced Walker to the other department heads and bureau chiefs of the Liquor Control Board to start the meeting.

It took Walker forty-five minutes, with twenty charts and graphs to say what could have been said in five. Enforcement efforts would concentrate on the usual roads into Pennsylvania from its bordering states-particularly Maryland - where liquor and wine was much cheaper than in Pennsylvania, whose citizens would make the short drive across the border for their holiday alcohol purchases. Many out of state towns had liquor stores – like Thurmont, Maryland just south of Gettysburg- sited a couple of hundred yards from the Mason-Dixon Line to provide easy access for Pennsylvanians. Walker announced his people would be in unmarked cars in many of these places as a new initiative even though Ben and everyone else in the room knew the same thing had been done for many years. The poor bastards who drove to Maryland to save ten or twenty bucks would be stopped and arrested as soon as they crossed back over the state line, their liquor confiscated and a big fine levied to boot.

Walker also talked about stolen product from the State Stores, licensed establishment raids and so on. He spoke confidently about the security of the warehouse systems and tried to take credit for that. Ben's ears pricked when he heard Walker state that enforcement would be reducing requests for warehouse audits so that manpower could be deployed to other problem areas. Ben immediately took this as a sign that audits were going to increase. Enforcement people were famous for trying to throw the staff off by stating one thing and then doing exactly the opposite. "I'm ready for you Colonel" Ben thought to himself.

It was good fortune that Ben's shipments to Arthur had slowed in September and October. The audit of the two Harrisburg warehouses came a week after Walker said they wouldn't happen. Ben's reputation for squeaky clean honesty, his brilliant inventory system that only he understood, and his mild and meek manner usually resulted in audits that were a breeze for him. Ben loved to tell the mystified auditors…low paid and under qualified civil servants…"Let me simplify this for you!" and then would give them the answers and results he wanted. As it turns out, even if an auditor would have wanted to verify certain damage or breakage numbers, Ben could always make the arithmetic add up just right.

He told Arthur this when they met a week prior to the next Robbins meeting for Arthur's regular pick up.

"I'm still waiting for official audit results but everything went well. We have a lot of inventory we can move, Arthur, if we get the orders, but if we have to keep things quiet for awhile, that's OK too. How is your family and the scrap business coming along? I hear from my brother that you have been doing a good job…too good they say; they were complaining that they had to "over pay" you for some things. Of course, I said nothing. I'm happy for you and keep raising your prices. My family will try to take advantage of you every chance they get."

"You know Ben, you are so much different from the rest of your family. I am very fortunate to have this relationship with you. You took a chance on me and our families have both benefited. We have found a way to be successful despite having some cards stacked against us. You know, if this LCB ever gets to be too much for you, we will still maintain our friendship. I know you feel the same way."

"I'll be there Sunday, Arthur. Make sure Claude has some extra help for the official work and you probably should have an additional truck available, as I expect a lot of transfers and shipments for the holidays. Might require your guys to work all the Saturdays, too. Good thing we wrote those double time pay provisions into your contract for Saturday, Sunday and holiday work."

"That was a very nice idea you had Mr. Cohen. See you Sunday."

30

"Chief, Sorry to call you this late at home, but we got a situation up on Christian Street." It was Lt. Hauser. "Colored guy up there just sliced up his wife; Fitzpatrick and Wilson are on the scene. They saw her before she got put in the ambulance and don't think she'll make it. We got the husband at the station; he's drunk. We just finished booking him and thought you should know."

"Things calm on Christian Street Hauser?"

"The two officers will be down here any time, but they reported by radio the scene is pretty much buttoned up. This happened in the kitchen of the home looks like. Patrolmen didn't report any trouble with crowds. It's pretty cold out, so that helped. There's a couple of kids and a mother-in-law in the home and the neighbors all seem to be helping out."

"Husband say where he did his drinking? What's his name?"

"Family name is Leland; Ronald L. He's pretty much out of it. Not sure he understands exactly what happened. We have the knife…big kitchen job, twelve inches maybe."

"I'll be down first thing in the morning, but call me tonight if you need me."

"10-4 Chief. I'll probably hang around until you get in. Good night."

Ernie put the phone down. Hauser would keep everything under control. Ernie was fortunate to have him as second in command. Hauser never complained when Ernie was hired over top of him. Hauser was a well regarded name in Steelton. One of the boys was the postmaster. The other a high school teacher who was also on town council. The three sons were active in little league sports, and many of the charities in town.

Ernie worried a little about where Leland got so tanked up. Arthur ran a pretty tight ship so he wouldn't allow a guy to get that drunk in his place, nor Bob's. If the wife dies, that's the first murder for the year for Steelton. Probably another funeral for Howard and another early Saturday morning at the station for me. Ernie's wife had been awakened by the call.

"Do you have to go in Ernie?"

"No honey. It's all right, go back to sleep."

"Trouble?"

"No, it's just the West Side."

Scrappy and Wallace were comparing notes as they made the return journey to Bethlehem. Wallace worked nine days straight through, he even went into the rail mill on second and third shifts two days. Scrappy gave him credit for dedication and hard work. Wallace made a couple of helpful suggestions to the PEP team but for the most part kept his ideas to himself. He constantly wrote into one of several spiral notebooks he always had in a large boxy cardboard- sided case he carried everywhere he went. Scrappy had taken him out to dinner one night, and had given him a full tour of Steelton. Wallace seemed particularly interested in the West Side and told Scrappy that he'd spent most of a full day walking every inch of Scrappy's neighborhood. Wallace had street maps of all of Steelton with principal buildings noted, but also technical layouts of power sources and lines, all utilities including water and sewer, rail sidings, everything. Scrappy was especially interested in an old report Wallace had on the flood of 1936, when fifteen feet of water covered the steel mill and most of Steelton. High water in thirty-six on the West Side was up to the second floor of most of the homes.

"Why all the interest in the big flood, Wallace?"

"In addition to my work on the PEP team, it's my responsibility to formulate recommendations to the executives when the decisions are made on capital investment."

"I understand that" Scrappy said as he braked for one of the many traffic lights on route 22. "That flood was twenty years ago, and everybody said it was once in a hundred year kind of event, with all of the ice jams on the river combined with that sudden thaw and heavy rains. I was just a little kid but I remember our own house had water in the second floor. Every place you go in Steelton has pictures of that flood."

"Risky to put a lot of money into a flood plain, Mr. Stone. Even riskier to live there."

"Well, it hasn't stopped Bethlehem during the eighty years there's been steel production on this site and it hasn't stopped the people from staying in the homes and neighborhoods they built."

"That was the past, Mr. Stone. I concern myself with the present and the future."

Scrappy was looking at three more days up at Bethlehem with their PEP group and thank God he wouldn't be seeing much more of Wallace. He planned to put in twelve hour days the next two days so that he could cut out around noon that Friday. He had a date with Susie, and Susie's parents would be in Pittsburgh for that weekend conference. He was certain Susie would find some way to get them plenty of time alone Friday and Saturday nights.

His schedule in Bethlehem did not fit with Bill and Cheryl Willis for dinner, but he was seeing them the following weekend after Thanksgiving. He did connect with Bill for an hour over coffee and doughnuts in the mining department that Friday morning. Bill asked about the project and Mark asked about Bill's work, and their house hunting. Scrappy was telling Bill about his time with Wallace and the work that Wallace had done in Steelton.

"You know, Wallace is one of Ledbetter's favorites. Guy is a working machine and smart. He probably kept everything to himself but Wallace is an M.I.T. graduate and has a master's too. He is assigned to a small unit that they call strategic planning. He gets lots of access to the very top men. The man has no personality at all, not married, no hobbies and the executives like that, because he has no feelings for anyone. It's all business and profits to Wallace."

"That all seems to fit, Bill. I gotta run. Kiss Cheryl for me and Susie and I will see you next Friday night. Give me a call once you get to Steelton and we'll confirm the arrangements."

Mark Stone guided the Rambler back to Steelton. Could this big opportunity for expansion at Steelton have any chance with a guy like Wallace in the mix? And if Steelton did win the prize, what would the effect of that expansion be? He thought about Wallace's map, his interest in the flood, and his walking tour of the West Side.

"This Rambler is a total piece of shit. No wonder they're going under."

The first thing Ernie heard when he got into the jail was the uncontrolled wailing of an anguished man who woke up and sobered up enough to realize what he had done the night before. Hauser had the preliminary report typed on the Chief's desk.

Mrs. Leland died before she got to the hospital. They had two kids, twelve and nine. Neighbors heard her screaming. She apparently tried to get away and collapsed at the front door, her pale green night gown covered in blood. Two neighbors got into the house and took the knife away from Leland, who was sitting in a kitchen chair. There was a half gallon of Four Roses and a quart of Ballantine on the table. Ernie's officers got to the scene in about ten minutes. Bill Schrauder, who lived half a block down the street and who was a medic in the war tried to help stop her bleeding. His officers handcuffed Leland and got him into the back of the patrol car. He was too drunk to give a statement. Ernie would take care of that, and then he'd go visit the family and talk to some of the neighbors. The justice of the peace would be in at nine, consult the officers, and complete the paperwork. Leland would be on his way to County by the afternoon.

The upper block of Christian Street was all colored. It was an odd street, Christian. The very lower end by Trewick Street was all colored on the east side of the street for about ten or twelve homes, then it was solid white all the way up to Conestoga, across Conestoga and past the alley where the Schrauder house was. The next three homes were white, and then all the rest up to the gas works were Negro.

On the west side of Christian near Trewick was a vacant lot that used to be used for parking when the passenger terminal was there for the railroad. Then there were a few homes, all with white residents, until the water works, which was a large pumping station and borough storage for all many of sewer and water pipes, cinders for the winter roads, and so on. From Conestoga northward, whites lived solidly side by side in the row homes until # 318 where the Kaufmanns lived. Next door to them was the Brown family, who were colored, and then Christian was colored again, solidly all the way to Franklin Street where there were homes on the south side, and a few on the north that backed up to the large UGI gas works. Steelton's most famous landmark was a giant round gas storage facility, maybe a hundred feet high, with a large red and white checkered pattern across the top twenty feet. This was to warn aircraft for the Capitol City airport, just across the river, and military aircraft using the Olmstead Air Force runways, situated alongside the Susquehanna down at Middletown. There was also a large power station, with oddly designed metal towers that stretched power lines across the Susquehanna.

"Mr. Leland. I am Chief Linta of the Steelton Police. Do you have anything you want to tell me?"

Leland sat on the edge of the chair in the holding cell, his head bowed. "No Sir. Just that I am sorry."

"All right, Mr. Leland. We have to keep you in here for awhile. You want water or coffee you ask one of the officers."

Linta moved back into his office and waved to Hauser. "Thanks, Mickey, for taking care of all of this. Do we know where this guy goes to church? I'd prefer to have a pastor tell him his wife is gone. See if you can arrange that, and call me on the radio. I'm heading over there to see the family. Let your relief know what's cooking."

The Chief's Plymouth pulled up to the Leland home. Several people were milling about and residents seemed to instantly pop out of their homes when a police car moved up the street. Ernie saw three men on the stoop where Mrs. Leland probably drew her last breath. The brick sidewalk was wet; somebody had most likely hosed the blood away.

"Good morning. I'm Chief Linta. Any of you gentlemen family to Mr. and Mrs. Leland?"

"I'm her brother." A middle aged man with a toothpick in his teeth said slowly.

"I've come to pay my respects. I understand there are children in the home, and Mrs. Leland's mother lives here too. Is that right?"

"The children been moved to my house" the brother said. "just up the street. My momma is in the living room here, but she don't want to see anybody."

"I understand that. Can you tell me, does the Leland family have a pastor or minister? I'd like to talk to the man if so."

"She sent the kids down to that Mennonite Church on Myers Street sometime. Ronald and his wife never went to church."

"Mr. Leland does not know that his wife is deceased. We have not told him. I usually like for a pastor or family member to convey that kind of news. I will follow the wishes of the family, but Mr. Leland is going to be formally charged sometime today. He will have to be told that his wife is deceased as he is facing charges. May I have your name, Sir?" Ernie asked the brother.

"I am Marcus James. Ronald was not a bad man, but sometimes when he drank too much he'd just be crazy. I ain't goin' down to tell him, I think you police better just do your jobs and tell him yourself."

"Do any of you know where Mr. Leland was drinking last night?" By now a crowd of maybe fifteen men and women had formed.

"He was up at Arthur's for a bit, but they threw him out. I was there. He was mad at the bartender up there for throwing him out, and I guess he came home and took it out on his wife."

"And who are you, Sir?"

"My name is Brown, my whole family live on this street; people know where you can find me."

Ernie looked across the faces that were looking up at him... brown and black faces every one.

"Thank you Mr. Brown. Ladies and gentlemen, I am truly sorry that you have to suffer this loss. If you will let me know when the family can see visitors, I would like to come back and pay my respects. Mr. James, maybe you could call me? Mr. Leland will be told of his wife's passing by me personally when I return to the station. If anybody has anything to add, anything you saw or heard last night, please call the police."

The Chief headed back to the municipal building. He patched a call through to Arthur through his radio.

"Mr. Howard? This is Chief Linta, Steelton Police. There was a lady killed on Christian Street last night. Have you heard about it?"

"Yes I have Chief."

"I will want to escort the funeral personally if the family contacts you for the services."

"A Mr. Marcus James already has. We will be handling all of the arrangements. I will call you about the Chief's escort as soon as I have the details."

They were always careful when on the radio. No mention was made for the next day's meeting at Robbins.

Tim spent the Saturday before Thanksgiving week with his dad – and just about every other resident of Steelton – up at Cottage Hill for the season ending Steamrollers and Williamsport rivalry game. Steelton, Williamsport, and John Harris High in Harrisburg each had one loss for the year in the competitive Central Penn league. The Williamsport ("Bill-Porters" to the Steelton gang) Millionaires were always a powerhouse team. Steelton prevailed 14-13 this year, and now the local fans just had to hope for a John Harris defeat in their annual Thanksgiving Day game against their rival, William Penn. After the game, all of the men repaired to their favorite watering holes to celebrate the big win. Most of them had hip flasks of their favorite bracer so they had a head start on the festivities. Most of the West Side boys piled into Yetter's Beer Garden.

It had been a good week at work for Tim, enjoying his three to eleven shift and his work on the PEP team. He was especially happy with Stone's pick of J.T. Squires, the union representative. Squires had been in final shipping for many years, which meant that he dealt with rails that were already QC'ed, fabbed if needed, bent or sheared and were ready to be shipped out to customers or other departments in the mill. Any scrap, rejects, customer cancellations, all of that steel was diverted before it ever got to Squires' department. This meant that Squires, who was very savvy and a dedicated worker, would have no experience or insight into the areas that provided most of Tim's products bound for Arthur.

When the latest inventory reports came out, Tim looked for the two remaining "ghost" gondola cars…they didn't show up anywhere. His time on day shift had slowed his shipments to Arthur, but the good news is there was a bounty of bad and lost steel scattered throughout the yards, and Tim spent as much time as he could getting it positioned to an area where he could load it onto rail cars for Arthur without attracting attention. He had all of his own records ready for the Sunday meeting.

Doris had Sunday dinner on the table right at noon. Two big dishes of what passed for lasagna in Steelton, two loaves of bread and some cut up ice berg lettuce with bottled Italian dressing. Harry had arrived about eleven and read the paper…Tim slept late as usual but came down the stairs a little before twelve.

"Do anything fun this weekend Harry? We missed you at the football game, helluva game, right dad?"

"We just need Harris to beat Penn, and we're league champs again. I'll probably turn the Eagles on this afternoon to see how they're doin'. You stickin' around Harry?"

"I might, dad."

"How are things at work?"

"It's pretty much more of the same. The boss there is trying to break a production record and a quality record at the same time. Everybody's a little on edge I guess you'd say. Several of the office guys wanted Friday off but the boss said no."

"How are things with the apartment" Doris wanted to know. "Do you need anything down there? There will be plenty of left-overs, I made two big pans."

"Thanks Mom…I got a little red wine down there, might go good with the lasagna this week."

Tim again, "Got anybody to have dinner with Harry? You never said how that Halloween party turned out. Still seeing the girl you took?" Doris' ears pricked up.

"She was very nice…has a good job down at the turnpike office. She's a college grad, too. It was a double date, nothing serious. Haven't seen her since; too busy."

The truth was that Harry had gone down to Bernardo Brothers pay phone last Tuesday and called to ask Patti out for this weekend, but she had other plans she said. He was hoping to try to catch up with Stone to see if there was anything he could learn from Patti's sister Susie. He planned to call Scrappy this week. He hadn't seen the Dale sisters or Scrappy at church all month, and he decided not to go this morning.

"I just wish you boys would find a good girl and settle down. You're both going to be old bachelors before you know it and no woman will want you. That Decker girl already found herself a man, that new butcher Kormy hired, so you both missed the boat there. Darlene was a nice girl, good family, I don't see what you two are waiting for."

"You're starting to sound like a broken record, Mom. I gotta go. Sorry I can't help with dishes, I'll make it up to you." Tim excused himself from the table and ten minutes later started up the Merc and took off.

"I'll take care of the dishes, Mom. I get plenty of practice these days."

"I know yesterday was a rough day, Dad, but we've got to go over these figures for this afternoon. I have everything ready for you."

"That's fine, Anthony. I didn't forget. Don't know where I'd be without you. Let's get started."

"First, for the family accounts. Lowry the tow truck driver dropped off his payment when he came in to see Cackovic about his taxes. He's paid through October. Weideman and Bernardo the same and that just leaves Lewis. He's paid through August but I haven't seen him since."

"That's OK, we know he's good for it. He gets busy with deliveries once the weather gets cold. Nobody wants to pay for their coal or oil until they need it. There is nothing like waking up in a forty-five degree bedroom to remind you to order your fuel. By the way, Peter handled everything perfectly for us in that Posetti situation. His dad would be proud of him."

"That brings us to Robbins. Revenues are down almost twenty percent on alcohol because of Sonny's lost accounts. The pick-up business at Arthur's, and shipping to his own outlets are steady. Arthur's kid dropped off the envelope for me along with some payroll tax stuff Arthur had for Cackovic; they had a real winning streak…a little over two thousand net in the scrap operation alone. We had just over two hundred profit from

Arthur's trash and trucking of Borough business. I have the shares calculated and I am holding back ten percent until we get a clearer picture of where the liquor business is going. Cohen is going to be nervous about inventory piling up at his warehouses."

"OK, Son, I want you to do a little more talking with the men tomorrow. I want you to start to play a bigger role in the meetings themselves. Explain the hold-back and the reasons for it. Let's try to get a clearer picture from Burger on what he expects for the next couple of months. How were his collections by the way?"

"His four accounts are steady. We will pick up some volume if that manager at St. Lawrence starts up his own bar, but then we have to worry about retaining St. Lawrence with a new guy. The Moose had a good month."

Ernie rubbed his eyes.

"Dad, you know we've done well for a number of years now that I have been working with you. The house is paid off. I make a good living. We have plenty of cash on hand. Maybe it's time to think about winding this thing down. I enjoy the work, it is important for me to do my part for you and Mom, but maybe that raid on Bob's last summer, this Sonny and Posetti business, maybe it's time to think about alternatives. And that's not to mention we still have an unknown with Arthur and his kid and that Parker boy."

"Anthony, I can see where you are going here, and I thought about it a little myself. But way back when I started some of these partnerships…Lowry and I go back to our childhood and our business relationship is at least ten years old now-same with Peter Lewis and his dad-I got into these arrangements because I wanted them to be durable, and because I trusted my partners one hundred per cent."

Anthony took a drink of his Coke. His dad wasn't looking

at him as he spoke...he was sort of looking off into the distance.

"When I started out as a Steelton cop, then those years on the Harrisburg force, a lot of guys supplemented their pay by taking payoffs or by letting something slide. We even had a code for it in Harrisburg, LOW money. The L.O.W. stood for 'look the other way'. Those guys – patrolmen and the officers too- took a couple of bucks here and there, maybe they ate and drank free in certain places where some kind of shenanigans were going on. I never did that. I always thought it was dangerous...some little guy gets nabbed, he blows the whistle, you're in big trouble. I wanted partnerships, where the other guy and me shared the risk but we shared in the rewards over time. If I could steer him some business, I got a piece of that...kind of like a commission, but always just enough, you don't get greedy. I wanted my part-ners to be profitable, and to find their relationship with me to be profitable for them, too. I wanted honorable men, hardworking guys in my circle, not some shopkeeper on my beat who gave me a free ham sandwich because I knew he was selling stolen bread. Take a guy like Mr. Lewis, he now has five trucks. They always have to double park for their deliveries, every coal truck in the state probably has fifteen broken or missing things a cop could write a ticket for. In Harrisburg, those kind of guys would get a bunch of tickets every month, and then have to scurry around to two or three different people to pay off to get 'em fixed. I figured, why not get out front of that. If I went to a guy like I did with Lewis and said, 'What would it be worth to you if you never had a ticket for any of your trucks? Wouldn't that be worth something to you?" Ernie paused and looked at his son. "I don't know how I got into all that. I want some discussion tomorrow on what we might do if Sonny wants to come back with something we can trust. And I'll need a couple of minutes alone with Arthur after the formal meeting…so maybe you can wait in the car for me."

"May I know what that's about dad?"

"I'll let you know after I talk to Arthur. Something hit me today, an idea, and maybe we can help ourselves and Arthur out with what I think is a problem with that big kid of his and our sports hero Parker."

31

Cohen sat in his Chevy with the motor running and the heater on. He had to sit on an old cushion that had an ugly green and red flower pattern so that he could comfortably see above the steering wheel. He always backed into the loading dock so that he could see who was coming up the abandoned road. "More potholes than the moon, that road" Ben thought to himself. Arthur decided to arrive in one of his unlettered green panel trucks and Tim soon followed in his Mercury, kicking up more dust and stones than Arthur did…not a smart thing to do, Ben thought. The last thing we need is any kind of attention back here. Tim and Arthur shook hands, and motioned to Ben. "Afternoon, Mr. Cohen" Arthur liked to exaggerate the formality of these business meetings. Arthur had a dress shirt and slacks, and a nifty sports jacket. Ben thought he looked like a Polish refugee in his thread-bare parka and woolen cap.

The three men entered the old shipping office that somehow felt colder than the air outside. "Our January meeting will have to be a quick one" Arthur said while he gazed out of the cracked and dirty window. "Here comes the Buick".

Nods all around and Ernie spoke first as usual. "We'll try to keep things moving since it's so chilly in here, but we've got to make sure we cover a couple of things thoroughly. Anthony has your shares and will have a couple of things he wants to say at the end of the meeting."

This sentence alone got everyone thinking because Anthony rarely said more than two sentences in any meeting no matter how much was going on.

"I thought I'd bring everybody up to date on the Sonny and Posetti thing. With Peter Lewis' help, Posetti is out of Steelton and out of our hair. His people took care of that. We shouldn't hear anything from him or about him. The money's gone for good, Anthony has written it off." With this, Ernie paused a minute and looked at Arthur. Anthony, Ernie and Arthur knew where the money was but no sense winding Ben and Tim up and complicating the meeting. "I think we need to talk a little about Sonny. He helped us out with Posetti, and took a pretty hard hit, not that he didn't bring it all on himself. I expect that at some point Sonny will come back with some sort of deal, what I'd like to know is how you feel about that. We would have to be sure that whatever he brought to us was air tight, and insulated from the Lombardi people and anybody else who might be watching Sonny."

Tim spoke first. "I don't think Sonny will ever be free from his big people. I thought he was a risk and I don't think we have to look any further than his trust in Posetti to prove my point. I think we're better off without him."

Cohen spoke next: "He moved products and we got a premium price at most of his accounts. Our choice is to find another way to fill that gap or just settle for less revenue. I can absorb the inventory on my end. What we need is one single customer who we trust who can take a significant amount of deliveries; deliveries that Arthur can make."

"My own businesses will take more over Christmas and New

Year's but then things slow down. There are some colored-owned bars in Harrisburg but I do not want to stray from Steelton. For one thing, we don't have the level of police protection we need. I think Tim has a point; Sonny will never be able to break free from the people above him. He also has a little lone wolf in him that does not fit with the rest of us. I say if he approaches us, we say no thanks. We don't make him angry, we don't hurt him. He knows too much about us and we need to maintain a good relationship with him…just not a business relationship with him."

Everybody was surprised to hear Anthony speak up. "I think we buy his friendship. He's probably hurting for money. I think we keep him on the payroll, maybe something small like a hundred a month to keep his loyalty. Enough where it really doesn't hurt us but is important enough to him to cooperate."

"Sounds reasonable. I'll find a way to get that message to him. We all OK with this?" Ernie looked around.

"We are losing a good piece of income and now we are increasing expenses, and an expense that doesn't generate any revenue. I don't like that direction, but I can go along with the decision" Cohen offered.

"Let me bring everyone up to date on the steel side. This big new project will not hurt us in the short term; I think my own supply to Arthur will continue about the same level. Over the next couple of years, though, there is bound to be improvement in these systems that track all of the raw materials, finished products, waste and so on. If I can't figure out a way to beat or trick that system, we will have a major shortage in my shipments. We do have one opportunity coming up later next spring: it's a contract year and people expect a strike come July. Some union guys start raising hell during contract negotiations, causing wrecks, purposely breaking equipment, hiding tools, that kind of stuff. There is always a big spike in customer demand the six months prior to the potential strike as customers try to build their inventories and get their deliveries before the strike. This combination presented a good situation for us in fifty-three and should again next year. The strike itself, if it happens and especially if it drags on, is bad for everyone. Plant security usually triples during a strike and the feds are called in to protect the railroads. Arthur and I do expect to try to convert two more rail cars over the winter, and that was good business for us."

"You know, Tim, those wheel assemblies on the rail cars have special alloy steel that Cohen's family was wild about. It killed them to dig deeper into their pockets, but they paid me a premium for them. Any chance you can just acquire the wheels so we don't have all of the expense and risk of stealing and cutting up the entire car? They make the wheels in Steelton, right?"

"Arthur, I can try to get down there at some point. It's a part of the mill I've never spent any time in. That department is down below the frog and switch area…let me see what I can find out." Tim offered.

The men went through the rest of their business. Anthony spoke at the end as his dad requested, handed out the shares and explained the ten percent holdback. Cohen didn't like it but said nothing. "Next meeting, last Sunday in January. Arthur, I've got something for you in the trunk of my car, and we need to talk about the Leland funeral arrangements." Ernie looked at Anthony who shook hands with everyone and then got into the Buick. Ernie and Arthur went back to the rear of the car and Ernie opened the heavy steel trunk lid. Inside, Arthur saw a large dark blue binder and a textbook. There were some pamphlets that had slid around in the broad trunk of the big Buick.

"Arthur, I have an idea. Just hear me out. I brought these

books for Charles Parker. We both know that young man has a good future if he stays with you, but I want you to consider something else for him. You have your sons to help follow you in the business. I'd like you to think about having Charles join me on the police force."

Arthur, who had perfected his ability to show no reaction or emotion in any circumstance, seemed shocked by what he heard. He just looked at Ernie.

"These are some materials I'd like you to give him to begin his studies. Those pamphlets are things I saved from my own orientation on the Steelton force, and then with the Harrisburg P.D. The binder is the official publication for what rookie patrolmen need to know to pass the entry exam. The book is the basics of civil and criminal law written for the police officer. I have had two new patrol positions approved by the Borough Council. Charles is tall, athletic, and his high school sports career gives him a head start I think. He has learned a little about professional behavior thanks to you, and he has been around some stressful situations, wouldn't you say?"

Arthur didn't say a word.

"And I have a couple of other reasons, Mr. Howard. First, it wouldn't hurt our little enterprise here if I had a patrolman I could assign to any sensitive cases or situations that might affect us. And last, I believe it is time for Steelton to have a Negro on the police force."

Arthur ground his back teeth. He turned his head to watch Burger and Cohen drive out of the Robbins lot.

"He ain't no Jackie Robinson."

"And I don't want him to be…except Mr. Robinson needed tremendous strength to do what he did, and he needed someone higher up to support and defend him. Charles would have that with me. You know his character better than I do, does he have what it takes?"

"Let me think about this. Let's talk about it after the funeral Tuesday."

"Will you take the books?"

Howard cleared his throat: "I'll take the books."

32

It was the Monday of Thanksgiving week and Bob Hernley stood at the rear of the office that Harry shared with the foremen and waited for the remaining staff to file in. He glanced at his watch twice in a thirty second period. This was the first appearance Hernley made in the office in well over a month. He had been working twelve hour days but rarely said anything to his people...preferring the company of his two student interns. All of his communication came through Karl Long, the general foreman. Harry had not had so much as a nod from Hernley since the Halloween party and Harry kept his distance when he saw the Hernleys at church.

"Purpose of the meeting is to give all of you a status report on our production and quality numbers. Since I launched our new enhancement program, we are two percent above the highest daily tonnage production rate that goes back to fifty-two. We don't have good production records for the time before the long strike. QC rejects are down about eleven percent during the same period. We need to keep on the pace through Christmas week to give us the best production and quality quarter the open hearth has seen. We are going to continue twenty one shifts per week schedule until New Year's. We will evaluate our production plans at that time, although with a potential strike next summer, we can all expect high demand through at least June. Any of you expecting to request vacation time between now and New Year's, I will try to be reasonable but don't expect every request to be approved. In order to keep variable expenses down, I will not be approving any overtime unless it's an emergency. Send your requests through channels to Karl Long. Any of you who have worked furnace shutdowns, particularly back when some of you may have been in union jobs, see Karl. Our personnel files that existed before I got here are in worse shape than the production records. We are building a skills inventory of experienced hands as we expect furnaces will be scheduled for orderly shutdown in anticipation of the strike. If we don't have a strike, we will do re-bricking and major furnace maintenance in July. Any questions? Good. Thanks for your attention."

Melton was sitting next to Harry. After Hernley and Long left the office, Melton complained to Harry. "We long service guys are used to having some time off around Thanksgiving and a lot of us take two weeks over Christmas and New Year. Sounds to me like I better get my request in now."

Harry saw an opportunity. "Mike, if you get a solid two weeks off, who does your job? Any chance you could teach me more about it? Maybe I could fill in and build my own experience. Hernley might go for it if I could prove I could do both jobs in a pinch."

"I'd be happy to work with you on that Harry, especially if it helps me get my vacation Okayed."

"Can you run the idea past Karl Long? If Hernley knew I was the one asking for this he'd reject it on general principles."

"How did you ever get so crossways with him, Harry? You did a good job on that project and as far as I can see you do a good job as pit recorder. You're here every day, you even put in off the clock time, don't bitch and moan…I don't get it."

"Mike, it's because of my work with Scrappy Stone. Hernley thinks I am reporting everything that happens down here to Stone, and that Stone is looking out for me with Willis. It ain't true. I haven't seen or talked to Stone in maybe a month. If you want to know the God's truth, Stone encouraged me to listen to and learn from Hernley. Somehow the situation just got out of control."

"Allright. Look. Come over to my desk around two. We'll spend a little time together and then set some time up every day if we can. You sure your own work won't slip?"

"Mike, truth be told I could probably get through everything in four or five hours a day. If the union guys on second and third shift did a better job in their log entries and stuff, it could go even faster. As it is I spend a couple of hours most days trying to figure out what happened and how they logged it for the previous two shifts. Mondays are full time though, 'cause of all the weekend entries…the shift foremen try to do their best on weekend and second and third shift, but they have other priorities."

"Tell me about it!" and Melton headed toward the coffee pot.

Harry got his time with Melton and some of what Melton did every day was familiar to Harry because of last summer's Stone project. That afternoon after work, Harry decided to stop into the St. Lawrence Club for two beers instead of following his usual routine where he went directly to his apartment for his post work beer and smoke. He knew a couple of guys at the bar who were nursing shots and beers. Somebody had played some rock n roll on the juke box, a recent and not entirely welcomed addition to the selection of polka bands and old standards. He was enjoying his time in his apartment and relished the independence and freedom it provided. He didn't mind the cooking and cleaning, his TV brought in four stations most of the time. He slept well. Between Doris and Peggy's mom –who took in washing and ironing and lived just up the street- laundry wasn't a problem either. He thought he'd miss women and dating more than he did. In his weaker moments he'd still swoon over the thought of Cindy Hernley, but he'd soon come back down to earth. He thought back on his night with the Dale sisters and Scrappy. He enjoyed being at the management club as much as he did Patti's company. He'd still like to see her again, but he'd have to work that through Scrappy he thought. He ordered his second Schmidt's and lit up a cigarette.

His money had been holding up OK. He spent more of his savings than he wanted to on getting some stuff for the apartment. The everyday cost of things he took for granted at home, not only the food but cleaning products, toilet paper, that sort of thing, it surprised him how much money that took. He had been counting on at least a little overtime pay to help out but that was not in the cards…nor was a car anytime soon. Tim said he could use the Mercury if he wanted it, but that just didn't seem right to Harry. There was no doubt that not having a car would cramp his dating opportunities, not that he had the spare cash to spend entertaining the kind of girl he hoped to attract. He couldn't imagine Patti Dale –who had a nice car of her own – dating a guy who didn't have wheels.

Harry walked the few blocks up Front Street and turned up Locust at the bank. He heard the satisfying sound of the dead bolt turn and walked up the steps to his apartment. He fished around the ice box and heated up some Doris leftovers. After the dishes, he stretched out in bed and clicked on the Bakelite that was tuned to 1460. He flipped through a couple of old comic books that he kept by his bed. The radio was turned off, the alarm set.

33

Harry had Thanksgiving off, Hap had Thursday and Friday, but Tim had to work the full week, three to eleven. Doris grumbled all through the morning, worrying about the vegetables and cursing her unreliable oven. She told Hap three times that she was getting a new oven before Christmas come Hell or high water. Hap got into the whiskey a little earlier than normal. Doris wanted dinner on the table at noon so that Tim could have a comfortable meal before heading off to work. It was a drizzly day, not too cold for late November.

Harry offered twice to help Doris in the kitchen but he quickly realized he was most helpful by staying out of her way. He did set the table for her, got out Hap's best carving knife, and opened the half gallon jug of wine Tim had brought home that was stored out on the back porch. Harry poured himself a water glass full and decided to join Hap in the front room.

"Well, Dad, a pretty good year overall wouldn't you say? Work is steady, we had a nice fall, everybody seems to be in pretty good health. I'm really feeling good about the new year coming up. I think Ike will win another four years in next year's election, and outside all of this Communism business, I don't see us getting into any shooting wars anytime soon."

"I guess, Harry. I don't think about that stuff. You suppose your Mom will have the turkey ready by twelve?"

"I think you better be shopping for a new oven unless you want cold cuts for dinner all winter."

"She's just in one of her moods. Everything always works out. She burned one of the punkin pies a little last night and that set her off about the oven." Tim came bounding down the steps, dressed for work.

"Wish I could join you for a drink. How's that wine Harry?"

"I wouldn't know good from bad. I guess it's OK. Sorry you have to work today, Tim. I'll pay for it tomorrow with the back-log but I'm glad to have the day off. I suppose you'll have a lot of guys calling in sick today?"

"The usual guys who loaf around anyway....better off without most of 'em. It's OK. I've got a routine down for my guys on holidays. I got a case of TastyKakes for 'em, and I tell 'em at the beginning of the shift that I'm happy if everybody works safe and stays awake. I don't push anyone. Most of the guys have a big meal before they come in so it's a major accomplishment just keeping everyone awake." Tim was thinking mostly about how quiet it will be and his plans to get the two gondola cars positioned to be moved the next day. He'd have one of his crane operators load one of the cars with about three tons of rusted rail he discovered two days ago that had been missed during last physical inventory. "Yep, kind of a sleepy shift; might get a snooze in myself."

The father and sons shot the breeze about nothing in particular until Doris yelled for them to come sit down. There was no prayer of thanks, just the silent passing of plates steaming with vegetables and potatoes, with Doris giving Hap advice on how to carve the turkey. Three hours after they sat down Tim was at work, Harry and Hap were asleep in the front room, and Doris finished putting away the dishes.

Tim mustered the thirty or so men who showed up for work. "OK men, listen up! I know most of you had a big meal and would rather be home with your families. Let's work safe today. Just take things as they go; we don't need to break any production records today. And don't forget the double time you're making by working the holiday; that will come in handy when you are shopping for my Christmas present. I got something for everybody at lunch break. I want to see all three crane operators for a couple of minutes before you climb up into your cabs. Anybody need anything special come see me in the office."

Tim had a couple of reasons for getting the crane operators aside. For one thing, he would matter of factly point out some old rails that had been "written off as scrap" that he wanted put into the gondola cars he had positioned on the north siding of the rail mill. Second, Tim had been thinking about his PEP project and wanted his bridge crane operators' opinion on an idea he had.

"Charlie, I want you to handle to gondola loading. Let me ask you guys, if we extended the supports and track, could we put the old maintenance section up by Trewick Street and the railroad to good use? I was looking at some old records, and that area was used by the Pennsylvania Railroad at one time for the passenger terminal and small station. It closed down in the mid thirties. We could use extra rail storage space but we'd need crane access."

Mike, one of the old timers, spoke up. "I was runnin' the crane when we first took that over. The maintenance guys just started using it, filling it up with old or broken machinery, supplies, that kind of thing. They also put those two picnic tables up there…there's a cool breeze in the summer so they took their lunch breaks there. I often wondered why we didn't use it for rails, especially when we are jammed up like we have been the last year or so. No reason why the crane couldn't extend to there. The other guys can speak their piece but it would help us because we are always scramblin' for storage."

"OK. Thanks Mike. That's what I thought. I'm going to work on that."

"You'll get a grievance from the maintenance guys if you try to move their picnic tables, you know."

"Yeah, I figured, but I have an idea about that too. The union wants this PEP project to work out as much as the Company does, there's a lot of jobs in the balance. If I can tie our plan into the PEP program, those picnic tables won't be such a big deal."

"Tim, the millwrights sleep on those tables too, you know. I can see 'em hiding in there. Just a heads up."

"Got it Charlie. Now you guys be extra alert for the men on the floor. Half of them look like they could fall asleep standing up today. Any of you see anything unsafe, you have my OK to stop everything. Just let me know."

Tim went back to the foreman's office and wrote out a request to see Pat Patterson Monday at shift change. He also put a similar note into Stone's mail slot, asking to meet with Scrappy to go over his ideas for improved work flow and storage expansion as part of the PEP.

Scrappy's Thanksgiving started in the main office on Swatara Street just after six in the morning. The security guy was the only other person in the office. His project was moving along well and he need both days remaining this week to get December off to a good start. He would have Monday after Thanksgiving at Steelton but then he was needed up at Bethlehem for the rest of the week.

He had been surprised at the level of efficiency, and the solid quality of the rail mill at Steelton. This was no doubt the result of the much newer and better designed equipment and machinery that Steelton had, a distinct advantage over the other company rail production centers. The principal issues surrounded special orders, customer or credit holds, custom steel formulations that some governments and especially the military required. When standard steel rails in standard lengths were demanded, Steelton's production could not be touched. Scrappy had his attention on system approaches to sorting out these special situations.

His rail mill PEP team was working well together. Pat Patterson, who Scrappy thought might be resistant, was in fact a big help. J.T. Squires, the union rep, knew more about the back end of the rail process than any management guy did. The only weak part of his team was the lack of trained data processing talent, an issue Scrappy intended to review with Willis in his briefing Monday.

The day flew by and before he knew it, it was nearly three. The Stone family would all be together at his grandfather's house, just a few doors away from his parent's home on Conestoga and it wouldn't do for Mark to be late. He waved to the security officer on the way out to his Rambler, the big "U" placard in the windshield.

Mark's mom had roasted the turkey at their house and Kenny carried it down the few doors to their grandma's. All the best old china was laid out. The old man said a prayer before the meal. The talk at the table covered all of the usual subjects, and everybody seemed to have a sense of satisfaction and well being. The tradition was for the three sons to do all of the clean up for their mom and grandma, except for the washing of the best serving pieces. Scrappy's dad and grandpa went into the front room to smoke their cheap cigars.

Scrappy took the opportunity to sit with his family the whole evening. He could have gone down to the St. Lawrence, where they opened at six, or maybe given Susie Dale a call, but he enjoyed listening to the conversation, having a beer with his dad, and helping straighten out the kitchen. Listening to his grandpa, who was on his fourth or fifth highball, was always the highlight of the day.

"We've had a lot of Thanksgivings in this house, and we've been damn lucky that most of 'em have been good. We've been able to put food on the table, and we all survived the wars and depression. I think back to thirty six, and how some of us wondered if we'd ever get back to a normal life. Every family on the West Side suffered through that flood, but I don't think any of them ever thought for a minute that they'd live anyplace else. Once the water, and the ice, and the mud went down, we were all back in here cleaning up and working to fix our homes. And it was more than the building, it was the family. It was important to get our roofs over our heads so that our kids could get back in their beds. We were one of maybe twenty families living on the second and third floors of the elementary school, no light, no heat. Men would work on their homes and then work on the school. Same as the mill. As soon as we at least had our homes to the point we could live in 'em, we all went back and helped the mill get back on its feet. That was our livelihood. That steel mill needed us and we needed it. One can't live without the other, and we all depend on one another. We've had the strikes and our disagreements that's true. But everyone knows in their heart that we are all in the same boat, and we trust each other to do right by the other. That's what makes Steelton different."

There were a few more people in the main office on Friday, but none of the senior people. Stone continued his work on the PEP and headed over to the rail mill just prior to shift change to check up on the first and second shift team members. He had his date with Susie and Bill and Cheryl set for the Old Stone later that evening, and reminded himself to be out of the mill by five.

Tim was getting his crew started and came back to the foreman's office about three-thirty. He was surprised to see Scrappy sitting at Patterson's desk, and a large set of drawings set out in front of him.

Scrappy looked up. "Hi Tim. Got your note. Pulled out these drawings to see the area you're talking about. Show me on the layout here what you're proposing and then let's go out and have a look."

Tim was happy to see Stone's interest but concerned that, if he hung around, Tim's plans to get the train engineer to move the gondolas up to Arthur's might be delayed.

"This area is almost a thousand square feet of yard space, but we stack rails up to twenty feet high. It's essentially unused now. The maintenance guys can get their junk out of there. I'll need some engineering help to figure our design and cost, but a couple of years ago we did a new sixty-foot section of bridge-crane tracks and supports and the whole deal was done in two weeks. It may not directly help the PEP project, Mark, but it would give us additional capacity and could help prevent some of the confusion we experience now when we are busting at the seams with inventory."

"Tim, when we have finished product that we can't ship right away, like a credit hold or a customer requests a delayed shipment, we don't have a designated area for that do we? That product just gets mixed in with everything else, right?"

"Well, Mark, not mixed in. But there's no special area or designated storage if that's what you're asking. Sometimes that stuff is on hold for months at a time, and that hogs up some of our best space…where we have fastest access. I didn't think about it, but yeah, a designated area for something like that would be good. Let me ask a couple of the guys on the floor and my crane operators about that…I'd like their opinion too."

Stone liked this about Tim. Very few of the management would ever consider listening to a union man's opinion, and here was Burger seeking it out. "Yeah, good idea Tim. Let me know. Incidentally, you know the main opportunity for Steelton in all of this is to get more rail production capacity. If you are busting at the seams now, where would all of the new equipment, machinery and product go?"

"Well, Scrappy, Jeez, I don't know. I guess we could push out east toward Front Street across the parking lot; we own as far as the alley but that would take out all of the employee parking plus we'd have to have all of the S&H rail tracks under roof. Can't imagine all of that diesel smoke in the building. Also can't see all those businesses on this side of Front Street welcoming the mill directly behind them, a lot of them use that alley for customer parking and deliveries….and there's apartments on the second and third floors of those buildings. People wouldn't get much sleep with the mill twenty feet behind them."

"Yeah, I can see that. OK Tim, get your hard hat and let's go take a look."

Scrappy spent the rest of the work day looking and listening. He motored down to his Highspire home to shower and get ready for his date. He was picking Susie up at six thirty and as he went out of his front door a little after six he realized he hadn't washed his Ford. The Rambler was full of crap for work. He slid into the Ford and took a deep breath. It smelled a LITTLE like fish, but not a lot. After their romantic weekend last week, Scrappy was hoping Susie would be in a forgiving mood.

The Old Stone Inn sat just back from Route 230 in Highspire. It had been a private mansion at one point, the limestone for the structure coming from the quarry in Steelton just a few miles away. Bill and Cheryl were waiting for Scrappy and Susie in one of the back booths, cocktails already in their hands.

"How was Thanksgiving, Susie?" Cheryl asked. She wore a pretty red and white dress with a black patent belt and shoes.

"We had a nice time. Dad roasted the turkey. Mom's not much of a cook. It was just me and Patti. Dad did open a couple of bottles of French wine somebody had given him and that was delicious. Patti and I made a pact to learn more about wine as a result…so I think I'll have some tonight. How's the house hunting going?"

"It's a little slow with the holidays, but we saw a really cute home just about fifteen minutes from Bill's work, and on the west end of town so we are a little closer to Steelton and upwind from the smoke. It's affordable but needs a little fix up, but nothing Bill can't handle. His dad said he'd pitch in too, so we are thinking about making an offer. It's a nice neighborhood, and the elementary school is brand new, just two blocks down the street. Great for kids when they come…you and Scrappy would love it!"

It was subject changing time for Scrappy. "We don't want to bore the ladies with work talk, but maybe you and I can get a few minutes after we eat, Bill?"

"Sure Scrappy. But you're not getting off the hook. It's a full court press to get you up to HQ and to Lehigh. Cheryl and I are team-mates on this one!"

Susie thought to herself "I'll have something to say about that."

The dinner went well with Susie ordering a bottle of white

wine with a French label. She had no idea what it was but every-body seemed to enjoy it. Conversation was full of Steelton, Beth-lehem, the upcoming holidays, their families. The check came and the couples decided to have an after dinner drink in the agreeable bar. The girls paired off to one side, the boys the other.

"I'll be up there Tuesday through Friday next week, Bill. I want to get some more time with Wallace. He's a pain in the ass but I think there's a lot I can learn from him. Also, in your mining group, do you have any decent people in data processing and anyone with experience in some of these automated processes we're looking at? I need help at Steelton, at least two more guys."

"Not in my group but there's a guy in Scranton where I worked –single guy named Brian O'Connell. Really smart and a college grad from King's. He's a native of the coal regions and wouldn't want to move to Steelton, but I bet he'd volunteer if you asked for him. Things can get slow in the middle of the winter at the quarry sites…he might be bored there. Look, I'll call him Monday. I know him; we worked together on a couple of things. You'll like him…he has a few beers now and then but he's a hard worker. I'll set it up for you."

"Thanks, Bill. Oh, and one more thing. As a friend, I've got to ask you and Cheryl to slow down on the me-and-Susie moving business. We had a lot of time together last week. She loves her teaching job and her dad is about to set her and her sister up in their own place. I honestly don't see her moving out of Steelton. I don't see marriage in the cards anytime soon, so maybe you can whisper in Cheryl's ear, please?"

"OK, sure Scrappy. I understand. Cheryl will not like to hear that, though. She's a little lonely up there, and she and Susie get along so well. And Cheryl knows how you and I are like brothers. I think we'll end up buying this house, and that will keep Cheryl's attention. We get settled in with our own place and my work continues to go well, I expect we will be trying to have a baby."

"I'm really happy for you Bill, but I have to get my own path settled here and I've got my hands full at work until spring. Let's try to catch up next Thursday before I head back to Steelton. And anything more you can find out about Wallace and his work, let me know."

"OK, Scrappy, I will. Guess we better get back. We've got an early start for Cheryl's parent's place tomorrow morning."

The four of them said their goodbyes in the parking lot. Scrappy looked over to Susie, who was staring blankly out of the passenger side window.

"Do you want to stop at my place for awhile before I take you home?"

"Not tonight, Scrappy."

34

It was a proper day for a funeral. The wind howling up the steel gray river could have chilled the bones of the dead. Snow aimlessly spit through the air. Mrs. Leland's mourners filed slowly into the church, her children with their uncles and grandmother, who had to be braced under each arm, her new pink shoes barely touching the floor of the sanctuary. Arthur's staff was dressed in their best white suits, Charles driving the hearse in his white tux. Arthur was in a navy pinstripe, a red carnation matching his bright crimson necktie. The Lelands were not very well known, and not regular church-goers, so the church was maybe half full, and just about everybody walked to the church as they had no cars of their own. Arthur's staff made a couple of trips from his funeral parlor on the West Side to give a lift to the older women and men… probably the only time they had ever been inside of a Cadillac.

Ernie Linta and his wife Marie entered the church with Mickey Hauser and his wife. Both men were in their full dress uniforms. Ernie would lead the procession up Lincoln Street to the cemetery. Mrs. Linta would ride at the rear of the motorcade with the Hausers. Ernie had seen to it to have one of his patrolmen and a cruiser ready at the entrance to the Howard Day burial grounds.

Ernie noticed a few white families in the pews, the Schrauder family and most likely some other neighbors. There were eight or ten members of the Steelton Mennonite Mission in attendance, the place where Mrs. Leland had sent her kids to Sunday and Bible School. The Mennonites were unmistakable, the men in their high collared plain suits and the women all in black with their black hair coverings.

The service itself was a short one; some hymns by a small choir, a solo, and a short message by the pastor. There was no eulogy. The pink-toned casket was wheeled out of the church and into Arthur's waiting hearse, where Charles Parker and Arthur's son Claude helped the pall bearers load the coffin into the Caddy. It was a short ride up Lincoln Street, a narrow one way street that dead-ended at the top of the hill at the entrance to two cemeteries…one black and one white. Baldwin, the white cemetery was on the left; William Howard Day on the right. It was important to Ernie to let all of the colored people of Steelton know that the police force was with them, and that a Negro life ended in a violent murder was just as valuable as a white life lost in the same way.

A short service of committal was performed at the grave site. As Arthur helped as many people into his cars as he could, Ernie approached him. "I can take two people in the police car and Lieutenant Hauser has room for two also." Arthur went off and came back with three elderly women and an old guy with a cane. Arthur and Ernie had a moment alone after the pastor shook hands and Arthur handed him an envelope.

"Think any more about Parker?" Arthur nodded. Ernie waited.

"I'll talk to him later today. I'll give him the books to look at. If he agrees, I will also talk to his momma…he don't have a dad at home. He's man enough now to make his own decisions about his life. I'll let you know what he decides."

"Thank you Arthur, but if he decides he wants to try for this, have him call me direct. You can let me know if he says no, but if it's yes I need to hear him say that to me himself. Charles and I are going to have to build an understanding. This is not going to be easy for him or for me, but it's worth doing. You have my word that I will keep you informed of how he is progressing...Lieutenant Hauser and I will help him with his studies. We should have him ready for his exam by February."

"Are you going to stop into the Leland's house now?"

"No. Hauser and I have to get back with our wives after we drop these people off."

"I'll see you at some of the Christmas events, Chief."

The two men looked one another square in the eye as they shared a firm handshake.

Arthur walked into the Christian Street home of the Lelands. The downstairs was full of people but everybody quieted down when Arthur walked in. He nodded and said his hellos, and worked his way back toward the kitchen. Marcus James, the brother of the deceased came forward and thanked Arthur for the fine service.

"Have something to eat and drink Mr. Howard. There's plenty."

Arthur noticed the tables full of food. He didn't see any beer or liquor, though. "This is quite a spread, Mr. James."

"The neighbors brought food and we received some baskets and trays from the people at the Mennonite Church. Mr. Howard, I know you probably came to get the rest of what we owe, but we are going to have to ask you for some time. Me and the family, we are good for it, if you can be patient."

"Let's step out onto the back porch, Mr. James...can I call you Marcus?"

Arthur and James moved out into the back yard, a small covered area that was next to what used to be the outside toilet.

"Marcus, you pay me when you can. I already took care of the ambulance people and the hospital…they will not be sending any bill to you on account of the way your sister died. How is your momma and the children?"

"The kids just don't know what to do. My wife and our little girl are going to move in here. We will get by OK."

"Do you work, Marcus? Do you have a steady job?"

"No Sir. I pick up some money fixin' people's cars, and the small motors on their boats. I help out the Chambers down by the river in the summer. I tried the steel mill for the labor gang and I hope they will call."

"What kind of education do you have?"

"Mr. Howard, we all just came up from Alabama a couple of years ago. I finished ten years of high school. I can read and write good, and I know my numbers and sums."

"All right. You stick by the phone over the next couple of days; I have your number. Keep that suit and tie you have on clean and ready. I'll see what I can do."

"Mr. Howard, I work hard. I ain't afraid of dirty work, and I know your jobs in your scrap yard is hard work, but if I get a chance you won't be sorry."

"You just stick near that phone. I have to be going. You take care of your family. Mrs. Howard and I are sorry for what has happened to you."

"Mr. Wilmot, Mr. Howard is here for your ten o'clock meeting."

Arthur was escorted into the gas company's operations manager's office.

"Hello, Mr. Howard. Good to see you again. Your message to

my secretary said you wanted to talk about Mr. Leland?"

"Thank you for seeing me on such short notice Mr. Wilmont. Yes, partly about Leland…my company handled his wife's funeral yesterday. Mr. Leland is in county jail with no bond. I came to see you about a couple of things that maybe you can help me with."

"Mr. Howard, I remember how you benefitted the gas company with that access road over through the north end of your warehouses there by Front Street. That gave us a second emergency exit for the gas works here as you know. Very important to everyone's safety."

"Mr. Wilmont, Mr. Leland is not going to be coming back to work. I want to help his family. He had two young kids and his late wife's mother is in poor health."

"What can I do? We have not terminated Mr. Leland's employment, but it is just a formality I guess."

"Can you see that his final paycheck, and any vacation he might have coming gets delivered to me. The family has asked me to handle it for them. Also, with Christmas coming, if there's anything the gas company can do a little special…maybe make sure the family gets their holiday turkey, that sort of thing."

"Of course. I will take care of it myself."

"There's one more thing Mr. Wilmont. With Mr. Leland gone, maybe you have a need for someone to replace him. His brother in law, Mr. Marcus James, needs a job. He will be taking care of Mr. Leland's kids plus he's got one of his own. I can vouch for Marcus. He's a hard worker, a strong young man. Lives just a block away from here. It would be a wonderful thing if you could find a job for him."

Wilmont paused. It was likely he'd need another favor from Howard at some time in the future…and he did need another laborer. "I can't help with any of the craft or skilled positions, they are union. I can find a place for him in the labor pool, though. Pay is decent and has some benefits. Have him come up here tomorrow morning and ask for me. He will need to fill out an application and take a physical…can he read and write?"

"He assures me he can. I also understand he's good with engine and motor repair. Thank you, Mr. Wilmont. I'll vouch for him…you have any problem of any kind, you call me and I will straighten it out. I'll have him up here first thing tomorrow morning."

"How is your business, Mr. Howard…the tavern I mean? I stop in there for lunch most every Friday for a fish sandwich."

"Business is good…here, take one of my cards. When you're in there for lunch, show this card to the bartender or cashier. You ever stop in for a drink after work?"

"Well, uh, I'd like to but I have a wife and four kids at home, so I usually head right home after I'm out of here. If I do have a drink, I'll have it at home with the Missus."

"I understand…where do you live? When you have a drink, what do you like?"

"I live on Sycamore Street in Harrisburg….thirteen hundred block. I like a cold beer like any other guy, but my wife and I enjoy a Seven and Seven when we can. With four kids, though, well…"

"I got three of my own, Mr. Wilmont. Thanks for your time here today. You call me if you have anything come up that I can help you with."

Arthur called Marcus once he returned to his office and told him to report –in a suit and tie – to Mr. Wilmont the next morning. Then he called in his son Claude.

"Get the address of a James Wilmot, thirteen hundred block of Sycamore Street. Take a half gallon of Seagram's Seven – the legitimate stuff we buy from the State Store – up to him this Saturday afternoon. Get your Momma to wrap it like a Christmas present. He'll know who it came from. And ask Charles to come in here when he's done cleaning the cars."

"Good morning, Harry!" George Clark smiled and Harry noticed George had on a heavy woolen coat for the first time this winter. "Expecting a snowstorm there George?"

"The Company provides these topcoats for a reason Harry. We're out here exposed to the elements for eight hours a day, not like you big shots sitting in the cozy warm offices drinking coffee and smoking cigarettes. How's everybody holding up in there?"

Harry walked over to George so they could talk instead of yelling. "I can tell you Christmas can't come fast enough. You got to admire Hernley, though. We'll probably make his goal and I've got to say, no one puts in more time than him."

"I hardly see him, Harry. The night shift guy tells me he gets in five or five thirty every morning. He's here on the weekend, too. You expect to get any time off over Christmas and New Year's?"

"Nah, I didn't ask. I'm way too junior. I offered to cover for Melton so that he can get his vacation in. Well, see you George, stay warm."

Harry punched in and headed toward the coffee pot. He saw a smiling Melton stirring some evaporated milk into his cup.

"I just saw Hernley. He okayed my vacation. I told him you could cover for me and that I had been training you. God forbid you screw anything up Harry, so let's spend the next week or so going over everything again. I also think we should get some time with the second and third shift foremen and make sure they know what's going on. If they would just pay a little more attention to the production sheets the hourly guys fill out, we'd all be that much better off. And by the way Hernley expects you to get everything done on your regular job too, no overtime."

"Don't worry Mike. It's our job to make Hernley look good. Maybe we finish up this year end push the way he wants he'll gain a little more confidence in us. That's what I'm hopin' for anyway."

After two long days at headquarters with mostly uncooperative people Scrappy welcomed dinner alone in the hotel dining room each evening. He'd taken to having a couple of glasses of wine with his meal, something he found quite agreeable. He'd have to thank Susie for that bit of enlightenment. He thought about Wallace, who had uncharacteristically shown some enthusiasm for Scrappy's invitation for dinner the next night; Wallace offered to pick him up and take him to his favorite German restaurant. Bill Willis had come through with the connection to the O'Connell guy in Scranton, and Scrappy had that meeting set up for tomorrow. He still needed one more technical guy to help him with the big machines in the basement of the Steelton main office, but his request for the guy he wanted from Bethlehem was turned down flat. Information about the HQ PEP was also slow in coming…made Mark wonder if they were all working for the same company. Bill's information was that it was in fact more competition than cooperation that the top guys at Bethlehem were driving. He'd find out more when he met with Bill for coffee tomorrow.

Stone also had his status meeting set up with Bill's dad for next week Friday, who told him not to be surprised if Mr. Stevens showed up for part of their meeting. The only part of Mark's schedule that seemed to be uncertain was this upcoming weekend; he and Susie had not made any plans at all. "Probably good to take a little break" he thought as he signed his dinner check.

35

"If you need any help with the menu, Mr. Stone, just ask; you may not be familiar with these German dishes." Wallace had secured a quiet table in the brightly lit and bustling restaurant.

"We have a pretty good Pennsylvania Dutch influence in Steelton, so I should be okay. The wiener schnitzel sounds good."

"Do you like wine, Mr. Stone? Perhaps a nice Riesling with our meal?"

"I am just starting to acquire a taste for it…I would be happy if you could contribute to my education."

Scrappy's plan was to try to build some trust with Wallace and to learn more about the strategic planning group he was a part of. He was on guard and expected Wallace to quiz him as well.

"I understand that you are in a group called strategic planning…we have nothing like that in Steelton. How is your department connected to the PEP projects in the different plants?"

"Well, Mr. Stone, it is something new. Just a few of us are there. We have the responsibility to think about the long term… five, ten years out. We try to anticipate the needs of our customers, the trends in the industry, and our capacity to meet the anticipated customer needs. We expect that automation will be critical to our competitive situation; therefore the PEP initiatives. Are you pleased with how things are going in Steelton?"

"I need more technical help. The operating and manufacturing components I have covered. My requests for temporary staff for the next couple of months have been turned down by the headquarters people. We have no local source for these skills in the Steelton and Harrisburg area."

"Yes, that is a restraining factor for Steelton. But those people might be recruited and then assigned to Steelton if your facility comes out ahead in this program for the rail mill investment. There are many other factors to consider for the approval of capital; these decisions are complex."

"That is another thing Mr. Wallace. We do not have the area for a significant rail mill expansion for the volume of production and storage that will be required should Steelton be selected as the site for this capital investment."

"Yes, I know Mr. Stone. Your current available space is locked in by rail to the east and west, and the existing operations to the south. Plant expansion is a challenge for Steelton. I have studied it. But I have something important to ask you. It is something personal if I may?"

"About me?" Wallace's question caught Stone off guard.

"About the way you work." Wallace eased his chair a little closer. "It is important for young executives like us to recognize our talents and strengths, but we also need to know where we need improvement. I have the education, and the engineering and technical skills, and I am fortunate to learn difficult concepts very easily. But I have trouble with people Mr. Stone. You have seen this yourself first hand. I cannot easily build these relationships…especially with employees who are very different from me. That, Mr. Stone, is a skill that you possess. I will reach a point in my career…perhaps sooner than later…where this weakness of mine will limit my growth. I would like to learn more from you and how you do this. Your PEP team, for example. You selected a union man for the team. I would never have thought of that. You get on well and receive cooperation and ideas from the working supervisors and the blue collar workers. I will have to learn how to do that if I want to be a leader in my field."

"It is not something I work on, Wallace. It comes naturally."

"Naturally? How?"

"I don't know. Maybe it's just the way I was raised on the West Side."

"Ah, your beloved West Side. There has to be more, Mr. Stone."

"I listen to people. I do not judge them. I try to find a common ground. I try to get people to see that all of our interests are the same when I can. I find if people think you are genuinely interested in them and their well-being, they will open up. On the two PEP programs…the open hearth and now rail mill…I first explained how our success will make life and work better for the individual involved. People generally act in their self interest as you know. I try to think of us all as equals. I expect that may be a basis for you to start if you are genuine in your question."

"Well, Mr. Stone, to be fair, I need this skill to advance my career, so I suppose you could criticize me for being selfish. But I am trying to make our Company successful and to increase our profitability, and that will mean more jobs and better pay and working conditions for all concerned."

Scrappy finished his wine. "Maybe, Mr. Wallace."

"We will be working together over the remaining two months of the respective PEP programs. I will be grateful if, from time to time, you could point out mistakes I make with people, or perhaps share some ideas with me to help me improve."

"I will do that, Wallace. I will need help from you, too. And now, with your permission, I need to get back to my hotel. I have another long day ahead of me. I liked the wine quite a bit."

On the drive back to Steelton, Scrappy would think back to all he had accomplished during the week, but his conversation with Wallace stood out. They were two very different men, but Scrappy knew he needed more of what Wallace possessed if he was going to be a success at Bethlehem. He also needed to finish his degree. Wallace needed him; that was clear. And then there was the conversation about plant expansion for the Steelton rail mill. No room to the east, west, or south. The only expansion available was to the north, but that was all residential. It was the West Side.

"I've studied that." That's what Wallace had said at dinner. Scrappy thought back to Wallace's walking survey of the West Side, and all of the maps he had…his questions about the great flood of thirty-six.

Scrappy tried to coax some heat out of the Rambler. "What a piece of shit this thing is" he said aloud.

"That should do it for this trip, Ben. We've also completed all of the warehouse movements you needed. Overall, we've done okay without Sonny's clubs. I'll have one more pickup prior to Christmas, and then one between Christmas and New Years. Same day and time?"

"Yes Mr. Howard. That will be fine. We have been fortunate. After that, I will not see you until the end of January. You can tell Mr. Linta that the audits here all came out perfectly, and I am not picking up anything about enforcement activity targeting Steelton. I have a very reliable man over there now."

"I will do that Ben. What do you hear from your family at Central? We delivered a very large shipment to them last week. The steel shipments have more than made up for the lost liquor accounts."

"I do not hear much, but our families will all be together over our holidays. Good bye Mr. Howard. Drive carefully."

"See you next time Mr. Cohen."

Tim's work on the PEP turned out to be much more fun for him than he thought. He had the opportunity to work on some new things. His proposal to take over the maintenance area for more rail storage gave him the chance to work with some engineers and to see how a capital request was handled down at the big office. Approval of the proposal looked promising.

His shipments to Arthur went smoothly, not one question about the two missing gondola cars; the third one would go to Arthur in January. Things were humming on the three to eleven shift, production demand continued to be high. His men were working safely and picking up some overtime. He enjoyed a good relationship with Pat Patterson, who had been the man who originally selected Tim for his promotion to foreman. Tim thought that Pat must be looking good to Willis and the others in taking a chance on such a young guy who seemed to be turning out to be one of the best supervisors in the department.

Tim bought a new oven for Doris for Christmas. He was pleased with himself. His life was just humming along and he saw no reason why things wouldn't just keep getting better and better.

36

The Main Office Christmas tree was decorated with the same garland, tinsel, lights and balls that had been on its predecessors for the past ten years. They were purchased after the end of the Second World War, and the fake wrapped "presents" underneath the tree were the same, too, stored fifty weeks a year in the boiler room of the Main Office. A nativity scene was in the same condition, but brightly lighted at the top of the marble stairs just outside the steel front doors. Scrappy bounded up the steps, choosing to walk the ten minutes from the rail mill instead of wrestling with the Rambler. He was immediately shown into Bob Willis' office.

"Be right with you, Mark. I read your reports and just need to send this quick memo out to be typed. Were you offered coffee?"

"Yes, Bob, but I've already had about a gallon, been up since five."

"All right, now look, Stevens is going to come in here in a bit. I have given him a synopsis of your report, but he wants to hear it from you direct. He also wants to know if we have any stumbling blocks or problems facing us. He and his wife are heading down to Florida for two weeks and he won't be back 'til after New Year's. Give it to him straight, just like you wrote in the report, especially about the lack of help from headquarters up in Bethlehem."

"I understand, Bob."

"And by the way, Mark, before Stevens gets in here, how are things with you and that Dale girl…you buy her a ring for Christmas?"

"Uh, no Bob, I didn't. Things have cooled off a little between us."

"COOLED OFF?" I didn't know that. My son didn't tell me. It's not ended is it? Who decided to cool things off?"

"It's just kind of mutual. Honestly, Bob, I got enough on my mind with this project and running back and forth to Bethlehem in that piece of shit Rambler you gave me – its God damned heater doesn't work by the way."

"Mark, you know you're pretty much like another son to Nancy and me. That Dale family is one of the best in Steelton, and her old man is damned important to the plant here. The turnpike just had several million in new bonds approved for road infrastructure and we have a meeting with Dale when Stevens gets back to make sure we secure that business for Steelton. We don't need a pissed off father if he thinks one of my best guys jilted his daughter. And what's wrong with her? She's pretty, family has money, certainly nothing wrong with her figure that I can see… and she's got a college degree and a good teaching job. I…"

Just then Stevens strode into the room. "Morning Bob, Stone."

"Good morning, R.M." Scrappy stood up and shook his hand.

"All right, this PEP status you wrote, am I right that things are going well from our end but we've got a problem with sufficient staff on those data processing machines? And HQ is not helping, that it Stone?"

"Operationally, we are exactly on track. My team is on top

of everything. There is insufficient staffing for the operations on the machines down in the basement. I stole a guy from Scranton mines and he started last week – good man named O'Connell. I tried to get two additional guys from HQ who had some training but my request was denied. There is no local talent that has any experience in this. I've contacted the State Labor office and the Harrisburg Chamber of Commerce. Skills like this are just beginning to be developed. I even checked out Mechanicsburg and Olmstead to see if there was anybody in the military doing this kind of work. Automation is brand new and anybody with any kind of IBM or similar training is hard to find. It's one of the two main issues that could keep us from being successful."

"Two?" Willis interjected. I only read one in your report. Something just come up in the last day or two?"

Scrappy thought to himself, "Well, here goes."

"The second major issue does not have to do with our project itself. It has to do with our rail mill capacity. If we are successful in this, and the Company makes the major investment for expansion you have been looking for, we have no place to expand. The rail mill is hemmed in on all sides, key railroad tracks and lines east and west, the rest of the plant operations to the south, and the residences of the West Side to the north. Even if we win this competition for the capital, we would be constrained by lack of expansion space."

Scrappy looked into Willis' eyes and then he took in Stevens' expression and posture. Stevens spoke: "We have the strategic planning guys in Bethlehem looking at that. We anticipated this. Your job is to get this project done right and on time. Don't worry about final implementation. Get us the information we need and support your conclusions and recommendations with the facts. I'll call Ledbetter to see if we can pry loose the personnel you need. We have any major problems, get a call to me, Bob. Stone, there's a lot riding on this for all of us; you've done well and you are the best guy to lead the PEP. I'm personally counting on you, and Willis here is too."

With that Stevens turned and left and it was a full two minutes before Willis spoke.

"Mark, let me know if there is anything I can do. Listen, on your staff shortage, how about those two guys who worked with the first PEP in open hearth? One of them we just hired… a pit recorder."

"You mean Harry Burger? No, he did well for me but he has no data processing experience. He couldn't help us on this….I need someone with technical knowledge. Besides, Hernley is on his production campaign and would shit a brick if we tried to yank someone away from him. Hernley already thinks I'm out to get him for some reason."

"All right. Just a thought I had. Yeah, Bob's on the warpath, but he's doing a great job down there. And by the way, sorry about jumping on you about Susie Dale. It's a personal matter, I know, but I'll say it again, but I really hope you and Susie get things patched up. You two make a helluva couple and I know my son has been looking forward to being best man. Hey, did you hear they got a house? Should know about the mortgage before Christmas. When are you back up to Bethlehem?"

"The Wednesday after New Year's for three days. If I don't die of pneumonia from that God-damned Rambler."

Ernie and Herman Klein took their customary table at the management club for their pre-holiday meal. Things had been going well for both men, and Herman in particular was in high spirits.

"Chief, my family can't thank you enough for getting Klaus into the position at that Italian Club. He is so happy, and he is working very hard. My wife now has her daughter and grandkids in our home, and what a change! It was just the two of us in that big empty house…now we have kinder laughing and crying and lots of laundry to do and big meals at the main table. I am in debt to you. Do you hear from your man there, are they happy with Klaus?"

"Marie and Anthony and I have been in twice for dinner. The manager, Cantore, is thrilled. The food is good and Klaus has put some good sausages on the menu. I am happy to have helped."

"After my beers, we are going to celebrate with a nice bottle of red wine…something Italian for you, Ya?"

"That would be wonderful. How are things at the mill…and your budget…all OK?"

"Things are good. I have a nice budget for next year…they are planning on another strike of course. I have a good staff and as you probably know our business is very, very strong. And you, Chief? I read about the murder, that black man cutting his wife. That is most unfortunate. I do not think I could handle such a thing."

"It was very sad. I can say also that my budget requests went well, I have been able to add new patrolmen, and can promote now one of my best men to Sergeant. And, Herr Klein, this may shock you, I have hired my first Negro police officer. He is in training and is doing well in his first weeks. I hope to be able to swear him in next month. My second in command, Hauser – you have met him - is a strong man, very good. He could easily have been made Chief back when the Council selected me. I feel bad for him that his career is probably at its top."

"I see, Chief. And for you, do you see that your career is also at its top?"

313

The question took Ernie by surprise. "I don't know Herman. I have not thought about that. I suppose that it is. I do not see Marie and me leaving Steelton, and my son Anthony lives at home. I must say, he has no interest in the ladies, it is all work for him. He is a good son, but shy. So I do not see him leaving home any time soon."

Their dinner plates had been cleared and Herman was about to dig into a large chocolate dessert. The Chief had his coffee and an anisette.

"I have something I would like you to think about Chief. I am not fond of working through another labor strike. Nineteen fifty two was a nightmare…and then again shorter but still trouble the year after that. I will be sixty-five next year, and I am thinking of retiring."

"That is wonderful for you Herman. I hope that you will stay in Steelton."

"Yes, of course, now with my daughter and grandkids thanks to you. And now, please: I am thinking that you would be a good candidate to replace me when I go."

Ernie could not believe his ears. This was one time when his training failed him, as his face betrayed his reaction. "Replace you? I am not qualified. I am not…"

"It's Christmas time, Chief Linta. We think about our families and we enjoy our homes and our lives. Then comes the New Year, and we think about our future. I ask you just think about your future. You said you have a good man, Mr. Hauser, who can replace you. I have no such man. It is a failure on my part. But you could do it. I would stay with you for a few months to help with your training. Just think about it. Your future would be much brighter with Bethlehem Steel, I am certain."

"Herman, it is a great compliment. It is totally unexpected."

"Let us enjoy our coffees. We have another dinner in a month or so, yes? I will call you to arrange it."

Christmas came on a Sunday and Yetter's was a quiet place on Christmas Eve. Only the old, the singles and the drunks found their way to the bar on Myers Street. There were maybe ten guys at the bar, not a woman in sight. Buddy himself told everyone he was closing by ten, and Harry ordered a last Schmidt's as Buddy reached up to turn the TV off…a sure sign that he meant it.

"We hear you are getting a color TV Buddy. Would be great to see the Rose Parade and Rose Bowl game in color." It was one of the Coleman boys from down at the end of the bar.

"Maybe next year. The only way to afford it is if I raise beer prices. That OK with everyone?" Buddy barked as he opened himself a quart bottle of Ballantine.

Harry had his Christmas shopping done. Two tickets to the big New Year's Eve show at the Moose for Hap and Doris, plus a new electric coffee pot for their kitchen. He bought Tim a navy blue wool sweater from Fromm's that Doris wrapped for him. He planned to get over to the house by ten the next morning to open the presents. He had a brisk walk down to Locust Street and had another beer at his kitchen table. He turned the radio on to get the Christmas music and smoked the last cigarette of the evening. The steam heat in the apartment kept the place nice and warm, and Harry cracked his bedroom window a bit even though it was in the low twenties outside. It was a clear, crisp night with no snow in the forecast. "All the kids getting new sleds for Christmas will be complaining about the lack of snow," Harry thought.

Doris had scrambled eggs and bacon ready for the men. Harry and Tim helped with the toast and coffee. Hap read the

Sunday paper. Hap had a small tree in the corner of the front room that he reluctantly helped decorate. Doris had Tim and Harry's old red Christmas stockings tacked to the side of the fireplace mantle. Inside the stockings would be the same crummy chocolate candy bars and jelly beans Doris had been putting in them since they were little kids. The presents were opened, the coffee finished, and breakfast dishes cleaned and put away by eleven. Hap had a CC and water around noon, a precursor to the inevitable nap to follow. Doris was headed up to Louise's house to see their tree and all of the nieces and nephews.

"The Saint Lawrence will open at one today, right after church, Harry. Let's take the car down and have a couple of beers. We haven't seen much of each other with me working three to eleven and you down at the apartment."

"Don't you ever get a day off, Mike?" Tim asked Mike Jamnov as they entered the bar, which was rapidly filling up.

"I have a day off scheduled next Fourth of July Tim" Jamnov said without much of a laugh. Kitchen is not open, and I'm the bartender too today, so what'll it be?"

Tim and Harry drank their first beers pretty much in silence, and after the second round came Harry asked about the PEP project at the rail mill.

"It's going real well. You were right about Mark Stone, Harry. The guy is as sharp as they come and a real pleasure to work with. I had an idea about converting some unused maintenance space to rail storage, and he got behind me and I found out a couple of days ago the big office okayed it. Turns out they had extra money left over in this year's budget. Engineering had the drawings and we're starting the new rail supports for the crane extension right after the first. I expect to stay on swing shift for a while, business is really booming. My guys are getting all the overtime they want. The PEP project is to be completed end of February, so I don't see myself getting any time off 'til then."

"All that work must be killing your social life, Tim"

"You know, Harry, I don't miss it so much. I still get out but I just don't have the time for what girls want. I mean, you have a couple of dates, you get 'em into bed, and then they want to get married. Screw that. And then you have all of this yelling and they get pissed off when they find out you're moving on. Who needs that? And how about you? I never hear you talk about a girl."

"I've had a couple of dates. Did like the girl I took to that Halloween party, but I don't think I'm her league. She was a college girl, worked in an office job down at the Turnpike building. I see one of the waitresses at Rea and Derrick once in awhile, that's about it. I think the kind of girl I'm interested in might be out of reach for me."

"Look, Harry, if the car's a problem use mine anytime. Give the turnpike girl a call…maybe try going out for an afternoon drive instead of a regular date. Take her down to Hershey for a nice lunch up at the Hotel. It's high class….women love it."

"Well, maybe I will after the first. We have just a couple more days before the end of the year until that boss of mine Hernley gets his gold medal. You know, I've tried everything I can think of to work with that guy and give him what he wants. I learned a second job so that one of the guys I work with could get his Christmas vacation in…so I'm doin' two jobs with no overtime. I tried to pick up some engineering knowledge to impress him. You never get a thank you or any kind of appreciation. Stone says I need to put a full year in the open hearth before trying for another position, I hope I can last that long."

"Can't Stone help you out, Harry? I don't like relying on other people for help myself, but seems like you and he have a good relationship."

"There's a limit to what he can do. He's helped me in a lot of ways. He's got his own fish to fry…big job, a steady girl, and now he's up in Bethlehem a lot of the time. I don't see him when I go to church anymore. You see him every week, don't you?"

"Just about. I told you he helped with that idea I had. We had a good talk a couple of weeks ago about the rail mill, and how we don't have the room to expand. He seemed worried about that for some reason. He's a funny guy. He is easy to talk to and to work with, but there's a point at which he just clams up. You can kind of see he's thinking hard, but you got no idea what he's thinkin' about. You can see the wheels turnin' though. Maybe he'll be in here later today for a drink."

"Tim, let's have one for the road and get back to the house. Doris will have the big dinner ready if she figured out how that stove you bought her works. Figure I'll have lots of ham left overs for my own dinners this week. What do you have going on for New Year's Eve?"

"There's a pretty big party at Catalano's that night club on the West Shore. Ten bucks admission, buffet dinner, a band, champagne at midnight. Couple of my friends will be there. Lots of single girls. You wanna come along with me?"

"Too rich for my blood, Tim."

"I'll pay. C'mon, it will be fun."

"I don't want to cramp your style. Let's get going. Hap will raise hell if we're late for Christmas dinner."

37

Bob Hernley had two general staff meetings set for the first Friday of the New Year…one at six thirty in the morning for the night shift foremen and crew, and one for three o'clock for second shift. All of the day turn men could choose their meeting, as there were quite a few more of them. Harry and Melton took the three o'clock session, although by then they had pretty much heard Hernley's story. Fourth quarter tonnage new record set and quality control rejects and returns also at a record low. Hernley uncharacteristically thanked everyone, including all of the union employees, but then naturally said that he couldn't see why the first quarter of fifty-six couldn't be even better. There was an audible groan from many of the men. The meeting lasted all of ten minutes.

Melton turned to Harry: "Harry, I really want to thank you for taking things over for me. It was good to get away for a couple of weeks. I know it wasn't that easy for you."

"It all went OK Mike. The foremen pitched in. The days were pretty packed but the time flew by, plus I enjoy learning new things and you taught me well before you went out. I figure everything I can add to my experience and knowledge will help me reach a management position someday."

Melton thought this over for a minute. "Harry, things come slowly here...they go a step at a time. You know, I really enjoy working with you, but maybe you should think about whether the steel mill is the best place for you. I think you've done a very good job, but you want things to happen faster for you than you're probably going to get here. Look around you....how many guys here –not just the union guys but everyone else – has been in the same job ten years or more? Most of 'em."

"My brother made foreman after just a few years in the union. I know he's the exception, but since the war I think the country has changed, and there's more opportunity. I think back to what things were like just before I went into the service...that was less than four years ago. Everybody now has TVs, clothes washers, new stoves and refrigerators, people get new cars, some people are moving off the West Side because they can have a better life somewhere else. Maybe I will have to go find another occupation to get what I want, but I'm going to keep tryin' my best here. Hey, Hernley's coming our way."

"Afternoon Mike, Burger. Enjoy your vacation Mike? Burger here did a good job filling in for you."

"Jeez, thanks Mr. Hernley" Harry could hardly believe his ears.

"Thanks for the time off, Bob. Harry and I are right back at it, though."

"Good. This is a strike year. Customers are going to want deliveries ahead of any work stoppage and the Company will be building inventory in rail, pipe, re-bar, structural, everything. We still have to keep our eye on costs though. It's all hands on deck 'til the summer."

The next day Harry walked down to Bernardo brothers with Patti Dale's phone number in his pocket. He was taking Tim's advice and it worked. Patti agreed to have lunch with him the following Saturday…Harry would pick her up at noon for the drive down to Hershey. That gave Harry time to arrange for Tim's car and to try to get to talk to Scrappy Stone to see what he could learn about the Dale sisters since last Halloween. Then he walked up to the house to catch Tim, who enthusiastically heard that his advice was taken, and that Harry was successful.

"By the way, how was New Year's Tim?"

"Harry, you missed a great night. There were a lot of Harrisburg and West Shore girls there. I got a date tonight with the same girl I took home last weekend. Get this: she's Jewish! Lives up above Division Street. I'm taking her to the Canton Inn. You have really got to listen to me and get out of Steelton to find the kind of girls you want. If this turnpike girl works out, maybe we can double-date."

"Have you seen Scrappy Stone? I'd really like to catch up with him. I called his house down in Highspire but no answer."

"I'm pretty sure he was in Bethlehem all week…maybe stayed there over the weekend. I heard they had some snow up there yesterday."

Stone had in fact stayed over in Bethlehem, but not because of the snow. He spent Saturday in the office and then visited Sunday with Bill and Cheryl Willis, hearing all about their new home. Neither Bill nor Cheryl said a word about Susie Dale.

"Gentlemen, please be seated. Before the Borough Council members come in to be introduced to you all, the Chief would like to say a few words. Chief Linta?"

"Thank you, Lieutenant Hauser. I am very pleased to take the opportunity for the first time to speak to our entire expanded force at one time. Thanks to you officers who worked overnight last night for coming in, when I know you'd rather be at home sleeping. I want to recognize Sergeant Michael Karmilov, whose promotion became effective January one. Mike has been with the force for six years, and our additional staff has allowed me to create the new Sergeant's position. I also want to welcome our four newest members of the team, Patrolman Anthony Maloney who has joined us with two years' experience on the Middletown force, and officers in training, Adams, Burkhardt, and Parker. All three of our trainees will be sitting for their qualifying exam at the end of the month, and we all wish them well. I also want to mention that we will be taking delivery of two new patrol cars in the next few weeks. We are just waiting delivery to Farina Motors, and then the outfitting with the radios, light and siren kits and so on. You will also soon be meeting another member of the Hauser family…a young man named Patrick. His father is known to many of you as the Postmaster and he will be joining us in a non-commissioned role supporting Lieutenant Hauser. This will free up the Lieutenant from some of his administrative work to concentrate on detective level assignments. I have also asked the Lieutenant to help prepare a five year manpower plan for the Steelton Police Force. And now, we will be bringing in all of the members of the Borough Council, to meet with you and to wish you well."

After the meetings and the drinks and snacks were served, Ernie returned to his office to check his messages and two caught his eye. One was from Hermann Klein, requesting a return call and scrawled on another pink "while you were out" slip: "Mr. Robbins called. Asked you to return his call; no number provided." For this one, Ernie would wait until the end of the day, and would use the phone booth down inside Bernardo Brothers. He liked the idea of showing up there unannounced once in a while anyway to keep the Bernardo brothers on their toes.

"Sonny, Chief Linta. What have you got?"

"Thanks for calling back so fast, Chief. Everything is OK…I got some news. I'm getting married and movin' down to Philly. My girl's family has a corner store on the South Side, and I'm going to help run it. They take a little action on the Philly sports teams, so maybe I can build that up a little. Anyway, I'll be out of your hair and I guess you won't need to be handing me any envelopes anymore."

"That's some news. I wish you the best Sonny. Good luck with the marriage."

"Well, they say third time's a charm, right? I got one more piece of news for you…maybe help you and the team there at some point. Remember that LCB enforcement guy? The big bald colonel named Walker? He's been givin' some of my associates in Harrisburg and Reading some heartburn with his raids and unreasonable attitude. We finally got to a guy who's now on our payroll and who's on Walker's staff…knows every move he makes. Turns out, Walker-who's a happily married man with a wife and daughter in high school over in Carlisle- has his secretary set up in a sweet place in the Riverview Apartments…eighth floor. His out of town trips he tells his wife about usually end up at the Riverview. Secretary's name is June Murphy…may be of use to you someday."

"Thanks Sonny…and look, if you're still here we have our regular meeting last Sunday this month. We'll have an envelope for you. Come a half hour early though so we can get that part of it out of the way."

"Thanks Chief…if I can make it I will."

"Good luck Sonny. Watch your step down there in the big city."

* * *

The rail mill PEP team was assembling in Pat Patterson's office and waiting for Mark Stone. Tim had come in a couple of hours early for the end of week meeting. Everybody was bullshitting about the weather as a big snowstorm was being forecast for the weekend.

Patterson spoke up: "While we're waiting for Stone, and since we have everybody involved here, why don't we get a quick update on the bridge crane expansion project. Tim, what's the latest?"

"The engineering guys had some existing drawings; turns out the original design was for the crane to go the full width of the yards, no one knows why it didn't. We've had the labor gang getting the foundations ready and the cement and so on is ordered. We just need the maintenance guys to get all of that old equipment out of there and we can start ground prep."

"Tim, I don't have anybody to move that shit out of there." It was Mahoney, the general maintenance foreman. "My guys are already pissed off about losing the picnic tables and anyway that's unskilled work and not covered by my guy's classifications."

Tim thought about this. There was a lot of value in those old machines…their motors full of copper wire and who knows what else. "Who owns all of that stuff anyway? Is it on anyone's inventory? Any of it any good or able to be repaired?"

Mahoney again: "If it could be repaired my guys would have fixed it. Some of those old rail benders have been sitting there six or seven years. I think all of that stuff has been written off as obsolete."

Tim saw dollar signs. "I'll help everyone out. I'll get my labor pool guys to clear all of that out and arrange for it to be hauled away as scrap. Mahoney, you know your guys could put their picnic tables down behind bay twelve…it's a little more quiet down there and the space is heated for the most part. You want me to have the tables sent down there?"

"Yeah, yeah. I'm expecting a grievance over this but that may take a little of the bite out of it for the guys. Let's do that."

Scrappy came in with his briefcase and a guy Tim didn't recognize. Scrappy said his hellos and got right down to business.

"This is Brian O'Connell. He's helping us with all the punch cards down at the office. He's from Scranton and agreed to give us a hand until the end of February. I brought him along to have him explain a couple of small changes in the coding process that you are using and also a small change in the color scheme of the order tickets…I think both of these changes will help us, and best of all, will make your jobs here a little simpler."

The meeting ended just before shift change at three. Tim collared Scrappy just as he was rushing out the door."

"Good to see you, Mark, I know you're in a hurry. My brother Harry's been trying to reach you. He asked me to give you the message when I saw you."

"OK Tim…I can't promise when I'll be able to see him. He get a phone in his apartment yet?" Tim shook his head no. "I'm bouncing back and forth between here and Bethlehem…I'm up there again all of next week. I used to see him at church some-times but I haven't been there in quite a while. You can have him call my house Sunday afternoon; that's his best bet. I'm working in the big office all day tomorrow."

Tim got busy with his labor gang on the maintenance area machinery. He'd walk up to Arthur's bar after his shift and get a message through the bartender that he needed to talk to Arthur. Since everybody at the plant knew about the scrapped machines,

Tim could be open about having Arthur's dump trucks come to pick it up in broad daylight and deliver it straight to one of Cohen's family yards. Tim was heading back to his office and saw Patterson heading out, on his way home.

"That was very good work with Mahoney, Tim. Good job all the way around."

"This is a nice car, Harry. We should have used this one Halloween instead of Scrappy's fish car."

"Thanks, but I'm afraid it's my brother's, not mine. I'm still saving up for one this nice."

"I see," Patti said as she looked out of the passenger side window. They exchanged some small talk as they went down the Hershey highway toward the Hotel. The skies were threatening. Harry had been to Hershey Park many times but had only seen the big hotel on top of the hill from the park below. Tim had given him specific directions and they pulled into the parking lot about twelve thirty. The hotel was not busy, and they were shown a nice table by the window in the big circular dining room.

"This is really a nice idea, Harry. Thank you. I love this place." She ordered a glass of white wine; Harry had a beer with his lunch. "Have you brought other girls here for lunch or dinner, Harry?"

"No, this is the first time I've been here. Been to the park many times of course. I really don't date much, to be honest with you Patti. I was a little surprised you said you'd see me for today. I had hoped to see you in church some Sunday to ask you out in person. I really enjoyed our night at the Management Club…I think Scrappy and your sister had a good time, too."

"My sister and I go to church only when our parents make us go, usually just special occasions. They don't attend as regularly as they used to. Speaking of church, have you seen Scrappy Harry? Has he been in church with his family? What has he been up to? You two are friends aren't you?" Patti looked down at her plate when she asked about Stone.

"Yes, we worked together on a big project. He's been very good to me, but I haven't seen him much for maybe the past two months. Haven't seen him in church since the day we all met. He has been on a big assignment and is up in Bethlehem a lot, but I guess you know all of that."

"Yes, I've heard. So you haven't really talked to him since Thanksgiving?"

Harry thought the question a little odd. "Maybe once at the St. Lawrence…I really don't remember. But your sister would know a lot more about him than I would."

"Yes, Susie and I have been so busy with our jobs and the holidays we really haven't had much time to talk about him."

Harry was not the most sophisticated guy in the world, but that just struck him as not believable…he figured sisters share *everything* between them, certainly their love interests.

"How's Susie's teaching coming along and how is your job at the turnpike?"

"We're both working hard and saving our money, too. My dad is helping us buy a house near Susie's school; it's under construction now. We might be able to move it by June."

They looked out of the window as the first flurries flew by. "Harry, I'm really enjoying myself but perhaps we should head back. When you picked me up my dad said it was snowing really hard in Pittsburgh and it was heading this way."

They got into the car and the snow was picking up. "Thanks for seeing me Patti, do you think I can call again?"

"Harry, I do enjoy our time together as I said, but I have been seeing a guy. It's not serious but we've been going out for a couple of months. He's a science teacher at Susie's school. He and his parents live here in Hershey as a matter of fact…he has an apartment just off Chocolate Avenue."

Harry kept his eye on the road. "I understand. I probably never had a chance with a professional girl like you anyway. I really appreciated Scrappy introducing us, and good luck with your teacher friend."

"Harry, you are a gentleman. One thing I like about you is your nice manners. You will find the right girl. We are not that much different from men, you know."

"That's news to me." Harry said, trying to force a laugh.

"No, what I mean is, it's clear you are working to make a better life for yourself. Susie and I saw that in you and Scrappy said the same thing. Times are good, and people our age are not satisfied to do just what their parents did. Susie and I were lucky to be able to go to college, and now we might have our own house. We both have careers. Our work is as important to us as yours is to you. And we want things to be better in every aspect of life…material things and our personal lives."

"There are some things I can change about myself but some things I can't. I can't change where I was born. I can't change what my Dad does for a living. I don't think I will ever be a college man. Maybe I've set my sights too high."

"Don't say that Harry. This is nineteen fifty-six. The sky's the limit for us. You'll find the right girl, and she'll be a lucky lady too. I really believe that. Well, we're here. Thanks for a nice lunch Harry; don't bother getting out of the car…you should probably get your brother's car home before the snow starts piling up." She leaned over and gave his a kiss on the cheek.

"Did Harry have any news on Scrappy?" Susie had been

pacing the living room waiting for her sister to get home.

"Not a word. Hasn't seen him or talked to him. Harry's a nice guy but that was not a fun lunch. I felt like I was taking advantage of him. He's so sincere. You really owe me for this. You want to get back together with Mark, you have to do it on your own."

38

Sonny was waiting at Robbins when the big black Buick pulled in. Despite the cold, he was standing beside his car, a station wagon, so that Ernie would not get concerned about a strange car in the loading dock. "New ride, Sonny?"

"Yep. Has come in handy for all those trips down to Philly. Heading back down there right after we finish here."

"Anthony has your last envelope. Thanks for the info on Walker. I had my contacts verify what you told me. His name's on the lease, the whole deal. You want to stick around, say good bye to everyone?"

"Nah, better to just take off. Tell everyone I said goodbye. You get down to Philly, look me up." The men shook hands. Sonny thanked Anthony for the envelope and got into the station wagon and drove out through the gravel road.

Cohen showed up at Robbins in his old Chevy, with Arthur and Tim close behind. They all hustled in to the freezing office. Cohen spoke first.

"We had a very good couple of months, Mr. Howard and I, both from the liquor side and my family's scrap business. Everything is OK at the LCB, too. There is a high supply of inventory I can ship, but it's no problem for me to hold onto it…after all, everything is where it's supposed to be, if you know what I mean? I'm the only one who knows where everything is."

"Mr. Cohen is being too modest. He has helped me with the prices we are getting from his brothers and father. We had a lot of legitimate shipments including quite a bit of overtime and premium pay days for the LCB shipping under our contract. And thanks to the good people of Steelton, our direct pick-ups from my place and all of our bars and clubs had a very good holiday as Anthony will confirm. Tim and I probably had two or three of the best months ever, including an above-board direct salvage job on machinery that netted us over two thousand with no expense from my end other than two guys and a dump truck for two days."

Tim was next. "I don't have much to add. We had some business fall right into our laps. I doubt that we'll be able to keep this pace up though. I'm staying on second shift and that helps. That big project I spoke about won't be that much of a threat to us after all….at least I don't think so. On the liquor side, we lost the Knights as you know, but everybody else is paid up, no problems."

"All right men. I had a call from Sonny; he's getting married and moving to Philadelphia. Anthony gave him his last payment, so that expense is gone. In the end, all of that headache we had with him worked out okay. We got an agreement through his people to stay out of Steelton, and Peter Lewis was a big help in that effort. Anthony and I have Peter in for another special cut as you'll see in a minute. Everybody still OK with our lines of communication? Anybody have any security concerns or anything we need to address? No? OK, use the lines if we need to be in touch, but no need to freeze our asses off up here in February. Let's meet the third Sunday in March, that's the eighteenth. Anthony?"

On the way back to Steelton, Ernie kept thinking about how he would break the news to his friends if he took the Klein job. There were a lot of arrangements that had to be planned for and made. He had not told his wife or his son. He needed to know more. He hoped to get his questions answered the following Wednesday when he again had dinner at the Club with Mr. Klein.

"Hello Scrappy, this is Harry Burger; glad I caught you. How have you been?"

"Harry, sorry I haven't been around. Between here and Bethlehem and the lousy weather I've been pretty much on the run. I'm heading back up to Bethlehem for the week early tomorrow morning. Is there something I can do for you? How are things at the open hearth anyway?"

"Mr. Hernley made his production goal...I even got kind of a thank you for doing my job and filling in for Melton. Everything else is about the same though. I did have one personal matter to ask you about, though. I had a lunch date with Patti Dale last week. It was kind of strange. She agreed to see me and then on the way home told me she was seeing another guy on a steady basis. She asked about you a couple of times, though. Said she hadn't seen you or heard much from her sister about you. That didn't seem quite right to me."

Scrappy thought this through. He and Susie had not seen one another all through the holidays; just one phone call Christmas Eve. "Unfortunately that's about the size of it Harry. I haven't seen much of Susie with all of this travel. She's been busy too. Her dad is buying them a house I guess...or at least helping them out and I know they've been working on that. Sorry to hear that things won't progress with you and Patti, I thought you two got on well."

"I liked her quite a bit, but, as she told me, girls want to marry up the ladder and that ain't me. My brother doesn't say much about the PEP but he did tell me he enjoys working with you, Mark, just as I did. So, good luck with that and I hope maybe we can get together for a couple of beers at some point."

'OK, Harry, that's a deal. This big rush should be over the end of February, so let's try for something in March. I'll get a message to you through Tim."

"Safe travels, Scrappy. If you happen to learn anything new about Patti I'd like to know. I did like her. 'Bye."

It was three full days of work and solo dinners at the hotel for Scrappy. Wallace had again invited him out but Scrappy preferred his time alone. He was not getting much cooperation from the headquarters staff, especially in the technical aspects of the PEP implementation. Any report or analysis Scrappy requested was either impossible to produce or delivered to him days later than he wanted it. Despite that, the Steelton operation seemed to be in the lead for the rail expansion prize. The headquarters location was having significant labor union problems with any new machinery or processes that cut out overtime, or threatened to cut jobs or job increases. The senior guys were concerned that this would be a major issue in the upcoming negotiations for the new contract. As Scrappy predicted, the Lackawanna plant went out of the running early, due to the political clout Bethlehem Steel Corporation had in Pennsylvania. Stone's plan was to work into the evening Thursday, have his weekly wrap up with Wallace Friday morning and head down to Steelton. He thought about calling Susie but set the idea aside.

Like most headquarters operations, the Bethlehem office that Scrappy worked in cleared out by five in the afternoon. Stone had completed most of his work, had several calls with the team back at Steelton, and had daily calls with Brian O'Connell, who had been a lucky find and valuable addition to the project. Stone had been waiting for the right time to look into the issue that had been troubling him for weeks, namely the physical expansion requirements for the Steelton plant if they were chosen for this capital investment. A little after six, he went up two flights of stairs and down the long corridor to Wallace's department. The lights were out and the door unlocked. He had been in Wallace's department and office many times, so even if he was discovered in there by himself it wouldn't arouse any suspicion. Wallace's office door was locked. Scrappy spent the next thirty minutes looking through inboxes, unlocked file cabinets, and anything he could find that might indicate contents about Steelton and the PEP. He didn't have any luck. He made certain that nothing he touched was disturbed and that everything he looked at was back in its place. As he exited the office, he walked past the department secretary's desk. Her name was Maureen and her typewriter was neatly covered and everything on her desk top put away. Knowing Maureen, Stone was certain her desk would be locked tight as a drum. Oddly enough, there were several items stacked in Maureen's in-box…probably placed there by the staff for typing after Maureen went home at four thirty. He rifled through the top two or three handwritten papers with their typing instructions attached and then he came to a spiral bound report with a clear plastic cover : PRODUCTION EFFICIENCY REPORT: WEEKLY STATUS. There was a handwritten notice to Maureen with Wallace's "From the desk of…" cover note asking Maureen to make the penciled changes to the report.

Scrappy opened the report to the table of contents. He noticed the status report was for the prior week, and had "Bethlehem Works" and "Steelton Works" sections. Each plant location had copies of locally produced status reports from the facility – Scrappy recognized his own work that had been sent by courier to Headquarters under Robert Willis' name. There was a separate section on the PEP budget toward the back of the reports, and as Scrappy turned to it, he noticed breakdowns-again by plant location – for operating expense budget and capital funds budget. He was highly interested in the capital budget…this would most likely be the money approved for all of the year for capital investment as determined by the PEP outline. He drew his eyes to line items for Steelton and immediately several caught his attention. He wiped his eyes and his breath shortened when he saw entries with six and seven figure dollar amounts in the following categories: North Boundary Expansion: Survey; Property acquisition and demolition; Initial facility site expansion preparation: utilities, transportation, infrastructure.

What he had feared was there in front of him. Tim Burger was right – there was no way to expand to the south, east or west. What Tim and many others would never have considered was that Bethlehem had its sights set on the West Side; that was the area the strategic planning group had designated for expansion. That explained Wallace's West Side walking tour, all of his maps showing the water, sewer and electric lines, the roads and rails, and the important elevation relief maps that detailed the depth of flooding in thirty-six.

"A successful PEP for Steelton means the end of the West Side" Scrappy thought to himself. With Bethlehem's money and political power, nothing would stand in their way. Not even the leadership of the United Steelworker's Union could be counted on to stand up for what's right if hundreds of new jobs were promised them. It became clear that R.M. Stevens knew about this and Scrappy wondered if Willis knew too.

Stone carefully replaced the report in Maureen's in-box, turned out the lights and went out through the main entrance where his Rambler was parked in the visitor's lot. He drove the three miles to his hotel and went straight to the bar. It was a five beer night, a cheeseburger and onion rings. Stone thought about his meeting with Wallace at ten the next morning and his long drive back to Steelton. The motor pool guys at the plant had fixed the heater and the defroster for him. The radio worked too. He'd get into Steelton by four, and he thought about heading down to the St. Lawrence Club to unwind. He had thoughts again of calling Susie; he'd go over the pros and cons of doing that on the drive back. Before he fell asleep, though, he did make one decision about his Friday night: he was going to have dinner on Conestoga Street with his family.

"Good evening Chief. It looks like the groundhog was right this morning. It certainly feels like six more weeks of winter. I think it best that they shoot that animal if he is afraid of his own shadow." Herman was enjoying his second Lowenbrau, served at the Management Club in a tall Pilsner glass.

"Herman, it's a Pennsylvania tradition. Besides it's supposed to be cold here in February…and it is good for our appetites."

"I have no difficulty there Chief Linta, as you can see by my belt. But yes, I think a big steak is in order for me, and perhaps a glass or two of red wine."

Ernie ordered his veal dish and the men had the usual talk of the weather, their work, their families. Ernie kept waiting for Klein to open the subject of employment…he was eager to hear more but he didn't want Klein to KNOW he was eager to learn more.

"And again, Chief, I thank you for the work for my son-in-law

Klaus…they are very happy and my wife is in *HIMMEL*. I owe you a great favor, and I think you owe me a favor as well."

"If I owe you a favor Herman, you must let me know what it is."

"Ernest, you can do me a great favor by agreeing to join me as Chief of Security. We will work side by side for two months and then I will retire. I have arranged this with my superiors in Bethlehem. You will have to meet a few people –I dare not call it an interview –it is a formality. You will also meet Mr. Stevens, but I believe you are acquainted with him. I would like to present you with a letter that details all of the particulars, but I think you will find them more than satisfactory. I do not know what a police chief in Steelton earns, but I comfortably expect your salary will more than double…and there are many benefits you will enjoy, this Club being one. And you can trade in that Plymouth police car for big new sedan…I have been driving a Chrysler and a new one comes every three years. You will need to buy some suits and ties naturally…this position does not require a uniform, or a cap!"

"Herman, this has taken me quite by surprise, but I have thought about it since our last dinner. I have not spoken to my wife or son. I would need at least 30 days to notify the Borough Council and to get my own succession in place. And, Herman, to be fair, there are some things that I believe we should discuss as professionals and gentlemen."

"I suspect you will want to talk about certain…*arrangements*, Chief? You may recall I have been a military officer, a police-man myself, and have been in security with many political and governmental considerations. I doubt that there is anything you could say that would surprise me."

"It is nothing serious. I will have to make an effective hand-off to my successor. He is a mature and trustworthy man but I must let him know about several, uh…"

"Arrangements."

"Yes, arrangements. Arrangements that exist that need to be handled with some discretion. In a small town there are also some political matters that require some special attention."

"Let me make this easy for you, Ernest. There are many temptations that come to my attention every day. There are also very delicate requests that I must make for information, and some information that is offered to me with a price tag. And I understand politics, believe me. We can go over this when you join me, but as a part of my budget I have special fund. It is a CASH fund. I spend it at my sole discretion. You will find, especially if we have a strike this year, that you will experience the need to pay to get certain information. You will also need to pay for some information to be kept quiet. The top people, they do not want to know anything about this. I suspect you encounter some things like this in your work."

"Yes, it is true Herman. I would be very pleased to accept your letter and attend the meetings you require. I will not speak of this to anybody except my family, with your permission."

"*Sehr Gut. Danke.*" And now Ernest, let's have a glass of port while I sign the bill. We have to have something in our bellies to fight that damned groundhog and his prediction."

The Sunday early afternoon dinners back at the house were a treat for Harry. He especially enjoyed the fact that it gave him and Tim a chance to talk. With their schedules –Harry daylight and Tim three to eleven- they just didn't see one another. After they helped Doris with the dishes, they usually watched Hap fall asleep and then opened a couple of beers and caught up with one another.

"Things about the same with the apartment and down at the open hearth, Harry?"

"Yep. I leave for work in the dark and get back to my apartment just as it's getting dark. I've got a little routine going. I have Doris' left-overs to warm up and I am getting better at doing a little cooking myself. Baked a ham last week so I had a couple of meals and plenty for sandwiches. Going to try a roast beef this week…figure I can burn it at least as good as mom does."

"And work, Harry? The same?"

"It's all predictable…very little new to learn and the same faces, lunch breaks and paperwork every day. I enjoy a few minutes each morning with George Clark. I watch everybody more or less go through the motions. I sure miss working with Mark Stone."

Harry was happy that his relationship with his brother had improved. Tim was always inviting Harry to join him for a night out in Harrisburg, or trying to fix him up with a willing girl. They also talked about their shared experience working with Scrappy Stone, and Harry thought how unusual it was for Tim to express admiration or respect for anyone, but he did for Stone.

"Yeah, Stone has been up in Bethlehem a lot. He is really sharp and easy to talk to. I've learned a lot from him in just the time we've worked on this PEP thing. How about the girls, big brother? You never say much about that. You should be living it up with your own place."

"I've been to church on and off. I hoped there would be a few eligible girls to meet on Sunday mornings, but it didn't turn out that way. I've picked up Mollie, that divorced girl who works at Rea & Derrick a couple of times. Sometimes I go down there just before closing to get a milkshake and then take her out for a beer or two. I think next time you invite me to double date I'll take you up on it, as long as it's not too expensive."

"OK Harry, let's plan on that. How about a nice rich Jewish

girl? Next Saturday?"

"What would a nice, rich Jewish girl see in me? Sounds like just another chance to be disappointed, Tim."

"It's just a date, Harry…it's not the first rung to climb on the ladder to success."

"Now that you are a police officer Charles, we will all have to watch our step around you, won't we, Claude?" Arthur looked down at the other end of the dinner table toward his oldest son. The Howards had invited Charles and his mother to Sunday dinner for a little celebration.

"Yes, Dad. I hope Officer Parker remembers who his friends and family are. I know we better not double park that hearse anywhere in Steelton!"

After dinner all of the women went into the kitchen and Arthur took his sons and Charles for a little walk down Francis Street. When they got to Christian Street, he turned left and walked down to the Leland home. He had something on his mind.

"You remember Thanksgiving weekend and Mrs. Leland being killed by her husband. Do you remember her two little children at the church service we did? I keep thinking about her and her husband. He'll be lucky if he don't get the death penalty. All those lives ruined. It made me think about how much of this kind of thing goes on here, women getting beat up by their men, but too afraid or too weak to do anything about it. You know, Charles, when that happens, they never call the police for help. You know why?"

"They don't want any police in their home. They are afraid their man will get beat up or locked up himself, probably both."

"That's right Charles, but with one exception. They don't

want any WHITE police in their home. If we had colored men in the police, maybe they would call. Maybe they would ask for help. If they see a brown skin man in a cop car going down the street, maybe they feel different than they do when they always have seen nothing before but white cops. So I am hoping that this changes. You are the first Negro police officer but there will be more, and it will help our community here. It is important for you to be a success and to show others the way. You can always count on me and my family to help you. And I know Chief Linta…he ain't perfect, but he's a man you can trust."

39

"Son, I've got some news. It affects the family and all of our business interests. I haven't told your mother about it; I want your opinion and suggestions."

Ernie's son Anthony leaned in across the small table in their downstairs family room.

"I have been offered a position by Herman Klein, the head of security at the plant…you have met him. He is retiring, and he wants me to come to work with him and then replace him when he goes. I have the offer letter, and a schedule of people to meet up in Bethlehem. The salary is almost three times what I am making now, plus there is a pension and a car. I think I am going to take it if the interviews go well, and Herman assures me they will. My plan is to have Mickey Hauser replace me on the force. I've thought through how this will affect our family businesses. The money from Lowry, Lewis and the few others we will just have to forfeit. I will speak to Hauser about keeping the police out of their way so that their businesses are not affected. We'll actually be in a better position with Tim and Arthur's steel business because I will have all of the security under me and can fix anything if Tim makes a mistake. Only the liquor protection is a problem, although we have a card to play with the head of the

LCB enforcement –that Colonel Walker –if we need it. That's it."

"I need some time to take this in Dad. When do you expect to tell Arthur?"

"Only after everything is settled. I have to have a confidential talk with Hauser too. I'm not going to say anything to your mother until I have the deal signed with Herman. I really need you to think through the liquor side of things with Cohen and the other guys. I can't ask Hauser to protect all of our spots and even if I could I certainly can't tell him why."

"Dad, I'll think some more but I have been hoping that you would take a little step back and maybe reduce the amount of risk we have all been carrying. I can take care of all the family business…all of our friends will be happy to have Hauser looking out for them without paying for it. One thing, if I talk to Mr. Lewis his son will find out…you have plans to talk to Peter direct?"

"Yeah, I thought about that. The nice thing is there's a petty cash fund at Bethlehem that I understand is for payoffs, hush money and political favors. I will control that. Herman told me all about it, so we can still support Peter."

"When are you going to Bethlehem?"

"Next week. If everything gets locked up and I sign the employment agreement I'll talk to Hauser. Herman will keep everything quiet on his end."

The new machine from IBM had been operating in the basement of the Steelton Main Office for about nine months. IBM employees did the maintenance and supplied all of the cards and the materials, and a new upgrade of a memory drum was supplied in December. Brian O'Connell had worked with similar equipment at Bethlehem's mining group in Scranton, but he felt that he was far from an expert…mostly he learned by doing and calling the IBM office in New York with his questions. As much as he felt he was a rookie, the newly hired employees he worked with at Steelton were real novices and the two men finally sent down from headquarters spent most of their time bitching about being in Steelton and counting the hours until they could leave. This was the biggest problem Scrappy had with the Steelton PEP process. The operating and manufacturing pieces were going well… the coded information getting to the machines was almost always high quality and right on time. It was this problem with the card processing machines that brought Stone down to the basement late Monday afternoon to talk with O'Connell.

"Brian, we're going to fix this situation this week, one way or another. Let's spend a couple of hours with you bringing me up to date and highlighting our priorities and your needs. Then we're going down to the Club for a big steak and a few beers. The rest of the week, I'm all yours to see what we can get done down here. Deal?"

"That's a deal, Mark. Let's get started."

The Club dining room was just about deserted when the two men walked in just after seven. Brian was staying at the Club bungalows, so he had dinner at the Club most every night. Stone decided to keep the dinner conversation on a light and friendly level…the two of them would be all business for long days the rest of the week. Brian talked about his college work at King's college in Scranton, and his home town Peckville a village smaller than Steelton. Scrappy asked him about his career aspirations.

"I'll probably try to make Bethlehem a career, especially if I can stay attached to the quarry and mining group. My family and friends are almost all coal miners…I kind of feel at home there. I'd like to get into a management position that has enough influence to keep the quarries and mines up there operating. It's the only way of life those people have…if those jobs would go away, there are whole towns that would just dry up and go away too…only thing left would be the bars and the churches."

"To get that, you're probably going to have to spend some time at the Bethlehem headquarters to get the right management training and to get to know the top people, Brian."

"Same as you, Mark, right?"

"Maybe. You know it was Bill Willis who recommended you to me. He had good things to say…Bill and I are very close. I was his best man. Maybe Bill would have something for you on his staff or in his department."

"I doubt that I have enough experience. After this assignment, it's back to Scranton for me. As it is, I expect to be laid off for a couple of months every year…just not enough business."

"Let me ask you Brian, you have any interest in working full time here in Steelton? I think I could swing it."

"Thanks, Mark. I really appreciate it. Working down in that basement with those machines is not for me. I prefer talking to people. You just can't reason with that noisy damn machine."

"How about your love life Brian…anyone serious?"

"Nope. There is no woman anywhere crazy enough to have two dates with me. I'm a very happy single guy. Plan to stay that way for awhile."

Stone and O'Connell put in twelve hour days the rest of the week. Scrappy took him to dinners at the Old Stone Inn, then to Martzie's tavern and to Buddy's for crab cakes. He told Brian to get an early start on the road to Peckville Friday and kicked him out of the basement at lunch time. He ate a quick tuna fish sandwich and then got on the phone to Bethlehem to call in his weekly status report to Wallace.

"Hello Mr. Stone. I miss our face to face meeting. How are things in Steelton?"

"We had a busy week. I want to give you a quick picture of our progress here. Things are still moving very well on the operating side. Production planning, inventory, the shipping schedules all going well. Quality control is at the same good level. Our main issue continues to be the punched card machine operation and the mechanical aspects of our coding, sorting, and the instructions from the machine to manufacturing. The man O'Connell is keeping things together single-handed. Our newly hired people here do not have the training yet, and I do not get sufficient staff from your office. I asked for four people, I got two, and I know I was given your worst employees…they're lazy and spend more time complaining than working."

"Yes, Mr. Stone, it sounds like a management challenge."

"We are in our final few critical weeks here…can you authorize either direct help from IBM or send a couple of trained, hard working staff here to help us?"

"Mr. Stone, we need the people here for the Bethlehem plant's own work. If you have the budget for more IBM staff that is your decision."

"Given those restrictions, I cannot guarantee that we will complete our project on time."

"Please send me your weekly status report in writing through Mr. Willis as always. These phone conversations cannot be considered part of the official record."

"I may not be up there next week Wallace. I'm needed here. Goodbye."

The first load of rails tracked down under the bridge-crane, its huge round magnets humming and its siren wailing as it crossed the safety walkway where the end of the storage yard used to be. Pat Patterson stood with Tim and several other management personnel and watched as the rails were gently lowered into the far bin, guided by the union hook-up crew.

"Congratulations, men, and Tim, special thanks to you," Patterson yelled above the noise of the crane that was rapidly returning for its next load. "We can use the space with this inventory build up, and I see all of the yellow tags on each rail bundle Tim. The color codes are a big improvement from the way we used to mark shipments and batches."

"Thanks, Pat. As soon as we get the bins filled, I'm heading down to double-check the order and batch numbers on the tags just to make certain everything is right."

"OK, Tim. When you're finished, stop down to my office. Try not to take too long, it's almost five and I want to get out of here...but I didn't want to leave until I saw the first load go into the new space."

"I'll walk down with you now Pat...I can get back over here later."

The two men entered Patterson's office and Pat sat down and invited Tim to do the same.

"Tim, I've got something for you to think about. You've done a helluva job here the past year or so, and your work on the PEP and some of the ideas you've had have really helped me and the mill. The other foremen like how you always pitch in, not to mention your volunteering to work second shift. People gave me a lot of grief when I appointed you foreman because of your age and lack of seniority, but I don't hear any complaints now."

"Thanks Pat. I owe you a lot too."

"Hear me out, Tim. I talked to Willis. You don't yet have the time in to make general foreman, that's too big of a step and I have a couple of other men to consider. But I have the OK to add a new position, an assistant to me …job title is Assistant Super-intendent. The job is yours. I got you a fifteen percent pay raise to go with it. We can make the promotion effective first of March. I want you to think about this a couple of days…we can go over what I expect next week. I want you to come in at one every day next week so that we get time to talk."

"Pat, you caught me by surprise. Is this in addition to my foreman's duties?"

"No, it's a new spot. I want someone who can take a look at all of our processes and procedures full time, evaluate efficiencies, quality, work flow. I see it as a natural extension of the PEP. And if we get this huge expansion everyone's talking about, I will need a right hand man to work with all of the engineers, someone who knows the operating requirements. I decided that's you."

"Pat, I can't see why I wouldn't take advantage of such a great opportunity. I'll be sure to see you Monday at one."

"Good," Pat stood and offered his hand. "don't say anything to anybody until we get all the paperwork done. See you Monday afternoon."

Harry dressed for church. He put on his big topcoat that was hanging just inside the entrance door to his apartment. It was a hat and gloves kind of day and Harry had a belly full of Quaker oatmeal as he walked up Second Street toward Pine. He nodded to a few people he recognized on the way into the church, hung up his coat in the vestibule and took his customary seat two rows behind the Becker family. He looked over to see Bob and Cindy in their usual spot. Whenever he was in church and saw the Hernleys he always made it a point to say hello at the end of the service. He hoped that a conversation would start, but it never did…just a few words of greeting and a goodbye. The Hernleys weren't rude; it's just as if Harry was an empty coat hanging around the cloak room with all the others.

Harry had no anger toward them. Over the past few months he had watched Hernley's interaction with the other men in the open hearth. Day in and day out there was no personal connection between Bob and Harry's co-workers of any kind, so in that respect Harry was on the same footing with men Hernley had worked with for years. Conversations with him were always about work and nothing but work. It was as if the weather, sports, food and drink, all of the things that filled up the conversations of working people somehow got checked at the plant gate with Hernley. Bob could not tolerate small talk. Harry had asked George Clark about this a couple of times and George's advice was essentially: don't worry about it, do your job, build some seniority, and then transfer out to another department. "You won't change him, Harry, and you won't get to know him either. Mr. Hernley has a wall built around him, and nobody – certainly not an employee of his – is going to get through."

Cindy Hernley was just as much a puzzle to Harry. She was probably the most attractive woman he had ever been around, and she was certainly pleasant enough. He remembered how he was totally taken with her the first few times he saw her, but it was clear to Harry that Cynthia Hernley would never be a woman he could talk quietly to, or touch.

Harry watched his shoe tops step by step. His Florsheims could use a polish. He'd put that on his list of things to do after Sunday dinner.

40

Scrappy took O'Connell into the St. Lawrence Club for hamburgers and beer. The first three days of the week had not gone well. The two men sent down from Bethlehem finally showed up at noon Monday and that gave O'Connell his first opportunity to see Scrappy raise hell. It had been a tense few days and now Stone was preparing to head up to Bethlehem the next morning for additional meetings with Wallace, and his second to last status report. Scrappy had been relying on O'Connell more and more as the project went along, and they had developed a bond. Stone wanted a final action plan and "red flags" from O'Connell so that he could include it in his report to Wallace, and then to Willis the following Monday.

"Scrappy, we have a big problem on the final printing of the shipping tickets. The information coming from the rail mill is still good and all of the initial errors we had with the coding have been sorted out. The main problem is the calculation that the machine makes for the final punching of all off those card decks…something is fouling that up and we can't figure it out. I called IBM every day this week, and they are sending a technician in tomorrow who has been working on one of their projects down at the air force base in Middletown. If you call me late

350

tomorrow I'll let you know how it goes."

"Brian, if we can't fix that, we are not going to meet our deadline. I expect to find out tomorrow that the other PEP guys are right on track…their only issue has been union objections and resistance. We have everyone pulling together on that angle…it's been a real plus for Steelton."

"Look, Mark. I'm going to hang around Steelton this weekend. I packed some extra clothes. I thought there was a chance you'd need me over the weekend."

"Thank you Brian. I'm going to have dinner with Bill Willis and his wife tomorrow, and I am going to do my best to give you a hand with your career in the mining group. I've really enjoyed working with you and honestly don't know where I'd be without you. I'll get the check…early start tomorrow."

"How's the Rambler running Scrappy? I don't hear you complaining about it anymore."

"Better than the IBM."

"C'mon in Mickey, and close the door."

"What is it Chief? We missed you Tuesday and I didn't see much of you yesterday, either." Everything OK at home?"

"Yes, thanks. Mickey I have some news for you…might as well give it to you straight. We've worked well together and you have been the best number two guy anybody could ask for. You have made me a better cop and supervisor, and I'm thankful to you for that. Last evening, I shook hands with Herman Klein on a job offer. I'm going to be resigning my position as Chief. I am going to give the Borough Council my hundred percent recommendation that you be appointed Chief. I'm giving them a month's notice. I have not told anybody except my family…I wanted you to know first."

Hauser sat stiffly in the chair. "I don't know what to say Chief."

"You can say you want to be Chief. A lot of people thought you should have had the job when I was selected. I've got an appointment with two members of the Council tomorrow morning. I'll let you know how it goes. Then, you and I will work closely together for the rest of my time here to make sure we have an effective hand-off."

"What's your new job? Are you moving to Bethlehem?"

"Klein is retiring. I'm taking his spot. We are staying in Steelton."

"Chief, I would be honored to take over. I have to admit it's been a dream of mine."

"Good. Keep a lid on this."

Scrappy had an afternoon of meeting and briefings, and spent an hour in the Bethlehem plant's equivalent to Steelton's basement operation. The IBM equipment Bethlehem was renting was nearly identical to the Steelton units, although it had been installed several months earlier. Scrappy learned that the entire operation was staffed by IBM employees during its first three months, enabling rapid training and start-up. Bethlehem also had arrangement with both Lehigh and Lafayette that provided recent college grads and interns who had already studied the new data processing approach that promised to revolutionize science, engineering and manufacturing. Steelton had none of these advantages.

O'Connell's call came in just before five. "Good progress made with IBM. Turns out their guy from Middletown discovered that we didn't have some kind of updated component we should have had. He ordered one from New York and they are sending a technician down next Monday with it. Will cost almost two thousand bucks though."

"Good Brian. See you Saturday, not too early. Having dinner with Bill Willis in a bit, bye".

At dinner that night, Scrappy told Bill about the great job O'Connell had done. He pitched Brian for any opportunity that Bill might have in his own group, or know about anywhere in Mines.

"You know, Scrappy. The things you just told me about O'Connell and what he needs to advance his career are the same things I've been telling you. I think I might have something for O'Connell in a couple of months but it would be a big boost if someone like Wallace was also behind it. Wallace doesn't show it, but he is kind of taken with the way you get things done. He's smart enough to know that all of the people skills you have – especially with the union and the shop floor guys – he doesn't have. You two would be a perfect one-two punch. And that Strategic Planning Group has a lot of influence and money to spend. Plus, they'd support you finishing your degree at Lehigh. I'm having a hard time figuring out why you're not jumping all over this."

"Let me think about it. I've got a big meeting with Wallace tomorrow and then I meet with your dad Monday at the end of the day. Probably work the whole weekend to boot."

Bill's wife Cheryl had been listening quietly and sipping her white wine. "Speaking of weekends, Scrappy, you don't mention Susie anymore. Is that over for sure?"

"We have spoken a few times but haven't been together since Thanksgiving. I've got two more weeks on this project and then I think we'll have time to have a good talk."

Scrappy's appointment with Wallace was for ten. He decided to take a new approach, to kind of go on the offensive with

Wallace. He still wanted someone to own up to the expansion plans that were in place for Steelton, but he didn't want anyone to know what he knew.

"Wallace, I'm prepared to give you the latest on Steelton, but I've got a couple of questions for you first."

"Mr. Stone, I have some for you as well. We have ample time through lunch; I have arranged for sandwiches to be brought in for us. And now your questions."

"I played football in high school. There are two expressions from football that apply to our situation here. One is home field advantage. Do you know that one?"

"M.I.T. did not have a football team but yes I know what it means. And the second?"

"A level playing field. I do not understand why the company is making these investments in Steelton, and then running parallel projects, but has not provided Steelton the same level of tools, personnel, budgets and training as Bethlehem. We were able to do well and compete on the open hearth project because all of the output was consumed internally by other plant departments. In the rail mill, we have over a hundred customers, so our project is in danger of failing on the back end…we cannot get the IBM machines sorted out on all of the final shipping demands. The main plant here has had home field advantage and we at Steelton have been fighting uphill."

"It is not folly to put these new machines into Steelton. All of our locations will have to have them to compete, and not just steelmaking, but mining, ship building and so on. Part of this is a test to see how much manpower we need and at what level of training and experience to perform satisfactorily…in other words how much human power does it take to match the machines? The other human element is something you know very well, Mr.

Stone, the union leadership and their members, the supervisors and operating management on the floor. Those human elements can also be a barrier to the machines' success."

These things made sense to Scrappy. "But why dangle this hope of rail mill expansion on a thread that you have made weak by design? The leadership at Steelton believes they are in a contest to win the capital to expand based on the outcome of the PEP. There has to be more to the decision making processes than this project alone."

"It's true. Steelton is the prime rail location now thanks to the modernization of the past five years there. It makes sense to capitalize on that. Some of our other plants do not have the same advantages of access to both raw materials and the final markets that Steelton has."

"But Steelton has no room to expand, Wallace. The current rail mill is hemmed in by railroad lines east and west, the rest of the plant to the south, and residential areas to the north."

"Do you know a Calumet Street in Steelton, Mark?"

It was the first time Wallace had called him anything but "Mr. Stone".

"No, I never heard of it."

"Calumet Street used to form the north border of the Steelton works. It was south of the current Trewick Street on your West Side. The plant eventually expanded northward to where it is today."

"So the block between Calumet and Trewick was all residential at one time, and the plant took it over?"

"All of the businesses and residences between Calumet and Trewick accepted a purchase offer from the steel works. And now, Mr. Stone, that line of questioning is over. Let's hear what you have to say about our progress."

Scrappy laid everything out as unemotionally as he could. Wallace took many notes. Scrappy told Wallace his formal report would be sent next week through Mr. Willis who he was seeing Monday. That gave him a bridge to talk to Wallace about O'Connell, and to ask for Wallace's support should Bill Willis request O'Connell for the main office.

The sandwiches arrived. Both men ate silently, Stone taking a look through the newspaper that was in the office and Wallace reading papers from his in-box. Wallace finished his lunch and broke the silent chewing.

"I suppose you will be heading back to Steelton now? I'll be interested to hear how things go with the IBM support. Your final report is due from Mr. Willis and I expect your Mr. Stevens will have something to add as well?"

"Yes, Wallace. He has taken a special interest in this. He wants that rail mill expansion. He believes Steelton is the best place for it, and wants this PEP result to help prove it."

"Yes, we know. He made his case before the strategic planning group several months ago. Did a reasonable job." Wallace looked for a reaction from Stone. He didn't get one.

"How did Stevens handle the question of where to expand? Your group, I assume, is at least as smart as you are, Wallace; they must have asked the question."

"You are returning to plow old ground, Mr. Stone. If I were you, I would be more concerned about yourself."

"In what way?

"When this current project finishes, you have no next assignment whether it succeeds or fails. If things do not work out, I can't imagine Willis or Stevens finding an important post for you. If the PEP succeeds, they will take all of the credit, you know. Something to think about on your way home."

* * *

"Happy Friday, Harry!" George Clark always had a warm greeting no matter how lousy the weather.

"Same to you George! You staying warm? What do you hear that's new?"

"Business is good up and down the mill and up and down Front Street. Everything else is about the same. I think spring is going to be late this year."

Harry didn't need to hear that. He felt a little achy when he woke up and couldn't seem to get warm on his usual ten minute brisk walk to work. A hot coffee and a TastyKake might do the trick, and he saw Melton by the coffee pot as he entered the office area. It was just before seven when Karl Long, the general foreman came in and informed everyone of a production meeting at ten. Harry got to work and before he knew it, men were crowding into the office awaiting Long and Hernley. Harry didn't feel much better.

"Good morning, men. This will be brief. We have some of the latest numbers from production planning and it looks like our current levels will continue through March and April. Our quality numbers are good but we have to reduce our costs. We've had some unavoidable overtime and our usage of material and supplies is way ahead of budget. Most of the overtime is to cover shifts for union guys calling in sick but we've had too much of that from the management and supervision people as well. I don't need to remind everyone that supervisory and management personnel costs are overhead. I'll be keeping an eye on this. I've got to get up to Swatara Street for a meeting, but Karl will go over the numbers with you."

Hernley left. Long read from some reports, there were no

questions, everyone went back to work with one thought in their minds: quitting time. For Harry, the clock seemed to be in slow motion. He had been planning to go up to Yetter's that evening, but by the time work was done he barely had the energy to get back to his place and put a can of soup on the stove. He had a seven and seven and was in bed, listening to the radio by nine.

Scrappy and Brian worked until mid afternoon on Saturday and figured they could do nothing more until the IBM guy arrived Monday. Scrappy offered to take Brian to dinner, but Brian said he was going down to Hershey to the hockey game. Scrappy pulled the Rambler into the driveway of his house, opened a beer and called his mom and dad to arrange for dinner Sunday. He had two more calls to make, the first to Susie. They connected and he asked her out for that night. She said it was too short of notice and couldn't possible make it. Scrappy was too tired to argue. He opened another beer and made the call he had been thinking about for two days.

"This is Mark Stone. Is Rocky at home?" Rocky's kid had answered and Scrappy could hear him yelling for his Dad.

"Scrappy? Where are you? Everything OK?"

"Yeah, Rocky. I've been up at Bethlehem a lot. The PEP program we've got – your guy Squires has done a great job by the way – is just about over. I've got something I need to talk to you about one on one. I'm coming up to have dinner with my mom and dad tomorrow. You got any time to meet? Has to be someplace where nobody sees us who knows us."

"Is this official Scrappy?"

"Nope, personal."

"All right, how about the small playground, the one in the back behind West Side School. Twelve o'clock?"

"Right, Rocky, that's good. See you tomorrow."

Rocky Garber was waiting for Mark. They were thankfully out of the wind, with the giant red brick edifice of the fifty year old West Side School between them and the river wind. The small play area backed onto a lonely alley between Main and Frederick Street. Both men had heavy top coats, hats and gloves. Rocky had a plaid scarf around his neck.

"Well, Scrappy, what's the big mystery?"

"Rocky, I said this is personal and it is, but it's also about the mill. So it's work and friendship, but in this case the friendship comes first. You know this big PEP project we have…I ran one in open hearth and now we are about to finish the rail mill, the one you helped kick off."

"Yeah, my guys keep me clued in. I know the rail mill took over some space the maintenance guys were using for lunch and sleep. I had to talk them out of a grievance on that, because I thought you and Tim Burger were doing your best to get us more jobs and production space."

"That's correct. And I suppose somewhere along the line somebody from your International leadership in Pittsburgh whispered in your ear about a lot of new jobs being created if this thing is a success…I guess that right?"

"You know how things work. That's also right."

"Well, I've got news. I've been up to the main office in Bethlehem. I also had a meeting here that R.M. Stevens attended a little while ago. I saw some reports I wasn't supposed to see. There's a group up in headquarters called strategic planning. They are behind this big mechanization work and the investment in all of these new machines to improve efficiency and increase production. What I've learned is that all of these efforts are to ELIMINATE jobs, not create them. They are trying to replace people with new processes and machines wherever they can…union jobs and low level management and supervision alike. I also saw a confidential report that all of this talk about the rail mill expansion at Steelton was to help convince you guys not to strike this summer. They intended to hold out this promise of big job increases as a way to get you guys to be easier at the bargaining table. It's like their version of the U.S. and Russia fighting a war with propaganda. They are using you Rocky, just like they used me. But I found out what's really going on…and I owe it to you to let you know, too."

"You sure about all of this, Scrappy? You saw all of this in black and white with your own eyes?"

"Yes I did. And my final report is due soon…I have a meeting with Willis tomorrow. We are having some problems with those punched card machines but not enough to stop the implementation of the PEP. By the way, your guys up in the Bethlehem local are less cooperative, there have been grievances filed and the strategic planning people said that the cooperation by the union at Steelton was a big advantage to them. They as much as said that your Local was rolling over for management."

Rocky lit up a cigarette and turned his head away from Stone. He took three long drags before he turned around to face his childhood friend. Garber did not shake hands, he didn't say a word. He set his jaw as he nodded his head. Neither man had to say what each already knew and understood: "This meeting never happened."

Tim arrived two hours ahead of his normal shift start to get his time with Pat Patterson. He knocked on Pat's door and let himself in. Pat had a cigarette going. Pat looked up at Tim and tossed some papers in his direction. Tim recognized the forms right way: grievances.

"Well, the shit's hit the fan. Did you know or hear anything about this? We've had nothing but cooperation from the union and now this?"

Tim looked at the grievances. Two were from the maintenance steward over the loss of their picnic area. One was from the union local –not the stewards- about a union employee – J.T. Squires – being forced to do management work. There were two other grievances all somehow related to the PEP program, including a safety grievance from the crane operators about their new track extension. "We were surprised when we DIDN'T get a grievance from the maintenance guys, so I understand that one although the timing stinks. These others are coming out of the blue. I didn't hear any grumbling the last week and certainly didn't get any heads up from anyone, Pat, including my crane operators. I have a great relationship with them….they had to be put up to this by the higher-ups in the union."

"I better call Willis. He's hyper about anything to do with the PEP. Jesus! Things had been going so well."

"This could all be from the union hall and not from the shop floor Pat. There's always a spike in grievances the months before the negotiations. Maybe that's what you tell Willis. Keeps his attention away from anything he thinks we screwed up here in the rail mill."

"Helluva idea, Tim. I'll do that. Jesus Christ!"

Stone and O'Connell worked through the day with the IBM technician. He installed the component and explained the process to all of the men of Scrappy's team. By three o'clock Stone and O'Connell understood what needed to be done to fix the final shipping cards. Stone had assigned the two men down from

Bethlehem to some general maintenance work; he didn't want them screwing things up for him. At four, Scrappy cleaned up a bit and went up to Willis' office where he sat until almost four thirty.

"C'mon in Stone." Scrappy knew Willis well and he could tell right away he was pissed off about something.

"Before we get into your report, you hear about these fucking grievances from the rail mill? Pat Patterson had 'em sent up here an hour ago. He says he had no inkling there was any union complaints. Now we have five grievances including one demanding a step three. All of them are related to the PEP one way or another. You know anything about this?"

"No Bob. I've been mostly down in the basement with IBM problems while I've been in Steelton, and I was up in Bethlehem end of last week. This is all a surprise."

"Well one of these is about that colored guy from the union you put on the PEP team...now they are grieving he's doing management work and insist he be taken off the PEP."

"This is all brand new to me Bob. Maybe it's related more to the contract negotiations than it is our operation."

"Maybe...that's Patterson's take on it too. All right. Let's get on with your report."

"Bob, I'll have to give it to you all verbal. I just didn't get time to write it out and have it typed. I can do that tomorrow. The highlights are things are going well but we have one major problem...if you don't count this new union resistance."

"I'm not telling Bethlehem anything about these grievances. It's a local matter."

"That's your call, Bob, but they are going to find out sooner or later. If this is related to the union negotiations strategy, you can bet all of the locals got the same memo from their H.Q. in

Pittsburgh. You know how they work…it's all about coordinated effort. You're risking the chance of the Bethlehem headquarters guys thinking you held back key information from them in order to make Steelton look better."

"Jesus Christ. Talk about bad timing. God-dammit. Other than this, what's the main problem?"

"It's experience and skill. I found out the Bethlehem group had a three month running head start on us with full IBM staff on site. Their budget must have been five times ours. They are using college grads from Lehigh and Lafayette and college interns to work with IBM. We have those two losers they sent down to help us…and some new hires with no experience prior to the open hearth project. If your son hadn't brought O'Connell to my attention, we'd be even further behind. The main risk to us is in all of the shipping documents and the customer details. I think it's probably another two months until we get that right. Then there's the longer term problem with people. We have no pool of trained or experienced candidates anywhere around Steelton. We have no local college for support. We can try to recruit some college grads from Pittsburgh or Philly, or maybe piggy back on Lehigh…but not a lot of college kids are going to want to move to Steelton. The lack of proper personnel is a competitive disadvantage for us and that will be the one major concern in my report."

"That O'Connell, you think he'd move to Steelton and come here permanent?"

"Not a chance. I already tried that."

"All right Scrappy. File your report tomorrow. Don't include the union stuff. I'll decide whether it goes in or not. I might talk to Stevens about it. Bill told me you had dinner with him and Cheryl last week. Have a good time?"

"Yeah, we did Bob. They are really excited about that new

house."

"I know. I'm going to take a week off when they move in to help out. How are things with Susie Dale? You two back on the beam?"

"Just the opposite Bob. I think it may be over. I called her Saturday…no dice."

"I had a feeling. Her old man's on the rag too. Made us go through a bid process and we think he's going to give half of the Turnpike business to Harrisburg Steel."

"Don't hang that one on me Bob, please. I'm doing everything I can for Steelton."

41

Harry had dragged himself to church Sunday. He spent the whole weekend in his apartment. He felt a little better and thought that a few prayers and Doris' home cooking might get him feeling better. She made pork and sauerkraut, mashed potatoes and corn. Tim and Hap ate like there was no tomorrow. Harry had a little of each, then helped Doris with the dishes. When the time came for Tim and Harry's Sunday beers, all Harry wanted was a ride back to his place.

"Mom, what do we have in the medicine cabinet? I think I'm getting a cold or the flu or something. Tim's going to give me a ride down to Locust Street."

"You sure you don't want to stay here Harry? Better than being alone if you're sick. I'll make some soup for you this week."

"Thanks Mom, but that's OK. Maybe you can put whatever medicine you have in with my leftovers."

Tim went into the apartment with Harry. "Listen, if you can't make it to work tomorrow, get a message through Dr. Becker's office to the house. I'll stop by and check in on you. How about giving me a call through the plant phone tomorrow afternoon if you are well enough to go in? You have some whiskey or brandy in the house?"

"I got plenty of booze. Right now all I want to do is get some sleep."

Harry made it in to work on Monday. He told George Clark he might not last until lunch time but in fact it was almost three when he pulled himself together and knocked on Hernley's office door. Karl Long was in there with Hernley and they both looked up, surprised to see Burger in front of them.

"Mr. Hernley, I've got to punch out. I've been fighting the flu or something all weekend. I tried to get through the day but I can't make it. I doubt that I'll be in tomorrow."

"You don't look too good" Karl said. "Better to go home than to spread that shit to everyone in the office."

"Well, I didn't want to take the time away, especially after our meeting last week. I haven't missed one day since I started."

"That's OK, Burger" Hernley looked up from his reports. "At least you won't cost us overtime. I can get Melton to cover for you. Get back here when you're a hundred percent."

"Thanks. I will. Sorry, I don't have a phone so I can't call in each day. My apartment is above an office and I can get someone to call in around eight though."

"Don't worry about it. When you show up at the start of your shift we'll know you're back. Go ahead and punch out."

Harry stopped in to Rea and Derrick to load up on anything he thought might help, relying on his memory of Doris' reliable nostrums. Then he walked the block up Locust to see Peggy, the Becker's receptionist.

"Peggy, please call my brother and ask him to stop by tomorrow on his way to work."

"You look terrible, Harry. You should get right into bed. I'll check in on you tomorrow myself. Maybe bring you some soup."

"I wouldn't turn that down, Peggy. Thanks a lot."

* * *

Ernie had a picture of the Punxsutawney groundhog in his mind as he moved from the back of Farina's garage to the basement entrance to Arthur's morgue. It was freezing, although Steelton did not have a lot of snow. March was just around the corner but there had been no signs of an early spring. He brought the Plymouth in to have Farina check the brakes even though there was nothing wrong with them…he needed a reason to have his talk with Arthur in a private place. Arthur answered his knocks and the two of them were alone. For some reason, Ernie felt colder inside the basement than he did outdoors.

"It must be important if it couldn't wait until Robbins." Arthur looked into Ernie's eyes.

"It is Arthur. I've got a Council meeting coming up and I'm going to give them some news, but I wanted to break it to you first. I'm resigning my position as Chief of Police. I'm taking over for the head of security for the steel mill, who's retiring. I figured you and I would want to discuss some things before we all get together at Robbins."

"You got anybody pushin' you out Chief? Any kind of trouble I should know about?"

"No. The job offer came out of the blue. A lot more money. I'll be in the perfect position to protect our steel business with Tim, but the liquor business we need to discuss."

"Who's going to take your place? Hauser?"

"I'm recommending him and I'm sure he'll get it. I'll be careful what I tell him but he will know that you are to get special attention. I'm going to base it on your position and influence with the coloreds. He'll leave you alone, plus we've got Parker. As for the LCB, I'm talking to Peter Lewis. We know all about the top enforcement guy- that Colonel Walker who Cohen hates-Walker's got his secretary shacked up in a nice apartment and he's paying the rent. Walker tries anything here in Steelton, Peter will whisper in his ear."

"Mr. Cohen is not going to be happy, and our accounts are bound to shrink you know."

"Arthur, you and Cohen have a special connection. My idea –and this is your decision – is to have you and Cohen take all the liquor business and revenues. You, me and Burger will run the steel. My son will keep all the books and handle the cash for both ends. You and Cohen can make your own decisions about the liquor. I'll still be around for help…I've got a special fund that I will control – all cash- if we need to spread some around to keep somebody quiet. We will still meet as a group at Robbins, but you will be running the show since you are the main guy with a stake in both ends of our operation."

"How do you want to handle this at Robbins? You son knows, right?"

"Yes he does. I figure you can break the news with Cohen during one of your pick-ups or transfers so that he has some time to think it over too. My guess is he'll like it."

"Maybe, Chief."

"Tim doesn't know but I don't see any reason to tell him until Robbins. I gotta get back to Farina's, Arthur. Your family doing OK? Business good?"

"Yeah, Chief. Everybody is fine. February is a good month in the funeral business. Some people would just rather lay down and die than linger for a spring that never seems to come."

Peter Lewis usually attended the monthly Borough Council meetings. He did so as a citizen, not as a lawyer. He was at the

Municipal building a half hour earlier at Ernie's request and found Ernie in his uniform on the phone and sitting behind his big wooden desk. Ernie waved for him to take a seat.

"Peter, thanks for coming, sorry to be so secretive about the reason I wanted to see you. We have an agenda item today that's going to cause a stir."

"It's OK, Chief. Which item?"

"You see the item marked Confidential-Police Personnel? That's at my request. Peter, I'm advising the Council of my intention to resign as Chief. I'm providing thirty days' notice. I'm taking the top security job at the mill; Herman Klein is retiring. I'm recommending Mickey Hauser replace me."

"I see. You certain about this, Ernie?"

"Yes. I have the written offer and have accepted. I wanted to give you advance notice and also wanted to go over a few things regarding my transition. I'll talk to Hauser about your Dad's business and Anthony will speak to your Dad directly. I understand I'll have a petty cash fund to use at my discretion in my new job, so I can still support you Peter. And I have two special situations I'll need your help on."

Peter started to stroke his moustache. "And they are, Chief?"

"Arthur Howard. You know him. He is my major link to the Negroes in Steelton. You know he sways a lot of votes. He and I have a special relationship. He helped me hire my first colored patrolman. In addition to his funeral and scrap business, he owns some grocery stores and a couple of taverns. You remember last summer you helped us with one of his guys who was running a little independent bar operation. I'd just like to ask if anything Arthur is involved in somehow gets cross-ways with the law or the LCB that you give me a call. I'll do the same with you for sure."

"I understand Chief. Just tell Mr. Howard to keep himself as clean as possible. I suppose the second special situation has to do with our friends at the PLCB?"

"Yes, Peter. If they plan a raid or some kind of enforcement action here in Steelton, they are supposed to give us a heads up. There may be a case where they plan to disrupt some businesses that have special importance to me. If that happens, I would like to call you so that you can get that guy Walker off our backs. I don't want him or his people in Steelton. I have good reasons."

"This is related to the apartment in the Riverview I checked out for you?"

"Yeah. Apartment 806. Walker pays for it and his name is on the lease. His secretary- her name is June Murphy-lives in it. If I get word Walker is causing trouble, I need you to place a private call to him on behalf of Steelton telling him that the newspapers and his wife might like to know about apartment 806. He should be informed that confidences can be preserved if he stays out of Steelton."

"I think you can rely on me to handle that in the right way, Ernie."

"Thanks Peter. Mr. Howard and I have a little something to help out with your charity work."

Ernie pushed an envelope with ten twenties in it across his desk.

"Thanks Chief. Best of luck in the new job. Hauser will do just fine. Good man and a good family."

Arthur and Claude had a regular transfer scheduled between warehouses and he called Cohen to arrange a brief meeting. While Claude helped a forklift driver load a marked Howard truck, Arthur got Cohen aside around the corner of the load-ing dock. He told Cohen about Ernie's plans and his idea to split their business into two distinct parts.

"That means just you and I work together, and just you and I share in our profits, is that correct Mr. Howard?"

"I imagine the Lintas will take a little something for Anthony's risk and his book-keeping, but yes. Our volume would be lower…essentially just my outlets. I'd handle the collections and the reporting to Linta. I tried to figure an estimate but it looks like our volumes will go down by close to half compared to last year with Tim's accounts all going away, and considering the lost Sonny business."

"And I would not share in any of Tim's steel business with you, even though my family buys most of your scrap?"

"I think it has to be that way. You have my word if something comes up that I need your help with your family and you come through, I'll see that your work is paid out of my own pocket."

"I think this will be satisfactory. I will want to hear more on the eighteenth."

"Thank you Mr. Cohen. You will still get your portion from our LCB contracts same as always and that will stay just between you and me."

The two men were too smart to take the chance of being seen shaking hands. Arthur returned to help his son, and Cohen walked the long way around the warehouse building, his woolen scarf wrapped tightly around his neck.

"Jesus Christ, Harry! You look terrible."

"I feel it too, Tim. I've barely been out of bed except to use the bathroom, and I've been in there plenty too the past couple of days."

"Have you been able to eat anything? How about Mom's soup I brought you Tuesday?"

"I'm not eating much of anything. If I don't feel better tomorrow, I'm going to see if Doc Kingston can swing by here. I've been passing notes under the door to Peggy in the office in the evening that she picks up the next morning. She's bought some medicine at Rea&Derrick for me. I don't want to get close to anyone in case this flu is catching."

"Look, let's not wait til tomorrow. I'll go down to Bernardo's and call the doc. We can set something up. I think you need to get some real attention."

"Don't tell Mom. And can you get a message to Hernley that I will try to come in Monday if I'm feeling better."

Tim arranged the appointment and went back up the hill to spend a little time with Harry. He sure didn't want whatever it was Harry had. "I'll call Hernley this afternoon, Harry. I'll stop in to see you on my way to work tomorrow."

Doc Kingston came by the next morning. Harry had another poor night, but he put some coffee on for the old Doc.

"You've got the same flu everybody else has. You've also got some fluid and congestion in your lungs. I don't want to see this develop into pneumonia. I'm going to give you a shot and a prescription. I want you to turn the heat up in here, and keep your chest warm. You've got to get on your feet and walk around. You can't lay in bed all day. You should start doing a little better in a couple of days. Take your temperature every four hours. You start running a fever over a hundred and one, call me."

"Thanks Doc. Can you give the prescription to Peggy downstairs. Here's a ten for her...that will cover it? And what do I owe you?"

"Your brother Tim told me to send the bill to him Harry. Have Tim or Peggy call me if that fever gets worse. Pneumonia is nothing to fool around with."

* * *

It was late on Thursday and O'Connell and Stone were in the basement working. It had been a long week, with continued problems with the IBM equipment, including the newly installed components.

"I'm sending those two loafers from Bethlehem back home after lunch tomorrow Brian. Everything they touch they screw up. I have my final meeting with Willis next Wednesday, then up to Bethlehem the end of the week for the last time I hope. I have to admit, I don't have a lot of confidence in our ability to keep things together here."

"Mark, we did our best but we never had the time or the manpower we needed. I'm not sure that last fix the IBM guys put on will hold together."

"In any case Brain, I appreciate what you did for me and for this plant. If we have any degree of success it's mostly due to you. I'm going to be telling everyone that. Maybe we can swing that headquarters position for you. And by the way, you're back to Peckville after lunch tomorrow too. You and I are wrapping it up tomorrow."

"Congratulations, Mickey. You are going to make a fine Chief. Count on me for any support I can give you. You have the Council and all of the patrolmen on your side, and I know the people of Steelton will be right behind you."

"Thank you, Chief. You said you might have a couple of final items to go over?"

"Just some minor suggestions. We have a couple of small businesses here that I kind of looked out for. The funeral parlors, Steelton Coal and Oil, and few others. You know Lowry and I go way back, so I hope you can keep his towing business contract renewed. The churches and family run taverns, and the social clubs I tried to go extra easy on. And Arthur Howard and his businesses. He is a valuable link to the Negro people. He makes an honest living and helps out a lot of people. You have any problems with him, please let me know. I encourage you to build a good relationship with him. I also used him as a source of advice from time to time. He has a hauling and salvage contract with the Borough I'd like to see him keep."

"Consider it done, Chief."

"And I think it would be a good idea if you and I had dinner every so often. Herman Klein did that for me and I learned a lot from him. Everything that affects Steelton affects the mill and the other way around. Plus there may be a strike this summer and we'll need cooperation both ways."

"I understand Chief. You can count on me."

Scrappy parked the Rambler behind the main office. It was deserted on a Saturday afternoon. He didn't sign in. He walked down the stairs to the idled IBM punched card machine. He had closely watched the IBM technician, and he knew exactly which terminals to cross connect. The entire job took fifteen minutes.

42

Tim stopped in to see Harry every day. The medicine Doc Kingston prescribed helped but Harry's fever would come and go. Harry worried about his lost pay. As a new employee he had no sick days and if he didn't work, he didn't get paid. He would have had a week's vacation coming this summer but he could not use that in advance. At Tim's request, Doc Kingston came in on Wednesday morning, and pronounced Harry improved and his lungs clearing. "If you feel up to it and have a good weekend, I'm writing you a note now that you can take into work Monday."

"Thanks, Doc, don't worry, please. If I can crawl in, I'm going."

Stone was in the rail mill as he had planned the following Monday morning. He had scheduled his final meeting with his manufacturing team before making his presentation to Willis two days after. Just as the meeting was about to start, Pat Patterson came out of his office, red in the face.

"There's a fire in the main office! I heard the Citizen's was called and the plant's own pumpers from Gate ten. Scrappy, you better get up there. Man called me and said the fire started in the basement where all your PEP equipment is!"

* * *

Harry was well enough Sunday to have dinner with his family. He got a good night's sleep and was pleased to see George Clark on the way through his gate.

"Harry. I heard you were down with the flu. Good to see you back. You OK?"

"I'm not a hundred percent, George, but close enough. How are you?"

"Things are about the same. I'll be happy when spring finally comes. Take care, Harry."

Harry saw Melton at the coffee pot and got caught up on the nearly two weeks he was out. Harry apologized to Melton for making him do double duty.

"That's Hernley's idea, Harry, not mine. I gotta tell you, he was on my case every day, sometimes twice a day asking me how it was going, was everything getting done right, like that. I hope you don't get sick again anytime soon. For one thing, it made me really appreciate how you filled in for me over Christmas."

"Maybe three months." Willis looked at Stone. "They say they have a six month backlog for their machinery and even for a good customer like Bethlehem that can't guarantee a replacement until June at the earliest. How the fuck did this happen?"

"Too early to say, Bob. Some kind of electrical problem. Our best guess is those two goofballs from Bethlehem screwed something up last Friday. It was their last day here and they were in a hurry to get home. I'm not suggesting they fucked things up on purpose."

"What? You mean there's a chance they deliberately sabotaged that thing? So that Bethlehem could win the rail expansion? You saying that they were put up to it?"

"Calm down, Bob. I didn't say anything like that. Those two clowns were bordering on incompetent. I tried to get them replaced if you'll remember. I asked for additional staff from up there. Wallace turned down every request. I told you in my last report we had the cards stacked against us."

"Well, we're fucked now. Stevens was in here yesterday and ripped me a new asshole. Your last report said we don't have the qualified personnel to effectively run this equipment, and now it goes up in smoke. IBM is pissed and I don't see us being able to blame them for the fire."

"Bob, we were doing great from the manufacturing side. Our operations were better than Bethlehem's and we had a big advantage on the union side until those grievances popped up out of nowhere. I have to go up to see Wallace tomorrow for our final report. Do you want to send something along under your signature as the official final word on this, or do you want me to handle it?"

"What would I say? This is your project Mark. You make the report to Wallace and his people. Then you send me a memo on what happened. Keep in mind whatever you send me will probably go to Stevens."

"I'll take care of it, Bob. I'll do as you say. I'll do my best to protect Steelton, as I always do."

"Burger! Hernley wants to see you in his office right after lunch." Karl Long didn't hang around to tell Harry why. It had been a long week, but Harry made it to Friday. He collected his paycheck that contained one day's earnings. His stomach still wasn't right and he had Campbell's chicken noodle soup and some peanut butter crackers every day for lunch. He finished his soup, washed out his bowl, and walked out to Hernley's office. No one else was in there.

"Come in Burger and sit down. This isn't going to be easy and I might as well get right to the point. Our expenses in the open hearth are above budget and I have to make some reductions in personnel. You're the most junior guy here. I'm cutting out three positions and yours is one of them. Over the past two weeks Melton was able to do his job and yours, just as you were able to do both jobs effectively over two weeks last Christmas. I can't afford redundancy in my department. So today is your last day. You'll get a week's notice pay. Go up to the main office and see Mr. Zimmerman in personnel. He'll go over everything. That's it."

Harry was frozen. He started to perspire. He felt dizzy.

"Mr. Hernley. Can you please give me a second chance? I worked hard and never missed a day until the past two weeks. I had a bad case of the flu. You saw the note from Doc Kingston."

"Sorry, Burger. Decision's final."

"You mean because me and Melton were dedicated, and took on double duty with no extra pay, that cost me my job?"

"Burger. It's over. Punch out and go up to Swatara Street and see Zimmerman. We'll arrange to have your stuff delivered to your apartment."

"I'm going to lose my apartment. I'm going to lose everything I worked for. Please, I'm asking you. Can you please give me a second chance? I'll take a pay cut, or work overtime without pay, anything!"

"That's it Burger. Go punch out. Go up to see Zimmerman."

Harry's mind was spinning. He went through the motions. He didn't say anything to anybody until he saw George at the gate.

"George, I just got fired. I got fired for being sick. I got fired for helping Hernley out when I did two jobs at once. Melton's getting stuck with my job and his. I got no idea how I'm going to explain this to my family."

"Harry, I'm sorry. You need someone to talk to call me. Come down to the Citizen's on a weekend, I'm usually there."

Harry spent his Friday night in his apartment. His head was still swirling. He'd have to go over his finances. He'd have to talk to Dr. Becker. He'd have to talk to Tim. He hoped to talk to Scrappy Stone. He'd have to tell his Mom and Dad. He reached for his cigarettes…he hadn't smoked the whole time he was sick but now it was one right after the other. He poured himself a Seagram's Seven and turned on the TV. He had no idea what he was watching.

"You had quite a week, Mr. Stone. My superiors tell me they have spoken with your Mr. Stevens, who does not want to give up his quest for the capital investment for your rail mill. This is despite your new labor problems, your poor prognosis for the qualified personnel to properly manage that investment and now this unfortunate fire. I'm afraid this presents too much risk for my group. We cannot recommend Steelton as the site for the deployment of our long term capital."

"I'm not surprised Wallace. I understand. I regret that all of those jobs will not be coming to my home town."

"Do you, Mr. Stone? Do you? You know, when I was assigned all of that time in Steelton, and the hours I spent studying and walking around your West Side, my understanding was that those of you born on the West Side think of that neighborhood as your home, and not the Borough itself. It was really quite clear. I saw it in you, as well. Your own family has been there more than fifty years, is that not so?"

"Yes. It's true. Look, Wallace, let's cut the bullshit. I have a proposition for you. I will file my report under my own signature. As you predicted, Willis will have nothing to do with it. It will praise Steelton but conclude that we are two years away from having the proper personnel and computerized equipment to handle any potential expansion for the rail mill. Where you decide to put your money is up to you. I will recommend that Steelton continue to receive a healthy share of the Company's money to continue its existing modernization. That makes good sense. And..."

"I can agree with that. You had something else?

"I'd like to have the opportunity to come up here and work with you in the strategic planning group. I'd like the Company to support me in continuing my studies for my Bachelor's degree." Scrappy looked for Wallace's reaction; it came in seconds.

"I had hoped that you would come to your senses and make that request. The successful completion of your undergraduate degree will be a condition of your new position. I have already briefed my superiors and I am confident that you can leave the arrangements for your new post to me. Have you said anything about this to anyone? Your friend young Mr. Willis perhaps?"

"Not a word to anyone."

"I suppose we should now begin to use our first names on a regular basis, is that OK, Mark?"

"You can call me Mark but to me you will always be Wallace."

"Very well, Mark. Before we close our conversation, I have something to say to you."

Stone looked at Wallace, who now stood up and moved closer to him.

"I have respected you almost from the start, even though you detested me. You have qualities and skills I do not have. Qualities and skills I will need to succeed in business. I would like to learn from you. I need to understand the human side of business. My mother has told me I need to understand the human side of life. You see, she has told me I will never find a good wife without this skill. I think we understand one another, don't we, Mark. You have things you want to learn from me as well, yes? We will work well together and who knows? Perhaps we will become friends. And you can be certain Mark, that no one will ever know who was responsible for saving your precious West Side. It is our bond, yes?"

"As you say, Wallace. And we can shake hands."

"Shall we say the first Monday in April as your starting date? I will authorize time in the hotel for you until you can find a place of your own. I will work out the salary and the title. Do you have any other requests I should know about?

"Two. I'd like you to use your influence to get Brian O'Connell a position with Bill Willis' mines group. Bill would like to have him. O'Connell is first rate in every respect."

"I see, and your second request?"

"I'd like to keep my company car -the Rambler."

"If these guys get a forecast right for a change we're in for one hell of a snowstorm." Ernie said to his son as they went over the Steelton-Harrisburg line where Front Street became Cameron Street. They turned the big Buick into the abandoned gravel driveway. Cohen's beat up Chevy, as usual, was already there.

"Let's just wait for Arthur and Tim. I think Cohen always feels better when Arthur's with him. You ready with everything, Anthony?"

"Yes, Dad. After we went over all of the personal family accounts yesterday, I prepared all of the numbers for today.

We are going to do just fine with this new arrangement. I think Cohen is going to be the happiest of us all. We may even get to see him smile."

"If he does, it will be the first I've ever seen, Anthony."

Tim barreled in with the Mercury and Arthur wasn't far behind. It was right around freezing in the office, and everybody kept their hats and gloves on.

Ernie opened the meeting and looked primarily at Tim. "I have some news. April one I am taking over from Herman Klein as head of security for the entire plant operations at Steelton: the mill, the quarry, railroad, everything. Tim, I know this is news, but it will give us every level of cover we need for our steel and scrap business. Mickey Hauser is taking over as police chief and he and I had a conversation about protecting our interests. Arthur, he knows that you and all of your businesses are a special case…he didn't ask any questions. With me moving out of the Chief's job, that cuts out our protection for some of the liquor outlets. Anything not directly sold or controlled by Arthur can't be protected. I've given this a lot of thought and my suggestion is that we break our relationship into two separate businesses…the liquor and the steel. Arthur and you, Mr. Cohen, will keep all of the proceeds of that…subject to a finance charge from Anthony for your reporting and cash management. Tim, that means no more collections or new business sales for you…you are all steel from now on. It will be your job to coordinate with Arthur on closing down the Moose, St. Lawrence and other accounts."

"Ernie, you're not going to believe this, but my news was to tell you all that I've gotten a promotion…assistant superintendent of the rail mill. My ability to move steel and scrap to Arthur should be improved. I think our business could easily double, so I'm happy to be out of the liquor trade."

Ernie turned to Cohen. "Mr. Cohen, are you in accord with this?"

"Yes. It will mean less risk for me and as I figure it, my income should be the same or maybe better. Mr. Howard and I can continue as we have."

Everybody turned to Arthur. "We have a deal."

"I forgot to mention I had a private word with Peter Lewis. He agreed to be available in case we need him. I think the group here should continue our support to him, plus I'm willing to kick in out of my own account. Anthony here has the money and the numbers. Anthony?"

"Gentlemen, take a look at my figures and as usual return all the paperwork to me. Your shares are in the brown envelopes. I think since we have a new arrangement we should meet in a month to see how things are going. Let's schedule April fifteenth…that's four weeks."

"It will be baseball season by then." Tim said.

"Yeah, if them Phillies can play in the snow." Ernie said half jokingly as he looked at the snow starting to fly from south to north. "We have an upriver wind, it's thirty-two degrees, and a solid gray sky. My advice to you, gentlemen, is to get to your homes, light your fireplaces, and get a nice glass of Mr. Cohen's finest in your hand."

Harry was not accustomed to having visitors. He had rarely been out of his apartment since he had the news from Hernley. A twenty inch snowstorm had brought everything to a standstill for three days. He answered the knock on his apartment door to see Mark Stone, wearing a wool hat with ear flaps and big rubber galoshes. "Scrappy, come in! Great to see you!"

"Hello, Harry. I'll just leave the boots outside at the top of the stairs here. I wanted to come see you when I heard the news about your layoff. Would've been here earlier in the week but I got snowed in like everyone else."

"Sure, that's OK. Can I get you something? A beer? Whiskey? Coffee?"

"OK, I'll drink a beer with you, why not?"

Harry turned off the radio and opened a quart bottle of Schmidt's. They sat at the kitchen table. Harry got out some beer pretzels.

"I feel terrible about your losing your job, Harry. That Hernley, what an asshole. I tried to get Willis to intercede on your behalf but my relationship with him isn't so good anymore."

"Yeah, my brother Tim told me about the fire and the PEP program for the rail mill. Too bad."

"Well, it's more than that. I told him I was taking a new job up in Bethlehem. He seemed more hurt than mad but, well, that's that."

Harry was crestfallen. His chin literally locked onto his chest. "I didn't know."

Scrappy looked at his glass of beer. "Sorry, Harry. I just had to do what I thought was best."

"That's OK Scrappy. If it's a good job I'm happy for you. You deserve it. It's just that, well, it's just that I was hoping I might be able to find a way to work again with you. I really need a job. I never had as much enjoyment as I did while working with you. I'm afraid I'm going to lose my apartment here. I really need to work. I thought I did everything a man was supposed to do. I worked hard, I kissed people's asses when I had to. I even went to your church trying to socialize with the higher ups. I could use some help."

"Well, you could go back to the union. I can help you with

Rocky Garber. Problem is there will most likely be a strike this summer, and after the strike, they'll lay a lot of guys off, and you'll be on the bottom seniority-wise."

"I'm not going back to a union swing shift job. No way."

"Well, there's nothing I know of that's open. I can tell you there's real need for trained men in working with the punched card machines…you know, the IBM machines you saw in the big office basement. It's a big problem for companies-no trained men. Why don't you use your G.I. benefits, get some training. I think the tuition is free. You'll get some unemployment benefits and G.I. bill benefits, won't you?"

"Do you know where I could go? I don't know of any place for that kind of training."

"Harry, you've got to get the initiative yourself and find these places. I think there's an institute starting up down at Middle-town…might be related to the Air Force's need for good people. Computers are the way of the future. If I were in your shoes, that's what I'd do. Then there's always the State. You have veteran's preference that puts you at the top of just about any test that you take. They're all office jobs, good benefits, all nine to five so no shift work."

"Okay Scrappy. I'll start to look into it. By the way, have you been seeing Susie? Are you two back together?"

"Afraid not. She has her life to live and I've got mine. Some things just weren't meant to be."

"I know, Scrappy. I know."

"Dr. Becker, thanks for seeing me. I think you know I had a long bout with the flu and unfortunately that ended up costing me my job in the open hearth. There's nothing else for me at the steel mill, and my plan is to go back to school under the Korean G.I.

bill and learn how to work with computers. I'm sorry to say I won't be able to afford my apartment. I'm certain you can rent it for more than I was paying. I want to thank you for being so kind to me and giving me a chance to get ahead in my life."

"Harry, you were a good tenant. We've known your family a long time. Is there anything I can do...maybe give you an advance or maybe let you pay your rent late for a couple of months?"

"Thank you, but no. I'll probably be a full time student for the rest of the year. I can move back home. If you want, maybe you'd be interested in the furniture and some of the kitchen things I bought? I won't have a need for the chair...it was second hand, or the bed, and there's a few kitchen things my mom gave me that work fine. You could really advertise the apartment as fully furnished with the bed and chairs. I'll want to keep my little TV though."

"Sure, Harry. How much do you want?"

"I bought the bed and chair on time from Miller's. I still owe forty bucks on them."

"How about we say fifty for everything?"

"Thanks, Dr. Becker. I'll be out by the end of March. Easter Sunday is the first of April this year. I'll be out before then, and maybe I'll see you and your son in church for Easter."

"Good luck to you Harry. When you come back for your next appointment with James, it's on us."

"I'll be sure to thank Peggy too. She was very kind to me. Thanks again for taking a chance on me."

Harry's Florsheims were shined and he had his grey jacket and blue tie on. Doris had pressed his best white shirt. Most of the snow had melted away and a weak sun tried to break through the overcast. Hap and Doris were up and dressed and headed to the Easter services at Church of God on Main Street. Tim was having his coffee with the newspaper at the kitchen table. As Harry turned to go up Pine Street he decided it was his last trip to church there. The idea of sleeping in Sunday mornings suddenly had a lot more appeal. On the way into church he saw all of the Beckers, beautifully dressed in their Easter best, and they all exchanged warm Easter greetings. He moved toward the cloak room to hang up his coat when he saw Cindy and Bob Hernley walking up the far aisle toward their pew. Cindy was holding her husband's arm and she wore a pink outfit with a matching hat. He lost sight of them as they slid into their seats.

Harry grabbed his topcoat off of its hook. He quietly moved toward the church's main door and pushed it open. A deep breath of cold air. He took the familiar path down Pine, and when he got to Front Street, he saw the Citizen's Hose House and remembered George Clark's invitation. He took two steps in that direction, stopped, and then decided to head home. "Why ruin George's Easter?" he thought to himself.

Doris had the traditional Easter baked ham with pineapple, scalloped potatoes and green beans and a big coconut cake for dessert. Tim opened a bottle of wine and they all watched TV as a family. Tim went out at seven to have a drink at the St. Lawrence. Hap went to bed at nine and Doris followed shortly thereafter.

Harry clicked off the TV and trudged up the stairs to his bedroom. The stairs creaked the way they always did. Doris had his old bed made with the same blankets and bedspread that she had used for twenty years. He looked around his room, took off his shirt, shoes and pants and slipped into bed. He lay there for a while listening to the radio. A commercial came on, interrupting the music. Harry turned toward his bedside table, reached over, and the pale yellow light of the Bakelite's dial flickered off.

About the Author

Keith Warner Hall is a native of the West Side of Steelton. This is his first novel.

Made in the USA
Middletown, DE
16 October 2018